MELDERBLOOD

THE MELDERBLOOD CHRONICLES
BOOK 1

E.A. WINTERS

Paperback ISBN: 978-1-958702-17-8

Hardback ISBN: 978-1-958702-18-5

DragonLeaf Press, imprint of Snowfall Publications, LLC

Sticks and stones may...
Who am I kidding? Words are powerful, with the potential to build
up or destroy.

To words.
May we respect them and use them wisely.

SOCIAL MEDIA

Connect with me on social media! [1]

- Website and newsletter: eawinters.com
- Facebook: facebook.com/eawintersnovels
- TikTok: @eawinters
- Instagram: @e.a.winters

---

1. Warning: connecting on social media may lead to exclusive content, behind the scenes snapshots, and joining a community that is way more fun than your daily to-do list. Engage with caution.

1

The art of womanhood ruled in shadow. Her curse was to never be praised for her effectiveness in the broad light of day, but her gift was to fill the palace with a web of eyes and ears, for people to scurry to and fro along the silk lines by night. Her spiders tripped over themselves to bear information to her waiting hands. The queen's blessing was protection, life, and the ear of the king; her curse was a death sentence.

The latter consumed the business of the day. Queen Satya leaned back against her carnelian throne and dragged long nails through the coarse fur of Mrtyu, the enormous hyena at her side. A deep rumble emanated from Mrtyu's throat, and the trembling man before her held up his hands.

"I have done everything you have asked."

Queen Satya cocked her head. "Did you now? And what did you think I asked of you?"

The sniveling man cast a furtive look to the columns lining either side of the empty stone room, as though escape was actually possible. A foolish thought. The man licked his lips. "Your Majesty asked me how the queen of Jannemar gained her power before magic returned to the world, and how she used it without any sign of siphon poisoning. Your Majesty asked me to find out if the king of that land had melderblood. You asked me if the princess had melderblood, and if they were strong enough to wield their power for war."

A pang of irritation curdled her stomach. She leaned forward. "And for which of these questions did you provide answers?"

The man threw up his hands. "Every single one! The queen of Jannemar is a dragonlord. Dragons are rare, and the connection between lord and dragon is bound in magic that does not require melderblood. There is no evidence of any housing artifacts being used in Jannemar before Queen Semra took possession of Aurin's spear from the wellspring at the origin of the world where it had been lodged, and magic returned to the world.

"There is no evidence that King Zephan has melderblood. The necklace of Raisa was with his sister Princess Avaya until three years ago, when it disappeared. Jannemar is likely to be in possession of it still, and it held windcaller magic.

"Princess Aviama has made few public appearances in the past three years since The Return. There was an incident at the castle, which I've told you about, three years ago—but the staff there is numerous, though not as numerous as here, of course, Your Majesty; they are a small kingdom—and there is no evidence that melderblood runs in the Shamaran line."

Queen Satya clenched her jaw. She loved the fear in his eyes—that was appropriate—but fear was supposed to motivate people to *do their jobs*. To be *useful*. She let out a long sigh.

"There's little evidence of melderblood in *anyone's* family line. It's been six hundred years since The Crumbling destroyed magic, and only three since The Return." Why did she have to repeat the obvious? She did it all day long with her husband. Must she do it here, in her own private judgment hall, as well?

Satya ran her fingers over Mrtyu's mottled gray fur, pausing over the rust-colored streaks along her head and ears. *I know you're hungry, my sweet. But the fool's failure will be your deliverance.* Satya snapped her eyes back to the man at the base of her throne.

"Does Princess Aviama have magic or not?"

He swallowed. "No one knows, Your Majesty. No one."

"Where in my instructions did I ask for excuses?" Satya turned her palms up in a resigned gesture. "I received this same information from three others. Your usefulness has run out. Mrtyu—dinner is served."

The man's scream echoed in the soundproof chamber as Mrtyu launched off the dais, the failed lackey's terror cut short by a snarling, ripping sound and the spurting of blood.

2

———

The storm hit without a cloud in the sky. Sailors ran to the rigging. Shouts filled the air amid the gale lashing against the sails and whipping Aviama's golden locks over her shoulders. She clutched at the rail, and her stomach lurched.

No, no, no. Not again.

She'd been nervous, sure. The closer their ship had gotten to Radha, the more Aviama's insides had turned topsy-turvy. She'd been standing at the prow, watching as the strip of foreign soil grew larger and larger, thinking.

And it was the thinking that had gotten her into trouble.

Snatches of raised voices whirled past her on the wind. The ship rocked, and she yelped. Her hand slipped from the rail, and she fell backward.

"We're too close to shore for a storm, Captain!"

"Scourge. Move! Get pressure off that mainsail!"

Strong arms wrapped around her waist and hauled her backward. The low voice of Enzo, her bodyguard, cut through the noise. "We need to get you below deck, Your Highness."

But how do I calm the storm if I'm below deck? But she

couldn't say that. No one could know she had magic, not even Enzo. Though a storm out of nowhere certainly didn't look good for keeping the secret.

Aviama nodded dumbly and tripped over her feet as Enzo wrapped an arm around her shoulders, covering her back with his and bending the two of them against the wind, while he half-led, half-pulled her through the storm across the deck and down to the lower level.

She should be better at managing her emotions by now, keeping her power in check. She was better, after training with Frigibar. Why was this so different?

The ship rocked again, and she threw a hand out to keep her nose from slamming into the wood siding. A sting told her a hundred splinters had buried themselves in her palm. *A hundred? No, that was ridiculous.* But she must have scuffed it pretty good.

"Are we going to crash?"

"I wouldn't know, Your Highness. I'm not a sailor. I'm sure they're doing the best they can." Enzo pulled her down the hall to her quarters and set her on the bed. The floor beneath their feet pitched. Aviama wrapped her arms around the bedpost, and Enzo skidded backward into the doorway. "I'm going back up to help. Don't open this door."

He slammed the door against the wind, and she threw her arms around the bedpost and squeezed her eyes shut. In a flash she was home, the outer ward of Shamaran Castle shimmering against the backs of her eyelids. Gusts of wind blasted from her hands and threw her backward. She threw her hands up in terror, and air ripped upward from her palms, blowing a hole in the roof of the smithy.

Screaming, screaming. People running. So much screaming.

The cyclone had spun over the smithy, weapons and tools

caught in its currents. Aviama cowered from a flying hammer and a sword blade still glowing from the forge. The blade sliced over her shoulder, and she cried out.

Someone tackled her to the grass. Semra! Semra, her dragonlord sister-in-law, yanked her behind the building and wrapped her in a tight hug. She was saying something into her ear, trying to calm her down, trying to tell her what to do, but Aviama's brain raced too fast to focus on her words. Semra had sent short bursts of fire to interrupt the gusts, and as Aviama began to breathe again and the wind began to die down, Semra had sent great swaths of smoke into the air to break up the currents.

That was three years ago. One of the servants had been killed by a hammer to the head as he carried buckets of grain to the stables. The hammer Aviama had ducked from. The hammer that should have hit her.

Incidents of power outbursts were not unique to Aviama. In the aftermath of The Return, people with elemental powers discovered their new abilities in the worst of ways: a fireblood burning down their home, a crestbreaker flooding the river and ruining the crops all along its bank, a tavern collapsing in on itself and trapping occupants as a quakemaker's power disrupted the foundation.

And then there were windcallers like Aviama. Not all of the newfound melders had blood on their consciences, but Semra and Aviama's brother, King Zephan, had had their hands full putting out fires within Jannemar's borders. Aviama's power seemed to crop up out of nowhere at all, and though she'd gotten better at controlling it since then, her magic still felt wildly unstable.

And then the summons had come.

Aviama tightened her eyes shut, as if closing them harder would block out the memory. No such luck. Her eyes flew open, and she stared at the opposite wall. The map fell off the wall and clattered to the floor. She could see where Shamaran Castle was marked, the Shalladin River at the base of the cliff on its northern side, and their journey the past three months up the river, out into the Aeia Sea on their way toward Radha. Jannemar looked so small to the south of the great nation. Even Belvidore, to Jannemar's south, looked insignificant in comparison.

Aviama took in a ragged breath and forced herself to notice things around her, things in the current room outside of the memories plaguing her. Map. Desk, askew from the rocking of the ship, her books scattered on the floor. Three trunks with gold inlay and stamped with the emblem of Jannemar on their lids.

The smooth carved wood of the bedpost. The smooth softness of the silk of her gown. She took in another, steadier, breath, and let it out. Hummed one of her mother's lullabies. The ship's rocking had eased, and the rushing in her ears was gone. Stampeding feet and shouted orders told her they were coming into the harbor.

She still had time before they landed. Aviama pulled up her sleeves and grinned at the throwing knives strapped to leather gauntlets on her wrists. Semra had insisted she carry something sharp. Zephan hadn't loved the idea, but Semra had worked with Aviama until her aim pacified him.

"I know Enzo's a good bodyguard," Semra had said. "So she won't need the knives, and she's good enough now that she won't hurt herself. But it'll make me feel safer sending her to Radha. Unless you think I should accompany her..."

That had squashed the argument, and the knives were sent with Zephan's blessing. Semra's coming to Radha was impossible, with the amount of magic-related concern still riddling the country. Not to mention the insult to Radha if another sovereign came uninvited to babysit their contestant.

Jannemar couldn't afford to cause international issues right now.

Aviama winced. To be frank, Jannemar couldn't afford much of anything. Not in the wake of the war with Belvidore.

She pulled the two knives from her forearms and threw them one after the other into the wall on the other side of the room. *Thwap. Thwap.*

The first landed almost exactly where she wanted. The second drifted left. *Biscuits.* Semra never would have missed.

She hopped off the bed and retrieved the blades, raising her arm and letting the blade fly just as the door opened. *Thwap.*

Enzo jumped back with a grunt and raised an eyebrow. "Feeling better, Your Highness?"

"If I'm not, will you let me stay here and tell the royal family I send my regards?"

Enzo pursed his lips, but the corner of his mouth told her he'd almost smiled. The man was old enough to be her father —slightly graying hair, well-muscled chest and arms, and a no-nonsense expression occasionally softened by her shenanigans. He had three daughters back home, and Aviama thought it worked in her favor. She could put up with gruff, but she hated boring, expressionless guards.

"I hardly think it would be productive to stay below deck after the journey to bring you here."

"Good point." Aviama threw up a finger. "Counterpoint. I shall pique the prince's interest and fascinate him with mystery by failing to appear with the other princesses. When at long last I emerge from the ship, he will be dying to meet me." She took the edge of her skirt and twirled in a circle, falling into a curtsy at the end. "And that will be that. Easy as pie."

"Please don't curtsy to me, Your Highness. Even in jest."

"Lighten up, Enzo. I didn't do it in front of anyone, and I was just kidding. You were obviously standing in for Prince Shiva. Didn't you ever play pretend when you were a boy?"

"I did, yes."

Aviama sighed. "Were you as bad at it then as you are now?"

Her chest tightened as she thought of meeting Prince Shiva and the Radhan royal family. She knew how to be proper, how to greet monarchs and diplomats, how to dance, all the basics of formal events—but flirting had never been a part of her education.

No small wonder. She'd been fifteen when her mother was killed, and it wasn't exactly like suitors were knocking down the door while assassins crawled the kingdom, war broke out, and her father was murdered. Aviama blinked hard against the moisture building at her eyes. She could still smell the smoke, hear the shouts of the soldiers.

The ground had shaken beneath her feet at the pounding of all those footsteps as her father, King Turian, was escorted to safety—and straight toward the explosive that would take his life. She'd been only three meters from her mother when the knife plunged into her chest, and a stone's throw from her father when the blast hit.

Avaya, her older sister, had always been a fantastic flirt. Manipulative and gossipy too, but men always seemed to fall at her feet. Not so much now, but certainly back then. Now she was on what was essentially long-term house arrest.

What had Semra said?

"Remember, you don't have to marry him. You don't have

to like him. Just stay long enough to find out their intentions toward Jannemar, and their military assets…"

Zephan had snorted. "You're not allowed to like him. He's a Tanashai. The Tanashais are greedy, power-hungry, and have been running military drills closer and closer to our northern border. If Avaya is to be believed, they want the Horon Mines. And based on our intel since The Return, they are not friendly toward melders. You don't need a target on your back. Don't tell a soul."

Enzo cleared his throat. "Your Highness?"

Aviama snapped her head up. "Hmm?"

Enzo blinked. He'd obviously said something while she'd been lost in her own world. "It's time to go. We've landed. Your escort waits on the main deck."

Her stomach wrenched. She slipped her knives back into the gauntlets on her wrists, let her long sleeves drop over them, and grimaced. "I could court him from here. I'll send him letters?"

"The prince is selecting a bride and therefore an alliance. Removing yourself from the running seems unwise."

He didn't say it, but she knew what he was thinking—and selfish. He thought she was here to really play the game, to enter into a contest with three other neighboring nations to be courted and wined and dined and examined for desirability. Suitability.

Radha was a powerful kingdom, and Jannemar was vulnerable. An alliance would be wise, and with Avaya castle-bound, Aviama was the only princess Jannemar had to build alliances with. Despite her father's marrying a commoner, and Zephan marrying a commoner ex-assassin, Aviama following suit was stupid at best.

But Zephan didn't trust the Tanashais and didn't want her linked with Radha. So she would play along, gather information, and smooth things over as best she could before returning home.

She'd never been a spy before. Maybe it could be fun. At last, an adventure of her own. Not shut in her room or escorted to an obscure farm to wait out the danger but having a mission of her own. If it were truly perilous, Zephan and Semra would never have sent her. But there was at least a little risk involved, and she could finally be helpful.

Aviama swallowed. It was time to be a princess. To act like a Shamaran. She lifted her chin, and tried to imagine what her meeting with Prince Shiva might look like. She would float in with her entourage and gifts—smaller than the gift Radha had given with the summons, but when they saw Aviama's remarkable poise and intelligent, gentle speech, they wouldn't notice anything else.

Prince Shiva would bow and take her hand and kiss it; Aviama would curtsy and dazzle them with talk of Jannemar, the glories of home, the beauty of Radha. She would mingle with the other princesses, become friends, and return home with connections to three other kingdoms in addition to the one with Radha.

Perhaps she'd become such good friends with the other girls, that whichever princess Shiva chose would let Aviama design her wedding gown. It wasn't traditional, of course, but what fun would that be! Hope blossomed in her chest, and she set her jaw.

You are Princess Aviama of Jannemar, and adventure is yours. You laugh in the face of peril! You are effortlessly secure, standing unmoved by frivolous attempts to undermine you! You wil—

"Your Highness. Please. Radha's welcome committee is waiting for us on shore."

Aviama cleared her throat. "Right. Yes."

She lifted her chin again and swept from the room with all

the grace and confidence befitting her station. Enzo fell in close behind.

The sailors stood at attention in an aisle on the main deck. Aviama blinked in the bright light of midmorning as she strode across the open space. The Jannemari flag fluttered from the mast in a gentle breeze. The wood planks sounded hollow under her feet, but familiar now, after so long at sea.

She'd come this far, hadn't she? She could do this.

But as she raised her head from the deck of her own ship to the shore of her destination, the sight before her sent a jolt through her bones. A whisper of wind gathered at her palms, and her heart pounded as if it might escape her chest.

Fear struck her like a hammer.

3

———

Theirs was a modest vessel, like a pony among warhorses. Aviama had heard that Radha's pride was their navy, but only now did she truly understand what it meant. Ships filled the harbor, orange and red flags snapping in the wind. Nearly every one of them depicted the symbol of the pakshi, the national bird—though Aviama did notice one ship flying a green flag with a black stripe down its center, and a second flying a white flag with one golden star in the center surrounded by three more.

She was not the first contestant to arrive. The white flag with the stars told her that Princess Marija of Tomos had come before her, and the green flag indicated the warrior princess of Batal, Princess Vanina. Only Princess Darra of Curion was missing.

Aviama winced. *Better than last.*

Beyond the harbor and the sea of sails, the coast city lay to the left, and an expanse of sand dunes to the right. The sun beat down off buildings colored in an array of striking oranges, reds, pinks, and even blues. Aviama had certainly heard of the city of Rajaad. She'd honestly heard little else in the past months. But seeing it was another matter entirely. If it looked grand from this distance, what might it look like up close?

Enzo stepped off the ship onto the jetty first and offered her his hand; she took it and gingerly transferred from the gently swaying ship to the first solid ground she'd set foot on in three months. Between her sea legs and her failure to look where she was going, it was a mercy she didn't fall on her face. She could thank Enzo's strong hand on her elbow for that. But she could hardly look away from Radha's welcome party waiting just off the dock.

Three dozen armed men greeted them, dressed in burnt orange, adorned with identical jewel collars, and mounted on horseback—except for two driving a cargo carriage and four mounted on massive yellow, blue, and green birds. Elaborate plumage decorated large heads and curved beaks set atop long, gracefully curving necks down to a large body set over thick legs that seemed to go on forever. And in the center of the party, two pakshi birds stood hitched to a cushion-seated chariot.

Aviama caught herself just before her jaw dropped to the jetty. She gulped. "Enzo...are they under the mistaken impression that I am riding in that thing?"

Enzo released her elbow and stepped to one side. "I'm afraid in this case, Your Highness, it is you that is under the mistaken impression that you might not. I see no sidesaddles, so you cannot ride a horse, and I imagine the few extra horses they brought are for your own entourage. The rest of our party will follow with our gifts and your luggage."

Alarm seized her. Jannemar would be seen as weak, ungrateful guests. Coming to the hospitality of a foreign nation with nothing to show for herself? Unthinkable. She shook her head. "No. Our gifts must arrive either before me or at the same time as I do. Not after."

"Of course, Your Highness. I'll speak to them."

"Where's Murin? If I'm going to die by birds picking my eyes out, I want a friend to share the experience."

"Here, Your Highness."

Aviama jumped and turned. Her lady-in-waiting curtsied just behind her, materializing out of thin air. "Murin! What would I do without you? Stay close to me, would you? I was just kidding about the dying by birds thing." She surveyed the creatures. Their talons looked large enough to rip her to shreds, but as they progressed down the jetty, she thought the beak would do just as much damage.

The feathers were more vibrant than anything she'd seen back home. Iridescent sunflower yellow contrasted with emerald and azure tones, shimmering in the sun, and harnessed in glinting gold. The sight was indisputably gorgeous. But the large, beady eyes gave her pause. She flinched as several of their heads swiveled toward her in sharp, jerking movements.

As she drew closer, Aviama realized the contraption the pakshi pulled was not quite a chariot. Long, curved runners replaced the wheels like a sled or sleigh. She wasn't sure what she expected to meet her, but this wasn't it. Chariots weren't exactly practical over the dunes, and pakshi *were* the national bird—but then, there was a dragon on Jannemar's flag, and she'd never seen one until three years ago.

The Radhan company drew their right fist to their left shoulder in a smooth, synchronized motion and inclined their heads from their mounts in a gentle bow. A man in the front, with a coil of ribbon sewn along the shoulder of his overtunic, dismounted and bowed low.

"Your Royal Highness! Welcome to the sparkling kingdom

of Radha, home to beaches, deserts, and forests, and the renowned House of the Blessing Sun."

Aviama dipped her head in acknowledgment. A curtsy in response to a soldier or guard would be inappropriate. "Thank you for your warm welcome. We are honored to see with our own eyes the shores with whom we've so long enjoyed successful trade."

Diplomatic. Vague. It was a princessy answer. She imagined her mother would have approved.

The man smiled, but the expression wasn't warm. "Yes, Your Highness."

What was *that* supposed to mean? Was it that trade had soured? Aviama stifled a grimace. Did she just out herself as utterly clueless as to matters of state?

Great. She'd been here all of ten seconds and already word would spread of Princess Aviama of Jannemar, the airheaded ninny who came from a needy nation to be courted by a foreign prince for an alliance. The *out-of-touch* princess who didn't even know how badly affairs stood in her own kingdom.

But she *did* know, didn't she? She'd heard from Zephan and Semra. She'd watched the generals and nobles stride this way and that at all hours, eyes tired, faces drawn. Maybe she didn't know all of it. Or maybe she did, and it wouldn't matter because now on the shores of Radha, rumor would spread of the desperate idiot contestant, and her chances of gaining a good-enough impression with the prince to gain his trust and learn Radha's intentions would go up in smoke.

Aviama scratched her head. Barely thirty seconds had passed since the man's response, but the man had a curious look in his eye as he looked at her. Aviama swallowed and followed the man's gesture toward the sand sledge.

"Your ship and crew are very impressive, Your Highness. The envy of your fleet, surely. Rarely have we seen a ship come to harbor as quickly as yours, and yet slow in time for a good docking."

Biscuits. Her wind brought the ship in too fast, and they knew something was off. But they had no proof it was anything other than impressive engineering...she hoped.

"Jannemar is blessed with excellent craftsmen. We are indeed in their debt."

The man's eyes narrowed a fraction, and her mouth went dry. One of the pakshi clicked its beak two meters from them, and Aviama nearly leaped out of her skin. Behind her, Murin shrank back, then recovered and drew herself up tall. *You cannot be more cowardly than your lady-in-waiting. Pull it together.*

Her saving grace was that her display of fear had not been in front of the Radhan royals. Aviama wondered how the other princesses had fared. She lifted her head and accepted the man's hand up into the sledge and onto the cushioned seat. Murin took the space beside her, and Enzo accepted the reins of a striking palomino. Aviama wondered if an army of palominos would blend into the sands when the sun glinted off their golden hides and white manes.

Aviama turned to look for Enzo, who spoke quietly to one of the men. Surely, he was arranging for their gifts to be brought ahead of them or added to their party to arrive along with her to the palace. But when he caught her eye, he gave a slight shake of his head. Aviama's lips parted to speak, but the hackman driving the sled clucked to the birds and they were off with a lurch, at a surprising speed. Sand flew up in every direction, and she squealed as the spray hit her face before evening out into a straight path.

By the time they finally pulled across the dunes and into Rajaad, Aviama's stomach was gnarled in angry, empty knots and growling like the starved stray dogs she saw slinking into the alleyways. But the dogs were the only visual of lack that she saw, though she knew their course into the city would have been carefully mapped out. Radha's wealth would be on display as a show of prosperity and power over the course of the contest for the princesses to take back to their homelands. Perhaps the navy had even been rearranged to pull as many impressive ships to harbor as possible to show off to their royal guests.

All through the city, colorful buildings, smiling men and women, waving children, and tall structures with domes, elegant archways, and murals peered out from one street to the next. People lined the streets to watch their entourage pass by, some throwing flower petals in their path to be trod down by the pakshi. One street after another showed the city unfolding like a flower, the colors of the buildings and the luxuries of the houses growing richer and richer the closer they grew to the city's center.

And then there it was—the House of the Blessing Sun. Aviama gasped as they turned the corner and set their sights on the palace. She'd seen it from other angles as they approached, but now it was suddenly both far and close at once, reaching four stories high in the middle, and stretching out on either side for far more meters than she could estimate. The palace midsection was colored in a gradient, with salmon reds at the top melting into coral on the third floor, peach on the second, and buttermilk yellow on the first, flanked by gentle sandstone the shade of a blushing desert, as if the sand itself tinged pink throughout the stonework.

Domes claimed every place a turret might have been run up on Shamaran Castle back home. Every corner was rounded, each archway swooping, patterned and carved, or scalloped. Gates studded in carnelian and pearl swung open to usher them into a grand promenade lined with trees and into a main courtyard filled with fountains, pools, benches, and curated greenery.

Not a plant grew in its natural shape, but the result was easy on the eyes. The pakshi came to a halt and fanned out long tail feathers in commanding shades. Enzo dismounted and came round to the side of the sledge in an instant, offering his hand. Aviama took it and stepped down.

The beautifully, tastefully ornamented halls of home shrank away in her mind before the grandeur of the House of the Blessing Sun. The palace grounds were easily ten times that of Shamaran Castle, if not more, and the imperial look in the eyes of the servants they passed did nothing to assuage her anxiety.

Had the other princesses felt this small, or was the weight of insignificance hers alone to bear?

Aviama grimaced at her reflection in one of the pools as they passed. Her golden curls were better described as yellow matted mass. Enzo's borrowed palomino had less tangles in its tail and mane than she did in her hair. She lifted a hand and ran it through a snarl next to her face. Her hand came away gritty. Apparently, half the desert had taken up residence in the bird's nest on her head.

Servants in identical cream tunics formed a short aisle on the steps leading up to the main entrance, smiling and bowing or curtsying. A short man dressed in ornamented teal blue padded down the steps in sandals, a cornelian cord wrapped around the shoulder. He bowed low.

"Your Royal Highness, Princess Aviama. The sun shines the brighter for your presence here. We are truly honored. I trust you traveled well?"

Traveled well. Was he joking? Did she look like the kind of girl that was accustomed to travel, dumb enough to let her hair flow over her shoulders to be snagged and twisted and snarled by the wind? Maybe it was her confident demeanor he referred to, and she'd managed to project a stronger presence than she felt. Maybe most people felt great after a few months on a ship and a pakshi-driven dash through the desert with a healthy dose of sand exfoliating her skin with every harsh breeze.

Or maybe he was merely being polite. His keen eyes watched her intensely, but the deep maple brown seemed warm enough. Reserved, but warm.

Aviama smiled. "Quite well, thank you." A twist in her gut reminded her of the gifts she had failed to bring, along with the rest of her escort. "My company comes behind bearing our gifts to the royal family. We thought we might present them at whatever time is suitable for the king and queen—perhaps at the formal introduction."

Better to make it sound like coming separately was the plan all along, rather than an oversight.

"Of course, Your Highness. I'll see to it." The man bowed again. "I am Amir, head steward of the king's house. Nothing happens in the palace that I don't know about, so if you have any need at all, please do not hesitate to bring it to my attention."

Aviama dipped her head. "Nice to meet you."

These were interactions she could manage. Things were looking up. Perhaps she'd reclaimed some dignity after her wide eyes as they swept into the palace grounds, and her ratty appearance after the ride through the dunes.

Just then, her stomach let out a long, grouchy yowl announcing its emptiness to the world. Murin shifted her weight at Aviama's elbow, and, bless her, pressed a hand to her own stomach.

Amir's gaze flitted over them, but his expression released no emotion to betray his thoughts. "You must be tired. I'll show you to your rooms, and you'll have a chance to rest and clean up before this evening."

Aviama clasped her hands together to keep from clapping. "That would be lovely, Amir."

Enzo and Murin flanked her as she left the courtyard behind and followed Amir up the steps and through the soaring archway into the palace. The inside was even more grand than the outside, a series of high scalloped archways painted in intricate designs so that hardly a centimeter went without color. Ornate as it was, it felt a bit busy to Aviama, but maybe that was only in comparison—she never would have thought to describe her own castle as simple, but here, next to this, it certainly was.

Cream-clad servants and men and women dressed in all colors crisscrossed through the palace halls as Amir wound them through the entryway and past another courtyard. Most took no notice, though several did turn to watch them. But as they passed a second courtyard, a line of pillars the only delineation from inside and out as the ceiling pulled back to reveal the open sky, a male servant shot daggers in a glare and muttered something under his breath.

A chill ran up Aviama's spine. She could have sworn she heard the word *melder*. She was opening her mouth before her brain quite caught up.

Don't make a scene. Don't be a fool.

She stopped.

Turned.

"A thousand pardons. What did you say?"

The man's eyes burned into her skull, not afraid to be a servant confronted by a royal for rudeness, not confused by an unnecessary pause in the princess's mission. Aviama blinked. He was *furious.*

His lip curled, and he spat at her feet. "Kingdom of melderblood. You infect us with your curses. *Curses!*"

Aviama drew back, and she'd hardly had time to process the insult when a flash of steel caught her eye. The servant launched toward her, and she screamed as an iron grip yanked her backward and two bodies collided on the marble floor.

The palace disappeared then, the Radhan servant replaced for a moment in her mind with the glassy eyes of the man on the outer ward of the castle at home, staring up at her. Sightless. Dead. The hammer lay next to him, in a mound of spilled grain.

Aviama's stomach knotted, and nausea threatened her. She squeezed her eyes shut, and opened them to find the Radhan man on his back at her feet, Enzo's blade to his throat—and the dagger the man had drawn laying harmless on the marble floor several paces away.

"Stop! Stop, stop!" Aviama stumbled back from the altercation before her, running straight into something behind her.

A woman yelped, and a silver platter clattered to the floor. Aviama spun to see a pile of round breaded delicacies of some sort rolling in every direction. The woman wore the cream-wrapped tunic of the servant women of the palace, and bobbed her head and dropped clumsily into a curtsy as her fingers snatched out to catch the escaping morsels. Aviama dropped to the floor and swept several of them into her hands, offering them to the woman.

"I'm so sorry, my mistake. Here, let me—"

The woman pulled back with a gasp and shook her head violently. "Please, Your Highness, no! It is no trouble, no trouble! I will take care of it, do not bend yourself to such a task!"

Aviama froze, then slowly rose to her feet. Beside her, Murin had gathered several more of the treats and replaced them on the platter, to which the woman bowed low several times while backing away.

She bit her lip and twisted back toward Enzo and the Radhan man on the ground. Amir stood to one side, eyes wide, palms together, his fingertips over his lips as if silencing himself from expressing a thought too direct to share with his esteemed visitor.

"My deepest condolences, Your Highness," he said at last. "Please do with this man as you see fit. His punishment shall be on his own head for daring to attack our honored guest."

Enzo twisted the blade of his knife, and the man on the ground swore. He held his hands up, eyes wide, glancing frantically from Enzo to Aviama and back.

She'd been in the palace all of ten minutes and had already been spat at, caused a fight, and made a cultural faux pas by assisting the servant—who was clearly mortified by her actions. At home, Aviama wouldn't have done servant work either, but the Shamaran family's relationship with their servants was more relaxed. She asked them about their lives, and those close to her answered honestly. If she'd wanted to help pick up a dropped item, they had learned to let her, not turn skittish like a deer at the scent of a huntsman.

The servant girl gathered her platter and disappeared around the corner just behind them. Murin straightened, and Enzo hauled the man to his feet. Amir, Murin, Enzo, and the Radhan man all stared at her, unblinking, glaring, gaping.

Her mouth went dry. *Words. Say words, idiot.*

She wet her lips. "Um, no, I...I don't think...not necessary." Aviama took a breath, but her pulse still pounded in her ears, and her heart still thundered in her chest.

Say something. Anything.

She tried again.

"Don't let him near me again. Deal with him according to

your own people. I'm not a monster, and I don't need blood on my hands." She drilled the man with what she hoped was a cool stare, but what she knew was more like a shaken gawk, and swept past the four sets of eyes boring into her back. Aviama traipsed down the hall in the direction Amir had been leading them, chin high, feet slapping the cool marble beneath the swirl of her silk skirts, as if setting a fast-enough pace could erase the insanity of her latest international debacle.

Couldn't she have thought of anything more intelligent to say? Amir had handed her a golden opportunity to build trust and credibility, to be gracious to her assailant yet assertive, reasonable yet noble.

Mercy. Try it sometime. No, too harsh. And if she implied that he should try to have mercy, it would mean she *deserved* his mercy, which would require that she had done something wrong. Nothing could be further from the truth.

Let this be a lesson to you in presuming to know a person. Yes! That would have been perfect. Why did she always think of just the right thing to say *after* the moment—

"Auugh!"

Her body slammed into a broad chest and her vision spun as she fell, filled with coral and emerald details on the ceiling, yellow fabric, and the white of the polished marble floors. Just before she cracked her skull on the stone, her world shifted again as strong arms caught her and twirled her torso so that she stared up at a chiseled face, parted lips, high cheekbones, and piercing pair of umber eyes.

 viama's breath caught—though whether from the fall or the obscenely handsome face before her, she couldn't say.

"Hello."

Biscuits, even his voice is beautiful. She became acutely aware of his arms around her, one wrapped under the small of her back, the other at the nape of her neck in a tangle of sandy birds' nest tresses. Her hands were trapped between her chest and his, and she tried to worm one arm free before realizing there was no position less awkward to place it than where it had been before.

She swallowed. "Hello."

Her rescuer pulled her upright and set her on her feet. "Are you all right?"

Aviama smoothed her skirts, hoping the action would camouflage even slightly the flush of heat filling her cheeks. "Yes. Yes, of course. I'm so sorry. We had an, erm, incident, and I guess in my hurry I turned the corner sharper than I thought and..." Her voice trailed off, and she gestured at his torso.

"Ran into me." He quirked an eyebrow. "I thought I'd have

to go through this whole contest, but if sharp corners are all it takes to have a beautiful woman fall into my arms, perhaps I can be done with the whole charade!"

Aviama gasped. "Prince Shiva?"

Her gaze swept over him, and she could have sworn—if it were ladylike for princesses to swear, that is. Zephan and Semra swore, but neither of them was a princess.

Goldenrod yellow stitched with red and orange swathed the prince's butter-smooth almond skin in a tunic to his knees, with dark pants underneath. The Radhan symbol marked both shoulders, the short-standing collar glistened in silken thread, and a bodyguard trailed him.

The evidence was so glaringly obvious now that she had little else to say.

He bowed and kissed her hand. "At your service. And you, my lady?"

"Princess Aviama of Jannemar. We only just arrived."

"Your Highness! Ah, the princess from the dragon witch's land."

Aviama bristled. Was magic all Jannemar was known for since The Return? Did it always sound so unfavorable? "No, we have no witches. I believe you mispronounced *dragonlord*."

He tilted his head, regarding her with interest. "So I did."

Aviama shifted her weight, the heavy gazes of Murin, Amir, Enzo, and the Radhan man in Enzo's grasp settling over her like a thick cloud, observing their exchange.

Shiva took a breath and scanned the space beyond her. "An incident, you say?"

"It was nothing."

Shiva glanced at Aviama, and his eyes narrowed. His attention flicked back to his steward. "Amir?"

Amir bowed. "This man spat at Princess Aviama and attempted to assault her, my prince. Her guard acted quickly enough to stop his insolence from causing harm, and the princess requested his life be spared and he be dealt with according to our ways."

Shiva's expression turned to flint, and he turned on the Radhan servant. "What do you have to say for yourself, fool?"

The man stiffened and dropped into as deep a bow as Enzo would allow. Enzo dropped his weight to allow the man movement, and the servant crumbled, touching his forehead to the floor. "I am at your mercy, Your Highness, my lord! I was not myself."

"You are at my mercy, you say. I have none. Our ways do not give allowance for assaulting a member of the royal family without penalty of death."

The man wept into the floor, and a shiver ran down Aviama's spine at his words. The palms of her hands began to sweat, and the lightest touch of breeze wafted from her hands and played along her fingertips. She pressed her hands together and bit her lip.

Shiva pressed his mouth into a tight line. He eyed Aviama, then dropped his shoulders and spread his hands as he turned back to Amir. "But, in honor of our guest, have him flogged and dismissed from service with his head still attached to his shoulders. This is mercy, man. Learn some respect."

The prince jerked his chin toward the man on the floor, and two guards materialized from behind columns to take hold of him and haul him away. Aviama twisted around. Had they been there the whole time? No, surely, they'd merely watched the scene unfold and approached to stand at the ready.

Shiva whirled back to Aviama and captured her hand in his, dirty as it was from the road, sand caked under her nails, and brought it to his lips. She nearly snatched it away in her embarrassment, and her hesitation earned her a questioning look from the prince as he glanced up in surprise from beneath long, dark lashes. She bit her lip, and he kissed her hand. A tingling shot of warmth ran goosebumps up her arm, and she'd never been more grateful for long sleeves.

"I take my leave," he said, dropping her hand. "I trust Amir will care for any needs you have. Do accept our deepest condolences for the barbaric behavior of our servant. Gracious as you are, I will ensure all our staff know that any further outbursts will not be met with the kindness of Jannemar, but with the justice of Radha. I look forward to seeing you again at the welcome banquet."

He turned to go, then paused and pivoted back to her. "Perhaps, if you don't mind—would you keep our meeting between us? I wasn't meant to meet any of the princesses before tonight. I wouldn't want the others to think I showed any preferential treatment."

Of course. Yes, naturally. How thoughtful of you. But to Aviama's dismay, none of those words made it out her mouth. She nodded dumbly, and he dipped his head in gratitude and disappeared down the corridor behind her.

Amir cleared his throat and recaptured her attention, leading them once again through a series of courtyards and long halls and up a flight of stairs until at last he opened a door, stepped inside, and swept his arm inward. "Here we are."

Murin sucked in a breath, and Aviama very nearly did the same as she came across the threshold. The entire room was a deep lapis-lazuli blue, thick with intricate white designs wrapping up the walls and across the vaulted ceilings. An archway led out to a balcony next to three more arched windows lining one side, afternoon light pouring in onto white couches and chairs. A set of pillars and gauzy drapes separated the sitting room from a large bed set low to the ground and dressed in vibrant-orange satin coverings.

Rich, sweet, decadent scents wafted through the air from the silhouette of a steaming bath just visible through the filmy drapes. A platter of berries and sweet cakes stood with a water pitcher and crystal glasses. Aviama's mouth watered, and her stomach growled again.

She cleared her throat to cover the noise and turned to Amir. "Thank you. It's beautiful."

Amir bowed. "Your things will be brought up when they arrive. Get some rest, Your Highness."

Enzo gave her a nod and took up his position outside her door. The moment the door clicked closed, Aviama threw herself down on the couch with a grunt.

This morning, her anxieties had whipped an unnatural storm into such frenzy that she'd nearly run her ship aground. She couldn't remember a time when her powers created something quite so strong, but maybe she was even more uptight about the contest than she'd thought.

Since the storm blew over, they had docked at harbor, sent her to the palace in a pakshi sledge that wasn't even covered enough to protect from the dunes, *without* her gifts to her hosts, arrived at the enormous palace, been spat on, insulted, and assaulted, broken the culture of the palace by trying to help a servant woman, and run straight into the prince himself.

Aviama flung an arm over her face and moaned. It had all happened so fast. Causing a scene is *not* how she'd hoped to make her first impression. But then, based on some of the glares she'd received, coupled with the outburst of the Radhan servant, maybe her first impression was made for her. Maybe the people simply hated Jannemari people, and would hate her for all she represented. But if Radha hated Jannemar, if they hated—what had the servant called her?—*melderblood,* then why invite her at all?

Still, she'd seen no disdain in Prince Shiva's eyes, even if he did call Semra a dragon witch. No, with him, she'd seen something else. *Felt* something else.

But that was ridiculous. She'd only just met the man, and he probably charmed every girl he saw. His ridiculous face and strong arms and silky voice would have seen to that. Besides, by the time she got to the palace, she'd looked like she was dragged *behind* the sledge rather than arrived riding *in* it. No man in his right mind would see her in such a state and think to himself, *there's a girl I want to stare at for the rest of my life.*

And after the bumbling idiocy that tripped out of her mouth, she also doubted he'd considered her as a confidante with whom to share all his military secrets.

Her stomach burbled again, but her aching muscles begged for reprieve. Her arms and legs felt as though they might crumble to dust if she made a move for the tray of sweets. Aviama lay on the couch, silently debating the pros and cons of what she should do first: eat, bathe, or swear never to move from this exact spot. Murin had busied herself checking the bath, wardrobe, and vanity to see that everything was in order, and she could hear her soft patter cross the room this way and that.

Aviama lifted her arm and squinted up at the lapis-blue ceiling, then pushed herself up on the couch. Sand trickled down her back and into the crevices of the couch. Her hair felt crunchy with sea salt, dirt, and sailing, and her body felt just as grimy under her dusty silks.

Bath it is.

Murin hurried to help her undress, and Aviama sank into the steaming bathtub with an audible sigh. Bergamot, jasmine, and sage swirled to her nostrils in a heavenly aroma as the filth of the ship and the dust of the road washed free from her body. Murin massaged her scalp and shampooed her hair until the dirty, scrubby feeling was replaced with freshness, scented oil, and perfume.

By the time she emerged, her skin was smooth, her hair was clean, and her aching feet were placated. The trunks of her wardrobe arrived at the door, and Murin received them and arranged the clothes in the tall armoire to one side of the bedchamber.

Aviama stepped from the bath and reached for a towel. "Tell me the truth. How bad was it today, Murin?"

Murin pulled the last of the gowns from the trunk. "Oh, the servant man certainly was angry, but you handled yourself well, princess. And Amir and the prince were on your side, precisely as they should have been."

Aviama pursed her lips. "And the prince? What did you think of him?"

Murin leaned back from the armoire and tossed her a devilish grin. "Oh, I think you'd make a fine match, Your Highness."

She laughed. "You know I'm one of four princesses, and he may not choose me, right? In the end, even if he does ask me, I may not choose him either!"

Murin dipped her head. "Yes, yes..."

The smile waned from Aviama's face. She wished she could have told Murin her real purpose here and the true state of things back home. But it wouldn't be appropriate, and Zephan and Semra had charged her not to tell a soul, and she'd kept her word.

But such secrets were lonely.

Aviama sucked in a deep breath and let it out. Sometimes lonely things grew lonelier with cheerful people about, no matter how comforting they were at other times. "Thank you, Murin. For everything, always. Why don't you go inquire about your own quarters, and get cleaned up yourself?"

Murin looked up. "Are you sure?"

Aviama nodded. "I'm quite capable of milling about my room alone without tripping into any unsuspecting royals, and Enzo is at the door to stop anyone from trying to stab me. I'll find something to wear for now and let you dress me for the banquet tonight. We're all good here."

The girl smiled and curtsied. "Of course, Your Highness. Call for me the moment you have a need!"

Aviama assured her she would and waited for the door to shut again before wrapping the towel around herself and crossing the cold floor to the armoire. She selected a simple pale-blue velvet dress with a draping silver girdle and wide, sweeping sleeves. It was beautiful, but it was also *comfortable*. A rare and wondrous combination, and a necessity on a day like today.

She scrunched her hair with the towel and let it fall damp over her shoulders to dry, then reached for the platter. Aviama didn't know what kind of foods the Radhans served at banquets, but when she bit into a red berry and pinched off a corner of the cake, she didn't care. Whatever it was surely would not compare with this.

It almost made her forget that she'd been insulted, attacked, been accurately accused of having melderblood (though she wasn't supposed to let anyone know about that), and had rammed into the prince for a stellar first impression smelling of sailors and sea and wearing her hair in the alluring style of the bird nest.

Almost.

Aviama crammed the rest of the cake into her mouth. Fluffy soft sweetness melted on her tongue, honey with hints of walnut mingled in with—she stopped. *Paper?*

The rude interruption to her flavorful taste, the sharp edge of the parchment poking the roof of her mouth where spongy cake should have reigned supreme, caught her off guard. She drew out the offensive intruder and found that it was indeed a slip of paper, neatly folded inside the cake.

I know what you are.
Midnight. Butterfly pavilion.
Come alone.

Aviama swallowed, and her throat constricted. *I know what you are.* Not who. *What.*

At least the location didn't sound so bad. But then the Radhan servant's face filled her mind, seething hatred and contempt in every muscle he moved to form the word: *kingdom of melderblood.* If that's how Radhans felt about her just for being connected with the kingdom that brought about the return of magic—and with it, elemental melders—how would they feel if they knew Aviama *was* a melder?

Her stomach soured. She knew exactly how they would feel. And more importantly, what they would *do.* If the sentiment against melderbloods really was so grim in Radha, and if someone really did know she was a melder and leaked that information...

She'd be lucky to live out the week.

5

Aviama brushed the crumbs from her fingers and lunged for the balcony. Air. She needed air.

Power pooled at her palms to the drum of her wild heartbeat. A breeze lifted the ends of her hair as she strode to the railing, eyes searching the courtyard below, the knives on her forearms suddenly bringing more comfort than she'd expected. Not that she was good enough with them to be particularly useful, but there was some small solace in not being completely helpless.

She took a breath and let it out slowly, but her thoughts sped along their course just as precipitously as before.

Someone was threatening to kill her. But if the person who wrote the note was also the one who wanted her dead, how could they expect her to waltz right into their clutches at the time and place of their choosing?

But then, if they wanted to kill her, wouldn't it be smarter to poison the cakes she'd scarfed down so thoughtlessly and be done with it? Why put in all the effort to get a message to her without anybody noticing?

Come alone.

A ridiculous suggestion. Her bodyguard followed her everywhere, and as a foreign princess at the palace, she was high profile—easily recognized, noticed by everyone, and not free to roam someone else's house. It was suspicious, not to mention rude.

Although getting the information about Radha's military plans might lead to some suspect behavior anyway. She was a spy, after all. But she didn't think it would start quite so soon, and she'd expected to have the element of surprise. Nobody had any reason to believe the eighteen-year-old Jannemari princess was anything more than a pawn in the game of kings —a broke kingdom wanting allies and security, and a magic-hating kingdom wanting...wanting what, exactly?

Information on magic? An alliance that provided access to Jannemar's mines that Radha seemed to want so badly? Or was it simply time for the prince to marry, and the king had decided any of the women from bordering nations would do, and he would make an alliance with whichever kingdom allowed his son the most marital happiness?

Enzo stood just outside. She could open the door, show him the note, and ask him what to do. But then she'd have to explain that she had powers, which Zephan had expressly forbidden her from doing. Not telling *anyone* meant not telling *anyone*. Not even Murin knew.

The windstorm off the coast would have given them pause. Surely some of the crew of her ship had realized someone on board had powers—or that someone on Radha's side did, and was trying to stir up trouble for their docking.

So how did this person, from across the sea, claim to know what her lady-in-waiting and personal bodyguard did not?

The fingers of Aviama's right hand dug into the rail of the balcony, her left hand crushing the slip of parchment in her fist. She stared out on the courtyard below, at everything and nothing, hardly registering anything in her field of view. Slowly the scene before her sharpened into focus—the pakshi-shaped pool surrounded by fruit trees and flowers, the benches nestled under their shade, the pillars lining the border where the courtyard ended and the halls of the palace began again.

The man standing under the shadow of the trees. A gem-studded collar lay over his ruddy chestnut chest, and golden bands adorned bare, corded arms. Clearly not a nobody—but also not Radhan, as the white linen wrapping his waist in a schenti and extending to his knees displayed a style she'd not yet seen. A neatly trimmed short, black beard framed his face, and his eyes—

With a start, she realized the man was staring at her. Glaring. Hard.

Aviama sucked in a breath and jerked back from the balcony railing. Those hard eyes...she couldn't shake their sharpness, their severity. Was this the man who'd left the note? Had he waited to ensure she'd got the message? If so, did he want to protect her...or kill her?

She squeezed her eyes shut. Too many possibilities. Too many variables. No way to know how many people wanted her dead, or how to tell friend from foe. But she needed information. Aviama looked down at the paper in her hand.

Information.

Aviama shook her head. *Don't be an idiot. Going to mysterious meetings alone without backup is how people die. Zephan will kill you. No, wait, he won't. Because you'll already be dead.*

She paused. If Semra were here, she would go. Addicted to danger, they called her. Well, maybe it was true, but Semra would go to the meeting. And Semra's way had saved Jannemar more than once.

Aviama spun back to the inner sanctum of her quarters

and perched on the edge of the bed, chewing her nail. Her gaze flicked to the balcony every few seconds as if the stranger under the fruit trees would spring to the railing like a frog and tumble in with swords drawn.

If he *had* written the note, she wasn't so sure she wanted to see him again. Her mind redrew the high cheekbones of his face and the curve of his arms as she considered it. *Biscuits. You're insane.* No, he looked like the kind of man who could tear her limb from limb and then casually eat pastries over her body. A chill ran down her spine.

No thank you.

But which was worse, really? Him writing the note, setting a meeting, and *not* wanting her dead; or him *not* writing the note, *not* setting the meeting, and plotting her demise?

She launched to her feet. *That's it. I'm talking to Enzo. I won't tell him what's going on, but I'll ask him about security measures, any rumors he's heard in the halls, anything he knows about the people here and what they might have against Jannemar.*

Her breathing ticked up a notch as she strode for the door. Even as her hand lifted the latch, she wasn't sure having the conversation was a good idea. But it was the best option she had.

The door swung open and—

Aviama stopped cold. Enzo was gone. And in his place stood an imposing, dark-eyed Radhan shorter than Enzo but at least as broad and busting with muscle. Ice crept along her skin and reached long, frosted fingers toward her racing heart.

"Who are you?"

He looked back at her with disinterest. "Ishaan."

"Where is my guard?"

Ishaan dipped his head in the shallowest of bows. "He took ill, Your Highness. He hopes to return in time for the banquet tonight, but until then, I am his replacement for your security."

Aviama's mouth went dry. "Can I see him?"

"No, Your Highness. Several of the men from the guard-houses have gotten sick, and the infirmary is off limits. If your guard comes down with the same illness, he will be quarantined until recovered. For your safety, and the health of our prince, whom you will be interacting with, we will keep sickness in the sick bay."

Aviama shut the door. It swung closed harder than she expected, and she jumped, then questioned the wisdom of rudely cutting off a conversation with the person solely responsible for keeping her alive.

She opened the door. "Um, thank you."

Ishaan dipped his head.

Aviama closed the door again. She poured herself a glass of water and sank onto the couch. A tiny eddy of air wound around her fingers, and she let it play along her hands, absent-mindedly spinning it from one hand to the other.

A knock came at the door. She squashed the air current. "Yes?"

"It's me, Your Highness. I'm here to get you ready for the banquet."

Murin! How long had Aviama been sitting? She ran to the door and opened it, eyeing Ishaan and ushering her lady-in-waiting inside. What if he didn't want to keep her safe? What if *he* was one of the people who wanted to kill her?

Murin floated through the room, laying out dresses and girdles and jewelry, commenting on the loveliness of the palace, the fine weather, the prince's gentlemanly manner when they'd met him earlier in the day. Aviama nodded and smiled and *mhmm*ed at all of it, but the parchment from the cake seemed to burn a hole in her gauntlet.

A rich amethyst purple gown was selected, and she liked it, though she wasn't sure if she'd agreed to it somewhere in her vague responses or if Murin had simply taken charge of the situation. The fitted bodice sparkled with metallic gold woven into the brocade, and her long golden curls were twisted and pinned up with a circlet set on her head. Aviama fiddled with the rings on her fingers, and her thumb brushed the hilt of the throwing knife through her sleeve.

Murin pressed her lips together. "They're very beautiful, but a bit too aggressive for a formal banquet in a foreign nation, don't you think?"

Aviama snapped her head up. Weapons at a dinner certainly did seem untoward. "Yes, of course. You're right." But she unbuckled only the gauntlet of her right hand, which she would be extending for greetings for people to kiss. The other hid well enough in her long flowing sleeve, and though she was confident she'd be incapable of using it efficiently if the need arose, having it close felt important somehow.

Maybe only because it was a taste of home.

By the time Ishaan knocked on the door to escort her to the banquet, Murin had asked Aviama three times if she was all right, and finally declared to her that it was normal to be nervous, that she looked every bit the stunning princess that she was, and that she would do great at the introduction dinner. Aviama murmured her thanks, but all she could think about was the Radhan servant spitting at her feet, the stranger in the courtyard glaring daggers, and imagining what style of death Ishaan might prefer if he was assigned to take her life.

She hardly noticed the ornate, colorful halls, arches, and courtyards as she left Murin behind and followed Ishaan through the palace. They'd already passed two pools by the time Aviama realized she should be looking for the butterfly pavilion.

Not that she'd decided to go.

Because that was a ridiculous plan. Especially now that Enzo had disappeared.

Lively music bounced down the corridor, and massive double doors stood open like glorious bronze sentries leading into a wide-open circular ballroom with soaring ceilings, dripping with crystal chandeliers. Long tables set with silver and arrayed with spires of tall vases of red and orange flowers lined the far end, leaving the center of the room empty. Servants bustled to and fro with platters, and dancers accompanied the musicians opposite the tables.

Well-dressed guests were already seated at the tables—nobles, visiting dignitaries, other men of state. The king and queen of Radha stood at the head of the long center table. King Dahnuk was draped in rich patterned gold and a long necklace of six strands of pearls, a heavy crown on his head, and a twinkle in his eye as he ran a hand through his graying beard. Beside him, Queen Satya was also dressed in gold and wore a similar pearl necklace and a second gem-studded necklace against her throat. Black hair topped with her own crown matched intense, black-lined eyes, and Aviama nearly faltered at the sight of them.

Their son stood at the right hand of his father, dressed in sun-kissed yellow and gold and looking the spitting image of his father. Aviama could see the queen in Shiva's strong cheekbones and penetrating gaze, but next to King Dahnuk it was clear whose likeness he favored.

What had he made of their unconventional meeting that afternoon? He'd smelled like spices. She'd smelled like sand and salt and sailor-sweat. Okay, so some of it was her own sweat, but the stink of the ship had certainly lingered. She bit her lip, caught herself, and released it, clasping her hands tightly before her.

When she looked up again, Shiva had been looking at her, but his glance quickly jerked back to the two women before him. He said nothing, but the ends of his mouth curved just slightly. Something in Aviama's stomach twisted, but she turned to follow his attention to the regal women in the center of the room.

The first was dressed in sky blue with green rimming a wide neck, short puffy sleeves, and lacing up the sides of her torso and sleeves. Her long, red hair was plaited back in a braided net containing the rest of her tresses, and a crown too big for her face sat low on her forehead. Large, green eyes peered out above a small, crooked nose and thin lips, and she reminded Aviama of a doe caught in the wood. Graceful, but flighty.

Her dress style was enough to identify her as Princess Darra of Curion. She curtsied into a neat, clipped curtsy and bobbed back up again as if she were on a spring. She must have been introduced just before Aviama arrived. Prince Shiva bowed to Darra and kissed her hand, and the king and queen dipped their heads.

The second woman wore a one-shoulder white dress falling not quite to the floor. A second swath of cloth attached at her left shoulder wrapped around her back and looped over her right arm like a shawl before drifting down toward the floor. Gold trim and an armband stood out against the white, and long earrings contrasted with deep-brown rivulets falling over one shoulder. A simple band set upon her brow, a single star affixed to her forehead. The symbol of Tomos. Princess Marija. She stood still as a swan, stunningly beautiful.

An announcer beside Aviama barked out her name, and she jumped. "Princess Aviama of Jannemar."

Aviama glanced behind her, but Ishaan made no gesture, no movement to follow, nothing. *You're on your own,* his bored dark eyes seemed to say. She pressed her lips together and swept into the center of the circular space with all the practiced grace of a thousand formal events before.

But this wasn't like a thousand formal events before. She'd never been expected to charm someone past a greeting and maybe a dance. She'd never had to hold the attention of a man or get him to tell her his secrets; she'd only had to represent her family decently and be a well-mannered host.

How was your travel? she might say. *Excellent, thank you,* they would respond. *We had the pleasure of touring your father's stables. What spectacular stock you have!* She would nod, and smile, and suggest an evening of sport to get a better look at the stallions. Laugh at marginally funny jokes. Dance with heavy-footed men and thank them afterward for the pleasure. Drift off to her chambers or her mother's sitting room when the evening was ended, letting her father and brother take over the hosting...

Aviama approached the royal family, smiled, and dropped into a curtsy, muscle memory carrying the movement while her mind spun daydreams of how her experience up to now could possibly be of help. *My, what delightful pakshi you have! I was particularly pleased when they didn't peck my eyes out. And what an impressive navy! Tell me, prince, are you and your father bent on invading Jannemar if negotiating for the Horon Mines is unsuccessful? Do you really hate melders and hope to destroy us, and if so, would you be so kind as to share a few key Radhan military weaknesses?*

Prince Shiva gave her a warm smile, and as he took her hand and brushed his lips across her knuckles, that warmth seemed to seep through her skin and trip down to the tips of her toes. Aviama felt her cheeks redden and winced. She smoothed her skirts in a vain attempt to hide the extra rosiness of her face, gave the king and queen another smile, and stepped backward to stand in line next to princesses Darra and Marija.

A loud *clink* sounded behind them, and Aviama turned toward the doors. She nearly fell over. So did the announcer, apparently, because he barely got words out before the woman before them strutted through the space.

"Princess Vanina of Batal."

Aviama had heard of the warrior women of Batal. But she hadn't imagined anything like Vanina. A glistening fitted silver breastplate wrapped her torso, long strips of cloth replacing a traditional skirt from its base so that snatches of her high silver boots and strong legs could be seen swishing beyond the skirt. Fur wrapped her shoulders and hemmed the cuffs of her billowing sleeves, and she held a longbow in her hand like a staff. The weapon stood as tall as she did, and at its sight several men from the court leaped to their feet.

Shouts filled the hall, but Aviama couldn't take her eyes off the forceful woman before her. Surely this was no pawn in a king's game. Dark hair wove back into thick braids, and her brow bore a silver horse head and serpent head wound together. A scar ran across one eye, though it hardly retracted from her striking features, and she wore white face paint in several streaks horizontally across her cheeks and the bridge of her nose, and vertically in dots down her nose and from her bottom lip to the base of her chin.

The shouts grew louder, but she held up a hand and passed her longbow to the guard at the door before sweeping into an elaborate bow with a flourish. Aviama shook her head. *What an entrance.* Nobody would remember anything else.

Prince Shiva bowed and stepped forward with his hand out, an invitation to allow him his typical greeting of a lady of her rank. She offered him her hand, gazing at him with her chin high as though this gift were the greatest he could hope for in all his days, as he kissed it and let her go.

The king clapped his hands. "Welcome! Your Royal Highnesses, esteemed women, neighbors, and—for one of you—future daughter-in-law and joining of nations. It is with great joy and honor that I welcome you tonight to Radha, our humble home. But here under the Blessing Sun we do not make speeches on empty stomachs! So sit, relax, and enjoy yourselves. And I'll give you your speech after a glass of wine or two."

The company laughed and roared, and Aviama smiled and clapped along with the women. The king gestured to four empty seats one table over from the royal family, and the princesses made their way over.

Aviama scanned the long tables as she took her seat, her pulse pounding in her ears. She'd survived the introduction, but the evening had only just begun. And someone in the palace wanted her dead.

Were they here? Was the person who wrote the note here too? Were they one and the same?

What if they weren't Radhan? What if the other princesses were spies too, and one of them was sent on a mission to kill her? Was her murderer sitting next to her even now?

Aviama swallowed. A knife flashed just over her shoulder, and she flinched away from the motion. Whoever wanted a meeting was too late.

She slipped one hand into her left sleeve. Her fingers grazed the handle of the knife.

Servants stepped forward and set down a small crystal glass in front of her. Then, in one synchronized motion, they whirled the knives in their hands in an arc, tossing up oranges, slicing them in the air, and finally setting an orange wedge on the edge of the ceramic cup. Whatever it was looked like pudding and smelled divine.

And apparently wasn't meant to kill. Aviama grimaced at her mistake, and smiled sheepishly at Vanina, who sat across from her with a raised eyebrow.

"Are you always so jumpy?"

Aviama set her jaw. "Just surprised me, is all. What a skilled display..."

She let her voice trail off and drew back her hand from the knife handle. Aviama stared into her pudding, then picked up her spoon and lifted her head—and looked straight into the eyes of the man from the courtyard outside her balcony.

6

———

Aviama fumbled her spoon, choking on nothing as her heart stopped and her stomach dropped to her toes. She snatched her spoon again before it hit the table and dipped it into her pudding. The man from the courtyard was seated at the king's table among other foreign dignitaries.

Was Jannemar hated the world over? Had The Return so sullied her kingdom's reputation? But then, if they only knew —if they only knew how necessary The Return had been to stifle a would-be dictator.

Aviama could feel Vanina's judgmental stare on her again. Maybe if she just ate her pudding and examined the tablecloth and place settings all night, she could escape without further embarrassment.

Too late. Staring at the plate will only make you look weaker than they already think you are. Aviama looked up again toward the king's table, avoiding the stranger. The king and queen of Radha sat at the head, Prince Shiva on the king's right, his three younger sisters on the queen's left, important guests filling in the seats down the line. Goblets lifted, good-natured talk and laughter floated up to the high ceilings, and the king looked nearly as excited as his daughters, who spent the evening giggling and talking quietly to one another while stealing glances at the princesses' table.

"How was your travel, Princess Aviama?"

Ugh. The same pleasantries as any formal event in the history of the world. Aviama dragged her thoughts from the king, the prince, and threats of death and turned to the speaker. Princess Darra peeped at her over a glass of wine, eyes too large for her face, expression sweet and expectant.

"Longer than I'm used to for sailing," Aviama admitted. "But the weather was favorable, and it wasn't half bad." *Except for the windstorm in the middle of that favorable weather.* She'd keep that part to herself. "And yourself?"

"Oh, not bad at all! But then, I've spent a decent amount of time on the sea. I just love it. The only thing I miss about home when I'm on a ship is a hot bath and a proper bed."

"Yes! And maybe a perfume that doesn't somehow end up smelling a little like fish by the end of the day."

Aviama smiled, and Darra laughed. "Exactly."

Vanina leaned in and dropped her voice low. "Have any of you met the prince before?"

"I have." Marija lifted her chin and drew the wine to her lips, letting all three of the women turn toward her before she spoke again. "He participated in one of our joust tournaments four years ago."

Vanina cast a sideways glance at the prince, her eyes roving over him before a mischievous smile crept across her face. "I think I could take him."

Marija scoffed. "He's got more muscle in one arm than you have in your whole body. Your war paint can't make up for brawn. He destroyed all his opponents in the joust, and he took down a few of our best fighters hand-to-hand, as well."

Vanina pursed her lips. "*Batal* women can fight just as well as men. We're trained from childhood. We don't sit around twiddling our thumbs and cooing over needlepoint."

"Oh, how the arts must suffer." Marija gave an exaggerated sigh and adjusted the bangles on her wrists, lingering to examine her nails. "I shudder to think of how ugly Batal must be to visit, with nothing valued but war."

Aviama drew back. Had the woman no tact at all? Or was she riling Vanina up on purpose? Aviama racked her brain for anything she remembered regarding Tomos' relationship with Batal, but came up empty.

Vanina opened her mouth, but Aviama heard herself talking before she could catch herself. "Women might have to work twice as hard to be as capable as well-trained men, but it's absolutely possible. I've seen it."

Marija screwed her face up in disgust. "Right. Your sister-in-law, the dragon witch. Is it true what they say? That she has more blood on her hands than most kings?"

Aviama's glare bore through Marija like fire, but the princess only smirked. She wanted to bite back, to tell her who Semra really was, what she'd done for Jannemar. How she cared more for her people than most monarchs ever did. But Semra and Zephan had warned her of others' curiosity about their situation. Better to stay quiet with someone like Marija.

Darra cleared her throat and turned back to Marija. "He came to Tomos, you said. What is he like?"

"Oh, he's the perfect prince!" Marija leaned back, glowing in the attention of the table, lighting up like a beacon at the chance to tell her story. "All the men adored him, and he had the most successful hunt of all of them. He knows his way around a bow—and word is he knows his way around a woman as well." She winked.

Aviama choked on her pudding. She glanced up at the king's table, and Shiva looked up at her in that precise moment. Her face flushed hot, and she jerked her attention back to her pudding. She jabbed her spoon into the crystal, but it was empty. Aviama lifted her glass and drained her wine instead. Also empty. *Biscuits.*

Darra's eyes bugged out, and her hand flew to her chest. "Doesn't that make him *less* perfect a prince?"

Marija's musical laugh floated up to play through the chandeliers. "How adorable you are. Oh, I don't mind my men having a bit of practice. Besides, anyone who pretends men of court aren't experienced with women are naive indeed."

The second course arrived, and the thought of Shiva gaining *experience* needled at her throughout the girls' next three topics. Did they come from large families or small? How did Batal's line of female monarchs impact its rule, if at all, and how had Tomos' trade exploded even beyond the borders of Ashwood?

Aviama gave short responses, smiling, nodding, or focusing on her own meal and pulling into her thoughts. Why did men do that—practice with other women and get praised for it? Women were not afforded the same treatment for doing the same. Was this male behavior an affliction of other nations, since her own father and brother never took consorts, prostitutes, or other sexual conquests? Or were Zephan and her father truly unique in the world of men?

Something in her stomach twisted. Is that what Shiva would be looking for in a wife? A conquest? Or could he be looking for something real, something deeper than he'd had before?

Her gaze slipped up to the king's table again and found Shiva laughing with his parents, completely oblivious to her observance. A small mercy. But an eerie feeling settled over her just the same, and as she scanned the table, she saw the stranger watching her again.

Again, the parchment burned from its hiding place in her gauntlet.

I know what you are.
Come alone.

Did *he* know what she was? Is that even what the message meant? Would Ishaan follow her every waking moment? Was Enzo still ill, and how long would it take for him to be returned to her?

The second course ended, and the king rose. Conversation died away as every eye turned to the head of the main table. King Dahnuk spread his hands and smiled.

"I think we'll all agree speeches sound better with some wine and good food. I do hope you're all enjoying yourselves."

Cheers. Applause.

He continued. "Again, I'd like to welcome our highly esteemed special guests this evening: Princess Darra of Curion, Princess Marija of Tomos, Princess Vanina of Batal, and Princess Aviama of Jannemar." He gave a slight bow, and those seated at the tables dipped their heads. Aviama gave a smile and an appreciative nod back to the king. All four of them responded as one with the same gesture.

"Radha has been profitable in recent years. Our navy continues to expand, our land armies are bored without battles. A good problem to have, yes? It is only with the return of magic that our land has suffered. Outbursts of the elements have cropped up throughout our lands, causing destruction and mayhem wherever they arise. The problem is becoming wider and wider spread, as magic seeps throughout the world from the origin point and develops into a global phenomenon."

Aviama's chest tightened as nods and murmurs rippled through the room. The origin point was obviously Jannemar —the wellspring where Aurin's spear had been removed. No one said it out loud, but she could feel the many sets of eyes flickering over her face for a reaction. She swallowed and stared harder at the king, smoothing her features into as smooth and calmly attentive an expression as she could manage.

Dahnuk held up his hands. "But in the wake of global catastrophe, nations come together. Common troubles invite collaboration, and as the Blessing Sun continues to shine on our great kingdom, there are few good things we have withheld from our children. What parents do not love to spoil their children!

"And in that effort, as our son Prince Shiva has come of age and grown into a remarkable man of strength, of strategy, of skill in combat, and of training in all areas of kingdom rule, taking on more and more responsibility—it is time for our blessing to be shared. It is time for our son to experience the blessing of marriage, and for the blessing of Radha to be joined to another kingdom, so that the strength of each might abound even more. And because of the generosity of our neighbors, representatives from four nations are here with us today."

Aviama shifted in her seat. Ah, yes—what a favor Radha was doing to whichever lucky girl and lucky kingdom Shiva chose. Except, clearly that *was* the case to some degree, or each nation would not have answered the invitation by sending their princess. Or maybe each kingdom simply could not afford to insult Radha either.

She looked at the three young Radhan princesses,

huddled together with excited sparkles in their eyes, ages ranging from maybe ten to sixteen. The queen shushed one with a stern look and then returned her attention to her husband with a graceful smile. What did they think of this selection process for the prince? Aviama found herself wondering if he was close with his family.

"And now for the rules." King Dahnuk clapped a hand on his son's shoulder, and Shiva gave him a good-natured laugh and shoulder shrug. Clearly, it was something they'd discussed. Aviama wondered how much input the prince had had, and how much he had simply been informed about.

Dahnuk held up a finger. "Evening dinners will be spent here, and we will offer you all the opportunity to sightsee and enjoy all that Radha has to offer, experiencing our culture together as a group."

A good time for the royal family and court to observe each of the women. Smart.

"The prince will have individual time to get to know each of our candidates. The order of the first round of dates will be selected at random, and he will have one date per week with each woman. That said, the prince may request additional time with any woman with whom he feels a particular connection.

"Out of respect for your time, Prince Shiva will spend two dates minimum with each princess, and after that, if he is sure he does not have the connection he would desire with you for marriage, he will send you notice that you are released from your agreement to participate in the contest and are free to return home."

Dahnuk's voice grew stern, and he looked intently at each princess in turn. "If you are not invested in this experience, and have no desire to join your kingdom with ours, say so at once and be dismissed."

Aviama froze under the king's grave stare, and her breath caught. Shiva was surprisingly handsome, but marriage wasn't her goal. She was here to keep from offending Radha, learn what they wanted from the Horon Mines, and gain military insights for Jannemar. Precisely the sort of thing one got hanged for if she learned it by snooping instead of being told freely.

Dahnuk's attention moved on to the next girl, and Aviama let out a breath. After a pause, the king's posture relaxed.

"Although I am sure that we will have no such unsavory experiences with the four of you, I would be remiss not to mention it—all candidates have entered voluntarily, and therefore any candidate who entered into this contest and is caught with another man will be regarded as in bad faith. An act of this kind will be considered aggression on Radha. A betrayal of the heart is just as great a betrayal as one on the battlefield."

The king clapped his hands, and Aviama jumped. Marija smirked. "And now, we offer you your first opportunity with our prince—a dance."

Aviama's mouth went dry. If anyone discovered she was sent as a spy, Radha could kill her and invade Jannemar. Forget philandering with other men, few things said *betrayal* like *espionage*. And now, on display for all of the Radhan court and foreign dignitaries, she must earn the prince's trust, learn Radha's intentions, and discover what plot there may be on her life—all in the public eye of the very people who may want her dead.

7

Marija's dance with Shiva was exactly what Aviama would have expected—smooth, beautiful, effortless. Marija followed Shiva's lead without a second thought, their movements all long lines and delicate turns. He spoke into her ear, and she laughed softly, then turned up to flash him a dazzling smile. It made Aviama's stomach turn.

Darra's dance was also somewhat predictable. She was hesitant and shy, but knew the steps, and Shiva held her gently through a relaxed, easy dance. Her tight shoulders softened by the end of the song, and her doe eyes were both relieved and grateful. Aviama found herself grateful, too, that Shiva had taken notice of the girl's nerves and slowed the pace. Darra seemed sweet.

Only two dances remained for the evening. Vanina stiffened as the announcer stood to announce the next dance. But it was Aviama's name he called, and her stomach squirmed under the gaze of the room as she stood from the table.

As a princess, she often drew the attention of important people, but she was never the most important person in the room. Never the focus of gossip, or intrigue, or international concern. Representing her people now for a contest of marriage she had no intention of going through with was the strangest situation in which she'd ever found herself.

Prince Shiva approached and offered her his arm, and she took it. She'd danced with a hundred men, but never in a romantic setting. Only at galas and balls and lessons, when good manners would dictate the men invite the women, and her status made her top of the list for positive connection with the royal family.

They fell into a waltz—*one, two, three, one, two, three*—and her feet took to the floor like butter, the feel of the music and the count of the beat the first true friends she'd found in Radha.

Shiva arced his arm to send her into a spin and brought her back with grace, her feet falling into step right where they'd left off. He smiled as his arm slid back in place at her back. "You're wonderful."

Aviama lifted an eyebrow. *A bit forward for a first dance.* "How would you know?"

Shiva blinked. "At dancing."

Heat flushed her cheeks pink at her mistake. "Of course. Thank you. You as well."

She winced. A smile tugged at the corner of his mouth, and those dark eyes pierced through her green ones.

"Did you get any rest before the banquet? Are you recovered from this afternoon's adventure?"

For a moment, the only adventure she could think of was her terror at finding a threatening note in her cake. Shiva turned her about the room, and the stranger from the courtyard flashed into view. An icy knife of fear panged in her gut, and she shivered. He tightened his hold in response, and she looked up at him.

The assault! The Radhan servant. She nodded. "Yes, thank you. I feel much more myself. And I'm sorry for nearly bowling you over this afternoon—and for any sand I dragged in and got on your clothes."

He laughed then, and the sound sent a tingle to her toes. "I *live* here. If sand sent me cowering, I'd be in trouble."

She gave a sheepish grin. "I suppose you would."

Another turn, and a dip. She let herself extend away from him with only the lightest touch on his arm to keep her position, and he caught her up in his arms again and spun away across the floor to the murmurs of seated guests.

Shiva had started all the conversation so far. She needed to be polite, pull her weight. *Say something interesting.* Aviama racked her brain. Nothing too controversial. Nothing political, not yet. Something personal, maybe, but not too personal. Maybe about his sisters? Yes, that would be a decent start. She opened her mouth, but it was Shiva who spoke again.

"It looked as though you had the chance for interesting conversation with the other women."

"Oh, yes, they're lovely."

He cocked his head. "All of them?"

The count continued in her head: *one, two, three, one, two three.*

Aviama shrugged. "They were all nice enough. If they were hateful this early, it would not bode well for a peaceful union, would it?"

Marija wasn't *nice enough,* exactly, but she didn't need to be labeled as the palace gossip on the first day. Better to be diplomatic. Besides, if Marija was to be believed, could she be faulted for merely mentioning truths? According to her story, it was the prince himself who wasn't acting quite *nice enough,* carelessly and without chivalry. Not the way Aviama would prefer for a future mate.

Something on her face must have given her away, though, because the prince pursed his lips. "Mhmm." He brought her close to whisper in her ear, and his breath tickled her neck. "You don't miss much, do you?"

Aviama drew back, startled. *People. Staring. Lots of people.* But then, he'd treated Marija the same while dancing, hadn't he? She swallowed. "Neither do you."

His lips twisted into a mischievous grin. "What were you ladies talking about?"

Aviama wrinkled her nose and tried not to imagine how she'd looked when Shiva had caught her eye during Marija's story. Tried. Failed. She decided to hedge the question. "Hmm? When?"

"When you were eating your invisible pudding."

No way was she telling him the answer to that. *He knows his way around a woman.* Aviama blushed again at the memory of Marija's sultry expression and the wink she gave as she'd said it. She shook off the thought and lifted her chin.

"Oh, well, we discussed the genius of Radha to develop an invisible delicacy. We thought it both a social and economic achievement, and debated the storage space required in your storehouses, and how you could keep accurate inventory without being able to see it."

Surprise flickered across his face, and Shiva laughed loud before he could stop it. He caught himself, sent her into a spin, and looked at her again with a sparkle in his eye. "My princess, you dance like a queen, but you talk with the ease of a sister."

"I *am* a sister. I've had practice."

Shiva's hand on hers and arm at her back gave subtle cues directing her this way and that across the floor, and she responded to each; their steps flowed as one, poetry set to music. Aviama studied the lines of his face, the light in his eyes as curiosity seeped through the practiced formal exterior. The song ended, and they broke apart, his hand brushing her skin to stay in contact for a lingering moment as they turned to face each other.

Shiva reached out and claimed her hand again, kissing her fingers and leaning toward her. "I'm going to make you tell me what you talked about."

Something about the roguish look he gave her made her laugh. It made her want to be an imp, too, just for kicks. She dropped into the most elegant curtsy she could muster, flashed her eyes up at him, and smiled.

"You can certainly try."

She could feel his gaze on her back as she floated back to her seat, and even as he invited Vanina onto the floor and the next song began, twice she caught him glancing her way. Of course, she was watching him, too.

He's the prince, in the middle of the room. He's the spectacle. You're supposed to be looking at him—but he's not supposed to be looking at you. Not when it's Vanina's turn.

Her mouth twitched, and Marija glared daggers at her from across the table. Aviama snatched the goblet of wine and took a sip, keeping the stem in her fingers to keep from fidgeting.

The contest wouldn't end in marriage—at least, not for her —but it might be a little fun. And maybe, if nothing else, she could find common ground between Radha and Jannemar and build a positive relationship between them.

Vanina's dance with Shiva was a bit jerky and halting, an odd contrast to her dramatic, confident entrance. Their expressions were pleasant, Shiva's polite and well-mannered, Vanina's cool and collected except for the moments when she stumbled and grimaced.

Marija clucked her tongue and leaned over to Aviama and

Darra. "Two left feet. A little focus on the arts would have benefited her today."

Aviama took a breath and let it out. What comments had Marija made about Aviama during her dance?

The last dance ended, and the king thanked everyone and concluded the evening. Each woman would be invited to their first one-on-one time with the prince this week, and King Dahnuk encouraged them all to rest from their long journeys and explore the main courtyards and library at their leisure. Amir would be available for any questions or concerns, and palace servants could also relay any needs they had.

Aviama's thoughts drifted back to the paper in the cake and the meeting that night. The water clock indicated two hours until midnight. Ishaan fell in step behind her again as she left the room, and one hall led into another hall, and another. She realized she could hardly make it back to her own room, much less have any idea where to find courtyards she had yet been to see.

Not that she was going to the meeting.

But she was, wasn't she?

Aviama stopped in her tracks and gave a heavy sigh. She glanced back at Ishaan and gestured for him to lead. "Do you mind? I'm not used to the palace, and I'm not sure where I'm going. Can you tell me a bit about where things are as we head back?"

Ishaan stared at her with an expression somewhere between boredom and disdain, but he dipped his head and took the lead. He rattled off general directions for various courtyards, the library, the throne room. A roar rattled the air from a distance, and Aviama jumped. Ishaan swept his hand in that direction and noted the menagerie of the king's collection of exotic animals was several corridors down.

Aviama's jaw dropped. "The king keeps exotic animals—inside the palace?"

Ishaan nodded. "Yes, from as many places as he can. It's a hobby and his great pride."

"What kind of animals?"

"All kinds. And down this way, the lotus pool, and that way, outside to the sparring area."

Ishaan could not have cared less, but how was she supposed to *not* be surprised by a king keeping all manner of dangerous beasts inside his house? An enormous house, but still. Aviama wondered if they ever broke loose, or if any of the residence rooms could hear them at night like she had heard them as she passed by.

It was then that she realized Ishaan had just mentioned the butterfly pavilion, and she'd missed it. Somewhere down the hall to her left...

Aviama made a mental note and did her best to track their steps back to her chambers from there. But directions were not her strong suit, and the path was already fuzzy in her brain by the time they reached her door.

But she had to remember how to get there. Because she'd already decided she was going. Enzo was missing. Half of Radha seemed to hate her simply for being *from* the kingdom that brought magic back. And between the stranger from the courtyard and the note, she'd never forgive herself if she didn't at least go and see *who* was waiting for her there.

All she had to do was slip Ishaan, find her way back through the halls, locate the butterfly pavilion, avoid whatever faceless enemies she might meet on her way, and return to her chambers unnoticed.

She stepped into her chambers and Ishaan swung the heavy door shut behind her. It latched with a thud of finality.

Biscuits.

8

Murin was waiting for her inside, plumping already-plumped pillows and smoothing the already-smooth comforter. She brightened as Aviama walked in, and Aviama did her best to smile. It wasn't Murin's fault Aviama didn't want to see a single soul.

She wasn't late for any meeting.

Aviama wasn't late either, but with Ishaan outside the door, Murin in her room, and only a vague idea of where she might find the butterfly pavilion, it was safer to assume she had little time to spare. How long had it taken to walk back from dinner?

"Oh, Your Highness! How did it go? Word already spread —your dance was divine. *Divine!* They say he didn't seem to want to let you go. Is it true? What did you think of it?"

Aviama walked in and poured herself a glass of water. She took a sip. "He was..." A great dancer. Handsome. Intense. Supposedly *experienced.* "Very nice."

Murin flashed her a grin. "You are so modest. Is it too soon to hear wedding bells? I'm kidding, of course, you know I am. You take all the time you need to make such important decisions, and I know you just met, but he does seem like a gentleman."

"He does." Aviama scanned the room. Wardrobe, bed, vanity, writing desk. Her trunks set at the foot of the bed. Across to the sitting area, sofas, chairs, and a low table stood out under the rich blue-and-white patterns of the walls and ceilings. But no inspiration struck as to how to get out of the room. "Have you seen or heard from Enzo?"

"I heard he was sick, and several of our sailors also." Murin's brow furrowed in concern. "They're in quarantine."

"Have you heard from him directly or seen him at all? How did you learn of it?"

She shrugged. "Just from the other servants."

Aviama twisted the rings on her fingers. "Did he tell you he was feeling ill? Did he look ill before today?"

"No, he didn't. Everyone seemed healthy. Is everything okay?"

It was probably nothing. The journey was long, after all, and perhaps he felt it was professional of him to hide his ailment until he was far too sick to ignore it. She'd known plenty of people to follow that trajectory. Her father came to mind. And Semra.

"I'm sure it's nothing. I'm just worried about him." Aviama crossed to the door and opened it. There he was, her latest shadow. "Ishaan, would you be so kind as to inquire about my guard and when I may have the chance to visit him?"

He gave a nod. "Yes, Your Highness. I'll find out in the morning."

Aviama dipped her head and closed the door. But the queasy feeling in her stomach didn't go away. When did Ishaan sleep? Who would cover her door in his absence?

Aviama flopped onto the bed and buried her face in the

pillow. "I'd love to tell you about the evening. But I'm exhausted. Can I tell you about it tomorrow?"

A pause. "Your Highness?"

Aviama lifted her head, then glanced down at the pillow muffling her voice. She cleared her throat. "I think I need to get some rest. But I'll tell you everything tomorrow."

Murin curtsied. "Of course, of course."

She turned to go, and Aviama sat up. "Murin?"

"Yes, Your Highness?"

"Could you...could you be here early tomorrow morning?"

"Of course, princess. I'll be here at first light."

"Thank you."

Murin slipped out, and Aviama fell back onto the bed. It gave her some comfort, knowing after whatever happened tonight, she wouldn't be alone in her rooms tomorrow. She could get dressed and go out to the courtyards, explore a bit, with a familiar face by her side.

Maybe she should stagger her routine, and keep from doing the same thing every day. Frigibar, the last Keeper of Magic, who had watched over the wellspring until Aurin's spear was removed and magic returned, had taught her how to mold her power and maintain better control. But he'd also told her about the dangers of a world thrown into magic after being without it for so long, how in some lands melders might be seen as superhuman or gods of sorts, and in others as pariahs, a curse to be blotted out.

People fear what they do not understand, he had said. *And with so many melders realizing their powers but having no knowledge to control them, chances are high the view of those with powers will be tainted early on in this new era.* An image of the older man stroking his long, gray beard filled her mind. *Tragedy on tragedy will strike, and who will be there to blame but the person staring at their hands, stuttering as they drown in their own fear?*

It was part of the reason Semra and Zephan had worked to conceal Aviama's powers, why Aviama had spent that first summer away with Frigibar to practice control away from prying eyes. Semra did her best to protect and train and inform those with confusing abilities cropping up throughout Jannemar, since she alone had experienced magic before The Return and learned to manage it.

So she would change up her schedule while in Radha, and avoid doing the same things at the same times every day. But dinners were served together, not to mention the sightseeing outings the king had mentioned, and as one of only four high-profile contestants, she could hardly sneeze without the whole palace knowing about it.

How long had it taken the servants to spread word about the princesses' dances, that Murin knew about it before Aviama had even made it back to her room?

But more pressing concerns loomed over her mind. She glanced at the door.

Aviama hopped off the bed and moved to the wardrobe, opening the doors and ruffling through dresses, girdles, ribbons, and nightgowns. The rustle of silk, the sheen of velvet, the sparkle of gemstones screamed *royalty* from every corner and drawer. She couldn't look like she was hiding her identity, but she couldn't afford to attract attention either.

Her fingers ran across a light, sage-green mantle with a hood. The hood was questionable, but so was blonde hair in a sea of dark-haired Radhans. Anyway, it was devoid of glitter and clasped in the front, so she could ditch the hood and cover most of her dress. And an extra layer made sense, given the chill settling into the air as night descended on the palace.

Aviama pulled out the mantle and slipped out to the

balcony. Several other second- and third-floor balconies overlooked the Pakshi Courtyard, where she'd seen the dark stranger glaring at her. She wondered for a moment if one of them were his, or if perhaps they belonged to the other princesses.

Moonlight spilled down onto the water of the bird-shaped pool from the open air above. Yellow, blue, and green tiles patterned the floor, only broken up by the cool white of the marble columns lining the edge of the courtyard at intervals. Aviama peeked over the edge of the balcony and sucked in a breath.

Something told her this was the stupidest thing she'd ever done. That thought grew as she peered into the vacant space below, looking both ways, as she looped her mantle around one of the balcony spindles, and as she hiked up her skirts to swing herself over the railing. She thought it as she gripped the edges of the mantle, and as she slipped off the edge and fell.

The mantle held her weight, and she dropped the rest of the way to the floor. A light wind from her palms buoyed her up to slow her fall, and she landed without a sound. It was a risk, but she didn't slow herself enough for anything to look out of the ordinary. Just enough for quiet.

Aviama slung the mantle across her shoulders and stole along the shadows of the pillars back in the direction they'd come that evening. Of course, that evening, they'd eventually wound up on the second floor, not the first. And her sense of direction was bad enough retracing paths she'd physically been down before.

Reds, yellows, blues, and greens intertwined in intricate patterns covering the walls and ceilings, occasional gilded embossing or metallic gloss catching the moonlight that made its way in from windows or open courtyards. The visuals were stunning, and not quite so cold as the simple sandstone of her castle home in Jannemar. The House of the Blessing Sun put on an excellent show. Still, as she passed one hall after another, she couldn't help but wonder how much the attention to detail and ornate splendor were just that—a show.

Did Radha really have so much disposable capital? Or was this the prize of generations past, its beauty now a showpiece for foreign visitors to gape and gawk and respect the great kingdom that produced it? Aviama was under no illusions that the Tanashais had only one palace. Their kingdom was much larger than Jannemar, and they selected the House of the Blessing Sun for a reason. Location or splendor, she wasn't sure.

But the image of the servant she'd knocked over when she arrived flew to her mind. Terror in her eyes. Wild concern. What would happen to a servant who permitted a guest to help them with their duty, even in a small way? What was the real story of Radha?

Maybe it was just the dark talking now, tainting her thoughts. Maybe it was something Frigibar said—*every house has two stories. The one it presents to the world, and the one hiding in the cracks of the foundation.*

A chill ran down her spine. She hadn't expected to see cracks so early. So who was so desperate to share them? Because the meeting was more than a threat to Aviama. It was a revelation: Radha was not all that it seemed.

She turned a corner and the soft patter of her shoes echoed down the empty corridor, lit only by two flickering lanterns. She blinked. Red ocher painted the walls like blood, delicate lines of gold leaf running through it in every direction.

Aviama's stomach turned. She'd seen this hall before,

gotten the same feeling she shouldn't be there, and chosen a different hall. She was lost.

What if this part of the palace was off limits? What if she couldn't find her way back to her room, much less to the meeting, and was caught having roamed the palace all night and accused of spying and taken prisoner, and they launched a war on Jannemar, all before she'd been in Radha twenty-four hours?

A dramatization, certainly. Her mouth went dry. Wasn't it?

She turned on her heel and retraced her steps. Ishaan had pointed out a pool close to the butterfly pavilion—if she could find it, she might regain her bearings. Aviama fiddled with the rings on her fingers and counted the stones set in the band. *One, two, three, four.* Her heart pounded, and her palms began to sweat. She counted the stones six times over. The number never changed.

In three more turns she found it, the pool in the shape of a lotus. A lump rose in her throat at the sight. Aviama stepped under the shadow of a cluster of fruit trees just beyond the edge where moonlight kissed the marble floor from the open air above. Water trickled from a fountain in the middle of the pool, benches sat forlorn and empty, and she racked her brain for the direction Ishaan may have indicated for the butterfly pavilion.

A deep rumble of a voice cut through the darkness behind her.

"Are you lost, princess?"

9

Aviama yelped and spun. A dark figure emerged out of the shadow, and by now, she would have known those piercing eyes, deep chestnut complexion, and muscular shoulders anywhere. She'd imagined him or Ishaan lurking around every turn—but finding the stranger now, in the flesh, struck fear to the core of her heart.

She shrank back, and her hand flew to her wrist. *Fat lot of good that will do you. That would be a great narrative—ditch your guard, run amuck through the palace, murder a dignitary of some sort.* She dropped her hand.

The man held up a hand. "I didn't mean to frighten you."

"Yes, well, you did." Aviama ran her fingers over her ring. *One, two, three, four.* She bit her lip, then released it, self-conscious.

"My apologies. Are you lost?"

Yes. I'm unguarded, alone, and completely unaware of where I am or how to get help were I to need it. Aviama swallowed. "I couldn't sleep."

"You're not in nightclothes."

Aviama stiffened. "You might prance about the palace

common areas in nothing but a collar and a schenti, but I do not."

His eyebrows soared, and her mouth dropped open. She clapped a hand over it and stepped back. *Biscuits.* "I'm so sorry. I'm afraid I'm a bit on edge."

If he was here to kill her, maybe she wouldn't be embarrassed for long.

"That seems to be a fair assessment." The man studied her. "I'm often in the courtyards and pool areas. They feel the most like home to me. That's why you saw me there earlier."

What was she supposed to do with that?

"Okay."

His arm moved, and she flinched. He hesitated, then crossed his arms and leaned back against one of the trees. "So. You're not lost."

"No."

"And if I left you right now, you'd know exactly where to go."

Aviama lifted her chin. "I'd figure it out."

Was he really going to leave? If he left, he must not be the person who wrote the note. Which meant he was still in the running for people who might want to kill her. He had definitely glared at her that afternoon in the courtyard, and again at the banquet. And she still didn't know who he was.

"Mhmm." He stroked his trimmed beard and turned to go.

Aviama steeled herself and cleared her throat. "You know who I am."

He turned back, the hint of an amused smile flickering across his face. "You mean one of the four princesses that was introduced by name in front of all the palace guests tonight? Yes, I know who you are."

Aviama huffed and rolled her eyes. "A polite man would have introduced themselves."

"A polite woman might have asked."

She gritted her teeth. Then, in a moment of filterless sass, she spun in a circle—letting all the practiced decorum of her childhood fall on her by the time she made the turn—and sank into an exaggerated curtsy. "May I have the pleasure of knowing your name, my lord?"

He bowed with equally mocking formality. "I doubt it is much of a pleasure, Your Highness, but the name is Chenzira."

Aviama blinked. "Chenzira?" The name rang a bell. "Chenzira what? Chenzira from where?"

He pursed his lips, and his eyes narrowed, as if debating with himself whether to answer. "Chenzira Bomani, though I'd appreciate you not reminding me often."

Aviama's eyes bulged. "Keket?"

Chenzira dipped his head in assent and gave a stiff bow. "Good night, Your Highness."

With that, he strode across the courtyard and disappeared into the palace with enough confidence that he might have owned the place—and she might have believed it, except for the knowledge Aviama had just gained. Because she'd called him "my lord" as a guess, but she'd woefully underestimated his position. Chenzira Bomani, the second son of the king of the island nation of Keket, had not been heard from in years.

The moment Chenzira was out of sight, Aviama dashed to the other side of the pool and down the hall. It took two tries, but finding the lotus pool Ishaan had referenced was what she needed, and a few minutes later, the palace opened up again to the sky above, and the moon shone down on what looked less like a pavilion and more like an expansive dome.

Mesh, glass, and greenery served as its only walls, so that even the inside looked like being outside, but the fluttering insects inside remained in their habitat. Aviama glanced this way and that, but she neither saw nor heard a living soul. The faint trickle of a fountain floated down the hall, and a chill night breeze rustled the leaves of the pavilion shrubbery.

Aviama padded across to the rounded glass door. The handle turned easily, and the door swung silently inward. She shut the door behind her and stepped through a tunnel of flowers and vines. Soft flitting wings brushed by her in the dark, and a whisper of velvet bumped into her hand as she walked.

Several more delicate butterflies perched on flowers in the dim moonlight on the other side of the tunnel. Aviama pulled her hands to her chest and took small steps, grateful for her long skirts to keep the insects out from underneath her feet. They were so beautiful. She would hate to harm them.

At the end of the tunnel, the foliage and flowers blocked the rest of the palace from the center of the dome, so that she might almost forget it was there. Two empty benches sat beneath the trees and climbing flowered vines. She breathed in the stillness, but her heart beat fast. It had to be close to midnight now, if not well past. Perhaps her host had given up and left.

A soft swish to her left caught her attention. Aviama twisted to see a middle-aged woman with shining black hair, still wearing the same gold attire she'd worn at the banquet. She'd taken off the crown, but Aviama would have recognized her stern eyes, red lips, and sharp nose anywhere.

"Princess Aviama. Welcome to the House of the Blessing Sun."

Aviama's stomach dropped as she fell into a curtsy and bowed her head. "Your Majesty. It is an honor. I did not expect to find you here."

The queen gave a lazy wave of her hand, granting her permission to stand, and sat on one of the benches in the center. "You did not expect to see someone in the butterfly pavilion at midnight, after being told to come to this particular time and place?" She arched a severe eyebrow and indicated the bench opposite her.

Aviama edged closer to it; her breath caught in her chest. Had the queen...disposed of whomever set the meeting? Was Aviama next on the list?

Queen Satya sighed. "Sit down, girl. I sent the message. I very much dislike waiting, and you were late, so I'd like to get on with it."

Aviama sat. Her head spun. *I know what you are.* She counted the stones on her ring three times before she spoke. "Your Majesty, I'm afraid I don't know what this meeting entails."

The queen pursed her lips. She folded her hands. "If you do not know what the meeting entails, then why are you here, princess?"

Warning bells clanged loud from the back of her mind. Aviama paused, searching for the right words. She couldn't afford to be wrong and hand the queen information she was fishing for but of which she had no proof. And she couldn't afford to insult Radha, or get herself sent home empty-handed, before having been here a full day.

"I have a vice, Your Majesty."

Queen Satya's eyes narrowed. "A vice?"

Aviama nodded. "Yes, Your Majesty. Curiosity. I'm afraid the message was so cryptic, and so strange, that I couldn't get it out of my head. Who was it that considered me a *what* instead of a *who*? And what rumors might the people of Radha think of me, that might taint my connections here?"

She leaned forward, as if sharing the deepest, juiciest of secrets. "And then to be told to come alone, in a foreign land, when my own guard has taken ill within hours of arrival? I had to know who could say such a thing. And now, to discover it is you—well, my concerns are lifted! I can only hope you have wisdom to share for my protection here."

The sweat on the palm of her hands and the number of times she had spun the rings on her fingers were evidence enough that her concerns were not, in fact, lifted. But her voice was steady enough, and her expression innocent and smooth. It was the best she could have mustered.

The queen sat perfectly straight and impossibly still, examining Aviama as though she were a gift horse from a neighbor with a grudge. Aviama spun her rings again. *One, two, three, four.*

Queen Satya held the silence until Aviama was ready to squirm, but finally tilted her head and spoke. "I do have wisdom for you, princess. My words bring life to those who listen, so listen well. You may think you have secrets. You may think you can fool the king, and the prince, and whomever else you encounter. But I already know what you are, and I will not have an abomination wed to my son."

Ice laced her words, and Aviama froze. Heat flushed her face and anger flooded her body like a lightning bolt to the heart. "I did not know our kingdoms were on such sour terms, Your Majesty. Particularly in light of an invitation, which we accepted in good faith to explore our options for an alliance."

Well, almost. Jannemar was invited to the contest, and they did accept.

The queen leaned forward so her face was level with Aviama's, close enough for her to see the vein twitch in the woman's forehead, even in the low light. Her eyes flashed, and her voice dropped into a low hiss. "Play your games, but know this: I never lose. You will ensure that you leave the contest after the minimum two dates with my son. And you will go back where you came from, taking your vile bloodline with you."

Aviama swallowed. Queen Satya lifted her chin and slowly straightened, beady eyes drilling into her like swords.

She knew. Aviama couldn't fathom how. But the queen knew Aviama was a melder, and she despised her for it.

Or did she only suspect? Why have the meeting at all?

The answer hit her like a sledgehammer. She didn't have proof. If she did, there were enough people in Radha against the idea of a melder in the Tanashai royal bloodline that Aviama never would have been invited to the contest. Or did the king want her here, and Dahnuk and Satya were at odds over who should wed the prince?

There was nothing for it now but to maintain her position and double down. Aviama drew her shoulders back and lifted her head. "Your Majesty, I would never dream of compromising the integrity of the contest. If I did, Jannemar could be in jeopardy—as the king himself said, a breach of faith could be seen as an act of aggression. I wouldn't dream of starting an international incident between my homeland and the mighty Radha across the sea."

Queen Satya bristled. "Come, girl. I'm not suggesting you find someone to have a fling with to get you tossed out. That was my husband's concern. Only that you lose Shiva's interest."

"I'd have to have it in order to lose it." Aviama folded her hands in her lap, mirroring the queen. "I've only just met His Highness."

Her lips pressed into a thin line. "Have you heard about the sickness sweeping the guardhouses? Terrible. If their conditions continue to deteriorate, they may not all survive."

Enzo. She was going to have him killed.

Aviama sucked in a breath. Spun her rings. *One, two, three, four.* Her fingers paused on the last stone. There was a truth she could afford to share that just might buy her time.

"Your Majesty, we received an invitation and accepted. I have no desire to beat out the other girls, no grand design to be joined to your house. I'm sure Prince Shiva will be more drawn to the others the more time he spends with us. But neither would I be wise to spurn any meager interest he does show, and risk insulting him or your great nation."

The queen looked at her for a long moment, her expression unreadable as flint. A butterfly landed on her hand, and she lifted it slowly to examine the delicate fibers of its wings. "Such a beautiful thing," she said softly, almost to herself. "It would be such a pity to destroy it. It's so fragile, so delicate. It doesn't even truly understand the danger."

Her gaze lifted to gore Aviama through, and the savage fire in her eyes sent goosebumps up her arms. With that, the queen stood and flicked her fingers toward the exit. "That will be all. We will speak again—and I will be watching."

10

Aviama rose from the bench, curtsied, and fled the pavilion. She hurried back through the tunnel of climbing vines and flowers and burst through the door—only to come to a skidding stop in front of Ishaan's judgmental glare.

"Ishaan," she choked out. "What a delightful surprise."

Ishaan's dark eyes glinted in the moonlight, and Aviama found herself wondering if the man emoted any more when he was about to kill someone, or if his victims simply never saw it coming.

"I'll save you the trouble of coming up with a lie. I'm here with Her Majesty. Shall we return you to your room now?"

Aviama opened her mouth, closed it, and dug her nails into the palms of her hands. She lifted her chin. "How thoughtful. Yes, that would be lovely."

Ishaan set a clipped pace, but it still felt tortuously slow to Aviama. He made her skin crawl as it was, but after having him confirm he was the queen's man—she shuddered. He might as well have said the rest: Ishaan was assigned to watch her every move and report to Queen Satya, and Enzo had been taken as collateral to keep her in line.

Where were they keeping him? Was he even sick? Did they poison him? Panic flew up from her belly and threatened to swallow her whole. *Murin. Where was Murin?* Her single remaining ally, the closest thing she had to a friend.

It would do no good to ask Ishaan, so when they got back to her room, she floated into her quarters and shut the door without a word before collapsing into bed and sobbing herself to sleep.

Even so, it was a fitful night. She dreamed of the queen, standing over Enzo's breathless corpse and sneering as Ishaan held Murin by the throat. The Radhan servant stood to one side, screaming, *melderblood! Melderblood!* Through the mirror on the vanity, Aviama caught a glimpse of Semra and Zephan in Jannemar, and though she called out to them, they could not hear. After all, months of travel by sea stood between her and them—and with the queen on the hunt, any mail she sent would surely be searched.

From the other side of the room, her father ran toward her, and Aviama flew to meet him, but just as he reached out his hand, the ground shook and an explosion blew at his feet. When she turned around again, Queen Satya walked through a sea of bodies: Aviama's father, King Turian, and mother, Queen Sharsi, soaking in their blood on the floor; Enzo, cold and gray, and the Jannemari servant she'd killed with the hammer still lying by his temple.

Please, she begged. *Please, let them lie in peace. No more. No more...*

Ishaan grinned, and the flash of his cunning smile was as quick as his blade against Murin's throat. She fell, and Queen Satya jabbed a long, pointed finger toward Semra and Zephan in the mirror as Murin hit the ground. *Melderblood, melderblood! Cursed, cursed!*

A scream tore through the air, and Aviama hardly registered the voice was her own until she was staring wide-eyed at Murin's worry-lined face, shaking her awake. "Your Highness! Your Highness, are you all right? Oh, did you have another nightmare? There, there...it's okay now, you're safe, it's okay..."

Aviama's chest hitched with sobs, and she melted into Murin's arms. She'd had nightmares before, since her parents passed, but they usually just replayed the memories. Her memories were nightmare enough. But she'd never had any like this.

Early morning light swept through the windows, playing along the metallic accents of her covers and warming the tiles with a bright optimism Aviama far from felt. Yesterday she had been looking forward to exploring today, getting out and seeing more of the palace grounds in the light of day. But today...

Aviama wiped the tears from her face and twisted to fall face first back into her pillows.

"Perhaps an early breakfast, Your Highness?"

Her stomach growled at the thought, but visions of sweet cake and parchments and butterfly pavilions squashed her appetite. She groaned.

Murin ran her hands through Aviama's tangled hair, smoothing out a snarl with gentle, expert fingers. "You've had a long trip. Travel is exhausting, and you were attacked just yesterday. You've been through an ordeal, not to mention the excitement of the contest and being in a new place. And with Enzo ill, it's just not starting out quite how you'd hoped, hmm? But he'll be all right. Perhaps so much time at sea did not agree with him. What if we get you a nice hot bath, breakfast, and then go exploring? It'll lift your spirits, Your Highness, I know it will."

Aviama sighed. She couldn't very well hide in her room all day. Not without arousing suspicion. And she didn't want to give the queen the satisfaction of holing her up. So Aviama sat up slowly and nodded, and Murin smiled at her.

"There we are. The brave princess I've come to love so much!"

Aviama snorted, but the weight on her shoulders eased just a hair. And by the time she'd bathed, eaten, and dressed, Murin flitting this way and that, twisting her hair into elegant knots and applying powders that removed all traces of her tears, Aviama felt the day might almost deserve the sun. Weather was fair, and the threats of night seemed not quite so overwhelming.

Murin arranged Aviama's golden tresses cascading over the sapphire blue dress, stepped back, and gave a satisfied nod. "Now then. I've asked around for things to do. We could visit the pakshi enclosure and see them up close"—here Aviama wrinkled her nose, and Murin grinned—"but *obviously* we would never dream of doing *that*, so there are also many courtyards and gardens to explore, and a rooftop with a beautiful view of the city of Rajaad."

Aviama laughed. "That sounds perfect. Not the pakshi idea. *Obviously.* But the rooftop, and the gardens." The roof could get her a better layout of the palace too. "Shall we start at the roof?"

Murin clapped her hands. "Yes!"

Looking at Murin's sweet face, Aviama couldn't help but smile back at her. Today might not be so sour after all.

Murin opened the door, and a Radhan servant woman stood on the other side, hand raised to knock. The woman stepped back in surprise. "Oh! Your Highness." She curtsied and held out a note. "I was sent to deliver this for you."

Aviama took it with a smile, but all her hope for the day crashed to the floor. "Thank you."

The woman disappeared. Did the queen need a second meeting so soon? A glance at Ishaan revealed nothing, so she broke the seal and opened the note. She blinked. "It's from the prince. He's invited me for a stroll and lunch."

She hadn't expected time with him so soon. She must be the first of the princesses to have time alone with Prince Shiva, unless he'd somehow squeezed in private time with someone by breakfast. Marija's lurid expression and wink filled her memory again, and she grimaced. Had Marija offered him more *practice* yet?

"Oh, but that's wonderful! Why the long face, Your Highness? He *must* have loved meeting you yesterday, to be chosen so soon!"

"I'm sure it's random, nothing to do with me," Aviama mumbled, staring at the note. She stole a glance at Ishaan, and her blood ran cold. She jerked her attention back to Murin. "Someone has to be first. It's nothing, I'm just—I was looking forward to the roof, that's all."

"Nonsense, Your Highness. You sell yourself short. I'm sure he took great notice of you, and there will be plenty of time to explore the palace after you return. Where are you to meet him? Is he coming here?"

Aviama re-read the note. "It says I am to meet him at the lotus pool. First floor."

Murin nodded. "Wonderful. I'll wait for you here."

Her lady-in-waiting stepped back, but Aviama's hand shot out and latched onto her wrist before she could go. "Walk with me, would you? And then I'll see you again this afternoon?"

Murin beamed. "Of course, Your Highness."

Aviama was convinced no one was as joyful as Murin. Her presence and excited chatter offered a much-needed buffer to the stone-cold silence of Ishaan's menacing company, and Aviama wondered if all Radhan servants were as terrified, invisible, or formal as those she'd seen so far. Watching Aviama with Murin must be a breath of fresh air for them. The two of them knew each other well enough for Murin to know when Aviama appreciated her talk, and when protocol demanded she drop back to a supporting, background role.

The corridors out of the guest residences, down the stairs, and past the two courtyards on the way to the lotus pool felt more familiar and far less intimidating this time, lit by the brightness of day and Murin's easy presence. Aviama tried to keep track of the halls they passed. She did decently at first, but by the time she reached the pool she'd forgotten half of it, and by the time she caught sight of the prince, the rest of her scrambled thoughts scattered like dust.

Prince Shiva reclined on chairs along the edge of the pool with three other men, laughing about something or other and tossing a pebble from the garden into the center of the pool's glassy-smooth surface. A light breeze blew his light tunic against his body, revealing the cut of his chest and curve of his arm. Aviama twisted the rings on her fingers and fought the urge to bite at her nail.

Ishaan stopped at the edge of the columns, abandoning Aviama to walk forward on her own. Murin had ended conversation as they neared the pool, and dropped back now to trail her at a respectful distance rather than walk close at her elbow. Aviama shifted her weight. Traitors, both of them. Even Ishaan.

One of the men, a middle-aged noble wearing gaudy emerald rings and cuffs far too large for his rail-thin frame, nudged the prince and nodded in her direction. Between the queen's threats and the squirmy feeling in her stomach when she looked at him, Aviama thought perhaps she should have stuck to her courting from the lower deck of the ship idea. Maybe if Enzo hadn't made her disembark, he wouldn't have fallen *ill*. They could have made their excuses and scurried back home.

A useless daydream now. Prince Shiva turned toward her, and his smile widened as his eyes locked onto hers.

"Ahh, my princess!"

He leaped to his feet and held out his hand. She took it and smiled back, and he drew her into the circle as the men followed their prince's example and rose to greet her. The skinny first man bowed, and the second quickly did the same. He was older, perhaps sixty, and dressed just as finely as the first, though more tastefully. They introduced themselves, but Aviama instantly forgot their names as the third man came into view from behind Prince Shiva.

Chenzira.

She focused hard on the face of each man as they spoke to her, though she didn't hear a word. General niceties seemed enough to pacify them, as she told them how pleased she was to make their forgettable acquaintances, and nodded and smiled as any decent lady would. Chenzira bowed, smooth and impassive, his languid movements revealing a man only as interested as the occasion demanded.

After her meeting with the queen, Aviama had nearly forgotten Chenzira existed. Now, his mysterious gaze was all she could think about. What did he make of her escapade last night? Had he told Shiva?

Prince Shiva clapped Chenzira on the back. "This man is one of the great hidden treasures of Radha! We can't seem to get rid of him, but he's been better to us than we deserve."

Chenzira's plastered-on smile hardened, but Shiva waved him off with a good-natured nudge.

Aviama dipped her head for the third time. "Pleased to meet you."

Prince Shiva turned from his companions and offered her his arm. "Shall we?"

"Of course." Aviama slipped her hand through his arm, and Shiva said farewell to the men and turned her away from the lotus pool and along the columns. Murin snuck a wave when Aviama glanced her way, and then disappeared into the labyrinth of the palace. Ishaan followed at a distance, but clearly a Radhan guard would not protect *her* from *him.*

Enzo would have. Real bodyguards would have. But lapdogs of the queen were only there to watch and tattle. And that's precisely what Aviama expected him to do.

11

Ishaan wasn't close enough to hear their conversation, but she grimaced at the sight of him nonetheless, trailing them like a circling buzzard—waiting for its prey to give up the fight and die. Aviama clenched her jaw and returned her attention to the prince.

"So, Princess Aviama." Shiva said her name slowly, as if tasting the sound of it. "What do you think of Radha?"

"I've not seen much yet, but everything I've seen has been marvelous. From the beach when we arrived, to Rajaad, and the palace. I've never seen anything like it."

The columns ended, and Shiva walked her through an emerald hall with vaulted ceilings and into a wide-open room with scalloped archways, finely-dressed people sitting at tables or reclining on benches, and a fountain in the center. Aviama wasn't used to large indoor common areas in a palace. She wondered who all the people were, and what tasks they might be busy with.

Shiva nodded. "Rajaad is one of my favorite places in Radha. Did you enjoy the pakshi sledge?"

"Um...they were...beautiful." Aviama scrunched up her

nose. "I think I prefer them from a distance. Their eyes are too beady, and they move so strangely. Like a cobra about to strike, but for every single motion. It's disconcerting."

Shiva laughed. "Are you easily startled?"

For three years now, yes.

"Are you telling me that sort of behavior puts you at ease? Should I try it, to make you more comfortable?" Aviama jutted her chin toward him in her most ridiculous imitation of the birds, jerking her head this way and that like a paranoid groundhog, then widened her eyes and stared at him with an awkward, unblinking gaze.

Shiva chortled. He used his free hand to cover her fingers on his arm, a blanket of warmth emanating from his touch. "No need, Your Highness. Perhaps if I find myself uneasy, you can use that technique again. As it is, I am already quite comfortable."

"Have you tried courting multiple women before? I wouldn't think such a thing generally relaxing to anyone."

The prince shrugged. "It's an effective way to meet you all, and when my father decides it's time to do something, he doesn't like to wait."

"Ah. And your father has decided it is time for you to marry."

For the millionth time, Aviama thanked her lucky stars she was the *third* born of the Shamaran family—unlikely to be called upon to rule, and spared the rigorous responsibilities associated with the heir. She could breathe especially easy now that Zephan was married and likely to have children. Aviama could relate to not having control over her life, but she couldn't imagine the weight of being a crown prince—neither the preparation required, nor the high demand to be and act just so until little freedom was left in any area of life.

She scanned his face as they crossed sparkling tiled floors, letting him lead the way and imagining what might be going on inside his head.

Shiva ran a hand through his hair and gave her a sideways glance. His mouth twisted up as he caught her staring. "Don't feel so bad for me. There are worse things than being assigned to spend a few weeks lounging by pools and strolling with beautiful women instead of being trapped in stuffy meeting rooms all day." He winked, and she blushed.

Aviama bit her lip and looked away—and caught a glimpse of Ishaan shadowing them from several meters behind. The blood drained from her face, and she stared down at her feet, watching the sapphire folds of her dress swish about as she walked. "I just know it's hard, being a crown prince and having so much dictated for you. I'm close with my brother, and watching him after our father died— well, it's been a lot."

She'd even gotten the brief chance to see what being next in line to the throne meant. When her dragonlord uncle took over the castle and Zephan was in danger, he'd signed a decree that Aviama was his heir. The pressure of that possibil- ity, bearing the weight of the kingdom's hope, proved to her how desperately she did *not* want to reign. Now, with Azi over- thrown and Semra and Zephan married, she breathed easier. Life was better as a younger child. Living in an elder sibling's shadow was better than ruling.

"And how is he adjusting to his new role?" Shiva peered down at her as they reached the end of the open space and went through double doors into a large courtyard. Four pools glimmered from each corner, colorful birds with spindly legs dotting the scene as they poked about for fish.

Aviama gazed across the courtyard. "Remarkably well. He's suited for it, you know? He and Semra are a good team. They support one another, like my parents did. I think that's how marriage is supposed to be."

"A queen having so much public influence on matters of state as your Queen Semra does is surprising."

"My mother was less public, but still had as much influence. Is it not the same in Radha —doesn't your mother have power in the palace?" Even as she lifted her chin to say it, she knew it was a mistake. Too pointed.

A shadow crossed his face just briefly, and then lifted to levity once again. He laughed. "Oh, at *least* as much as my father, I would say! But not publicly. My father is the king, and he needs no one's permission to make decisions. At the end of the day, what he says goes."

And what did Queen Satya think of *that?*

They walked quietly for several minutes, Shiva occasionally pointing out a bird or flower, and Aviama murmuring back her compliments. He plucked a sprig of lilac blossom and twirled it in his fingers, then pointed at a canary in the tree above them. She tilted her face up to get a better look at it, and he tucked the flower behind her ear.

Her cheeks reddened, and she swatted playfully at his hand, but she couldn't help a sheepish grin. He laughed, and something in her stomach flopped.

Ishaan glowered at her from the shadows of the trees. At least, she assumed it was a glower. He certainly didn't look pleased, but he always looked like he had a case of indigestion.

Aviama cleared her throat and turned back to the path. "Are you close with your parents?"

"Close enough."

The lightness of the mood deflated, and Aviama examined Shiva. His jaw tightened, and she lifted an eyebrow. She knew she shouldn't push, but Shiva had seemed so close with his family at the banquet—was it all for show? Or was he friendly with his father, but not his mother?

After meeting her, she certainly couldn't blame him.

Shiva's voice dropped low, like the whisper of silk when he spoke again. "I heard you did not sleep well last night."

Now it was Aviama's turn to clam up. Her chest constricted, and she took a breath. Had someone told him? Or had he actually *heard* how poorly she'd slept last night? Shiva glanced at her hand on his arm, and Aviama followed his gaze. Her fingers dug into his arm, and she jerked her hand back.

"Sorry. It's nothing to worry about. I'm sure I'm just adjusting."

From my parents' assassinations, and from current, ongoing threats of death. How was one supposed to *adjust* to something like that, exactly?

Shiva gently caught her hand and returned it to his arm. His hand lingered over hers for a moment before dropping back to his side. "If there is anything we can do for you, please let us know. If there's anything about the rooms…"

"The rooms are very comfortable. I'm fine."

Aviama lifted her chin, and Shiva let out a breath. He pursed his lips. "Well. We are quite a pair, aren't we?"

She grimaced. At least Ishaan should like their weird, terse interaction. Let him go tattle to the queen about *that*.

Shiva ran a hand through his hair again. Aviama shifted her weight. She glanced back at Ishaan, but he hadn't moved. When she turned back to Shiva, he was watching her.

"I think," he said slowly, "that courtyard strolls are not for us."

Aviama blinked back at him. "What?"

"Yes. I think they are much too boring. Something any man might do with any woman, don't you think?"

Any noble, perhaps. After having traveled just a little with

Semra, Aviama knew *most* men would not be strolling through courtyards, even in Radha. But then, it was silly to expect him to talk about commoners when he was a prince. She shrugged. "I suppose."

"I'm going to ask you three questions, and I'm going to guess something you've never done. And if I'm right, you have to agree to do it with me."

Her lips parted. "But what if—"

He shook his head. "No buts. And I'm not going to ask you if you're ready either. Princess Aviama, I'll bet you know all sorts of princessy things. We already know you are a magnificent dancer. Can you ride a horse?"

Aviama arched an eyebrow. "I'm not an imbecile. Of course I can ride a horse."

Shiva grinned and drew her down the path again, this time the slow meandering pace replaced by a spring in his step. "And do you read?"

"I love to read. It's become one of my favorite things to do." She had little else available to her while in hiding or practicing control over her magic with Frigibar. But there was no need to mention that.

"Me too." Shiva paused, then lightly touched her hand. "This doesn't count as my third question, but what other things do you like to do?"

Aviama frowned. She used to love to sing, but she hadn't done it in a long time. It used to calm her, make her feel at home. But it reminded her of her mother, and with everything going on, she'd done it less and less over the past months. No need to share that either. Why highlight her kingdom's tragic loss of stability?

She chose another hobby. "I like to draw. Sketches, really. I helped design Queen Semra's wedding dress."

Shiva's brows soared. "Impressive."

"Thanks."

The mischievous light from last night returned to his eyes, and he leaned toward her. "Have you ever seen a hyland troll?"

Aviama rolled her eyes. She'd read about them, but only in Mox's fairy tales. Not in history books. They lived in the Crater Wood, where they'd broken off from the peaks of the mountains, rolled down into the valley, and left deep impressions in the forest where they landed. The sun rose and they turned to stone, but when night fell, they sprang from the earth and roamed the wood. "They're not real."

"Oh, they're real."

"No, they're not."

"Dragons are real."

"Yes, but trolls aren't."

"I've seen one. I've *touched* one."

Aviama made a face. "Do all Radhan men exaggerate as much as you?"

"I'll make you a deal. If I can prove they exist, you have to tell me something I want to know."

She laughed. "What do you want to know?"

"You owe me an answer from last evening. I want to know about the ladies' privileged conversations." He flashed an impish grin, and Aviama laughed in spite of herself.

"If I told you, it wouldn't be privileged!"

"Nonsense. If you told me, *I* would be privileged to know it. See?"

Aviama shook her head. "Fine, but if you point to a rock and tell me it's a troll, I'm not going to believe you."

Shiva led them past the last of the pools in the courtyard and into the arch of the double doors on the other side. "I accept your terms. There's only one catch. Where we're going isn't exactly for guests, so I'm going to have to dismiss Ishaan from following us. Unless of course you feel unsafe with me without him...?"

Her heart leaped. Free of Ishaan's imposing supervision? She nodded. "My own guard is ill. I feel safer with you than with Ishaan."

"Surprising. He has such a sunny disposition."

Aviama snorted, then clapped a hand over her mouth in horror. Shiva smirked. Aviama dropped her hand.

"Where are we going?"

"My father's private menagerie."

12

———

Aviama's heartbeat pounded in her ears as Shiva ushered her against the wall. He opened the door before them just a sliver and peered around the corner. He'd dismissed Ishaan, and the man's condescending observance had deepened to a murderous glare. But he was a bodyguard, and Shiva was the prince. He could do nothing but bow and disappear, which is precisely what he had done.

Shiva had led her through several corridors and archways and past two bronze double doors with sentries on either side. "The menagerie's main entrance," he'd said.

He'd opened a door two doors down and slipped inside. When she hesitated, Shiva had snatched her hand and pulled her after him into what appeared to be a conference room of sorts, then produced a key from his waistband and proceeded through another door into the adjoining room, where they now stood.

Aviama leaned in toward Shiva. "Who are you looking for?"

Shiva kept his eyes on the crack in the door to the room beyond when he whispered back. "My father took a few nobles hunting this morning. He should be gone a few more hours, but his private office is on the other side. And sometimes he shows off his collection to his guests."

She gasped. "You're taking me past the king's private office? Are you trying to get me killed?"

The prince gave her a sideways glance and smirked. "Relax. He'd kill *me* before he killed you." He took one more look into the room, then grinned and pushed the door open. "If you would, Your Highness."

Aviama gawked at him. Everything in her told her this was a terrible idea. It was in this precise moment that she realized just how terrible of a spy she would be. "No way."

"Do you never break the rules, princess?"

He grabbed her by the hand and tugged her through the door. She tripped after him and froze, and the sight spilled out before her. Cages and habitats lined each side of the room, with an aisle down the middle leading to a single gold leaf door on the far end. The king's private war room.

All memory of the soft trickle of water and floral smell of the courtyard vanished, a mingled smell somewhere between the woods and the stables assaulting her nostrils in their place. Excitement tingled along her skin as marvelous animals and beasts chittered, screeched, and roared from every corner. To her right, four monkeys leaped up on the netting of their enclosure to get a better look at the intruders, and to her left, a meter-long glorybird of paradise hid her face beneath her wing to sleep, swaying softly on her perch.

Next to the bird, a bundle of something fuzzy hid under a pile of hay and dirt, burying itself in the ground. On the opposite side, a lizard slithered from under a rock behind the glass of its habitat, opening its mouth and shooting bright-red light at a leaf high above it. The leaf burst into flame, and a bug dropped from the plant into the lizard's open mouth.

Aviama sucked in a breath. "Oh, they're incredible! How beautiful!"

"That's nothing." Shiva slipped his hand into hers and pulled her along with him, the formality of the public eye melting away in his excitement. "I have a bet to win. This way."

They passed cage upon cage of creatures, the smaller ones toward the entrance, and becoming grander and more unusual as they progressed. Something encased in glass ran the length of the far right side. A shriek split the air from the left, and Aviama screamed. A clatter sounded from down the corridor, and the handle to the golden door at the far end of the hall began to turn.

Shiva clapped a hand over her mouth and dragged her backward into the narrow space between two enclosures on their right. The space was large enough to walk, but only single file. Aviama stared wide-eyed across the open space to the opposite side of the aisle, where the shriek had caught her off guard. A huge beast the size of a pony paced back and forth. Black fur covered huge, clawed feet and a deep-chested body. Two sets of ears swiveled in every direction, and spines lined its haunches like daggers.

She'd never seen anything like it. Never *heard* of anything like it. Her pulse pounded in her ears, and her chest heaved from fright. A soft click warned of someone's presence, and Aviama's eyes bulged as Shiva wrapped his arm around her waist and lifted her off her feet to drag her around the narrow corner between the enclosures and out of sight from the aisle.

Footsteps echoed down the hall, clear at first, then muffled as the sounds of the animals covered them. Shiva eased her to her feet, his hand still smothering her mouth, and she twisted in his arms—only to come nose to nose with a pair of eyes staring directly at her. Aviama's body jerked against Shiva's iron grasp, and she clamped down hard on her tongue to keep from screaming.

Thick glass separated Aviama from the woman on the other side. But it *wasn't* a woman—at least, not quite. Piercing lavender eyes bored into her, bright stars in the most exquisitely beautiful face Aviama had ever seen. Pure white hair unfurled through the water behind her over what looked like a seal pelt top, clinging to her curves in a tight band around her torso and over one shoulder. Silver scales framed her face and glimmered across her skin, bouncing soft light in every direction. From the waist up she was like a woman, but below the waist a long, powerful pewter tail cut through the water with the flowing grace of a ray or dolphin.

Aviama reeled back on her heels, but there was nowhere to go but further into Shiva's broad chest. He was already pressed up against the bars of another enclosure at their backs, and the aquarium hemmed them in with a long glass wall running from where they stood to the end of the room on one side. The narrow way they had come was the only exit in or out from their position.

She knew she should care about the footsteps—if it was the king who had come from the office, or someone else, and whether or not they would be found. But nothing could tear her focus from the captivating creature glaring back at her from behind the glass.

Biscuits, how had King Dahnuk gotten his hands on a mermaid? Regardless of how he'd done it, she didn't look too pleased about her situation. And from the scathing look in her eyes, she blamed Aviama for the whole thing.

The mermaid shifted her dagger gaze to the prince and struck the glass with an open hand. Webbing ran between her fingers, and a long scar curled around her palm and up her forearm. Perfect lips curled back in a snarl to reveal razor-sharp canines. She drifted slowly backward in the water, and Aviama sagged against Shiva. His arms relaxed, and she could breathe again.

Shiva dropped his face down to her ear, his breath tickling her neck. "Stay here."

Aviama spun to object, but he'd already slipped away and was creeping down the side path toward the main aisle. She bit her lip and turned the rings on her fingers. Counted the stones. *One, two, three, four.* A small school of yellow and blue fish swam by in the pale blue of the aquarium, and her gaze darted from one movement to another as Shiva stepped out of view, and an eel emerged from tendrils of seaweed along the aquarium floor.

This was taking too long. Where was he?

Aviama peered around the edge of the aquarium, but the narrow pathway was empty. Her heart hammered against her ribs, and Ishaan's murderous expression filled her mind. What if the queen had decided to dispose of her? What if all this, the menagerie, was her plan, and Shiva was in on it? Lead the princess into the menagerie, abandon her with beasts four times her size, leave a cage door open...

Or let Ishaan know where she was, slit her throat, and toss her to the zegrath to rip apart the evidence.

It would be so easy. So explainable. Her mouth went dry.

"Shiva?" she croaked. Her voice was barely above a whisper, but felt loud against the gentle ripple of aquarium surface above her and the distant chattering of the monkeys on the other side of the menagerie.

She turned her head, and a blinding flash thrashed against the side of the aquarium. Silent as death—the flicker of a tail, the glint of scales—and the mermaid was upon her, the base of her tail crashing into the glass. Aviama's yelp of surprise cut short as a rope slipped around her neck and yanked her up against the enclosure.

Aviama's hands flew to her neck to pry at the rope, her cry for help reduced to a desperate gurgle. Her fingers clawed for purchase against slick, slimy fibers. A burning seized her lungs, and she kicked against the air, but the mermaid's grip was unbreakable. She could feel the blood draining from her muscles, and two thoughts permeated her brain as weakness threatened to take her:

Shiva had abandoned her. And the queen ran the palace after all.

Cold water dripped down the back of her dress. A chill washed over her body, and her heart rate began to slog like a wheel turning in mud. If she didn't do something fast, she was going to die. And her secrets didn't do her much good if she was dead.

Aviama threw her hands up, calling magic to her palms to blast the creature from its place as it held her against the aquarium hanging half-in, half-out of the water. A tingling sensation pooled at her hands, but the wind refused to answer. Her vision swam, and a ringing in her ears seemed to scream *betrayal.*

She pressed her feet up against the slick glass and pushed upward with all that she had, writhing against the mermaid's hold—and then her thoughts began to break apart, like the cake that had crumbled in her hands just yesterday, leaving her with a single message:

I know what you are.

13

A shout pulled her from the dark, and Aviama's eyes fluttered open just long enough to register Prince Shiva bolting around the bend. He snatched a spear from its mount along the beam of the opposite enclosure, ran at the glass, and leaped up to grasp the top of the aquarium, plunging the spear down on the mermaid's tail.

A hideous screech filled the air, and Aviama dropped to the floor like a sack of potatoes. The mermaid flailed backward and disappeared with a slap of her tail on the surface, sending a splash of cold water over the edge onto Aviama's head.

Aviama jerked backward as the icy water seeped through her hair into her scalp, then collapsed on the floor again in a coughing, spluttering heap. Her breaths came in ragged gasps as her frantic lungs attempted to fill once again. She pushed herself up on her elbows, chest still heaving, and her fingers brushed that same slimy texture she'd felt against her throat.

She snatched her hand away, but when she looked down, she saw that the mermaid's rope had been long strands of braided seaweed. Shiva placed a tentative hand on her back.

"I'm so sorry. I'm sorry. I thought you'd be safe here, while I looked—I didn't think—"

Aviama dragged in a long breath and shook her head. "Not...dead. I'm fine. But if"—here she convulsed on the floor in another coughing fit, then tilted her head up to look him in the face—"if you leave me alone again, I just may have to kill you."

Shiva offered her his hand, and she took it. The corners of his mouth twitched as he pulled her to her feet. "You really think you'd survive another round? And that killing me would solve your problem?"

Aviama shrugged. "You wouldn't have to worry about who to marry."

"How would you do it, if you had to kill me?"

"Oh, I don't know. I'm sure I'd think of something." A trickle of water ran down her spine, and she shivered. "Can we get out of here?"

Shiva nodded and took her hand to pull her away, then paused. He spun around and pointed at the enclosure opposite the mermaid and pointed. "Before we go—hyland trolls."

Two large, rounded rocks sat motionless inside metal bars. Aviama arched an eyebrow. "She choked me, but I didn't hit my head. Those are rocks, just like *someone* around here predicted. Can we please go?"

Shiva spun the spear in his hands and shoved the butt of the shaft through the bars and into the smaller of the two rocks, rolling it out of the stream of sunlight coming in through a narrow window and under the shade of a short overhanging shelter. The rock stood about a meter high, and as it came to a stop under the shelter, it trembled and broke open.

Aviama's eyes bulged as the boulder began to uncurl, revealing short sturdy legs, a moss-covered back, and grouchy, exaggerated features in a round, stony face. If a gargoyle had the figure of a dinner roll, Aviama was sure this was precisely what it would look like. The thing wrinkled its nose, snarled, and started to roll toward them—but just as it left the shadow of the shelter, it froze, hardening into a paralyzed statue state.

Aviama stared back at it in wonder, but Shiva had gotten what he came for and was already tugging her back down the path. "They turn to stone in sunlight, so we added a window with natural light leading in all the way from the roof. These are young ones, and they don't grow at all in the sun. So we keep them as well-lit as we can. Luckily, they don't fit through the windows or bars, and they're too stupid for any complex escape schemes when they do wake up at night."

The prince led them back out into the hall, down the corridor, and up a tower staircase. He glanced behind them three times on their way to the tower, and twice more before opening a door spilling out to a rooftop terrace. His unease made her muscles tense, and she found herself scanning her surroundings, but she found nothing out of the ordinary. Not that *ordinary* had any meaning in a new place exactly.

Two sofas and several chairs sat in the middle of the terrace on a red-and-yellow rug interrupting the white of the stone floor, and a railing ran along the edge of the terrace, forming a square. Aviama broke free from Shiva and rushed to the balustrade, spinning her rings and twining a damp blonde curl around her finger. Her heart pummeled her rib cage, and she sucked in the fresh air like a starving child wolfed down bread.

The prince's footsteps slowed, then approached slowly. His hand brushed the back of her neck, and she cringed away from him. Her hand flew to cover her neck before she could think about it. The skin still stung over her trachea where the seaweed rope had dug into her flesh.

Shiva looked down at his hands and then lifted them palm up toward Aviama. "May I?" He gestured toward her injury. A lump lodged in her throat, but she nodded.

She'd been through worse.

But now that she thought about it, that wasn't strictly true. She'd *seen* much worse. She hadn't experienced it for herself. This was her first real brush with death. She was far enough down the line of ascension to be lower risk for assassination. Kidnapping, yes, slaughter of the entire royal family, certainly, but individual hits? Who would bother? And of all the threats her family had been through over the years, she'd never been so close to the end of her life. *Seconds* from the end.

Aviama never would have guessed it would come at the hands of a mermaid. She almost laughed at the absurdity of it. But then Shiva's hands were on her chin, tilting it up and gently turning it, and her thoughts grew hazy. His nearness arrested her attention, and her skin tingled as his fingers softly traced the raised mark the mermaid's attack had left.

Something in her belly squirmed under the intensity of his gaze, and she tried to take in the palace and its courtyards, the distant roofs of the city of Rajaad. It was a stunning sight —she knew it was, somewhere in her mind—but it hardly registered.

"It looks superficial. I don't think it'll scar." The prince turned her face toward him, letting his hand linger against it. "Are you all right?"

She nodded, trying not to focus on the curve of his jaw, the strength of his hands—the intensity of those umber eyes. "I'm fine. A little shaken, that's all."

Shiva stepped closer. She swallowed as his thumb skimmed over her bottom lip, and his other hand slipped back to the nape of her neck. "Perhaps she was jealous. It isn't every day an Iolani mermaid is the *second* most beautiful woman in the room."

Aviama rolled her eyes, even as her heart skipped a beat. "Hardly."

"She's not human, I know, but the sentiment remains." He paused. "You're lucky the menagerie is lined with *magna*. It stifles magical powers to protect us from some of our more... exotic exhibits. She hasn't tried anything in quite some time, but when she did, she had to resort to non-magical means."

He'd misunderstood what she meant, but she let it go. Two other things he said took precedence. One, she now knew why she was unable to call the wind in the menagerie. And two...

"Lucky." Aviama pursed her lips and leaned away from him. As intoxicating as his presence was, that very fact also scared her. She cleared her throat, still raspy from her ordeal. "She might not be human, but she's not just an *exhibit*. Isn't it wrong to keep anyone penned up like that for show? I'd probably get desperate too if I lived in a small box."

Shiva sighed, and his hand dropped from Aviama's neck. This wasn't the first time he'd heard such a complaint. "She's not an *anyone*. Anyones are people. She's not a person. She's a mermaid—a murderous one who nearly killed you just now. Besides, I don't hear you complaining about the zegrath or the monkeys."

An edge crept into his voice, and Aviama shifted her weight. She'd hit a nerve of some sort. Aviama winced. He'd sent Ishaan away, showed her something special that was off limits, and saved her life, only to be scolded now. She was being ungrateful. Perhaps there was more to the mermaid story than she knew.

Aviama dipped her head. "True. And the animals are all incredible. It's an impressive collection, and I'm grateful you showed me, honestly. I just—the way she looked at me. She *feels* things like we do. I don't know. It surprised me."

Shiva's expression softened, and he leaned his forearms on the railing. Aviama followed his lead, bumping her arm into his in silent apology. He nudged her back, his eyes sweeping over Rajaad, then turned to look at her. "The collection is my father's. He's a collector, and he likes trophies from various conquests and lands."

"You don't like trophies?"

"Oh, I love them. But as exciting as the menagerie is, I prefer to wear mine." He grinned and tapped the right side of his chest, where medals might hang.

Aviama smiled, but she couldn't shake off the image of the mermaid glaring at her through the glass. Lavender eyes of hate. Silver tail of destruction. Beautiful, but deadly. A chill ran down her spine, and her neck stung.

"Thanks for saving my life and stuff."

Shiva shrugged. "Don't worry about it. But...please don't tell anyone what happened. If you don't mind." He sent her a sideways glance, and Aviama nodded.

"No problem."

"Thanks."

Aviama gazed out over the palace grounds and the city beyond. Colorful buildings climbed several stories high, staggering the landscape at various heights and sweeping from one end of the horizon to the other. Below, the salmon reds and corals of the roofs burned bright beneath the sun. Aviama closed her eyes and let the warmth bathe her face, slowly drying her damp hair and removing the constant reminders of the attack.

Shiva suddenly straightened and slapped the balustrade. "Well, enough of that. Let's change the subject—I won a bet, and that's the important thing here."

Aviama turned to stare at him. She'd forgotten all about the bet. Her lips parted, but no sound came. She fought a grin, and pursed her lips.

"Hyland trolls exist. I won, fair and square."

She waved a hand. "Okay, okay. It was no big deal, really."

"I don't know about that. Your face turned cherry red."

Aviama grimaced, and to her dismay, heat filled her cheeks. *Biscuits.*

"See?" Shiva crossed his arms. "I'm wildly intrigued."

She rolled her eyes. "The girls were asking if anyone had met you before. Marija said that she had, when you came to Tomos, and talked about your hunting skills."

Aviama spun the rings on her fingers.

He arched an eyebrow. "And?"

"And they talked about your, ah, reputation with women. That all men of court have experience with women, and that yours is particularly..."

"Particularly what?"

Couldn't he read between the lines? Did she have to say it? Aviama groaned and threw her hands up. "I don't know. *Experienced.*"

Shiva laughed. "Is that all?"

Aviama drew back, face hot. "Is that *all*? You're not bothered by that, or embarrassed?"

He made a face and stiffened. "Why would I be embarrassed? I've got nothing to be ashamed of. I've done nothing any other man in my position would not do."

So he was entitled to it, was he? Everything was okay for the prince, was it? Aviama's eyes blazed, and her tone ticked up to a higher pitch. She jabbed a finger at his chest.

"You invited us here to determine if we are a good fit as marriage partners and kingdom alliances. Your father charged us with a national act of *aggression* if we are caught with other men. If I had other entanglements, I would not have accepted the invitation. And yet *you* have no qualms at all about a reputation bragging of your sexual exploits? Are all the men here so debased, or only the royalty?"

Shiva's brows rose, and his good-natured humor soured so severely that Aviama took a step back. "How *dare* you insult me! Are all princesses so pretentious and self-important, or only you? Did you ever consider that a rumor might be just that, and that I have a thousand rumors of all sorts swirling about me at any given moment? Did you ever consider that I might not be allowed the freedom to court any random person I like—say, a lovely murderer from the common villages, as your brother has done—but am tied to traditions more appropriate to a monarchical family?"

Aviama sucked in a breath, and a curl of wind wisped around her fingers. She took a step forward again and opened her mouth, but Shiva placed a finger on her lips and shook his head.

"No. You will not insult me *and* start *more* rumors today by shouting on my terrace and alerting every servant in the palace. Considering what they say about their own prince, I'm sure you'd hate what they'd say about *you* if they pick up on a lovers' quarrel after only twenty-four hours in the country."

Aviama knocked his hand away, furious, and stormed across the terrace for the door. Shiva caught up to her in three long strides, captured her hand, and set it firmly on his arm.

"You must be overwhelmed from your terrifying ordeal today. I'll walk you to your rooms." He dropped his voice low. "I will not be made a fool of in my own home before my own people."

The butterfly feelings of a few moments ago vanished in the burning furnace of anger hanging in the air between them. Aviama surged forward as they hit the first corridor, but Shiva slowed their pace.

Appearances, appearances. She ground her teeth, but the harsh hiss of his voice as he gave her a warning had rocked her to her core. How could he be tender and funny one minute, sweep in to save her life the next, and utterly terrify her the moment after?

Ice set into her bones as they walked, cold and paralyzing. Her mind spun with the events of the day. Shiva tucking a sprig of lilac behind her ear. Grabbing her hand and pulling her into the menagerie, watching her shock and delight at seeing so many exotic creatures. The flutter in her stomach as she'd been pressed up against him, hiding between the hyland trolls and the mermaid.

The mermaid's savage expression. Her own feet swinging through the air as the braided seaweed cut into the soft flesh of her throat.

Darkness.

Shiva.

He hardly seemed the same person, so stoically did he walk the halls.

She wondered if she felt the same to him.

They reached the guest wing, and as they turned the corner, Ishaan came into view, waiting outside her door. All levity she'd enjoyed in the last unsupervised hour or two, all anxiety over her burnt bridge with Shiva, evaporated like mist. The blood drained from her face. Shiva kissed her hand outside her room, and she murmured a minimally polite farewell. As soon as the prince had gone, Aviama fled into her chambers and shut the door without a second glance. Her heart dropped like a rock. The queen was going to kill her.

14

On the one hand, although she'd gotten *far* too close for comfort on the romantic end with Shiva, Ishaan hadn't seen it. At least, he hadn't seen the extent of it. Shiva had dismissed him when they were relaxed in each other's company, which couldn't have made him happy. But on the other hand, by the time Shiva returned Aviama to her rooms, the two of them were at a cold standoff. It would have been clear to anyone with a brain that something had not gone well, and Aviama was quite sure Ishaan did indeed have a brain behind those hollow eyes. It was probably good at plotting murders, for example.

Aviama headed for the sitting area but caught a glimpse of herself in the mirror and paused. Her hair stuck out from her braids in every direction, and the skin at her throat was still raised and red.

Fear struck her in the chest like a hammer. What had Ishaan thought of her mussed hair? What had the servants thought of it as they passed? Why hadn't Shiva said anything?

Aviama yanked at the pins and ties in her hair and raked her fingers through her tangled mane. She got only the worst of the snarls free before going through the drawers of the vanity for the powders Murin used to get her ready in the morning and carefully dabbing some along the red semi-circle at her neck. It wasn't perfect, but it would do.

She returned the powders to the vanity, flopped onto the sofa, and turned a throw pillow over and over in her hands. The man who saved her, the man who threatened her. The man who poked fun at her and dragged her behind him to break the rules, and the man who demanded public respect. An enigma.

Ishaan seemed easier to read. Dark, brooding, and waiting to run to the queen with every move she made.

Queen Satya, bent on keeping melderblood from polluting the Tanashai line. Willing to do whatever it took to make that happen.

Four light raps on the door told her Murin had returned. It hadn't taken her long. Aviama invited her in and let her fix up the room, though it needed no fixing. She told Murin about the walk through the palace with Shiva, about the courtyards, and the conversation on the terrace. She left out the menagerie, and mentioned only that he was defensive about having experience with women and she was worried she'd made him angry.

Murin listened with rapt attention, consoling her that each princess was afforded a minimum of two one-on-one opportunities with the prince before he made any decisions. Aviama still had a chance to make things right if there was a misunderstanding. The thought made her stomach turn.

Did she want to be alone with him again?

She had learned nothing of value to Jannemar so far, and couldn't go home empty-handed, so it would be advantageous to smooth things over enough to buy time. Not to mention that a bad relationship with the crown prince of Radha did not bode well for future trade relations between their kingdoms, alliance or no alliance. Aviama clenched her jaw at the memory of what he said about her brother. He didn't understand. He didn't try to.

But she hadn't either, had she? Rumors always surrounded great men. Her own family had dealt with enough of it that she should have been more sensitive. She'd assumed the rumors were true—why, because Marija seemed so trustworthy? Aviama buried her face in the pillow with a groan. The silver lining was that if Shiva decided she was pretentious and self-important and hateful, the queen would be pleased and might leave her alone. But Aviama couldn't afford to leave things tense with a kingdom as strong as Radha, and she wasn't sure what she would have to do to make it up to Shiva. And she had a feeling Ishaan would be watching closer than ever after today.

By the time Aviama had told Murin everything—that is, everything she felt inclined to share—she was sick of the four walls of her room, and her stomach growled. When Murin recommended lunch in the courtyard on the first floor just below her balcony, Aviama heartily agreed.

Murin called for lunch, and Ishaan shadowed them out of the room, down the stairs, and around to the courtyard beneath her balcony. Darra, the doe-eyed princess from Curion, seemed to have had the same idea and sat with two of her ladies along benches by the pakshi pool. Ishaan hung back as they approached, and Aviama made a mental note to engage with other royals or high-profile guests whenever she needed him to back off.

"Princess Aviama! Would you sit with us?"

Murin dragged over another bench, and the two of them sat opposite Darra and her girls. Darra folded her hands daintily in her lap and leaned forward. "Did you sleep well last night? Or did the screaming wake you up?"

Aviama blinked. Had everyone on the guest wing heard her nightmare scream? "I slept all right...until the screaming." Aviama grimaced. "And you? What have you done this morning?"

"Oh! We visited the stables this morning, and then the pakshi enclosure. They are so incredible, don't you think?"

Stunning. Creepy. Frightening. All the above. Aviama nodded and let Darra take control of the conversation, sharing her favorite horses in the stables, and the horse training she'd enjoyed back home. Aviama asked about the stables in Radha and the riding style in Curion. Darra lit up at the topic of horses and asked her questions about Jannemar in return. Curion was more open to magic, it seemed, and more interested in training melders than getting rid of them.

A more reasonable approach.

Aviama liked Darra. Maybe they could both stay in Radha long enough to get to know each other a bit.

Darra glanced to either side and lowered her voice, leaning in with such intrigue that Aviama edged forward in return. "The servants tell me the prince has already met with one of the princesses, and they seemed quite friendly. What do you think? Do you think he'll be like that with all of us, romantic and such, that it's all part of the process? Or do you think he only does that sort of thing with women he is truly drawn to and likes?"

The girl looked so bright and excitable, Aviama didn't have the heart to ruin it. A weight settled in her gut, but she mimicked Darra's cheerful optimism and only shrugged. "I don't know. I don't guess we know him well enough for that, but we'll have the chance to find out."

Darra giggled, then sighed. "I don't think there's any hope

for me at all. I bet it was Marija that he was with. He wouldn't be interested in someone like me."

"I'm sure he could be. But remember, it matters whether *you* like *him* too. Not just the other way around."

Darra gave a weak smile. "Not for me. Curion will be much stronger with a Radhan alliance. If Prince Shiva won't marry me, my father is hoping to unite one of my brothers with one of Prince Shiva's sisters, once they all come of age. But if I can secure an alliance now, they'll have less pressure on their own marriages."

Aviama winced. She knew she was lucky, having more freedom and less pressure regarding who she might marry. It really hadn't been a topic of focus yet, what with managing the grief over her parents and trying to keep the kingdom together. And now that Aviama was eighteen, though it would be strategic for her brother to arrange something for her to strengthen Jannemar, his focus had been elsewhere.

She doubted he had the heart to force the issue. Not after their father married a commoner for love. Not after Zephan himself married Semra—a commoner by birth, even if their father had granted her noble status before he passed. Still, with their older sister as a wildcard and not trusted to leave Shamaran Castle after all the destruction she'd brought to the kingdom, Aviama was their only hope for an alliance by marriage union.

It wouldn't be fair to expect her to marry for duty when Zephan had married for love. But even that union had a political spin on it to make it make sense. She was a dragonlord, a symbol of hope for the land. The people adored her and felt safer with the great blue dragon swooping overhead in Qalea. Everyone knew her name. She wasn't just any commoner.

But Aviama *was* just any other princess. A shadow in the Shamaran family, the youngest, the least important, least influential. She hoped she'd get some say in what happened to her, but if Jannemar's financial and political situation remained somewhat unstable, her king brother may be left with little choice.

A weight settled over her chest, and she reached out to touch Darra's arm. "I understand. It would be a great kindness to your siblings if you were able to form a valuable alliance before they come of age."

Darra nodded, tears welling in her eyes. "I don't want to disappoint them."

Aviama patted her arm. "We can only do what we can do."

Lunch arrived, and Aviama chatted with Darra, inviting Murin and Darra's ladies into the conversation whenever possible. They were shy, but willing, as Darra seemed just as relaxed with her women as Aviama was with hers.

After a while, Darra and her ladies withdrew, and Murin disappeared to find Amir and ask whether Aviama could visit the stables also, or even go for a ride. Ishaan stood sentry in the shadows of the pillars, and Aviama's stomach soured at the sight of him glowering from the edge of the columns. Surely, he would go off duty eventually, and another guard would take his place.

Not that it mattered. Queen Satya would no doubt ensure anyone watching Aviama would be equally as unpleasant and bound to her bidding. Aviama sighed and slouched against the reclining chair. She thought about slipping off her shoes and dipping her toes in the water, but an image of the mermaid flying up at her through the water gave her pause.

All she could see was koi, but the notion of the mermaid and the sting of her neck was enough to make her keep her distance. She watched the fish for a while, their orange and white scales glinting under the sun of the open sky above, and tossed a few bread crumbs into the water. The fish surged at the crumbs, mouths bobbing open and closed. But as harmless as they were, the flash of silver scales still made her queasy.

A door slammed somewhere on the second floor, the sound carrying down over one of the balconies. Aviama snapped her head up, and Marija swept out onto the balcony, her dark hair flowing over one shoulder. "That's *not* how I wanted it," she said to someone behind her. "I've told you a thousand times."

Marija's room seemed to be around the corner and several doors down from Aviama's, so her balcony overlooked the far side of the courtyard. Marija eyed the pool down below, and Aviama shrank back into her chair.

Not far enough. Marija spied her. "Princess Aviama! What a delight."

Her tone did not indicate any delight whatsoever, but the plastered-on smile oozed the sort of syrupy diplomacy Aviama had come to despise. Marija leaned one hip against the balustrade. "I'd come down and visit, but I am meeting the prince tonight and must prepare. I've got the most hideous bags under my eyes. Tell me, did you sleep better than I did last night? Did you find out who the banshee was, or was it you?"

Aviama ground her teeth. She dusted breadcrumbs from her fingers and gave a halfhearted wave up at Marija. "Don't trouble yourself to visit. I hope you sleep more soundly tonight."

No need to answer the banshee question.

Marija smiled. "Oh, I know I will. An evening with Shiva is always *so* relaxing. It's just what I need." She tossed her hair over her shoulder and disappeared into her room. Aviama rolled her eyes and dropped her head back onto the long chair.

What was it Frigibar used to say? *There's a hawk in every dovecote.* Well, *biscuits*, Marija was no dove. Aviama was grateful Darra had left before seeing her.

"Jealous already?"

Aviama startled and jerked upright, twisting toward the voice. Chenzira strolled to the fruit tray with lazy, reptilian indifference and snatched an apple. Aviama set her jaw. "Stop doing that!"

"Doing what? Standing in courtyards? Or eating fruit?" He tossed the apple in the air and took a bite. She made a face.

"Appearing out of thin air to scare me."

"Oh, well, be at ease, then, Your Highness! I didn't come for you at all. You just happened to be here. It's not my fault you jump out of your skin over nothing."

Aviama crossed her arms. "If you didn't keep showing up right next to me, maybe I wouldn't jump."

Chenzira took a bite of the apple. "I'm pretty sure you'd be frightened by a feather at this point. In any case, you were too busy glowering at the esteemed Princess Marija to notice me."

"I wasn't glowering."

"If that's what your pleasant face looks like, I'd hate to see you angry." He paused and regarded her a moment. Heat flew to her cheeks, and she clenched her hands into fists. Chenzira held his hands up. "No, see, *that* face is heftier than the one Marija got. I suppose *now* you're angry. Well, I'll take my leave and let you stew in peace. I imagine I'll see you tomorrow night at the games. I'll count myself lucky we will only be watching, and you won't be in the arena to kill me with your dagger eyes."

Chenzira took another bite of the apple and turned on his heel, chucking it at Ishaan as he passed. Ishaan caught it, then grimaced, and wiped his hand on his trousers. Aviama twisted in her seat to gape at Chenzira as he disappeared, then dropped back into her chair as Ishaan looked up.

Who did he think he was, popping up in random places to scare her, mock her, and run away like that? Perhaps she should have given it back to him, put him in his place somehow. She racked her brain, but even now that he was gone, suitable clever comebacks eluded her.

Aviama plucked a juicy piece of pineapple from the plate and popped it in her mouth. *Prince Chenzira of Keket.* Why had he left Keket? And why had Shiva poking at him earlier made him so upset?

A prince ashamed to be called a Bomani, staying for long periods of time in Radha…

How could hosting Chenzira make him a treasure of *Radha*? That's what Shiva had called him. Aviama sat up. Radha was going to ally with not one, but two nations. One of its neighbors, through marriage—and Keket, through overthrowing the government there and establishing a ruler of whom they approved.

A second son would never rule, but with enough support, the intel on all the infrastructure of Keket, and an agreement with King Dahnuk, Chenzira had a shot at the throne. By making a deal and handing over his family.

Planning such a thing would take time, and Keket was the only surrounding kingdom with a naval force to rival Radha. Radha would need as much backing as possible, and a new alliance through marriage would bring in the military support required for a large-scale invasion.

Aviama's stomach dropped.

If Radha took Keket, they would own the seas.

15

The rest of the day passed uneventfully, save for the spinning of her mind in a thousand different directions. Outwardly, she visited the stables with Murin under Ishaan's watchful gaze, walked the grounds, and retired to her room. But inwardly, image after image filed through her brain: the queen storming down the halls to kill her, and Ishaan's willing grin; the mermaid rushing her through the glass of the aquarium, fanged teeth bared and hands reaching out for her neck; Chenzira handing over his family to be murdered while he sat on his father's throne.

She lay awake much of the night, tossing and turning, as if by restlessness alone she could stave off the visions dancing before her every time she closed her eyes. Aviama buried her face into her pillow, and a new image appeared: Shiva, tracing his fingers lightly over her cheek, brushing his thumb over her lips—and then his eyes hardening from tenderness to flint. His hand shot out to grip her wrist in an iron vise, and he dropped his voice to a low growl. "I will not be made a fool of in my own house."

Aviama yanked the blankets over her head. She shook off

the figments of her overactive imagination, but when she squeezed her eyes shut again, she saw Marija.

Shiva wound his arm tightly around her waist, and Marija beamed up at him. He kissed her then, and she smiled—then turned to cast a sly glance in Aviama's direction. She winked. Aviama's skin crawled.

What did she care if the prince in a melder-hating kingdom preferred someone who actually wanted a union? After all, Aviama was only in Radha to pacify King Dahnuk and gain information. She didn't come with the same pressures Darra did. She didn't need a husband.

She didn't *want* a husband. And even if she did, Shiva was the last man alive she would marry.

Unless...

What if he didn't hate melders? What if *that's* what he disagreed with his mother about, and she could gain his ear, show him how melders only need to learn about their powers, not be treated like criminals? What if she was the link to protect melders in Radha from the hatred the servant had given her when she arrived?

The coldness of their last meeting did not bode well for Shiva's listening ear. The queen would be pleased, but Jannemar's diplomatic relations with Radha might suffer.

One way or another, she had to make it right.

But what was she to make of his sudden, aggressive change when she'd accused him of—what *had* she accused him of exactly? Enjoying the company of too many women, though it was typical in his circles? Was it possible Chenzira was right, and she was already jealous?

Aviama rolled her eyes and tugged the blanket tighter around her. No, it was the double standard that the visiting princesses were not to be with men, but the prince had rumors floating everywhere about his multiple encounters.

Still, they were rumors. He hadn't denied them, but he also hadn't confirmed them, or said that he was currently seeking out such experiences while getting to know the four princesses who had come to meet him.

Perhaps *debased* was too strong of a word. And stabbing her finger at him was probably uncalled for, as diplomatic choices between royals went. As much as she hated to admit it, she needed to apologize.

When Aviama finally drifted off to sleep, she dreamed of Enzo. He was dying in a barracks full of sick men, lying on a bed, racked with coughs and ghostly pale.

Morning came, and she woke slowly, luxuriously—with nowhere to be and nothing to do for the moment but shut out the world and pretend the world beyond her room did not exist. Rays of sun danced across the marble floor, and she imagined herself in a mythical underwater kingdom, the intricate blue patterns of the walls and ceiling forming her watery abode in a place where no foreign king, threatening queen, baffling prince, or self-important princess could find her.

Aviama thought of Mox's fairy tales, the story of the sea king whose sons lassoed the winds, and whose daughters sung sailors to sleep to keep a perfect society untouched. She'd loved that fairy tale as a child. The thought of swimming through the open ocean, swirling among the depths with a tail of her own propelling her through the water at top speed, was enchanting.

After yesterday's experience with the mermaid, it seemed less like a fairy tale and more like a nightmare.

Aviama closed her eyes and whispered to the wind, a silent pull in her heart, and it answered like a soft breath winding through her fingers. She opened her eyes and passed the trace of a breeze across her fingertips, then added air to it and tossed it from palm to palm.

Thanks to Frigibar's tutelage and Semra's mentorship, Aviama's magic was more controlled than anyone in Jannemar except for Semra. Her haphazard entry into Radha flew to the forefront of her mind. *Then why was there a windstorm as they came into harbor?* What was wrong with her? Everything seemed tame now, the wind following her command properly...

A soft knock pulled her focus, and Aviama dissipated the ball of air and sat up just as Murin slipped into the room carrying a breakfast tray. "Your Highness! You're up! It's already midmorning. You must have been exhausted."

Aviama rubbed her eyes. She never slept this long. "I was, but I feel better now. What's for breakfast?"

"Fruit, rolls, sweetmeats, and a letter from the king." Murin set the tray down and grinned.

Aviama snatched a roll and lifted it to her mouth, then hesitated, and broke it open with her hands instead. No secret messages. She took a bite. "A letter?"

Murin nodded and handed it over. Aviama broke the seal and slid the parchment from its envelope. She scanned the letter. "We are all being treated to a Radhan demonstration of skill tonight in the king's private arena. This must be what he meant when he said he'd see me today at the games..." Aviama spun the rings on her fingers and chewed on her nail.

Murin clapped her hands. "Prince Shiva is already looking forward to seeing you again, even in a group outing! He mentioned this yesterday?"

Aviama worried her lip. "I heard about it."

But not from Shiva. From Chenzira.

Halfway through breakfast, another knock came at the door, and Murin went to open it. She spoke to someone outside and opened the door wide, and two servants came in carrying an easel, large sketchpads, and an assortment of drawing utensils.

Aviama stood. "What's all this?"

The servants brought the materials into the sitting area and bowed. "A gift from His Highness, Prince Shiva, Your Highness. Is this all right?"

Aviama gaped at the gift, and nodded blankly. "Yes, of course. Thank you."

The servants bowed and made their exit, leaving Aviama standing in front of the couch, staring at the easel, mouth open. What did it mean? Had he sent gifts to all the girls? Was this an apology, or simply a way to buy back her good graces? Did it mean he still *wanted* her good graces?

Her heart skipped a beat, and she stepped forward to examine the gift. She ran her hands along the large sheets of thick paper. Exquisite quality. Her fingers itched for the pencils, or maybe the charcoal. Was she so easily bought?

She bit her lip and lifted the top leaf of paper. A note fell from between the sheets. Aviama picked it up off the floor and flipped it open.

For my hot-tempered lilac.
You look like a dream, but you talk like a firebrand.
Perhaps that's why I feel sparks when I'm with you.
I'd like to try again.

Her mouth went dry, and her chest exploded in a torrent of flutters. She spun her rings at a feverish speed. One, two, three, four. One, two, three, four.

An apology, then. More than an apology. A declaration of —of what, exactly? Did he mean it? She'd overstepped and spoken out of turn. Perhaps he understood that he had also.

Shouldn't she lend him the same grace she expected in return?

She re-read the note. Twice, three times.

"Good news?"

Aviama jolted, glancing up at Murin, who had perched herself on the arm of a chair and was watching her closely. "What makes you say so?"

Murin laughed. "You are smiling, Your Highness, though it seems you did not know it. That's the best kind, isn't it?"

Aviama blushed, and this time she couldn't help but over-analyze the uncontrollable sheepish grin that took over her face. "I wouldn't know."

Impossible, ridiculous man. Sending his stupid gift and his stupid note and expecting her to forgive him. She picked up a stick of charcoal. She'd been planning on apologizing to him anyway, but it was even better that he had apologized to her first. Well, he'd recognized his error. It must be difficult for men of power to remember to feel first, rather than be constantly caught up in the role they've been born and bred to play. To remember that the people they command are people.

Maybe he just needed reminding. And not only had he remembered her humanity—he'd remembered her hobbies and sent her a little piece of comfort to her room.

She touched the charcoal to the paper and dragged it lightly across the paper in long, arcing strokes. Aviama lost herself to the motion, drawing and blending and touching up, adding shadows and details, humming to herself as her arm swept across the page from top to bottom. By the time she stepped back, her hum had blossomed into song, her stomach complained for food, and her hand hurt.

"Your Highness, it's good to hear you sing again."

Aviama glanced up. "What? Why?"

"You haven't sung much since The Return. You used to sing often."

Something squeezed tight in Aviama's gut, and she swallowed. "I still sing. Don't I?"

"No, Your Highness. Sometimes I catch you humming your mother's lullabies, but you used to sing all the time. You sang when you were alone, and I would hear you from the hall. I counted myself honored that at times you felt comfortable for me to hear you while I was in the room. It is like the music takes you over when you sing, Your Highness. It is beautiful. And when I hear it, I am glad, because I know my princess is well."

Now that she thought about it, Aviama couldn't remember the last time she really sang. She hadn't quite noticed she'd stopped. But after Liben died—the servant who'd been hit by the hammer caught in Aviama's windstorm—the world had seemed a bit darker. Murin's observance moved her, and a lump rose in her throat.

Her mother, Queen Sharsi, used to sing. It had always soothed Aviama as a child, but her favorite was when they'd sung together. Weaving harmonies with her mother was about as close to a perfect moment as Aviama could picture.

The day wore into afternoon, and Murin recommended a cherry blossom pink dress for the evening, paired with gold jewelry set with rubies. Murin had just set the last pin into her hair when someone pounded on the door.

"Time to go."

Aviama let out a deep sigh at Ishaan's voice and took a breath. She lifted her chin and walked out the door. As the door latched shut behind her, Ishaan leaned in toward her.

"Watch yourself, Highness. Today you learn what happens to people who displease the crown."

A roar went up from the private arena of the House of the Blessing Sun, a thunderous noise that shook the bronze doors before them. Ishaan had led Aviama up two flights of stairs and down corridor after corridor so that she thought the kingdom's opulent display might never end. Did money grow on trees in Radha, that their sprawling palace by the sea went on and on, each hall as intricately painted as the last?

Aviama spun the rings on her fingers and shifted her weight from one foot to the other in the narrow hall above the arena. It was positioned only a hall over from the menagerie, but up two levels, and Aviama stood now in line with the other princesses as a booming voice on the other side announced their arrival.

Ishaan had said nothing since his ominous warning outside her door, but when they came to the double doors, Darra had greeted her with a hug and told her that much of the court and nearly anyone with a title had been invited to the evening's event.

Vanina, the warrior princess of Batal, tossed a dark braid

over her shoulder and leaned back toward them. "Marija looks like a painting. The stilted, pompous kind that you're not allowed to touch as a kid, but you've always secretly wanted to rip off the wall."

Aviama stifled a snort. Marija stood at the front of the line —no surprise there, and Aviama rather wondered how early she'd arrived to secure the honor—and was busying herself examining her nail beds and arranging the gold at her throat, which was already perfectly arranged. The woman was a vision, but Aviama would have been happier with her as a mirage.

Marija must have reciprocated the sentiment, seeing how she'd edged forward toward the door when they arrived rather than stand too close to them. Marija shot her a glare, and Aviama sobered. Vanina smirked.

Aviama felt a little guilty for mocking, but Marija deserved it. She was a gossip trollop wrapped in linen, and besides, she probably approved of any conversation that centered around her. It wasn't Aviama's fault Marija lived for dramatic insult and seemed to beg to receive it in return.

The doors opened, and Darra kept close to Aviama, hanging back for a moment as Marija paraded into the sun. Vanina snapped her head forward and marched after her, and Aviama nudged Darra to follow. The girl tripped over her shoes on the way through the doors, and Aviama winced, grateful when she recovered and made it down the walkway toward the seats.

Sunshine glinted off rows of seats set in a circle overlooking a sand pit down below. Tall stone doors were set in its walls, and three large poles lined one side of the pit. Nobles sat around its edge, and servants came to and fro with trays of food.

King Dahnuk sat on cushioned seats at one end, his wife

and daughters to his left, his son to his right. Four seats waited for them next to Prince Shiva, and a row of nobles sat on elevated chairs behind the first row.

Aviama let out a breath of relief as Ishaan disappeared into the standing room several paces back, but her heart stopped as she scanned the seats and made eye contact with Queen Satya. The queen pulled her lips back in a mirthless smile, and a chill ran down Aviama's spine.

The king nodded and grinned, waving them over and indicating the seats to his right, and Prince Shiva stood to greet them. Aviama's gut twisted, heart hammering in her chest as Shiva kissed the hand of each princess and took their arms to guide them into their seats.

Would his gaze be harsh and unforgiving as it had been last? Or had the tenderness returned, as his note might suggest? She bit her lip, released it, and twirled the rings on her fingers. *One, two, three, four.*

Ahead of her, Marija had flounced into the seat next to Shiva, Vanina perched stiff as a board on the edge of her seat, and Shiva reached for Darra. The Curion princess nearly melted away from him, and he laughed lightly, a low, warm sound. Aviama pursed her lips and glanced away.

Into deep-brown eyes. She sucked in a breath and jerked her gaze back to Shiva. *Biscuits,* was there no corner of the palace where she could escape Chenzira's unflinching leer? Her mouth went dry, and the last thing her embarrassed flusterment needed was to stare at Shiva's comforting softness toward Darra. Aviama ripped her chin sideways, and found the queen scrutinizing her from the other side of her husband.

Aviama dipped her head and gave a weak smile, but her knees knocked beneath her skirts as the reality of her position for the evening settled over her.

Queen Satya would expect her to keep her distance from Shiva, to remain cold—to show only minimal interest, in respect for her threats. Shiva himself would surely want to know if his gift and impossibly confusing note was received well, or spurned, and if she didn't encourage him, she might lose forever his attention, and, therefore, her welcome in the country. Ishaan stood at the back, watching it all like a hawk. And Chenzira, the missing prince conspiring to feed his family to the wolves for his own aspirations of power, would laugh at her from the seat directly behind her, patting himself on the back for calling out her jumpiness and jealousy.

Something touched her hand, and Aviama nearly jerked in surprise, but managed to stay herself and turn toward the something.

"Your Highness?"

Shiva brought her hand to his lips, his eyes kind but firm, a guarded diplomacy. Ah, of course. He would be neither harsh nor tender. Not here.

Her heart sank, and she dipped into a curtsy. "Prince Shiva."

Was there a question in his eyes, or was she projecting onto him her own curiosity?

Shiva guided her to her seat beside Darra and turned away, passing Vanina and Marija on his way back to his seat. Aviama swallowed. She leaned back, and flinched as a server she hadn't noticed brought a tray around on her right. A low chortle came from the place behind her, and her stomach soured. She took a bowl of a purple substance with shrimp around the rim and smiled at the servant in thanks.

She wouldn't give Chenzira the satisfaction of seeing him rattle her. Aviama plucked a shrimp from the bowl, dipped it into the sauce, and popped it in her mouth.

Fire exploded on her tongue, and she gasped. Hot tears

sprang to her eyes, and the shrimp lodged somewhere at the back of her throat. A hacking rasp took her over, and her shoulders shook as she choked and gagged.

An announcer was saying something, but she didn't hear a word of it. Heads swiveled in her direction, and Vanina leaned over across Darra.

"Geyser shrimp. You don't like it? It's so flavorful!"

Darra put a hand on her back. "I don't think she's okay. Are you okay?"

Aviama doubled over, and with a final cough, the offending shrimp hurtled onto the floor at her feet.

"It burned off my taste buds," Aviama wheezed. "I don't think I'll be able to taste anything for weeks."

Darra patted her back, and Aviama sucked in clean, cool air—her only relief from the fire. She glanced in each direction, but the servants were far around the bend of the arena, and she seemed to have missed the opportunity for a water glass.

Vanina plopped a shrimp in her mouth and licked the excess sauce from her fingers. "We enjoy spices in our food in Batal."

Shiva gave her a quizzical look from over Vanina's shoulder, and Marija arched an eyebrow. Aviama rubbed her still-burning throat and dropped her voice low. "Do you also eat lava and eat soup while it's boiling?"

Someone tapped her on the shoulder, and Aviama turned to her right. Chenzira held out a glass of water. It was as if he held out the nectar of heaven itself. Aviama reached for it like a parched dog finding his first puddle, and drained the glass in three long gulps. She hesitated, staring at the sparkling glass, and winced.

"Thank you. Sorry." She offered it back to him, but he held up a hand.

"It's yours."

Of course it was. He'd offered her a sip, and she'd emptied it completely. Why take it back? *Biscuits.*

Aviama bit her lip and slumped into her chair, but her mind chastised her the moment she sunk into her new position. *Stop it. You're a princess. Act like it.* She sighed and sat up. And craned her neck forward, because after whatever announcements she'd missed, two unarmed men were now facing off in the sandpit below.

The first man danced forward and struck the second man on the jaw. Before Aviama could blink, two writhing bodies were rolling in the sand, and when they finally broke apart, blood stained the ground. Which one had the injury? What were the rules?

To her left, Marija giggled and sidled up to Shiva. Aviama rolled her eyes and glanced down. The shrimp she'd choked on mocked her from the floor at the edge of her rose-pink skirt. She kicked it under her chair.

When she looked up again, one of the men was on the ground. He wasn't moving. A bell rang.

The winner threw his arms up to the cheering crowd. The loser was alive, if only barely, and was helped onto a stretcher and taken away. Vanina clucked her tongue. "He didn't keep his hands high and tight. Left himself wide open. Idiot."

"As if you could do any better," Marija scoffed.

Vanina tapped the scar across her face. "I *have* done better. Against better skills than that."

Shiva grinned. "You'll like the next cycle, then. First cycle, rounds of hand-to-hand. Second cycle, weapons. Third cycle, man against beast."

Aviama's jaw dropped. "Beast?"

The next match started then, and her question went ignored. Aviama knew tournaments, jousts, and general sparring and fighting were typical entertainments the world over. Jannemar's contests seemed more...civil. Regulated. Reasonable. But a man against a beast? What if the man lost? Why would they fight? And if the animal was weak, how was it allowed to be sent to its death for the sake of cheap sport?

To her left, Vanina critiqued the fighters' forms. Marija whispered something into Shiva's ear, and he laughed. Behind her, a servant made his rounds with a new appetizer. Darra watched the spectacle with mixed interest and shock, and Aviama fiddled with the rings on her fingers, staring into the sand beyond the combatants.

Wasn't there enough fighting and death as it was, without the need to simulate more? The first man's blood still stained the sand, and she found herself staring at it. The fighters dove at each other, one after the other, contestants for—for what? Glory? The privilege of living another day? Money?

Is this what Chenzira saw when he looked at Aviama and the other princesses? Contestants jealous over a prize, with no more morals or depth to them than that? The thought made her uncomfortable. She shifted in her seat. *One, two, three, four.*

A man fell. The bell rang. This time, the loser did not get up.

The crowd cheered. The weapons cycle began.

Aviama stared at the growing blots of blood across the pit. In every stain she saw a body—her mother, with the knife still protruding from her chest. Her father, and the guard's detached arm flying through the air with the debris of the explosion. Even the men Semra had killed, when she fought their way out of Shamaran Castle to save Aviama's life.

While Aviama did nothing, obviously. Nothing but sit and wait. Because she had no skills and was worthless in battle.

A Jannemari mourning song sung in wartime tugged at the edge of her mind.

> *Sing for the men, the dead, the dying,*
> *The families left, the hollow, sighing,*
> *The ground where you lie will flower forever*
> *And we will remember your noble endeavor*

But there was no mourning here. Only cheering. And there was nothing noble here. Only frivolous entertainment at the expense of someone else's blood.

One of the fighters in the pit whirled a mace over his head and struck at his opponent. The other man was shorter, but twice as fast, and ducked under the man's arm, letting the momentum of the mace pull him forward. The shorter fighter popped back up behind the mace-holder's dominant arm and smashed him in the temple with the hilt of his saber.

He dropped like a stone, the mace falling to the sand with a muted thud.

Aviama sucked in a breath. His face, his glassy, unseeing eyes—he looked like Liben. And in that moment this fighter in Radha became the servant in Jannemar, lying not next to a mace but a hammer. A lump lodged in her throat and she swallowed, blinking back unshed tears.

It wasn't Liben. Obviously. But what did it matter? Both were dead. One died for a dinner show, killed for a king's guests. The other died at the hands of an unstable new melder, a princess, for no reason but lack of control.

The ship came to mind again. Ever since her training with Frigibar, Aviama's control had been good. Better than good. Not close to Semra's, but better than most of the melders she'd met back home. So how had she whipped up a windstorm powerful enough to toss the ship too quickly to harbor, without even noticing?

What was wrong with her?

Aviama glanced to her left. Shiva caught her eye and smiled. She managed a weak smile back. Queen Satya leaned into the king, sharing some commentary or other over the festivities. Aviama snapped her head forward and stared at the body.

What was wrong with the world?

The announcer's voice boomed over the pit. "And now, a special treat—our generous king has chosen to allow his honored guests to see select beasts in action from his marvelous collection. In order to demonstrate, we have the ciraba monitor, native to Radha—and the criminal Darsh Mushkil, charged with destruction of property belonging to the crown, the murder of a royal guard, and unregistered melderblood."

Aviama's stomach wrenched. *Melderblood.* She was going to be sick.

17

———

A gate lifted on one end of the pit, and a man was shoved into the arena with a long prod. His hands were tied in front of him, but his feet were free. Even from her vantage point two stories above, Aviama could see the whites of the man's eyes. Darsh's chest heaved, and he tugged his bound wrists against his body.

The king lurched forward and gripped a servant by the collar. "I ordered his hands tied behind him. *Behind* him. He's a melderblood! Find out who is responsible for this."

It was the most serious Aviama had ever seen King Dahnuk's face. Except, perhaps, for the moment when he charged the princesses not to engage in outside romance during their participation in the contest for Shiva. A chill ran down her spine.

The second gate lifted. Its entrance was dark, and the space of that moment seemed to stretch on and on. Aviama held her breath. And then a long, rasping hiss echoed out from the tunnel beyond.

In a flash, an orange-gray streak flew across the open arena. Long, odd-angled legs tore over the sand, elbows straight out on either side, making for a strange waddling gait as it dragged its massive lizard body toward Darsh. The thing was five meters of muscle, its tail slashing back and forth behind it like a rudder. When it opened its mouth again, its hiss sent a tremor through the watching nobles.

Darsh dove to one side, but the ciraba was too fast. It lunged and seized Darsh's foot in its mouth. The man cried out and crashed to the ground. The ciraba shook him back and forth and choked up higher over Darsh's foot, claiming his ankle along with it. Darsh threw his hands in front of him, trying in vain to stabilize himself, but only raked futile fingers through grains of sand.

Darsh aimed his palms at the ciraba and blasted it in the face with wind strong enough to snap its head to one side. Aviama lurched to the edge of her seat and clutched the edge of the wall in front of her for a better view. The startled beast released Darsh's foot and dropped its head down against the melder's gale. Aviama's mouth went dry.

He wasn't just a melder. He was a windcaller. Just like her.

Darsh limped to one side, but his ankle collapsed beneath him in an unnatural bent. He'd never be able to outrun the ciraba. And even if he could, he had nowhere to go.

The ciraba tasted the air with a long, blue forked tongue. Darsh's face twisted into a snarl. He stood on his good leg, palms out, beckoning the beast. "Come on! Get another taste!"

Marija pressed into Shiva's side. "He actually attacked the palace?"

Shiva nodded. "He's one of our local extremists. They've been causing trouble all over Radha, but nothing we can't handle. This last was the most brazen attempt so far."

Darra's doe eyes bulged. "He wasn't working alone?"

"No, but we hope to make him an example. I can't imagine they'll die for their cause when it's obvious they cannot win."

Marija shook her head in wonder. "He's crazy."

"He's melderblood."

The last comment was spat out like venom, and all heads turned to acknowledge the new speaker. Queen Satya.

Aviama peered back over the wall to the pit, anxious for any reason at all not to look in her direction. Below, the ciraba charged Darsh. He shoved the corded binding of his wrists into the animal's mouth and pulled, the fingers of his one visible hand hooked as if on a fishing rod. The animal thrashed backward but would not release its hold. Blood poured from a gash in Darsh's forearm.

The queen spoke again, lifting her voice loud enough for anyone on this side of the arena to hear. "Crazy would be better. There is nothing worse than a power-possessed person who believes they are above all law. And that is what melderbloods are. Elitist, destructive anarchists."

Aviama's blood boiled, and she could almost feel Queen Satya's accusing glare settling over her small frame. Goosebumps fled up her arms, even as the sun beat down on the fabric shade overhead and filled the air with its heat.

Down in the pit, Darsh had managed to wrangle his bonds from the ciraba's mouth. Long cords still hung from one wrist, but he could move freely. He jumped on the creature's back, slipped the long cord into its mouth, and yanked backward. The beast writhed beneath him, making Darsh look a bit like a rag doll. The ciraba's smooth reptilian scales offered no place for the man to secure himself, and the shifting sands beneath his one good foot were even worse.

Despite his best efforts, the monster was winning the battle. Aviama spun her rings and chewed her lip. *Unregistered melderblood.* It was listed among his other offenses as if it were just as evil to exist as a melder as to attack the palace or kill a guard.

What did Radha do with the list of melders, if it were so important? Jannemar had no registry. They had resources and opportunities to train, education to minimize the damage and promote peace, to help people sort out their confusing new abilities.

It had only been three years since The Return. There were still accidents. But they had a good system in place, and things were improving.

What had happened with Darsh? Was he a criminal before The Return, or was all of this the aftermath of a man waking up one day with strange new abilities, met with fear and punishment instead of guidance? What could his life have looked like if he'd been in Jannemar when magic returned?

Aviama hardly noticed when she first leaned out over the wall, so lost was she in her thoughts. The ciraba snapped to one side and knocked the Radhan into the sand. Darsh rolled onto his good leg, hopped up, and summoned a mighty gale of wind. The air gathered beneath him, and he propelled himself upward on it—aiming straight for her.

By the time she registered what was happening, it was too late. The wind wasn't strong enough to carry him over the edge of the pit's wall, but he got just high enough to throw the cord around her neck. Her feet ripped from the ground and she toppled over the edge with a scream, plummeting down to the arena below.

Aviama crashed into the sand, her fall broken only by Darsh himself as he hit the ground hard a split second before her. She rolled right off him, her forearms burning as they met the harsh sand, and every muscle screamed in painful protest. But none of it mattered. Not when a blue tongue flicked out to taste the air and a roar rocketed across the arena.

The beast's enormous head swiveled in Aviama's direction. Her heart stopped. Sweat broke out across her forehead.

The ciraba charged.

Aviama screamed and threw up her hands. Wind sprang to her palms like moths to a flame, and the creature skidded backward to the far side of the pit. She gasped, and nausea swept over her as she realized what she'd done.

If you make it out of this alive, they'll kill you. Melderblood.

Of course, if she didn't make it out, her caution would be her death.

Beside her, Darsh dropped his hands. He'd called the wind too, at just the same time, from right beside her. It was conceivable that he had sent the ciraba scrabbling backward on his own, rather than inadvertently joining forces with Aviama.

Darsh hobbled toward her a step as she gathered her feet under her and rose. "You're one of us," he hissed. "Get me out."

Her heart battered against her rib cage. She shook her head. "I don't know what you're talking about."

Darsh's magic wasn't strong enough to get him over the wall, and Aviama had never tried to propel herself upward with her magic. She was unlikely to find success in that approach.

Flight was not her favorite mode of travel anyway. Aviama dropped into a miserable fighting stance, the kind that might improve her balance against a dog or small child, but utterly worthless against a monumental lightning lizard.

Darsh swung an arm around her neck and cinched it tight, dragging her backward against himself and leaning heavily on her to offset his bad leg. Aviama gasped and gagged, but he loosened his grip around her throat just enough for her to breathe. The ciraba charged again, and Darsh threw a gale at him with his free hand.

But the ciraba had learned a thing or two. A one-handed

call for wind wouldn't cut it anymore. It ducked its head and flew low along the ground like a snake in a river, cutting through the sand like butter.

Shouts and screams went up from the audience above them, and for an instant Aviama wondered what her foreign overlords thought of her latest failure—but all thoughts of Ishaan and the queen fled from her mind as the ciraba spun, its mighty tail knocking Darsh and Aviama to the ground in a single stroke, and lunged straight for her face with a wide-open mouth.

Aviama screamed. Semra wouldn't have screamed. She would have taken the hit like a warrior. And Vanina probably would have attacked the ciraba before her feet hit the sand. But Aviama was nothing but a castle-born princess cowering before a giant lizard.

A lizard that, from the size of it, could fit her entire head in its mouth with room to spare.

A blur dropped from the sky, knocking her sideways and sending her sprawling. She spit hair and sand from her mouth and tried to make sense of the world past the ringing in her ears.

Blood on the sand. Grit under her nails. Dark orange and gray scales hit her square in the chest with the weight of an ox, and she doubled over, clutching at her burning chest, begging for breath.

Don't die on your knees, lily. Never on your knees.

Frigibar. Even his nickname mocked her—he'd called her fainting lily after an embarrassing episode when they'd first met. Of course, the reality was he'd choked her out. Anybody would have lost consciousness, right?

Anybody who didn't know how to defend themselves.

And Frigibar had been adamant that if she ever faced

danger alone, if the world ever seemed to buckle around her again, she was not to give in to the gentle call of night.

It'll sing you lullabies. Night is easy. Surrender is easy. But to stay and fight...ah, that is where you learn your mettle. And if you don't have any, that is where you come to the end of yourself and get some.

Aviama gritted her teeth and launched to her feet, catching a glimpse of commotion as she stumbled forward. Two men backed the ciraba against the wall, pushing it toward one of the gates. The first was Darsh, hobbling forward and throwing whatever gusts he could manage, interfering with the animal's footing whenever he could. The second, to Aviama's shock, was Shiva.

Shiva struck the animal on the snout with a spear and, when it roared in protest, plunged the spear into its mouth. The ciraba let out a gagging, hissing rasp and knocked him off his feet.

"The gate!" Shiva shouted. "Now!"

The gate behind the beast rattled upward, and Darsh threw both hands forward, palm out. Aviama rushed to Shiva's side, using the motion of reaching for him to disguise a gust of her own adding to Darsh's. She slipped her arm under Shiva's and yanked him upward.

"Aren't you supposed to be on a cushioned seat somewhere?" she murmured.

Shiva snorted. "Aren't you supposed to be beside me?"

Sure, next to the other three women at your "side."

The gate on the far side of the pit opened, and two guards ran forward.

"A little late, don't you think?" Shiva growled, as they drew their swords.

Darsh twisted backward, and his eyes flicked from Aviama to Shiva to the guards. A shadow crossed his face, his expression shifting from fear to flint. Her mouth went dry as the resolve hardened in his eyes.

The criminal leaped for Shiva, palms outstretched. The prince's focus was on the guards. He wasn't looking. Aviama flew at Darsh, catching his wrist and redirecting his hands. She wasn't heavy enough to knock a grown man to the ground, but he only had one good leg. Her body collided with Darsh's, and his wasted gust of wind blew a guard several steps backward before escaping uselessly up into the sky. He started to stabilize himself, and she whirled and stomped her foot down hard on Darsh's injured ankle.

He cried out in pain and wrapped an arm around her waist, ripping her feet off the sand. An impressive feat for a man with virtually half the legs he'd had that morning. Aviama's breath caught. Darsh dragged her into the mouth of the tunnel and held up his free hand toward the prince and guards.

"You're going to let us go," he snarled, "or I'm going to snap her neck and feed her to the ciraba."

18

———

Aviama ripped at Darsh's arm, but he held her fast with little effort. She tried to twist to look over his shoulder into the tunnel, but it was no use. "Aren't you at all concerned the ciraba will eat us anyway?"

His back was to the creature. He either knew something they didn't, or he was daft. Maybe both.

The shouts from the nobles in the seats overhead rose to a roar, but Aviama could hear only the pounding of her own heart and the voices of those down on the sand along with her.

Prince Shiva lifted his chin and adjusted his grip on the spear, leveling Darsh a dark glare. "The only neck you should be concerned with is yours. You kill her, I spear you through. Simple."

"You would defile her body? Will the king of Jannemar look kindly on his beloved sister sent home with a Radhan weapon through her middle?"

Darsh's voice against her ear sent her skin crawling. A menacing hiss bounced off the walls of the tunnel behind them, and she froze. *The ciraba.*

Her captor dropped his voice to a harsh whisper for her alone to hear. "You're one of us. Act like it."

Aviama gritted her teeth. "I am *not* one of you."

They might both be windcallers. But she was no criminal.

The guards spread out on either side. Shiva stepped forward. He cast a glance into the tunnel behind Darsh, and Aviama swallowed. Shiva made eye contact with her and gave a slight shake of his head.

Her heart sank. What was *that* supposed to mean? It could be anything from "Don't move, I have a plan" to "Bad news, the ciraba is about to eat you."

The guard to Aviama's left ran at Darsh, but the motion caught the wrong kind of attention. Darsh twisted out of the guard's reach and yanked her further into the unknown abyss behind them, leaving the sand behind for stone as the ciraba launched itself at the guard and dragged him back into the dark of the tunnel.

Shiva and the remaining guard seized the opportunity and rushed Darsh. A gale of wind hit the prince in the chest, and he skidded backward in the sand, leaning forward and bracing himself against the blast.

The guard on the right was almost on top of them. Four paces. Three. Two.

And then the ground broke apart.

With a thunderous crack, the mouth of the tunnel rocked upward. The yelling overhead turned to screams, and the ground splintered and rolled. Darsh's arm ripped from Aviama's torso, and she pitched backward—or forward, or sideways; she really couldn't tell—and smacked into smooth scales, someone's foot, and the stone of the tunnel.

A rumbling echoed down the passageway, and the tunnel slanted into a ramp that sent her sliding downward. Shouting voices competed in the air around her.

"Darsh! Here!"

"Get the girl!"

"We don't have time."

"Kill him! He's getting away!"

And then the light winked out.

Aviama shook like a leaf in the thick dark, sucking in ragged breaths and willing her mind to focus. The extremists had a quakemaker. For an instant she thought maybe Darsh had two powers, but of course that was impossible. Only four melder types existed: windcallers like her, firebloods, crestbreakers, and quakemakers. Air, fire, water, earth. And whoever he was, the quakemaker was powerful. Maybe they had more than one.

And they wanted to kidnap her.

A shriek split the arid space, followed by a sickening pop. The scream cut short, followed by a thrashing, scraping sound and a ripping of flesh. Aviama estimated it came from just six meters away.

She swallowed. The palms of her hands were sweating. She couldn't just sit here, but she couldn't be loud enough to draw the monster's attention either. At least it was busy.

With the guard's mutilated corpse.

Aviama shivered, and slowly uncurled her limbs from the cold, dusty floor. One side of her head throbbed, and her forearms stung, but she seemed okay otherwise. She stuck her hands out and found a wall to one side. Aviama straightened and found that she could stand. She spun the rings on her fingers.

One, two—

"AUGHHH!!"

Aviama leaped back as something brushed her arm, but an iron grip found her wrist in the dark. Another hand swept up her body, hitting her arm and running over her upper chest and neck as it searched to smother her mouth.

"Shhh, it's me! It's me."

Shiva. Aviama nearly collapsed into him, and he released her wrist and mouth and folded her into his chest. The sound of a familiar voice in near-death experiences was more soothing than anything she'd expected. She was still shaking, and he hugged her closer.

"I explored the far end. We're in a space about six by ten meters, and this is the tallest area. I think the ciraba's tail is pinned under part of the collapsed wall, so it shouldn't be able to get to us."

Aviama cringed at the thought. "Your confidence is inspiring. How sure are you?"

She could feel the rise and fall of his shoulders as he shrugged. "Sixty percent."

Aviama gasped. "How sure were you that I'd be safe next to the mermaid?"

"Probably eighty."

"Spectacular."

Shiva chuckled, then sobered. "I'm pretty sure it's stuck. But cirabas slit the ankles of their prey first, then gulp down chunks at a time. It was starved before today's event, so it should be... motivated. Even if it isn't trapped, it should be busy for a while."

Aviama bit her trembling lip. "And Darsh?"

"Gone. We can only hope our guards pursue before they make it off the grounds. If they make it to Rajaad, they're in the wind."

She wasn't sure what to make of that. Was she grateful that a melder escaped? Or angry that a criminal was free to wreak havoc another day? Especially one that planned to kidnap her.

Aviama grimaced. "What now?"

"The rocks are too heavy on either end to break through, so we'll have to wait. The guards will find the best pathway out and dig their way to us."

Wait? Alone, in the dark, with a dead man and a half-starved, half-pinned ciraba—and the handsome prince she couldn't stop thinking about? Aviama jerked her head up off Shiva's chest, suddenly aware of their closeness. She shouldn't feel so comfortable in the arms of a man who wrapped them around three other women in the same week—and who knows how many others before that.

But the next moment, guilt broiled in her belly. The steel in his eyes when she'd insulted him, the threat in his voice, it had all been lined with sadness, hadn't it? She hadn't tried to understand. They were past it, weren't they? Or *were* they? This was the first chance they'd had to talk since he commanded her to keep up appropriate appearances through the halls of the palace and warned her about rumors.

She'd called him debased. He'd called her pretentious. A fair name-calling trade, really. His jab was probably more kind.

But then the easel...and the note...

Had he meant it?

Shiva tightened his arms around her waist. "You're making quite a habit of trying to get killed."

Her stomach flopped in a bed of butterflies, and her breathing quickened as he pressed her body against his. Against every reasonable bone in her body, she slipped her arms around him in return. "You're making quite the habit of saving me." Aviama winced. Cheesy. Stupid. She shouldn't have said it.

"I don't know." Shiva's voice was soft as silk, the voice of a man who might have written a sappy love note and hidden it in a gift. "It was you who saved me at the end, wasn't it?"

Shiva freed one hand and ran his fingers lightly up her arm, leaving a trail of goosebumps. A shiver took her over as his hand caressed her neck and tipped her face up toward him in the dark. "Thank you."

She could feel him moving in, every muscle surrounding her drawing them together. Aviama stiffened.

He paused. "Do I frighten you?"

"No," she lied. Aviama shifted her weight, and something in her chest twisted. She found herself wondering again if he was like this with all the women, or just with her. An image popped to mind of Marija worming her way against his side.

And was replaced by the memory of his eyes hardening to black on the terrace, his voice thick with warning. Aviama pulled back. "Which Shiva am I getting today?"

A beat of silence weighed down the space between them, and Aviama was sorry to hear a guardedness return to his voice when he broke it. "What do you mean?"

"I've decided in our short time together that there are three Shivas. And I'm not sure which one I'm talking to at any given moment."

Not that it mattered. If he loved her, the queen would kill her. If he didn't, spying for Jannemar would be that much easier on her heart.

A twinge of guilt sprouted in her gut as she remembered she was supposed to be spying. She'd done a terrible job so far. It was time to learn about Radha's intentions with melders.

19

The prince shifted in the dark. "Three Shivas?"

Aviama cleared her throat. "Yes. There's the soft, romantic one. He might be my favorite, if I could trust him more. Sometimes that one even drops the romantic stuff and seems really real, and that's better still. Then there's the diplomatic one, the formal one. I have a version of that too, and it's probably as boring a part to see as it is to play. And then there's the angry one. The one that feels...dangerous."

Aviama winced. If he didn't like being called debased, he probably wouldn't love being called angry and dangerous.

To her surprise, Shiva laughed. "You don't miss much, do you?"

He ran a hand from her neck up the side of her face, feeling his way in the dark, and brushed the hair back toward her ear. Sharp pain stabbed at her as his hands met the spot on her head that still throbbed. Aviama flinched, and he stilled.

A moment later, he tilted her head with both hands and gently felt along the sides of her injury. "You're bleeding."

"I mean, I was, at some point. It's nothing."

"I doubt it."

The ciraba's sickening ripping and chewing stopped, and a scuffling, grunting sound followed. Aviama tensed, ready to run—or die, more likely, in the narrow space. She held her breath and listened to talons scraping at stone but gaining nothing. Then silence.

It seemed Shiva was right, and the monster was trapped. She let the air out of her lungs in a rush.

Shiva slipped his hand down to find hers and pulled her further into their cave-in prison. They had to duck as the ceiling dropped low, and Shiva began pushing and pulling at rocks at the end where the tunnel entrance should have been.

Aviama grimaced. "Are you sure that's a good idea? Couldn't it compromise the...sturdiness or something?"

"I'm being careful."

"Oh good. At least if we die, it'll be while you're being careful."

"It doesn't hurt to try. We need to get air in here."

Aviama's stomach dropped. He'd sounded so confident about the guards getting them out, but he wasn't sure they'd get to them in time.

"So." Shiva continued his knocking, pushing, and feeling along the wall. He let out a grunt as he threw his weight against the pile of stone, then cleared his throat. "I'm danger-ous, huh?" He sounded amused, and it did sound ridiculous now.

She pursed her lips. "You might be. Sometimes."

"I think I like being dangerous," he mused.

Thud. It sounded like he was trying to dislocate his shoul-der. Aviama bit her lip. "Um, speaking of dangerous people. Darsh. I have a question."

"He never got close to any of the guest residences. Only the outskirts of the palace and a guard barracks."

Aviama considered this. Why the barracks? She shook her head. "No, not that. He was charged with multiple terrible crimes, but right along with murder and destruction, he was charged with being an *unregistered melderblood*. But melders can't help that they have powers. It's not their fault."

"What do you know of The Crumbling?"

"It happened in Jannemar. I know everything."

"Humor me."

"There were four elemental melders. People emphasize Aurin over the others because he was the one who actually thrust the spear into the wellspring at the origin of the world, stopping magic at the source. But in reality there were four, one for each element: Dru the crestbreaker, Garjan the quakemaker, Raisa the windcaller, and Aurin the fireblood.

"When Jabir Korjik was born with position and power, and learned to wield multiple powers through unnatural *sifal* magic, he was unstoppable. He destroyed the *Tabeun* Tournament, plucked the skilled, and gathered an army to overthrow and enslave the powerless. The Four were not strong enough to stop him head on, and the overuse of magic caused a poisonous imbalance in the atmosphere. More and more people grew sick and died. But the Four stopped him for good by removing the weapon that made him so dangerous. They destroyed magic and restored the land to peace."

Aviama let out a long breath. It was a fantastic summary. And it focused on the important thing, which was stopping a dangerous threat. A dangerous *person*. The Four had ended magic for the same reason Semra had brought it back—they had no other choice.

"Yes. Magic brought division, pollution, and death." Shiva paused. "When the Four put magic to bed, they knew they were giving up their own power to do it—a sacrifice few would have been willing to make. The heart of mankind is so fiercely wicked, it can hardly see past its own nose.

"Radha was not innocent in the time before The Crumbling. Our royal line was nearly snuffed out. If it hadn't been for a small child and his courageous nurse—my forefather—it would have been. But when magic was eradicated, that child had seen more destruction than any young person should see in a lifetime. He swore never to allow such a thing to happen again and charged each generation after him with the same responsibility. Even now, six hundred years later, we swear to it at each coronation."

A solemn weight edged into Shiva's tone.

"Magic is dangerous. I know your country was in a bad position, but you never should have resorted to bringing it back. There's a reason magic was destroyed in the first place, and we lived in a safer world without it for six hundred years."

Heat flushed her cheeks, and Aviama clenched her jaw. "What happened back then to your family was wrong. But no matter what you think about magic, melders shouldn't be punished. They should be helped."

"The best thing we can do for them is stop them from using magic and destroying us all. Any melder that sees that power and uses it for their own gain is just like the extremists. They want Radha to be ruled by melderbloods and to enslave everyone else. They think people without powers are less than those with them. They're dangerous."

Aviama shook her head. "You can't believe that. Even if some of them are crazy, like Darsh. You can't judge them all by a few."

"We can't control them, and we never know where the next tragedy will spring up. Melderbloods have to register because ever since The Return they've been wreaking havoc throughout the kingdom. Buildings collapse, crops burn, rivers flood—farmlands are destroyed, livelihoods endangered. We have to know where they are so we know how to protect our people. But some of them, like Darsh, refuse. They're extremists who have decided that having power makes them better than everyone else, and they use it to hurt people. What would you have us do?"

Aviama threw her hands up, though he couldn't see it. "Help them! Teach them! They're terrified and confused! Yes, they can be dangerous, but they can do good, too!"

She thought of the moment the magic in her own blood had come alive. The moment when the magic at the origin of the world had seeped through Jannemar with enough strength to awaken what had lain dormant for so many years. It had hit her like a sledgehammer, like an explosive packed with accelerant as a fuse was finally lit.

The power rolling through her had been insatiable. Impossible to contain. She hadn't understood what was happening, or even that it came from her, at first. When the wind picked up and the storm started, all she knew to do was hide—but her own terror had whipped it into a cyclone with enough power to tear through the smithy and kill a man.

It had happened throughout Jannemar, too. Without living legacies of the powers to train new melders, with no one to pass down knowledge to melder children, it had been a disaster. But they would learn. And the world would be better for it.

Power could be used for good, too. Semra was proof enough of that.

"You don't have to control them. You have to *train* them."

"Nobody knows how to train them. If nobody has had powers before, and none of the melderbloods know what to do with themselves, how are we supposed to help them understand what they don't understand either?"

Aviama rocked back on her heels. It was a good point.

She'd been lucky to have Frigibar and Semra. Semra's magic came from her dragon, but it operated similarly. And Frigibar was the last living Keeper of Magic, a scholar of old texts of melders.

Not that she could share that. Not now. The hate in the Radhan servant's eyes came back to her. And the disgust in the king's face as he demanded the melderblood be bound with his hands behind him and thrown to the ciraba to be killed for entertainment.

No, foreign royal or not, it probably wasn't even safe to advocate for melders. But to *be* one? A chill ran down Aviama's spine. If Queen Satya would rather die than see a melder in her son's bloodline, she could only imagine how the country would receive such news.

Aviama grimaced. She had no answer to his question. And she'd said too much already in favor of melders. "I don't know."

"Do you always concern yourself with politics?"

Aviama stiffened. "I concern myself with people. Shouldn't everyone?"

Shiva brushed against her side, and she jumped. He'd moved so quickly, she hadn't noticed him coming close again. "If I had a little light, maybe I could see weaknesses. As it is, I don't even know where I'm wasting my energy." He sighed and leaned back beside her against the wall. She wondered if he planned to abandon the conversation, but after a minute he spoke up again.

"I'm not the enemy. I don't hate melderbloods like so many Radhans do. We're friendly with any melder that registers and works with us. But these extremists are a huge problem."

Aviama bit her lip. She didn't like the way he called them *melderbloods*. It always sounded like a curse. She could feel him shutting down on her, his tone clipped and measured. But she steeled herself to push one more time.

"Jannemar has a plan, and it's working. There *is* training back home. Does your father look down on us for choosing a different solution?"

"My father is short-sighted. But I can see that melderbloods serve a purpose."

Aviama's mouth went dry. She thought of King Dahnuk smiling at her during the introduction banquet—and then screaming at the servant over Darsh only today. The switch reminded her a little of Shiva.

What did *short-sighted* mean for Dahnuk? Did he want to kill the melders? To cut off trade with Jannemar? To invade and stop the training? Would Shiva be able to talk him out of it?

Aviama spun the rings on her fingers. Her chest tightened, and the longer she thought, the worse it got. How dare they treat melders this way? Shiva sounded so reasonable when he spoke, but *what* he was saying didn't change. He defended putting "unregistered melder" next to murder on the list of Darsh's crimes.

Because, apparently, existing as a melder was just as bad as destroying property and killing people.

It was a terrible idea. She shouldn't have done it. But as a burning resentment grew in her chest, Aviama spun the tiniest breath of air between her fingers. She could almost feel the open air beyond the tunnel, bumping up against the collapsed entrance, asking to come to her.

With a whisper of a call, she tugged ever so gently for more air through the wall.

A soft rumble moved through the wall as a few of the rocks resettled—and then a small pebble rolled out from its place and bounced down the stones, leaving a pinhole of light in its wake.

Aviama squealed and clapped her hands. Someone on the other side shouted, and a chorus of male voices and running feet drifted through the sliver of space.

Shiva lurched to his feet, bending under the low ceiling.

"Ha! See, that dirty Darsh and his magic men didn't kill us after all. We'll have the tunnel repaired in a week. They think they can beat us without a fair fight, but we didn't need to cheat to get free. And we'll take them down without melderblood, too."

Even as Shiva started barking orders and their rescue was underway, Aviama's heart sank. She'd gotten her answer. Radha didn't just fear melders. They despised them. And they would take any opportunity to wipe them out.

20

———

The process to dig them out of the tunnel still took some time, but with the weakness in the wall exposed, the diggers knew where to focus their energy. Aviama wondered what Shiva would say if he realized their escape *was* in fact with the help of so-called cheating. After all, it was her windcalling that had shifted the rocks and exposed the vulnerability in the wall.

Two hours in, Shiva wiped his forehead with the back of his hand and came to check on her. "We're making good progress. There's a beam from the tunnel that's causing some trouble, but it looks like they're going to be able to get it out from the other side. It shouldn't be long now. So I thought I'd come ask what I've been waiting to ask you."

Aviama arched an eyebrow. Her stomach growled, and she wished they'd served anything sensible for dinner before she toppled into the arena. The scrapes on her forearms still smarted, and she could feel crusted blood on the side of her temple. Unless he was going to ask her what he could order the kitchens to make her for dinner, she wasn't in the mood.

Shiva plunked down beside her in surprisingly high spirits. "Did you get my gift?"

Her heart skipped a beat.

The queen's burning anger and Ishaan's evil glare burned in the back of Aviama's mind. She'd given one command: lose Shiva's interest.

Aviama bit her lip. "I did. It was lovely. Very thoughtful of you to remember my hobby."

"And...was there anything else?"

The note. Aviama's cheeks flushed, and she was grateful for the low light. "Yes."

"That's all you're going to say? It took quite a lot for me to write what I wrote, after our last interaction."

Aviama looked away. She swallowed. Was she more interested in protecting herself from the queen, or from her own swirling emotions? What if she could get Shiva to understand melders, and unite their kingdoms, and remove the barriers between their nations? The threat to Jannemar would be eliminated, and if they actually got married, what could the queen do then?

Wasn't that kind of benefit better than spying? Wasn't it her patriotic responsibility to explore if it was possible?

She examined the lines of his face, just visible now in the pinprick of light as the men on the other side of the wall moved back and forth, first blocking the light, and then revealing it again. Shiva pursed his lips and looked down at his hands. "I hope you didn't mind. I meant no harm. Lilacs make me think of you. That purple dress you wore at the banquet...the flower I put in your hair..."

An ache set into her chest, and the squirmy feeling was back. She'd thought there were three Shivas, but now she saw another one; not the romantic, suave side, not the mischievous side, not the formal side, but a young boy only hoping his admiration was returned.

Could it be that a man like Shiva could earnestly care for Aviama? Despite their differences and all their obstacles?

At the very least, she couldn't afford to insult him. She'd told Queen Satya so. Relations between Radha and Jannemar were uncertain, and Jannemar was vulnerable.

Aviama reached out and put a hand on Shiva's arm. "I saw it. I wasn't sure what to make of it at first, after...after how tense our last interaction was. I was flattered and confused at once, so I wasn't sure how to take it. Perhaps this is how Romance Shiva treats all the women."

Shiva captured her hand and turned toward her, his deep-brown eyes searching hers with a paralyzing intensity. "If I had no intention of an actual connection, why would I go through this charade at all? We would have weighed the political pros and cons of each potential union and issued a proposal. Instead, we opted for the opportunity for both diplomacy and love. And you—well, you puzzle me."

Aviama swallowed. "I'm sorry."

Biscuits. Was that really all she could think to say? What sort of imbecile was she? She grimaced and stared down at her lap. Shiva leaned forward, and she jumped.

He tipped up her chin and brought his mouth to just the corner of hers, and she sucked in a breath at his sudden close-ness. "I like puzzles."

Something inside her squirmed. She pulled back. A rumble and crash yanked her focus to the wall, and Shiva released her as a large broken stone toppled from the top and guards whooped and hollered at their success from the far side.

Aviama squinted and threw a hand up against the evening light, bright to her cave-adjusted eyes. The hole was four feet up and looked to be just wide enough for someone to wiggle through. Shiva held out a hand and winked at her, his back to the opening so that only she could see it as three guards peered down into the hole at them.

She let him pull her to her feet and clambered up the wall to the opening. The guards took hold of her wrists on one side and Shiva pushed her feet through on the other until she tumbled down into the sand pit in a heap. Shiva made his way out next, but somehow landed more gracefully.

The king and queen waited outside the entrance with ten men. Queen Satya ran to Shiva and took his face in her hands, looking him over. Satisfied, she kissed him on the cheek, and Shiva wrapped an arm around her shoulders. Aviama tried not to stare, but it was a weird experience, watching a sweet moment between someone who wanted her dead and someone who had just declared romantic feelings for her. Satya cast a dark glare at Aviama, and her blood ran cold.

King Dahnuk stepped forward and embraced his son, but their interaction was more businesslike. Odd. She expected the opposite, based on her observations so far.

Dahnuk rubbed his hands together. "We've caught one. Not Darsh, but another of his radical accomplices. Considering the lengths to which they went to free Darsh, I'd say the group might just be crazy enough to attempt another rescue."

Shiva nodded. "That's good news. What's the plan?"

"We're offering an exchange for two of the guards they took in the last hit."

Queen Satya glanced between her husband and her son. "And if they take the bait?"

The prince and his father exchanged a glance, then Shiva nodded at some unspoken understanding.

Dahnuk turned to his wife. "We kill them all."

Aviama clenched her jaw tight to keep from screaming,

but she bit down hard on her tongue as she did so. Tears sprang to her eyes at the pain, and she blinked them away before they dared expose her emotion to the people in the arena.

Shiva caught her eye and left his mother to step up beside Aviama. "Are you all right?"

She nodded. "Just...tired, is all. It's been a long evening." Her stomach growled, and she winced. "It's possible I could also use some dinner."

Shiva grinned. "We'll get you taken care of. You don't need to worry yourself about the extremists. They barely made it to the guard house, and there's no possible way they could reach the guest rooms. You're safe here."

Aviama blinked. She'd almost forgotten Darsh had mentioned kidnapping her. It made sense Shiva might assume that was her worry.

Well, it was now. Spectacular.

And if they only barely made it to an outskirts' guard house, how exactly had they gotten so far inside as to save Darsh?

No. These people were far more capable than Shiva gave them credit for. Or at least more capable than he was letting on.

The prince turned back to the queen. "Mother, Princess Aviama has some injuries. I'll talk to Amir myself about the food, but would you make sure a healer checks her out? I'd like her assessed tonight, and I think my time will be taken up by helping Father with the radicals."

A small sneering smile appeared across Queen Satya's thin lips. "I'll see to it personally."

Aviama's lips parted, and she hardly dared to breathe. She couldn't possibly think of a worse scenario than the queen's close personal supervision after being trapped alone with her son for a couple of hours. Ishaan stepped forward from behind the other guardsmen, his uniform utterly devoid of sand. What had he done this whole time? Twiddled his thumbs?

Satya glided over the sand toward her, and Aviama tried not to stiffen as the queen snaked her arm around her and dug long nails into her shoulder. "Come. Let's see what we need to do about you."

The woman's fingers were like icy daggers, and her voice dripped a sort of honeyed poison. Aviama was entirely sure she wouldn't die of her scuffs and bruises, but she was absolutely terrified of how her injuries might worsen under the queen's care.

She glanced back at Shiva, but he was already deep in conference with his father and two other men. The queen steered her through the opposite tunnel and wound them back inside the palace, shadowed by Ishaan in all his detestably impassive glory.

They made their way through several halls, the queen's arm never leaving her shoulders. Aviama was struck then by the similarity between Shiva escorting her to her room after their argument and the queen directing her through the palace now. To servants and guests, the caring queen hovered over the unfortunate, injured princess. But the pain in Aviama's shoulder told a different story, and Aviama suspected she was bleeding.

Ishaan rushed forward as they turned a final corner and pulled open a bronze door. Queen Satya glided inside, and Aviama's eyes bugged at the blandness of the stone room in contrast with the intricate rainbow of colors leading up to it. A rust-red gemstone throne sat on the far side, high horizontally slit windows angling light down on it from above, flanked by two rows of columns running the length of the room.

Satya strode forward so that Aviama nearly jogged to keep up with her, before the queen unwound her arm from Aviama's shoulders and threw her to the ground ten paces from the throne. She landed with a smack and rubbed her knee. *How could a woman so small be so strong?*

The queen floated the remaining steps toward the red throne and spun back to face Aviama, jabbing an accusatory finger in her direction.

"You lied to me."

21

Aviama's eyebrows shot up and her jaw dropped. "Excuse me?"

The queen's lip curled. "You didn't care about your guard. I told you about the sickness in the guardhouses, but you didn't listen."

Aviama launched to her feet, fists clenched. "What have you done with Enzo?"

Satya sat on the throne and crossed her legs. "Oh, now you care, do you? You asked about him one time, never received an answer, and forgot he existed. Something else pull your focus? Chasing my son, perhaps?"

Her stomach dropped like a sack of rocks, and guilt seeped into her chest. She *had* forgotten. She should have followed up, demanded to see him.

But she hadn't.

Aviama swallowed. "I've not been chasing anyone. I'm participating in the contest at the level expected of me."

"Your lies have no end! Would someone only trying to be polite have a spat with my son? If you didn't care, would you have gotten angry? Why did you have the prince command Ishaan to leave you that day when you disappeared?"

Satya's tone rose to a fever pitch, and she leaned forward until she perched on the edge of her throne. "Not only have you been chasing my Shiva, not only do you want him for yourself, but you intend to pollute the Tanashai royal line and twist it to your own ends. You've come for political power and will destroy my son in the process. You disobey me to your peril, girl."

Aviama reeled and took a step back. "Queen Satya, I honestly thought the argument I had with the prince would please you. You wanted him not to like me, and I made him angry. What's more, I didn't tell him anything about Ishaan. What the prince did, he did on his own."

She dug her nails into the palms of her fists. *Biscuits.* She was shaking. This cowardly creature was *not* the representative Jannemar needed.

The queen had no right to accost and question a visiting royal. Not without evidence.

Aviama rolled her shoulders back and lifted her chin. "Wild accusations will not serve you well. I want Enzo brought to me at once, sick or not, or I will make a formal complaint to the king and send word home of my treatment here."

Satya laughed. The thin, mirthless sound sent a chill to her bones. "Girl, don't you know I *own* the messengers?"

Aviama froze. She hadn't thought of that. If she was cut off from communication back home, and from her guard, then she was truly alone—and at the mercy of these hostile strangers.

The queen waved her hand. "Rumor is as good as gold here in Radha. And I've heard plenty about *you*. Well, let me fill you in on me. Nothing happens in the House of the

Blessing Sun without my knowledge. No one moves. No one breathes. And *no one* threatens my family."

For a moment, Aviama wondered what rumors the queen had heard about her. But Shiva had mentioned that, hadn't he? They were all bound to have rumors spread about them. There was no reason to believe any of them.

"Between the two of us, Your Majesty, I don't believe I am the one needing a talking to about threats."

"How *dare* you!"

The queen leaped to her feet, and a seething, snarling blur flew to her side from somewhere in the shadowed recesses of the room. Aviama's heart skipped a beat, and she gasped at the sight of an enormous hyena spewing spittle from its growling razor-lined jaws. The beast hovered under Satya's touch, and its disturbing presence seemed to soothe her.

She closed her eyes, running her hand along the raised fur on its hackles, and took a breath.

Aviama's breath caught, and her chest caved in, unable to tear her wide eyes from the massive creature before her. She'd never seen anything like it, and she wondered if Dahnuk had given the thing to his wife as a gift from his menagerie. What other insane family would have monsters for pets?

Queen Satya raised a quivering finger and jabbed it in Aviama's direction. "You're melderblood!"

Aviama flinched. But if fear was the queen's game, Aviama was losing. Weakness would get her nowhere. And Satya's finger betrayed her—she was scared too. Scared of *her*.

She ripped her gaze from the beast and drilled the queen with a dark glare. "A baseless accusation. And even if I were, it is permitted in my country—and I was never informed that being a melder, which one cannot control, was illegal here."

Satya sniffed. "Being a melder is not the problem.

Disrupting life as we know it and presenting a threat is the problem."

"In that case, breathe easy, Your Majesty. I am no more a threat than a fly, and spend my days reading and drawing rather than learning any overly helpful strategies for self-defense or war." Aviama winced. She probably shouldn't have emphasized how helpless she was, but it wasn't like she had an imposing stature anyway. Her ineptitude was obvious.

"If you are not a threat, why do you carry a knife everywhere you go?"

Aviama shrugged. "My sister-in-law is protective. Is that a crime? I've not used it once since being here, even as a letter opener."

"Wearing weapons in the prince's presence is threatening, is it not?"

"Not at all. Prince Shiva is a trained man of war, and I'm told his reputation is excellent. Is it my height or my muscles that frighten him so?" Aviama nearly laughed aloud at the thought. Shiva's feelings about her might be confusing, but the one thing he was *not* was afraid.

The hyena let out a yowl, and Aviama jumped. She shook off the shiver running down her spine and continued. "As for weapons in the presence of the prince, my armed bodyguard would have been permitted in his presence, though he is far more capable and dangerous than I. Besides, I didn't even wear the knife today. But if my sister-in-law had known my bodyguard would be taken away from me, replaced with a foreign guard whom I do not know, and then that I would be accused like a criminal without evidence, she would have sent me with far more than a knife."

Satya's knuckles turned white as she gripped the arms of her throne. "You dare speak to the queen this way?"

Aviama regarded her for a long moment. The woman's

thin lips pressed almost to nothing in her furious expression, eyes dark as coal to match the beast at her side. The long, empty stone hall.

Empty.

No courtiers. No king.

"I think, Your Majesty, that if the queen had evidence of wrongdoing, she would accuse me in public." Aviama spread her hands. "As it is, you've accused me of being melderblood, which is not illegal, though you still have no evidence of my being a melder. The only remaining accusation you've made is of participating appropriately in the contest to which *your* husband summoned me."

Queen Satya launched to her feet, every muscle taut, eyes blazing. "You drank from the same glass as Prince Chenzira at the pit. A gesture of familiarity."

Aviama blinked. Her jaw dropped. But the shock of the assertion gave way to a calming realization.

Satya was reaching. Desperate. She'd seemed so calm and collected that night in the butterfly pavilion. The sight of Queen Satya so frazzled now settled over Aviama like a warm blanket.

Aviama allowed herself a small smile.

"With all due respect, Your Majesty, the only crime committed in that scenario was the shrimp. Anything with the power to burn your lips off needs to be served with water. If a convicted murderer had been sitting behind me at that moment, and offered me relief from the geyser shrimp, I would have taken it." Her gut wrenched at her own wording. How close was she to the truth? If Chenzira really did plan on giving up his family, she may well have taken the glass from a murderer.

The queen opened her mouth, but no sound came. Aviama pounced on the silence, afraid of what might fill it if she did not. "I'll see my guard now, Your Majesty. No need to tend my wounds as the crown prince instructed. I'll see to them myself." She cringed at the edge to her own voice. She'd gone too far, and she knew it even while the words streamed from her brash mouth.

Satya's lip curled, and she barked out a single word in a foreign tongue. The hyena leaped from the dais and stalked forward in a low crouch.

Aviama felt the blood drain from her face as she retreated, beads of sweat tracing the gash on her temple and slipping into her matted hair. The hyena snapped its jaws, and at the queen's word, the beast cut left and herded her back toward the doors.

The stillness of the air clung to her skin, asking, asking...

No. She couldn't afford to prove the queen right. She couldn't afford to be a melder today.

Aviama tripped over her feet and bumped into Ishaan at her back. The hyena let out another yowl, and Ishaan reached for the heavy door.

Down the throne room, from the cornelian throne, Queen Satya left her with one final word: "Everyone who crosses me meets the same fate, Your Highness. Enzo is dead. Your move."

22

Aviama fled from the throne room, down three corridors, and around the corner. By the time she reached the end of the hall, she was breathing hard. Ishaan followed with no trouble, his long strides easily making up for her short ones. Her gut wrenched. Her overseer. Prison guard.

Orange flickering light emanated from torches along the walls, casting an eerie glow on the patterns underfoot. Ishaan gave no direction, and Aviama refused to ask for any. She caught her breath, glanced in both directions, and took off down an emerald hall she thought she recognized, then pulled up short as one of the pools appeared on her left.

Clouds obstructed the moon, and the courtyard was left in darkness. Her head throbbed. The tattered shreds of her dress blew back against her legs as a soft breeze wafted over her and through her tangled hair.

A reminder of her power. Her hamstrung, restrained, target-on-her-back melderblood power.

A lump rose in her throat, and she blinked back tears. She

couldn't let Ishaan see them. Not when he tattled everything to the queen.

Three nobles exchanged grave words in the courtyard under the shadows of the fruit trees. Her slapping feet against the marble mustn't have been stealthy, because one of them twisted in her direction.

Chenzira. *Biscuits.* Did the man follow her everywhere she went?

Heart hammering in her chest, Aviama settled for as fast a walk as she could manage, keeping to the shadows. She didn't want Ishaan to see her crying, but she didn't need the handsome judgmental killer prince to know it either.

Sure, maybe he hadn't killed anybody *yet,* but he was probably planning on it. Why else would the lost prince of Keket be holing up in Radha?

And what did he know of her so far, other than as a jumpy girl who gets lost easily, pines after Shiva from a crowd of melting princesses, and nearly dies when offered spicy food?

She grimaced. The worst part was he was right about almost all of them. But there was no reason to let *him* know that.

And she *didn't* pine after Shiva, no matter what he thought.

She didn't pine after anyone.

And that was another reason to stay far away from Prince Chenzira of Keket—Queen Satya would love nothing more than to contrive an excuse to get her kicked out of the contest. Better to avoid all appearances of literally anything with other men, however innocent, and keep her hounds at bay.

Or, more importantly, her hyena. Aviama shivered at the thought and focused on forcing one foot in front of the other. She chanced a sideways glance at the three men in the courtyard. More than one of them stole glances at her as she passed.

What rumors had spread about her since the pit? Did everyone think she was a melder? Did they believe she was somehow in league with Darsh, or just remarkably stupid to have allowed herself to tumble into the arena with a criminal and a savage beast?

What did they think of her time with Shiva, trapped alone in the dark with their prince for so long?

The memory of his warmth, the strength of his arms, his light touch against the skin of her neck and tracing along her face, sent a different kind of shiver through her. The note...he said he felt sparks when he was with her. She couldn't deny she felt them too.

Butterflies burst in her stomach, then wilted just as fast. No, it was ridiculous. If she liked Shiva that much, Chenzira would be right about *everything*. She couldn't possibly have that. But it was strategic to get close to the Radhan prince. That was why she came, wasn't it?

Aviama picked up her pace, anxious to be out from under the nobles' scrutinizing gaze. She shook her head and ground the heel of her hand into her forehead. If Enzo was dead, she had bigger problems.

It would also mean she was a big fat selfish hypocrite. How could she be thinking about Shiva when one of her own was dead? How could she *not* have followed up when she never heard back about him?

Another thought sailed to the forefront of her mind. If the queen really did kill Enzo, Murin would be next. If she wanted to kill Aviama tonight, she would have, but she didn't. Aviama was high profile, and despite what she might claim about all her power in the palace, Satya would have to be careful about how she went about it.

Not to say she couldn't kill Aviama if she wanted. She'd just need a little more time to put something reasonable in place. But if her injuries from the pit were exaggerated—if she said something got infected—well, it wouldn't take much.

Aviama needed to get word home to Semra and Zephan about what was going on. She needed help. Advice. Maybe rescue.

And in the meantime, she needed to spy out some intel before she wound up dead.

Aviama swept through the halls back to her room at a clipped pace, Ishaan only once redirecting her down a new hall when she got turned around. As soon as her door was in sight, she sped to open it, shut herself inside, and sagged back against it.

Tears spilled down her cheeks. Her chest caved in, and her empty stomach turned over. *You've bungled everything. You failed. And now a man is dead.*

Aviama stared out into the dimness of her room, illuminated only by a sad little sunken candle by the bed. Shiva's gift still stood in the sitting area, her obnoxiously optimistic sketch open to the room—a ship on the seas, a dragon in the sky, and a sun shining down on them both. Radha and Jannemar, in harmony.

A burst of heat rolled through her, and she clapped a hand over her mouth to keep from screaming. Coils of wind swirled around her, and she flew to the balcony. That much moving air could not be so close to the door. Not with Ishaan standing on the other side, begging for indications of melderblood.

Breathe. Breathe. You have to stop before you get yourself killed.

Something in her core bucked at the instruction. Was she bowing to Radha's insane policy by restricting her power?

What Shiva had said about melders didn't add up. On the one hand, he said he believed there was some use for melders, but on the other, that the best solution to melderbloods was making them register and stopping them from using their powers. It wasn't right.

Her sketch was a sham. It would never happen, not with King Dahnuk alive. Not with the queen ruling the shadows of the palace. Maybe not even with enough time to convince Shiva.

Time was running out.

A soft knock came at the door, and Aviama took a steadying breath and stilled the air around her with a wave of her hand. Murin slipped in carrying a lantern and, bless her, a tray of food.

"I thought you might be hungry after your unfortunate—oh!"

Murin froze as the lantern light hit her princess. Aviama winced and glanced down at herself, more scrapes and bruises appearing with every step as she left the balcony behind and moved closer to the light.

"I'm fine. We have more important things to talk about. Like where you got the dinner tray, and how quickly I can eat it."

"It's late, Your Highness, and the staff are in bed. I arranged it myself from the kitchens. Eat, and I'll look you over."

Aviama nodded and followed Murin to the couch. Murin set down the tray, and Aviama barely made it to her seat before snatching pieces of fruit, cheese, bread, and cured meats and stuffing them in her mouth.

"Your Highness, are you sure you're all right?"

Aviama twisted her arm to get a glimpse of the scrapes up and down her forearms from hitting the sand. The gash on her head probably looked nasty, but aside from the throbbing, she felt okay. She popped another piece of cheese in her mouth and ran to the vanity to grab the mirror, returning to view herself in the light of the lantern.

"Yeesh. Okay, so I don't look my best." Aviama tilted her face to one side. It wasn't pretty, but it was mostly dried blood. A fresh bruise on her neck from Darsh's arm paired nicely with the aging red mark the mermaid had left with her seaweed rope of death.

Matted, gritty hair fell in tangles over her dirty dress, its hem torn and scuffed. Blood decorated the rose-pink fabric at intervals from her shoulder to her feet.

Aviama snorted. "I look even worse now than I did when I first arrived. I didn't think that was possible."

Murin pursed her lips. "You're lucky to be alive, Your Highness."

Aviama sighed. *A short-lived blessing, if the queen had any say about it.*

Murin picked up a brush and started raking it through Aviama's impossible bird's nest. Grains of sand shook from her hair to the floor, and Murin *tsk*-ed before tossing the brush to one side and fetching a warm bowl of water and a cloth to start cleaning Aviama's injuries instead.

Aviama watched her work, eyes intent, hands gentle but firm, mouth twisted to one side as she examined the damage.

"Murin. We're not safe here." Aviama took hold of Murin's hand and brought her around to sit on the couch beside her. Her heart sank. She didn't want to bring Murin into this, but she deserved to know the danger. And Aviama needed help.

Murin leaned forward, searching her face. "What do you mean, Your Highness?"

"What I am about to tell you is for your ears only." Aviama paused, and Murin nodded. She continued. "The queen hates melders. The whole royal family does, but especially her. She hates me, she threatened me, and she says she killed Enzo because I didn't stay away from Prince Shiva."

Murin drew back. "Enzo? Are you sure? But...but isn't that why you were brought here? To spend time with him, and ascertain whether you would make a good match?"

"Yes, but the queen must not have approved of my invitation. I don't know if Enzo is really dead, and I need help. I need to know everything that happened in the guard house these last few days. I need to know everything I can about Darsh and the extremists. And I'm going to write a letter home to Zephan and update them on what's happening. Not all of it —but some of what I've learned."

Aviama hesitated. She didn't want Semra storming to Radha on her dragon, or Zephan starting a war with a much wealthier and stronger kingdom. But she couldn't warn her brother about Radha if she was dead either.

Murin stared, eyes bulging, mouth agape.

Aviama twisted the rings on her fingers. "And I need homing pigeons from our ship." Better to have more than one way to get word out, in case a messenger was intercepted.

This time, Murin nodded. Good. She'd need to get it together or the whole palace would know something was wrong.

"Murin, you have a better chance at listening to servants and laypeople than I do. You have more freedom. I need you to make friends, network, find out who knows what." Aviama cleared her throat, the words she knew she must say next nearly sticking to the roof of her mouth. "And I need to get away from Ishaan for a few hours. There's something I must do."

23

A homing pigeon was delivered to Aviama's room by midmorning the next day, interrupting her mad pacing back and forth across the marble floor. Aviama set down her pen and chewed a nail. She re-read the slip of parchment.

Bad news from Radha. Unsafe. Enzo missing. QS untrustworthy. And still, it's ME they find troubling.

A little abrupt. Thinly veiled. Aviama ran a hand over her face. No, not veiled at all. But what could she do when the pieces of paper for the capsule were so small? She couldn't very well tie a book to the bird's foot.

Aviama stared at the bird as it pecked the scattered grain on the bottom of its cage. It should have come as no surprise that Radha was riddled with the same weasels Jannemar had been plagued with several years prior. Another kingdom, another palace. Another threat, another dovecote.

Morning sunlight glinted off its wings, its green and

purple feathered collar shining as bright as any amethyst hair pin or emerald necklace. She spun the rings on her fingers. *One, two, three, four. One, two—*

She eyed the door. Amir had brought the pigeon himself. Just one. They'd want to know exactly how many messages she was sending at any given time, and how often she asked for a new bird. But it was more than that, wasn't it? The queen's haunting threat hovered in the back of her mind. *I own the messengers.*

Aviama gritted her teeth, crumpled the paper, and fed it to the candle burning beside her. She'd left it on since early morning when she'd given up on sleep, and it was down to a nub.

No way would she be allowed to send messages home.

But there was only one way to know for sure.

Aviama snatched another small slip of paper and picked up her pen.

This doesn't look like Jannemar. What do we have here?
A lost pigeon.
A missing guard.
And a liar.

She read it through twice, rolled it up, and set it inside the tiny capsule on the vanity next to her. The bird swiveled its head in her direction. Its unblinking round eyes carried a crazy, haphazard look that reminded her of the pakshi. Aviama opened the cage and carefully removed the pigeon, holding it against her chest to attach the capsule to its leg.

Now or never. If the bird was from Jannemar and the message *did* make it home, they'd know something nefarious was afoot. And if not...

Aviama crossed to the window, threw it open, and scanned the piercing blue sky. The sun climbed in the east, Jannemar lay to the southwest, and Murin had told her the dovecote was positioned on the northern side of the grounds. She tossed the bird into the air, and it took off in a flurry of feathers.

To the north.

Aviama's mouth went dry. The queen wasn't bluffing. Under the surface of her husband's rule, it was Satya who owned the staff and servants at the House of the Blessing Sun. Which meant there was no servant she could give a letter to and expect it to be delivered, and no bird she could acquire that wouldn't flutter right back into the queen's expectant hands.

Long chill fingers of fear worked their way up from her stomach to choke her. Satya's sneering face appeared in her mind's eye, laughing at her. *You are alone.*

But the queen was still just the queen. And she refused to give Satya the satisfaction of winning. *Your move,* she'd said. Aviama set her jaw. *Fine, then. My move indeed.*

She spun from the window and took in the room. The bed in the far room, still unmade. The vanity with its writing utensils and papers. The easel with her stupid, over-optimistic sketch. And the morning's breakfast tray, its contents already devoured except for a terrifying red mystery sauce she had refused to try.

Not after the geyser shrimp debacle. No thank you.

Murin had brought some basic medical supplies last night and gotten Aviama cleaned up. This morning, she'd set off on her mission to learn whatever she could about Enzo and the guard houses, leaving Aviama alone for the day. But Aviama had her own mission, and the pigeon situation only solidified her resolve. It was time to ditch Ishaan and do some spying.

Aviama glanced back at the abandoned tray. Someone would come to clear it eventually, but she needed someone with a bigger cart than one for breakfast trays. Her gaze halted on the mystery sauce. She crossed the room and picked up the bowl. Whatever it was, was thick and opaque. That would do. Aviama carried the tray from the sitting room and threw it on her bed. Crumbs scattered harmlessly on the sheets, but the sauce only barely oozed from its bowl, supported by her pillow where it fell.

She rolled her eyes and knocked it across the mattress. Red spewed across the pristine linens. *Yes.*

Aviama stalked to the door, drew it open, and poked her head out. Ishaan met her gaze with a deadpan expression, and Aviama arched an eyebrow. "My, what great favor you must enjoy from the queen to hold such an esteemed position."

His eyes narrowed. It was the only sign he'd heard her at all.

"I bet all your friends are so proud. Do you regale them with stories of your exploits?" Aviama drew herself up tall, puffed up her chest, and deepened her voice. "I followed the princess to four different rooms today. I counted our steps to keep my mind busy—five hundred and seven. I am renowned across the kingdom for my shadow-leering and statue-standing."

She'd already sent an insulting message back with the pigeon. Might as well push her luck to the limit.

Ishaan's upper lip gave just the hint of a snarl before smoothing over once again. "What do you want?"

"I've spilled my breakfast. I need another tray."

"You're the clumsiest princess I've ever met. How they ever let you out of your room back home, I'll never know."

"Yes, well, I also spilled it on my sheets. I'm really sore

today after yesterday's...events. I need a hot bath drawn and new sheets, because after I melt my muscles in the water, I plan on burrowing into my bed and never coming out."

Ishaan folded his bulging arms. "You have muscles?"

"Wit is not your strong suit, Ishaan. Don't hurt yourself." Aviama clapped her hands. "Send word *now*, please. My rippling biceps can't wait all day."

She shut the door before she could second-guess herself, and stared at it with awe. Had she really talked to Death Machine that way? Was she insane? A bubbly giggle escaped her lips, and she threw a hand over her mouth. A beat of silence passed, but no signs of retribution came from the other side of the door.

Within the hour, her bath was drawn, and the servant who drew it left just as another arrived to gather her sheets. Aviama peered out from around the curtain and smiled as the servant tugged a large laundry cart stacked with various dirty linens behind her. The woman looked up, wide-eyed, and gave a shaky curtsy. To her surprise, Aviama realized it was the same woman she'd knocked over her on first day at the palace, sending pastries flying in every direction.

Most likely not the normal launderer, then.

Aviama tilted her head. "What's your name?"

The woman swallowed. "Sai."

"It's nice to meet you, Sai." Aviama pulled back behind the curtain and tested the water with one hand. It was too bad she wouldn't be enjoying it. The temperature was divine. "How long have you worked here?"

"Six years, Your Highness. I am honored to serve." Sheets rustled on the other side of the curtain as Sai gathered Aviama's mess off the bed.

"That's a long time. What would have happened if I had

kept helping you with the pastries that day? When I knocked you over?"

"Oh, Your Highness! Our guests are not to trouble themselves. It would have been improper. I would have been disciplined."

Aviama picked up a dress she'd set aside for herself and dropped it to the floor next to the tub, as if she'd just taken it off. She pulled the skirts of her blue satin dress between her legs and tucked the hem securely into her belt. "Radha seems to take discipline rather seriously. Would you say so?"

Sai hesitated. "It's nothing to worry yourself over, Your Highness. Nothing happened, after all."

That was a definite yes. Consequences were severe. Aviama could hardly believe her luck.

"Thank you, Sai. I would hate for something bad to happen to you on my account."

"Don't mention it, Your Highness."

"I'm exhausted. I think I'll just settle into the bath and close my eyes, and—oh, would you grab the towel on the other side of the wardrobe? I'm afraid I left it there yesterday and forgot all about it."

"Of course."

Aviama waited for Sai's footsteps to trail away toward the wardrobe, padded out from behind the curtain, and hoisted herself up over the lip of the laundry cart. Linens swallowed her like quicksand. Her heart dropped to her toes as she wiggled herself down deep inside the cart, tugging the rest of the bulky laundry over her head.

Footsteps returned, and a soft *fwup* signaled the towel being added to the pile on top of her. A door unlatched and swung open with a creak to make room for the laundry cart. Aviama clutched at her chest, heart hammering. What would Sai do when she felt the extra weight? Would she assume the cart was stuck, then realize too late that she'd been an accomplice to an escape? Would she rip off the laundry right away, discovering her in front of Ishaan?

Why did she always seem to think through her plans *after* she started them?

The cart jerked, then stopped. Aviama held her breath. A bead of sweat gathered on her forehead under the linens and slipped down her temple into her hair. Sai gave a grunt, and with a shove, they were off. The wooden door of her room closed with a thump, and the cart wheels rumbled down the corridor.

Aviama waited for the screaming. The shouting. The ringing steel of Ishaan's sword slinging free to wallop her head from her shoulders. But it didn't come.

Instead, Sai progressed down the halls further and further. Aviama's breath came faster, adrenaline coursing through her blood, with every step the servant took—every step away from captivity.

The cart stopped. Aviama froze. And a small, hushed voice spoke into the abyss of sheets and towels.

"I hope you know what you're doing, Highness. I don't want any trouble, and I won't be caught up in whatever you're up to. Please don't accuse me of something I didn't do. I did my job."

Guilt blossomed in Aviama's gut. She'd set Sai up to fear blackmail on purpose, with the severe consequences Radha seemed to dole out on its servants—but she never wanted to really scare her.

But of course she did, didn't she? If Sai wasn't scared, she would have turned Aviama in or shown her to Ishaan. Luckily for Aviama, Radha seemed just as inclined to favor the story of a royal over the story of a servant as most any other place she'd heard of.

"I never saw you get in the cart," Sai continued. "For all I know, I'm talking to a pile of laundry, and they're simply heavier than I remember. I've done you a kindness. Please, don't repay it with wrong. I'm going to get some more laundry soap. I'll be back to empty this cart in five minutes."

Sai's soft footfalls left in a hurry, and Aviama was alone.

Alone and free.

24

S ilence reigned in the depths of the laundry cart, in the mystery room where Sai had left her. For a moment, Aviama wondered how likely it was that Sai had pushed the cart to the queen's throne room to be torn apart by Satya's hyena, but she dismissed the thought. The queen wouldn't wait around for her to emerge. She'd rip her from the cart and gloat about her victory before having her ripped to shreds.

Aviama straightened in the cart, tripped, fell, and tried again—this time gripping the edges to stabilize herself. *This is it. Now or never.*

It was too late to go back, so *now* would have to do. The option for *never* was way back inside her room, by the steaming bath that would by now be growing cold. Aviama clambered out of the cart and found herself in a long room with vats of laundry, a row of clean gowns and tunics hung up on one side and a row of servants' attire on the other. Aviama snatched a servant's tunic dress and its paired trousers, ripped her gown over her head, and hung it neatly among the other gowns. Who's to say it hadn't been among the last load of laundry done?

Shrugging into the servant clothes, Aviama couldn't help but grin. *This* felt like spy work. Her skin was paler than Radhan skin, an unfortunate variable she could do nothing about, but she might escape a casual glance if she covered her hair. After all, she'd seen the occasional non-native serving in the palace, so perhaps she might pass as one of them. She snatched a long cloth off a shelf and wrapped her wavy blonde tresses tight in its folds, careful to pull it tight around her face to hide her gash.

By now it was nearly midday. Sai would be back any minute, and she could hear clanging as servants bustled about in what might have been kitchens down the hall. Aviama steeled herself with a deep breath in and stole out of the laundry and away from the kitchens.

Two servant women passed, one giggling to the other over some gossip morsel or other, each balancing a large ceramic vase on one hip. Aviama kept her eyes fixed on the floor just beyond them, hardly daring to breathe as they passed—but they showed no interest in her at all.

Face unpainted, hair wrapped, body dressed in the uniform servants' garb rather than royal silks and satins, she was as good as invisible. A man carrying four trays of abandoned food platters stared at her, hard, on his way to the kitchens, and something in her stomach soured.

Okay, so maybe not invisible. But if she kept moving and stayed out of sight until night, she could return to her room without issue. Murin would be back by dinner, bringing Aviama's supper tray when she got back, and remove it at the proper time, after emptying it into the bottom drawer of the wardrobe. It would have been smarter to have Murin eat it herself, so the food was *actually* gone, but Aviama couldn't bear the thought of returning to her rooms starving and eating nothing all night. She might be new to espionage, but she had the feeling she'd be much better at it on a full stomach.

Aviama rounded the corner and exited a narrow door straight into a large common area swathed in emerald patterns on soaring ceilings, with lounge seating in each corner and pillars lining expansive floors. The contrast from the simpler service hallways was a jolt, in an instant dropping her back into a world of flowing dresses, tinkling crystal glasses, and the airs of nobility arrayed in every color under the sun—every color except the color *of* the sun, ironically. It seemed yellow was reserved for members of the Tanashai line.

A beautiful woman with gold on her arms and a long white dress held four men captivated as she laughed and smiled, perched on the edge of the fountain in the center of the room. The nobles laughed along with her, one scanning her up and down with thinly veiled interest. Her head turned, and Aviama jerked her head in the opposite direction. Marija.

Aviama gritted her teeth. So Marija could flirt with the entire court, out in public, and Queen Satya would count it as innocently building international relations, was that it? But *biscuits*, heaven forbid Aviama accept a drink of water from someone when she was choking to death.

But Satya didn't care a lick about the king's propriety rule. She cared about getting rid of Aviama, by whatever means—or, more specifically, lies—necessary. Aviama rolled her eyes. Well, the queen would have to do better than a glass of water if she wanted such an outlandish claim to hold up.

A distant banging caught her attention from the far side of the space, and she realized Shiva had walked her through this room on his way to show her the menagerie. She was already close to it.

Perfect. It would be entirely too awkward to ask for directions. *Excuse me, but could you point me in the direction of the king's private office? The one he does all his secret military strategizing in? Yes, that one. With the wild beasts and killer mermaids out front. Precisely, yes. Why? Oh, no reason. Just curious...*

Ugh. Aviama winced. How did Semra do it? She seemed to swap identities and meld into each new situation with such ease. Had secrecy and street smarts always come easily to her, or had she struggled in her assassin training?

All Aviama had been trained on was dancing, manners, and the few responsibilities of her station. And, through Semra, how to throw a knife with moderate success and pick a lock maybe three out of five times she tried it.

Aviama touched her left wrist, suddenly a little sad to find it empty. Last night was all the more reason to keep her throwing knife with her at all times. After this mission, she'd be sure to strap it on.

Marija's musical laugh floated across the open room, drawing in her simpering admirers and reminding Aviama of all that *experience* she claimed Shiva had. Was it really just rumor, or did she know from personal experience?

Aviama shook her head and hurried to the other side of the room, grateful for the increasingly thunderous cacophony of construction work emanating down the hall ahead. Noise, busy workers, distracted minds, and a close proximity to the menagerie—she couldn't have planned it better herself.

All sound of her pattering feet disappeared into the din of hammering, crashing, and whatever else the builders were doing to clear away the collapsed rock and metal and reconstruct the tunnel. The hall was empty, presumably because nobody else appreciated the noise.

The hall ended, and Aviama hugged the wall in the open area that followed. Doors lined the right side, but the left side was solid all the way up to the ceiling except for small windows set high in the wall. Natural light flooded the windows through an enormous skylight almost the entire breadth of the ceiling above her. She must be on the outside of the menagerie, as the windows were either barred or netted at the top depending on what creature was held in that area on the other side. Halfway down the long room, lumber, metal poles, and a box of nails were heaped against the wall, and a pile of rubble ruined the smooth marble aesthetic and ruby designs on the far end.

Three builders picked their way through the rubble, collected a stack of boards, and retraced their steps. If they saw Aviama, they paid no notice. She scanned the narrow windows along the ceiling.

She'd thought to try to get into the meeting room Shiva had led her through, but she couldn't be sure what to do about the key to get into the menagerie, not to mention that that hall carried much more traffic. But the last window on her left had no bars at all. If she remembered correctly, it was the enclosure with the hyland trolls—and, it now being nearly noon, the sunlight from the window would keep them safely turned to stone.

Aviama eyed the narrow opening, took a breath, and struck out for the pile of building materials. She set what she hoped was an ambling pace, snatched two of the narrowest nails from a box, and stowed them in the folds of her headwrap. Three out of five was not an impressive lock-picking statistic, but it was better than nothing, and all the hope she had.

She twirled a ring on her finger. How often did the builders come through? How soon before someone came to check on the project? Someone like the king, or Shiva, or any number of the queen's spies?

Aviama bit her lip, wiped her palms on her dress, and

leaned backward to peer around the rubble one more time. Nothing. With a flick of her wrists, she summoned the wind, propelled herself up to the window, and seized the ledge.

A tingling sensation hummed along her skin as her right elbow hooked the top of the opening. The trolls sat motionless, balled into harmless boulders in the sun down below. Good. Now for the door.

Holding onto the ledge of the window with her right arm, her legs dangling down the wall, she lifted her right hand toward the locked door of the troll enclosure and sent the wind to propel it open. Nothing happened. No response. No whisper of wind. Only the tingling along her arm.

But only that arm. Of course. The menagerie was treated with magna to deaden magic. Aviama glanced back over her shoulder. Footsteps echoed toward her from somewhere, though she couldn't see anyone yet. They'd be upon her in moments and see her dangling from the high ceiling of the king's private menagerie.

Her mouth went dry. With a grunt, she pulled her left arm free of the window and outside the walls, aiming for the lock from beyond the menagerie. Strong fingers of a willing breeze flew to her aid, opened the locking mechanism and unlatched the door with a quiet click.

It was then that she noticed her new position in the window blocked out the sun from the trolls beneath her, releasing them from their statue state. A rumble struck fear in her bones, and she watched in terror as the trolls unfolded from their spheres and glanced around. The small one was closer to the enclosure door—and turned its head just as the door swung free.

Voices drifted toward her from the room at her back, and her mouth went dry.

"Your Majesty, the tunnel was not the only structure the melderbloods destroyed. It seems their powers are growing."

"I want them found and their heads on a spike decorating my gate. Was my decree unclear? *No* unregistered melderbloods, *no* active use of magic, and—well, not only has Darsh's crew spit in my face, but they've used their abilities for murder, mayhem, and assault on my family. The House of the Blessing Sun is sacred."

That was all she needed to hear. Aviama's stomach churned. The smaller troll reached for the door, and the larger one had noticed Aviama and screwed its face up into an ugly grimace. But she had no choice.

She slipped through the window and fell to the floor in a heap just as the troll swung a giant stone fist at her head. The stone fist smashed against the wall, and Aviama was sure the thing would have crushed her skull to a pancake had she been just an instant slower. She rolled to one side and sprang to her feet, but when she turned to face her rocky assailant, she found it frozen in place.

Aviama scratched her head and swiveled toward the other side of the cell. The smaller of the trolls stood statue still, its hand on the open door. Beyond it, colorful fish swam by in the aquarium, and exotic birds trilled in the distance.

Invisible, indeed. Aviama straightened. Semra might even be proud of her accomplishment, getting in so unnoticed! She reached out a tentative hand and rapped the smaller troll on the head with her knuckles. True to its statuesque state, the thing made no sound, no movement, no acknowledgment whatever that it felt her touch.

Good, because she had to get the troll out of the doorway, so it wasn't so painfully obvious that the door was unlocked. She threw her weight against the troll, but it didn't budge. Aviama winced. She tried again.

Biscuits. Perhaps Zephan and Semra should have sent someone with a little more muscle do the spying stuff.

In a sudden stroke of inspiration, she jumped up and gripped the bar of the doorframe, swung back and forth, and kicked the troll hard in the head. It must have been positioned just right, because it toppled over and the door clicked shut.

Aviama let out a breath. She did it. She did it! The trolls in their cage, and her free in the menagerie. Aviama drew herself up and tapped the enclosure door with a small smile. *Take that, Queen Satya. My move, you said. My move! Well, how do you like me now?*

She turned on her heel—and flinched away from the silver mermaid staring back at her through the aquarium glass. Those pale purple irises cut to her core, the mermaid's perfect white hair swirling through the water around her stupid, flawless face.

Aviama took a step forward and jabbed a finger at the creature. "No! No, not today. I have no quarrel with you, okay?"

The mermaid tilted her head, the pewter scales of her tail shimmering as the light played off their smooth surface.

Aviama shook her head. "I'm serious. You hate Shiva, right? The royal family? Radha?" The mermaid stared back at her. She made no sign of understanding, but her eyes were too sharp and intense for Aviama to believe she wasn't listening. Shiva had said she was only a creature, like any other beast for the menagerie, but looking at her now... Aviama cocked her head.

"Or did you really just want to eat me for lunch the other day?"

A slow smile crept across the mermaid's face. Goosebumps broke out across Aviama's skin, and she swallowed. "I escaped my room in a cart of dirty laundry, so I'm pretty sure I wouldn't taste great. Leave me alone, and I'll leave you alone, and neither of us has to cause any trouble, okay?"

Aviama set her jaw and hurried down the narrow hall to the main aisle of the menagerie. A flash of silver caught the corner of her eye. The mermaid was following her. Aviama quickened her steps, fled across the open space to the door of the king's study, and pulled the two stolen nails from her hair.

She fitted them into the lock and felt for the pins, but the nails were two straight to reach. Aviama grimaced, scanned the animal cages on either side of the room, and ran down the aisle to the lizards that had burst into flames. "Don't bite me. I don't care about you, okay? You've got weird abilities, I've got weird abilities. Here in Radha, I'm basically reduced to be an exotic trophy too."

An orange lizard licked its eyeball in response, and she stuck her tongue out at it, selected a sturdy twig with a bend to it from inside the bars, and ran back to the king's office. Aviama fumbled with the lock for a full two minutes, but at last was rewarded with a click. She turned the knob and slipped inside.

And was slammed against the wall.

25

———————

The force of a solid body colliding into hers and ramming her back against the wall knocked the wind from her lungs. Aviama opened her mouth to gasp for air, but a hand smothered it just as she sucked in a breath. Her body ached from the fall from the window, and the collision with the man before her had done nothing to improve matters.

She jerked her gaze up to her captor, and the fiery rage she found there seemed shaken as they glared at one another. He dropped his hand, and they both let out the same sharp hiss:

"You!"

Aviama jolted up off the wall, but Chenzira shoved her back into place and planted a hand on either side of her head. "What are you doing here?"

Her insides squirmed, and she shifted her weight. "I could ask you the same thing. And why does everyone insist on putting their hands over my mouth?"

Chenzira smirked. "Because you're jumpy and you scream a lot."

"Am not."

He raised an eyebrow. "I've personally witnessed you do both more than once."

Aviama's face flushed hot, and she gritted her teeth. "You've not seen me scream more than once. And I think it's perfectly normal to scream when a murderer rips you from a high place down into a sand trap of death, thank you very much."

Chenzira pursed his lips and straightened. "How've you been sleeping?"

Her nightmare. She must have woken half the palace that night. Aviama looked away.

The missing prince grimaced and folded his arms. "You haven't answered my question. What are you doing here?"

"Same thing you're doing, it looks like," Aviama mumbled. She peered around him to take in the room. A heavy wooden desk served as the central focus to the room, with a painted pakshi peering out over the king's affairs from the royal crest on the wall behind a wooden chair cushioned with yellow fabric. Maps stuck with pins hung on one wall, and fully stocked bookcases lined the opposite side. A gilded box in gradient sunset colors sat in the center of the desk, flanked by a writing kit, three books, and several loose-leaf parchments.

Aviama jutted her chin toward the desk. "The king's been busy."

"He's a king. He's always busy."

The bitterness in his voice surprised her, and she glanced back at him. Chenzira rolled his eyes. He looked her up and down, and his gaze flicked to the door. "Who knows you're here?"

"Nobody. And the king just went by to check on the repair work."

"You're telling me you escaped under Ishaan's nose, and

your pitiful attempt at a disguise went completely unnoticed? By anyone in the palace, in the middle of the day?"

Aviama lifted her chin. "Nobody notices servants here. I'm not done up or anything, and I covered my hair. I made it this far."

Chenzira groaned. "Women are always overestimating the impact of makeup. Do you wear it for men, or for each other? You look like you. Besides, you weren't all trussed up when I first saw you either. You wore a blue dress, damp hair, and a natural face."

He'd noticed what she was wearing? "I might not have been dressed up, but *you* were hardly *dressed* at all."

She regretted it the moment the words left her mouth, but it was too late.

Chenzira arched an eyebrow. She could see him considering whether or not to address her comment. Gratefully, he dismissed it. "My point is that you weren't done up or anything and, shock of all shocks, I still knew who you were when you waltzed into the welcome banquet."

"Well, I'm here now. And the king is looking at the repairs, but I'm not sure how long he'll be, so tell me why you're spying on him, and let's get a move on."

"I'm not spying, I was—"

Aviama crossed her arms, mirroring his stance, and gave him a look. "We're past that, aren't we?"

"Okay, so I'm spying." Chenzira turned on his heel and strode to the desk, rifling through several papers and replacing them carefully in their original position. "But I guarantee I have a better reason *and* a better alibi than you do. And as annoying as it is that you're here, you add nicely to my story. If they find *you* here, you're dead. If they find *me*, I rescued them from your pernicious espionage. So keep your mouth shut."

Fire blazed in her chest, and she turned her back on him to stalk toward the maps. "Don't worry. Someone usually has a hand clamped over it anyway."

How dare he? Who did he think he was?

The esteemed prince of Keket, obviously. The missing one. The intriguing one. The one with the power to bring the island nation to its knees, and hand Radha the keys to the sea.

If so, Radha needed him. It didn't need her—there were far more suitable options for Shiva. Queen Satya had been clear enough about that.

Who was Princess Aviama but a flirty tool in the hands of men manipulating international relations? She wasn't really much of a flirt, but delicious rumor was somehow frequently more believable than mundane truth.

Aviama ran her fingers along the edges of the map before her. Pins of four colors burst from Radha at the center and wound to the north, south, northeast, and southeast, dotting strategic positions along their borders and beyond. The sea formed a natural barrier to the west, but each of the four colors led to a kingdom: one to Batal, one to Tomos, one to Curion, and one to Jannemar. Aviama leaned in close to a cluster of blue pins well within Jannemar's northern border. Was that what she thought it was?

Her fingers trembled. The Horon Mines.

What if this was Queen Satya's game after all? The whole charade, the entire contest? She could pick a fight with whichever nation had the most desirable resources, and frame that princess for something or other, and manufacture a reason to take what they want.

Even if it wasn't Satya—well, it was the king's office. And it looked like he was planning attacks on all four of his son's potential in-laws. Aviama stepped back and stared at the map, murmuring almost to herself. "Is he going after all of them, or has he not decided which one to hit?"

"Based on this, I'd say he's out for blood and wants to pit his options against each other for the best deal."

Aviama turned to find Chenzira crouched on the floor on the far side of the desk. She rounded its corner and knelt next to him as he examined the paper. "Was it on the floor?"

"Mhmm. Halfway under the desk. Which was lucky, because I can't figure out how to open the official box he's got up there with all the most important orders of business. There's not even a keyhole."

"What does the paper say?"

"Aviama Shamaran is a melder, and we must take her out at all costs."

Aviama's stomach dropped. "Does not!" She snatched the paper. He was trying to get a rise out of her, and she wouldn't give in—but she still scanned the document twice to ensure her name was absent. When she glanced back at him, he was watching her.

"Jumpy," he muttered.

She pursed her lips. "What did you see in here? It looks like Batal denied a trade deal for steel." Aviama squinted at the corner of the document. "Dated last year."

Chenzira nodded. "Steel, bronze, titanium. Metals used in weapons, shields, and chainmail. And he's reviewing it from a year ago. Why would he be doing that?"

"To strike a new deal?"

"Maybe. Radha is after herbs, spices, and magna from Curion too. From what I've gathered, they want something from each of their neighbors." Chenzira plucked the parchment from her fingers. "So what do they want from you?"

Her heart sank. The mines. Wyronite.

Aviama shrugged. "I don't know."

She must not have looked convincing, because Chenzira gave her a long look, then set the paper back on the floor where he'd found it. "How'd you get in here?"

Aviama bristled. "None of your business."

"Do you have a plan for getting out?"

"Sort of."

Chenzira took a breath. "A crappy plan, then. Well, I can't have you botching it and landing a guard outside the office door, now, can I? Come with me."

Alarm bells rang in her mind. Semra had taught her never to let an assailant move her to a secondary location. They would gain cooperation only to kill their prey more conveniently elsewhere. Of course, he wasn't really an assailant— yet.

But Prince Chenzira was obviously up to no good. And if the queen saw them together, she'd spark a war with Jannemar. She cleared her throat.

"I would really rather not."

Chenzira stood. "I don't care. Come with me like a good little Radhan servant girl—you know, the invisible kind with expensive rings on her fingers—or I'll chuck you over my shoulder and get some rumors started about the prince of Keket and his unscrupulous activities with Radhan maids."

Aviama's jaw dropped. That was precisely the sort of rumor that would get her killed. And her family attacked, for an *act of aggression* against Radha. She spun the rings on her fingers, then sat on her hands. How had she been stupid enough to forget about her rings?

The prince held out a hand to help her up. "That's the gentlest blackmail you'll get from me. I would take it if I were you."

She tilted her chin up to look at him. "You have more blackmail in store, then?"

He regarded her for a moment. "Yes."

Aviama swatted his hand away and stood up on her own, nostrils flaring, heat flushing her body. How dare he? How *dare* he?

She stabbed a long finger at his chest, stopping just short of touching him. "I will not be going *anywhere* with—"

A momentous splash and a yell from the menagerie rocked the air. The king's booming voice cut through the door of his private office, sending a chill down her spine.

"It's not too late for beheading, mermaid! Not all my trophies have to be *alive*."

Aviama could almost feel every last drop of blood drain from her face. She tucked an escaped piece of hair back into her hair wrap, but her fingers trembled. The menagerie was the only way out. How many charges would they bring against her? Espionage, conspiracy, theft, and breaking the contest agreement by philandering with another nation's prince...

She'd be dead by morning. Sooner, if the queen had anything to do with it.

Chenzira dropped his voice. "You were saying?"

"Shut up and get me out of here." Her voice quivered, and she backed against the wall opposite the door.

"As you wish, Your Highness."

Chenzira seized her by the shoulders and set her to one side, reached up toward the pakshi painting behind the king's chair, and stuck his finger right in its beady eye. The painting swung open to reveal a hidden space just as the king inserted the key in the lock of the door behind them. Aviama gasped and hiked up her skirt to clamber over the waist-high wall beneath the opening when Chenzira scooped her up and dumped her over the wall to the other side.

Aviama landed on her bottom with an unceremonious thunk. Chenzira landed infuriatingly gracefully on his feet and jerked the painting back into place behind them—plunging them both into darkness.

26

———

The sound of a door closing in the room beyond sent gooseflesh up Aviama's arms. Footsteps brought the king within a meter of their hiding place. A mere meter from certain death.

Aviama pressed her ear to the wall. The hole Chenzira had dropped them into was utterly black as it was, but she still closed her eyes to listen. The chair scraped backward and a heavy object was set on the desk, followed by the nearly-imperceptible mechanical sound of clicks and rotating gears.

A hand touched her waist in the dark. She startled, and it jerked away, as if it was just as shocked to find itself in such an intimate position as she was. A moment later, the hand groped along the floor, found her hand, gripped her wrist, and tugged.

Using her free hand to feel her way forward, Aviama scooted along a dirt floor in the narrow space. A ladder led them down beneath the palace, entirely swathed in inky black. Her heart raced, and her palms began to sweat. The tingling of the magic-preventing magna that lined the menagerie was gone.

For several minutes, her only companions were Chenzira's

fierce grip and the sound of their quickened breathing inside the tunnel. He adjusted his grip, and Aviama realized his palms were sweating as well, despite the chill of the underground.

He broke the silence first, and his voice was as cold as the tunnel. "How long have you been a melder?"

"Never said I was."

"Never said you weren't."

Aviama set her jaw. "Melders are born melders. It's nothing new. It's actually something quite *old*. So asking somebody how long they've been a melder is ridiculous. People either have been their whole lives, and discovered it when magic re-entered the world, or they never were in the first place. Just because I live in a place that understands that doesn't mean I am a melder myself."

"Yes, but you made your way *into* the king's study without a problem and didn't know how you'd get *out*. Getting in is fine and dandy if you've got powers, but getting out when the menagerie and study are lined with magna is problematic. And don't take this the wrong way, but I don't think you're clever enough to come up with a way into the menagerie without some assistance."

She tried to jerk her wrist free, but he held it fast. "How could I possibly *not* take that the wrong way?" she retorted. "You think I'm stupid?"

"Ah, well, I suppose you did take it the right way. Yes, that's what I meant."

Aviama shook her head, seething. "If you're so smart, how come you don't know how to open the king's box?"

"Nobody knows how to open it."

A small smile tugged at the corner of her mouth. "I do."

Chenzira stopped, and Aviama bumped into him. *"You?"*

"I know. Hard to imagine, what with my rampant stupidity."

The silence filled her with an unreasonable glee. *That's right, mister know-it-all. I know something you don't know. Soak it in.*

"How?"

Aviama shook her head. "*Tsk, tsk.* I don't tell secrets to snooty people."

"You must not talk to yourself much, then."

Still riding the high of having shocked him, the insult didn't even phase her. "That wasn't nearly as good a jab as your other ones."

He chuckled. The sound surprised her. "Maybe I'm losing my touch."

Chenzira's grip relaxed, still firm enough that she doubted she could pull free, but loose enough for the blood to flow again. Her shoulders dropped, her aching muscles loosened, and they fell into an easy pace side by side. Presently the passage narrowed so that their arms touched from shoulder to elbow, and something in Aviama's gut squirmed. She couldn't take the quiet.

"So you're not friendly with the Radhan crown, huh?"

His fingers dug into her wrist. An involuntary reaction. He caught himself and softened them again. "I have a mission. One that's more important than any single person's life, so keep that in mind."

"No judgment. Just trying to understand you. I thought maybe you were going to sell Keket's secrets to gain Radha's support in putting you on the throne." Aviama clapped her free hand over her mouth. *Biscuits, keep your thoughts to yourself!* The hairs on the back of her neck stood up as she contemplated all his possible reactions. Would he yell? Scream?

Threaten? Decide she talked too much and wasn't worth the trouble of keeping alive?

Instead, his voice was even. Quiet. Sad. "You thought I would have my family slaughtered so I could rule."

Aviama bit her lip. *Yes.*

The passageway curved, and his free hand reached across his body to take her elbow and guide her up over a ledge. "Honestly, it's a decent hypothesis. Nobody knows the real me."

"Well, that can't be what you're doing now. You're snooping in the king's office."

"So were you. And I thought you were after Shiva. If that was an act, it could have fooled me."

Aviama winced. It would be far safer for her if it *were* just an act. After being with Shiva on the terrace—and after the pit, when Shiva spoke about *melderbloods*—well, she was growing more and more convinced that the man was dangerous. "I was invited here for a contest to be his wife. Acting interested is rather important."

"And Shiva...is he also...interested?"

The question caught her off guard. Why would he care? He couldn't possibly be jealous. Could he?

"Sometimes it seems like he is. But he has his own show to put on, so I'm not sure."

"Has he expressed any interest, explicitly?" Chenzira caught her elbow to lead her over another ledge in the dark, then paused.

Aviama stuck her hand out and found a dirt wall. They'd reached the end of the tunnel. She swallowed. "Um...yes. He has."

A sliver of light fell from a crack overhead, and she could just make out his features. He grinned. "Excellent."

Aviama's head spun. His reaction ruled out jealousy, which

hadn't made sense to begin with. But this? She pressed her lips together. "Why is that excellent, exactly? I need information, but I don't want to marry him."

He waved her off, his mind clearly somewhere else. "Yes, well, he's a pig, so it's reasonable you wouldn't want to marry him. He's slimier than a salamander fresh out of water. But you could get information."

"That's quite literally the whole point of me being here, and so far I've been wildly unsuccessful. He hates melders, he wants them all to register so he can get them to stop using their powers altogether, and the king is planting bait for Darsh's people so he can kill them all, but I've learned nothing about—"

Chenzira's lips parted. "He's doing what?"

"I said he's setting up an exchange for two guards, and he's going to kill them all." Aviama threw up her hands. "Seriously, if your hearing is this bad, it's no wonder you didn't hear the mechanism in the box."

He stared at her. She shifted her weight under his gaze, suddenly uncomfortable. "Stop that."

"Sorry." He cleared his throat, glanced at his feet, then back up at her face. "I was wrong about you. And you're exactly what I need."

Aviama grimaced at the light in his eyes—not a romantic light, or a wicked light, but the spark of treacherous mischief. "What for?"

"Information. Get close to Shiva. Find out what he wants from Jannemar and where his weaknesses lie. If you don't, I'll create rumors that will end your little spying stint in a heartbeat."

Her stomach dropped. "What kind of rumors?"

Chenzira gave a wicked grin, and in an instant, he'd pressed her back against the tunnel wall so they were nose to nose. His voice came in a low husk that rattled her bones. "The kind that might make a prince jealous."

Aviama's mouth went dry. She shrank away from him, then dropped to the floor and spun across the narrow space, popping up on his other side. By the time he turned, his expression was unreadable—and Aviama was breathing fast.

"I'll get you information. But no one can see us together. No one. And I need something from you in return."

He gave a short nod, eyeing her intently. Waiting.

Aviama bit her lip. "My guard. Enzo. They told me he fell ill almost immediately after we arrived, and the—um, I was told he was dead. But I'm not sure if it's true. I want to know what happened to him and where he is."

Chenzira ran his hand over his face. "I'll see what I can do. We'll be in touch. Can you make it back to your room from here?"

"From this dark hole somewhere in the palace?"

"We're under the courtyard beneath your balcony."

She blinked. Was she supposed to know that from their wanderings in black tunnels? She twisted the rings on her fingers, then grimaced as she remembered how poorly they matched her servant's attire. "Can you draw people away from the courtyard so I can get back in? It'll take me a minute."

Chenzira arched an eyebrow. "To...to your balcony? That's quite a jump."

"Ishaan is outside my door, so that's not an option. I'll manage."

The prince's expression darkened. "Careful, Highness. You're sounding an awful lot like someone with tricks up their sleeve. Deadly ones."

Her chest tightened. She needed to be more careful of sounding like a melder. Aviama swallowed. "If you want me to get information for you, you'll leave me alone."

"Listen, I'm not who you need to worry about—not unless you interfere with my mission. Give me two minutes, and I'll have the courtyard clear."

He reached his hand up to the low ceiling, feeling along it with nimble fingers. When he found what he was looking for, he paused and looked down at her one more time. "Convince him you're interested. Find out what he wants from Jannemar and what his next move is for the extremists."

With that, Chenzira pushed something along the ceiling, and a panel slid to one side with a gentle scraping sound. A fountain burbled nearly on top of them, and mist drifted down over Aviama's face. Chenzira planted his foot in a hole in the dirt tunnel wall, poked his head out, and disappeared, sliding the panel not quite closed behind him.

Aviama held her breath in the small space, straining her ear to hear anything over the sound of the fountain. A tunnel entrance in the middle of a courtyard seemed unnecessarily risky, but the running water covered the scrape of the tile moving in and out of place over the opening. Muffled, murmuring voices came from the courtyard above, but she couldn't make out the words. Then footsteps. And silence.

Aviama slipped her fingers into the sliver of space Chenzira had left for her and slid the panel back. Copying his motion, she climbed up the footholds and hoisted herself up out of the hole under a small grove of fruit trees with a bench next to the fountain. She slid the square back into place, a tile fitting seamlessly into the rest of the floor, and paused at the bench.

Smart. Immediately, there was another reason to be in this particular spot. She glanced around, but Chenzira seemed to have done his job—the space was clear. Aviama stole across the courtyard, called to the wind, and leaped for the base of the banister at the balcony of her room. The wind was just enough to boost her jump, and she pulled herself up, swung a leg over the railing, and tumbled to the floor on the other side.

A loud banging reverberated through the room, and Aviama spun to scan her rooms.

Someone was banging on the door, and Murin stood with her shoulder to the wood screaming back at them as if her own small frame could stop a Radhan soldier from knocking it down and bowling her over right along with it.

"She's not feeling well! Respect her privacy—she's been through quite a lot!"

Aviama sprinted across the marble floors and dove for the bed behind the curtain, ripping her hair wrap from her golden waves and stuffing it into the covers just as she buried herself in the sheets and yanked the blankets up to her neck. The hair wrap found itself uncomfortably wadded up in the small of her back, but the door burst open before she could fix it.

The force of it sent Murin stumbling backward, and Ishaan stomped into the room with all the fury of a burning fire set to dry kindling. He towered over Murin with a snarling growl. "When I tell you to open a door, you open it."

Aviama propped herself up on her elbow, careful to tuck the sheets around the servant's dress she still wore, and raised her voice. "Hey!"

Ishaan pivoted toward her. His glare registered surprise as he took her in, bundled in bed under the blankets. Aviama envisioned her older sister's pretentious airs and did her best to channel them, turning her nose up just a hair.

"What gives you the right to storm into a lady's bedchamber and assault her lady-in-waiting? I hear the king is protective over the contest for Prince Shiva's hand. What reason could you have for intruding so inappropriately while a princess is in bed?"

The man hesitated. "I thought you were missing, Your Highness. I was concerned for your safety."

"You've been standing out there all day, haven't you?"

Ishaan set his jaw. "Yes."

"And did I go out?"

"I didn't see you depart." His word choice did not escape her. He did not intend it to. He didn't *see* her depart.

Aviama sniffed. "With your keen eyesight and quick wit, I'm sure nobody could get past you. I have no plans to go anywhere at all today, so my recommendation as you continue your elite standing responsibilities is this: don't lock your knees."

"Why did you not answer when I called?"

"You mean when you made demands and extreme tantrumming banging sounds?"

Ishaan crossed his arms. "It's the middle of the day. Why would you be in bed?"

She snorted. "Did it never occur to you that after being attacked, threatened, dropped into a sand pit with a murderer and a carnivorous beast, and trapped under a collapsed tunnel, that I might be tired? That I might not be interested in seeing your face? The prince suggested I take care of myself. Remember this?"

Aviama tapped the gash on the side of her face and lifted her scraped, bruised forearms for good measure. "Your presence is not healing, and your happiness is not my concern. Get out."

Ishaan glanced at Murin, who was shaking like a leaf, and locked eyes with Aviama once again. He seemed to be mulling over his options, his gaze never leaving her face. A vein twitched in his thick neck. And then he spun on his heel and strode from the room, shutting the door behind him.

Aviama stared at the closed door. She did it. He was gone. For now.

She turned to Murin. The girl was standing stock still in exactly the position she'd been in since Ishaan burst through the door—her eyes the size of saucers. Aviama waved her hand, and finally snapped her fingers.

"Murin! I need a dress. Any dress. And dinner. And I need to send a message to Shiva." Aviama paused. "And I need to know what you found out today."

27

D inner came, and evening found Aviama sketching at the easel with Murin beside her, talking through the day's events. Murin had spent the morning making excuses to worm her way through the servants' halls and listen to gossip, followed by sending herself to the guard houses with soup from the kitchens, claiming it was ordered for Enzo and could someone please direct her to him.

Enzo was gone, the men were squirrely about it, and she was not permitted entry. On her way out, one of the guards had caught her arm and pulled her aside. Murin squeezed her eyes shut, trying to remember the man's exact words. "'I know they took him. I want in. I have information. Tell the shadow to come back for me.'" She opened her eyes and spread her hands. "That's what he said. I didn't know what to do, so I nodded and left."

Aviama's hand paused on the lilac blossom at the edge of her pencil. Could Enzo really be alive? "Do you know his name? Did he wear rank? What did he look like?"

Murin's face fell. "I didn't catch a name. Brown hair, brown eyes, average height."

Biscuits. Every man in Radha met that description.

Suddenly, Murin snapped upright. "Moon-shaped scar across his left hand. Around the meat of his thumb."

Hope burgeoned in Aviama's chest. It could be a trap, of course. He could have been planted to see what they did with such an admission. But what was the shadow, and why would he think Murin would know how to communicate with it? If he *wasn't* planted, he didn't want his intentions to be discovered by Radha. And he trusted Murin. Which meant he could be used.

She seized Murin's hand. "This is good. Really good! Great work."

Murin beamed. "Really?"

Aviama nodded. "Yes. I never would have made it to the guard houses."

"But I didn't get any further than that. The captain of the guard found me, told me servants weren't allowed in the guard quarter, and escorted me back. That's why I came back early."

"And thank goodness you did, or Ishaan would have found out I was missing."

Aviama blended the petals with her finger and sat back to admire her work. A lilac blossom caught fire. *Firebrand,* he'd called her. She wondered if he'd pick up on the symbolism. That she felt the spark too. Aviama jotted a note along the base of the sketch, tore it from the easel, and folded it up tight. She handed it to Murin. "Get rid of the servant's clothes. And don't let anyone see you deliver the note to Shiva. We leave in an hour."

Murin dipped her head, tucked the note into her sleeve, and slipped out the door. Aviama stared at the empty space her lady-in-waiting had occupied just a moment before, her stomach clenching as she tried not to wonder what the queen might do to Murin if she was caught. The note had to be passed in secret.

From what she knew of Shiva, he'd be too curious to ignore her riddle. His face filled her mind—eyes intensely gazing into hers, his lips grazing the corner of her mouth as he whispered into the breath of space between them: I like puzzles.

She could use that. Fishing for information for Chenzira was really no different from fishing for information for herself and for Jannemar. And if doing so motivated Chenzira to get information for *her* that *she* needed, well, all the better!

The riddle was the best way to catch Shiva's interest and motivate him to meet her sooner rather than later. It was also the best way to keep the queen off her back. Aviama could only hope he'd take the bait and meet her, and that she could shake Ishaan in time.

She ran the riddle through her mind again. Was it too clever, and he wouldn't figure it out? Was it too obvious, and he'd find it boring? Did he care enough to come at all? She repeated the lines to herself over and over.

> *The more I take, the more I leave*
> *Somewhere they are not perceived*
> *Lilac, lilac, rock and boulder*
> *All in eye of the beholder.*

Not that she'd be able to get into the menagerie a third time. But if he'd meet her just outside it, in the room where they'd been free before...where he wouldn't want Ishaan lurking, and where no guard would dare to look...

How many times could she escape a royal bodyguard before they chained her to him?

By the time Murin returned, Aviama's shoulders were as

rigid and tense as the rocks she'd written about, and her chest felt as though coils of rope squeezed around her rib cage. She wrung her hands.

Murin poked her head around the curtain where Aviama paced. "You ready?"

Aviama wiped sweaty palms on her violet dress and took a breath. "Yes."

They both knew it was a lie. But no other answer would do. Aviama grimaced, pulled her shoulders back, and strode for the door. Murin pulled it open and Aviama swept through and down the hall. Ishaan imitated a statue until they passed, but his trailing footfalls soon haunted her along the corridor.

Aviama considered asking him if he ever slept. Someone must replace him for the night shift, or he wouldn't be available to leer over her every movement during the day. But no good could come of her opening her mouth. If she did, she'd only antagonize the man, and killing her would likely be wildly more interesting than his duties of late.

Ishaan, do you have indigestion, or is that just your face?

So glad to see you took my advice and didn't lock your knees. It would be a shame if you collapsed one of these days.

Aviama arranged her hair over one shoulder and sighed. "I can't decide which is worse—staying in my room or coming out."

"It will do you good, Your Highness," Murin answered from her place three paces behind. "You've been cooped up all day. If we get away from the guest hall, we're less likely to run into anyone."

Aviama groaned. They'd discussed what to say, and Murin's nature was so sincerely encouraging that it was easy to believe her. Frustration and anxiety over leaving her room was decently honest for Aviama, too, so she hoped she sold it.

Biscuits, what was she doing? The queen would have her

head if she knew Aviama was setting up a secret meeting with her son and slipping him messages of romantic interest. And Chenzira would have her head if she didn't.

But Chenzira might be able to find Enzo, and Queen Satya certainly wasn't interested in doing that. Besides, if she didn't satisfy Chenzira, he'd circulate enough rumor for the queen to have her killed anyway.

And what was this business about *the shadow*? What would they want with Enzo? Was Enzo even the *him* the guard had mentioned when he spoke to Murin? How could she find out without exposing her snooping?

Maybe Prince Shiva wouldn't even come.

Maybe he would, and he'd keep Ishaan around, and make advances.

Aviama's gut wrenched. She was no expert, but it sure felt like she relied on a lot more luck than was reasonable for espionage.

Hall after hall, emerald greens after salmon reds after ocean blues, Aviama's heart sank little by little. Every step took her closer to one doom or other. For the first time since arriving in Radha, she almost wished these ornate corridors would never end.

Fading daylight left a gentler touch to the vibrant colors of her surroundings. They passed two courtyards, a fountain, and a man lighting lanterns along the walls before Aviama stopped short. Murin collided with her, and Aviama glanced right and left. She took a step forward, then paused and bit her lip.

Ishaan cleared his throat. "Is there someplace in particular you were hoping to go, Your Highness?"

Few sounds irked Aviama more than Ishaan's dry voice and mocking tone. She shot him a dark glare. "I'll find where I'm going, thank you very much."

Murin shifted her weight. "Maybe someplace with high ceilings, to sing in? That would be nice, wouldn't it? Or someplace open to the sky, after being stuck in one room for so long?"

"I do love to sing, Murin, but I'm afraid Ishaan's face rather flattens my aptitude for it."

Ishaan pursed his lips but said nothing, and the next instant his typical impassivity cloaked any possible humanity. She eyed him, but he gave no reaction. How badly did the man want to kill her? Was he well controlled, or did he simply not care about anything?

Aviama turned in a circle and struck out down a new passageway, came to the end, and halted before what appeared to be double doors leading out to a terrace. Curious, she turned the handle and poked her head out.

To her right there was only a wall, but to her left a long railing ran thirty meters down one side, with steps leading down to a garden. Columns adorned with carved pakshi heads supported an overhang dripping with flowered vines, and a maze of tall bushes graced the center of the garden down beyond.

A figure leaned against a column, tossing an icing-glazed pastry in the air. She expected him to catch it, but he let it fall, and a tiny hand shot out through the railing to pluck it from its descent just before it hit the floor. A giggle rippled over the greenery on the other side, and the figure turned away with a grin.

Aviama's jaw dropped as their eyes met, and the beautiful smile vanished from the man's face. She wheeled around and shut the door behind her, her heartbeat pounding in her ears. Honestly, did Chenzira know where she was going before she herself did?

Except he had looked about as pleased as she to have run

into one another. Murin opened her mouth, but Aviama held up a hand, spun, and marched down the hall in the opposite direction. "This way."

This time Ishaan smirked, and Aviama wondered if he might be human after all. But there was now a more important question. Had he seen Chenzira? Her guess—and prayer—was that he hadn't. Murin had stood close behind Aviama as she opened the door and looked out, but Ishaan stayed several paces behind. It was probable he hadn't seen anything beyond the door.

She swept down the hall, setting a pace only a hair's breadth away from a run. Murin broke into a jog to catch up.

Chenzira Bomani. Why did the man have to be everywhere? Couldn't he just live his own life someplace else?

Although perhaps that's what he was doing. Radha *was* someplace else for someone who started out as a prince in Keket. What was he running from? Was he running at all? What did the Radhans think he was here for that allowed him such a long time at the palace? Had he been here ever since he disappeared?

Aviama shook her head to clear it and picked up her pace, accelerating to a few jogging strides before catching herself. *Appearances and rumors. The palace lives and breathes by them. Calm yourself.*

She set her jaw and slowed. Everything was fine. All she'd done is get herself lost in the palace, open a door, close a door, and retrace her steps. It was all rather mundane—nothing to lose her hat over, as it were.

None of it was true, but it was the story she was selling. And fleeing through the corridors like a dog with its tail on fire would do nothing to support the ordinary problems she was supposedly having.

The menagerie was close now, and a monkey's screech

reached through the walls. Aviama fixed her eyes on the colors of a melting sun gradually fading away on the wall ahead. She'd pass through the open gathering area with the fountain, which she hoped would be abandoned for the evening, and reach the passage on the far side that opened up next to the menagerie.

The hall ended and dumped into the wide-open space with its soaring ceilings, thick columns, and burbling fountain. Two women, one decked in royal blue and the other in burnt orange, passed Aviama, Murin, and Ishaan with a giggle. Aviama offered them a forced smile, and they gave a rote nod before they disappeared behind them, the cheerful gush and bubble of the water feature carrying away all sound of their receding feet.

Her stomach twisted, and she twisted her rings. *Ignore them. They weren't laughing at you. Probably.* Aviama took a breath and stared at her feet. *Just get to the other side and find somewhere to waste time near the entrance.*

Another giggle floated through the space. Aviama snapped her head up, but the room was empty. Had she imagined it? No, there it was again.

So what if people were enjoying themselves? Perhaps there were friends sharing secrets and gossip, or forbidden lovers meeting in the romance of dusk. Just because Aviama was miserable didn't mean everybody else had to be. She steeled herself, passed the fountain, and angled toward the double doors on the far end still twelve meters off.

Eleven.

Ten.

Aviama rounded the last column on her left, and ran smack into Princess Marija—her arms wrapped tightly around Prince Shiva.

28

———

Faking being lost in the palace had been easy after being truly lost multiple times in the House of the Blessing Sun. She'd done it for Ishaan's sake, as they wound their way toward the menagerie. But there was nothing fake about Marija's beaming smile as she pulled her lips from Shiva's and turned gloating eyes on Aviama.

The woman's perfect slender arms snaked around Shiva's neck, holding him close, and his hand was on her hip. "Oh dear," Marija cooed. "It seems we've been caught."

Aviama's heart plunged to her toes, and her mouth went dry. Shiva's lips parted—perhaps because that was the activity they were most recently used to—and his eyes widened. She tripped over her feet backing away, glancing right and left for an escape. The way she'd come was too long of a flight to be in the same room, whether their eyes were on her back or on each other. Only one option remained.

Her throat tightened against an unreasonable lump of emotion as she dropped into a halfhearted curtsy and fled toward the doors ten meters off. What did she care if the man flirted with all the girls? What did she care if he kissed them?

After all, breaking into the king's office for restricted information was a higher betrayal than being romantic with someone one was considering for marriage. Aviama was the one guilty of treachery.

What *Shiva* was doing was merely part of the game. The contest. The thing she'd been summoned for.

But she hadn't accepted the invitation to seek the prince's hand. She'd accepted to seek his secrets.

Aviama flew through the doors, past the large space she'd used to break into the menagerie only a few short hours ago, and under the skylight where the first of the stars made their grand entrance. She'd opened herself up, written that stupid note, and come like a puppy to wait for him. And for what?

Curses of curses, she was even wearing a purple dress. Heat flushed her cheeks.

It wasn't like he could honestly like her. It wasn't like her ridiculous sketch of the Radhan ship and the dragon in the sky, the partnered nations and freed melderbloods, could exist. Not the way both his parents despised them. Not the way Shiva had spoken about Darsh. Not with Aviama guilty of treason against the royal family.

The lump in her throat grew, and she swallowed hard. She'd burn the sketch when she got back to her room. Before anyone saw it, before she let her mind deceive her with ludicrous daydreams. Why did she care?

Aviama flicked a tear from her eye and marched out from the open room, past the corridor where she'd hoped Shiva would meet her, the one with the door to the adjoining meeting room they'd used before, and down another hall. She wanted someplace small. Even someplace enclosed, where Ishaan might be willing to stand posted outside the door instead of laughing at her as they walked.

The sounds of Ishaan and Murin's footsteps watching

every moment of her humiliation set a burning in her chest. A whisp of wind curled around her fingers, and she clasped her hands together tight. She spun her rings and bit her lip. And stopped.

The shadow footsteps also stopped. Aviama turned to Ishaan and lifted her chin.

"I'm sick of running into people I don't want to see. I want someplace to go where nobody will bother me. And where you can stand outside the door and leave me alone. What nearby room is there like that?"

Chenzira wouldn't have to know her attempt was a failure. She'd tell him she hadn't had the opportunity to see Shiva yet. She'd tell him she had a meeting set for another time, and stall until Chenzira got information on Enzo. Maybe Enzo would even know what to do, once she found him.

At least the queen would be happy to see Shiva so interested in another woman, and Aviama awkwardly running as far away from her son as possible. Chenzira had said he was a pig. That seemed extreme. But he was certainly playing his little field of women to the fullest.

Ishaan dipped his head and raised his arm to the right. "Down this hall, last door straight ahead."

Aviama turned on her heel and moved down the hall as if in a dream. Or a nightmare. She'd avoided Murin's gaze. The girl was too good. Too kind. Too *worried.*

Aviama took a deep breath. *Abort mission. Collect yourself. Cry alone where no one can see you. Go to bed and try again tomorrow.*

Maybe she could get information for Chenzira and her own kingdom by other means. Maybe she was on the right track when she broke into the king's office, and she needed more connections rather than banging her head against the brick wall that was Crown Prince Shiva Tanashai. The brick wall that kissed all the other princesses. The brick wall that threatened her on terraces, sent love notes to her bedroom, and teased her in collapsed tunnels.

The pristine white-tiled floor beneath her feet transitioned to black marble ten paces from the door at the end of the hall. Light swirls of gray interrupted its deep ebony, rolling like a storm cloud through its pure night. Aviama turned the knob on a black painted door and swung it open.

The room beyond was circular, the walls black, the floor a mirror reflecting the stars from a vaulted glass ceiling overhead. The style didn't fit anything else in the palace, and it was furnished only with cushioned curved seats against the walls. Aviama's jaw dropped, and the ache in her chest eased to see the glory of the sky come alive from the firmament above to the floor beneath her feet.

Tears brimmed her eyes, and she blinked them back. "Thank you, Ishaan," she murmured, not daring to turn. "This will do. Murin, please wait outside."

Standing outside with Ishaan was not the kindest of assignments for her lady-in-waiting, but Aviama didn't need to be inside long. And as she shut the door behind her, the overwhelming need for a quiet calm washed over her like a wave reaching a parched land. She stumbled forward and sank to her knees.

Solace.

The world shut itself away, and no sound traveled through the walls or door. Perhaps the room had thicker walls or was coated with some treatment or other. It would almost have been eerie, if the stars had not kept such beautiful company. They'd come out in majesty tonight, so quickly it was as if a curtain had been snapped back, rolling up the day and unfurling the night in a single sweeping motion across the heavens.

Aviama breathed in, every muscle tense, her arm still sore from her fall in the troll enclosure. But of all the ailments of her physical body, it was her heart that weighed heaviest. Her lungs filled and pressed against her ribs, and when she could hardly hold any more, she took yet another breath in and held it. Her lungs began to burn, her throat to feel its limits, every cell bursting for the air of life, and she let it all out in a rush.

Something about it soothed her smarting soul. She did it again, this time not holding her breath at the end, noticing the way her lungs expanded and contracted each time, never failing to serve her waiting body. What fragile things humans were. It took so little to throw her off-balance, threaten her security, make her feel crazy.

And yet in other ways, she could trust her body to watch over her when she was too consumed by the world to notice. The beating of her heart continued without her asking, air flowed in and out, the scrapes of her forearms from the pit's coarse sand had begun to heal on their own. Even now, could hope survive the darkness?

Aviama stared up at the diamonds twinkling in the expanse above. Out of darkness, light. In the abyss, hope. A star did not wait for dawn, for some other light to grant its blessing on the earth. Even knowing that its brightness offered harsh contrast to the depths of night, it stood its ground. Swallowed by day, it was invisible, but here its qualities showed all the more.

What qualities did she have that needed to shine? What resiliencies must rise to the occasion? With no way to contact home, and no allies, she could not afford to wait for the sun. So she would make her own hope. If only she could figure out how.

Resolve hardened in her chest as she ran her fingertips along the stars in the mirror. Aviama strained her ear, but heard nothing—and let a quiet hum whisper through the room. The soft echo bounced pleasingly to the high ceilings, and she looked up with a smile. Warmth lifted her spirits from within. She took a breath and raised her voice in gentle, quiet tones.

> *The beauty of a land with you*
> *Is lovely not with one, but two*
> *Through every shadow, you're my shield*
> *A song of love in every field*

She loved this song. It was one of her mother's favorites, and every time she sang it, she could almost be transported back to a joyful time when her family was whole. When assassins, dragons, and foreign kings did not threaten, and life was normal.

But Aviama was a royal. Life was never normal, and any safety she'd felt was only because she'd been too young to understand whatever threats had occurred back then. No monarchy was ever truly safe. And her mother was dead. The song trailed off to nothing, and a tear slipped down her cheek.

> *The beauty of a land with you...*

Her mother and father had found a love for the ages. A partnership to weather any storm, like Zephan and Semra had created together. Was it too much to ask for Aviama to find the same?

She wouldn't find it with Shiva. That was for sure. But why then did his face encroach in her mind again? And why did Marija appear next to him now, each time her thoughts returned to him?

A new song floated through her brain, almost plucking its

own strings as the notes formed together. Something in her soul broke, wound back together, and settled into an ache as the song took form.

> *In the silence of these halls*
> *Such beautiful prison walls*
> *When I turn and see you there*
> *I don't know if I should care*

> *When my heart goes out to you*
> *Is this part of what you do?*
> *Is it charm and grace and guile?*
> *Could it all be just your style?*

> *You save me now and then*
> *You hurt me once again*
> *I wish that I could know*
> *Whether I'm to come or go*

SHE CLOSED her eyes and let the music call her to her feet, her hands moving with the lilt of the tune as starlight fell gingerly on her face. Aviama sent a final note high and long, opening her eyes to the glassy ceiling as she let it build stronger and stronger. She'd forgotten how this felt. Music was her medicine. She hadn't been taking it.

The song resolved, its ending yet unwritten, and she let out a sigh that melted away the tension in her shoulders.

"You can sing."

Aviama squealed and jumped back, twirling to the door

with her heart in her throat. Shiva leaned in through the cracked-open door, watching her with a pensive expression. Her cheeks flushed hot.

"It's polite to announce oneself, not stand spying and gawking on a person's rare moments of solitude."

"I'm to understand you had solitude in your room all day, did you not?"

Aviama eyed him. He was checking up on her? She swallowed.

Shiva stepped inside, his hand lingering on the handle, Ishaan and Murin just visible in the hall beyond.

"I did not announce myself, because I was rather enraptured by what can only be described as the song of a siren."

She glared at him, hating herself for being almost complimented by the stupid sappy drivel coming from his stupid handsome mouth. Her gaze locked onto his, then dropped to linger on the curve of his lips for a moment too long. An image of Marija wound around him shook the vision free. Her stomach soured.

He tilted his head. "I didn't know you could sing."

"Yes, well, anybody can sing," she snapped.

"Not like that." Shiva took a step forward, swinging the door almost closed behind him.

Aviama had to concede the point. She'd once heard Saeb, the housekeeper in Shamaran Castle, croak out what was probably supposed to be music. It had reminded her of a cow she'd once seen, bemoaning getting stuck in a hole on the side of the road.

Aviama twisted the rings on her fingers and stepped backward. Her heart began to hammer. She wiped her hands on her dress. *Biscuits*, why had she worn violet, of all colors?

"Is it a song from home?" he asked.

His eyes were unnecessarily intense for a man who had

just had his arms wrapped around another woman. Aviama shifted her weight. "Yes, just another song from back home. One in a million."

Nothing I wrote. Nothing mortifying. Aviama looked away.

The door clicked shut, and long fingers of terror nearly choked her at the silky-smooth words that escaped him next.

"Lilac, are you jealous?"

29

"Jealous? Of the prince making out with every princess he's busy courting?" Aviama snorted, and she hoped it was convincing. By the look on Shiva's face, it wasn't.

A fair assessment. Her statement stank of bitterness, even to her. Aviama winced.

Shiva stepped closer, and Aviama stepped back in a perfect mirroring step. She'd never been so aware of a closed door in all her life. He took another step, and Aviama moved again. They could have been doing a very awkward, very distant waltz.

"I've not made out with every princess."

Only Marija, then. Was that supposed to make her feel better, or worse? Aviama shot him a glare, and he held up his hands.

"I got away as soon as I could. She rather accosted me."

Aviama pursed her lips and crossed her arms. "Yes, you did look powerless to stop her."

Shiva arched an eyebrow. "And this from a woman who is not jealous?"

Biscuits. Aviama dropped her arms and clasped them behind her back instead, spinning one of her rings out of sight. She lifted her chin. "You got my note?"

He grinned then, and something exploded in her chest at the sight of it. At the knowledge that *she* had caused it. "Yes. It's why I was in there in the first place, when Marija found me. I was headed for the menagerie. To find you."

"You figured it out, then?"

Shiva shrugged. "The more you take, the more you leave...footsteps." He spread his hands. "Lilac and boulders —you, and the trolls. I'm not sure what the last line was about. Perhaps it simply rhymed, and you needed a fourth line."

Curses, she should have made it harder. He'd even pegged the issue she'd had with the last line.

"I told you I like puzzles," he said, his voice dropping into the silk tone that stirred something inside her he had no business stirring. Shiva stepped forward again, and she tripped on her way to backing up, suddenly unable to tear her eyes away from him as he advanced. "But my favorite part was the drawing."

To her dismay, he reached his hand into his breast pocket and produced it then and there. Dancing calligraphy letters mocked her in her own handwriting, but the lilac could just as well have pointed and laughed. The burning lilac, the firebrand, the spark lit to flame between them. Her own idiocy set to a sketch.

Aviama stared at it dangling from his fingertips. If only she were a fireblood, she could incinerate the cursed thing in his hands and dispose of the evidence. The evidence that she'd tried to woo a man who spent his life floating through women, and somehow making *her* feel bad about judging him by the time they spoke again. Evidence that it might not all be a ruse, and she might care a little too much. Evidence that she was a fool.

Shiva crossed the space between them and slipped an arm around the small of her back. She let out a gasp as her calves hit the cushioned seat against the wall behind her, and she fell onto it in her haste to get away. Shiva didn't let go, instead following her to the seat.

Irritation burned her chest, and she held up a hand. "I'd hate to tarnish your memory of Marija with other romantic pursuits. Like a wine tasting. Let it breathe."

"She's not who I chose to be with tonight. I told you. She found me."

Aviama scowled. "Yes, you were clearly heartbroken about the situation. In lieu of recent events, I thought I could share something else with you tonight."

"In lieu of me kissing Marija?" Shiva drew back, scanning her face. "You're really upset."

"I'm not upset." The lump in her throat would say otherwise. Aviama gritted her teeth.

"Yes, you are. Are you crying?"

Aviama groaned and turned her head away, blinking hard to bring herself under control. She hoped any remaining glisten could be owed to the starlight, and turned to drill Shiva with a withering glower. "No. That would be stupid. You're not doing anything unusual for men of your station." Her stomach churned to say it, but she was sick of the topic.

Shiva eyed her for a moment, then pulled his arm from her waist and settled in beside her on the bench. "If I let you change the subject, will you talk about us after?"

Aviama hesitated, then slowly nodded.

Shiva rolled his eyes and gestured for her to continue. "I'm listening."

She took a breath and turned toward him, some

semblance of confidence returning now that the sappy, intimate look ebbed from his face in favor of a sort of irritated curiosity. "I've been thinking about your dilemma. With the extremists, I mean. And as someone with experience with magic—from my sister-in-law, I mean, not myself—I think I can help."

Shiva laughed. "You summoned me to talk politics?"

Heat flooded her cheeks. She dug her nails into the palm of her folded hands, but she kept her voice even. "They need training. Purpose. What if, instead of banning magic altogether, you gave them a productive place to channel it? To feel important, helpful? If you partnered with them—not the extremists, but melders in general—maybe fewer of them would feel they had to go so far to be heard. Maybe Darsh's men wouldn't have so much support."

He tilted his head, and for an instant the light in his eyes went out. A play of the light, a note of danger, a hint of the man on the terrace. Aviama held her breath, but the next moment it was gone. *You're all keyed up. Relax.*

The corner of his mouth tipped up. "See, Marija would *never* have come up with something like that."

Aviama stiffened. "If you were smart, you might stop talking about her."

"Says the impassive lilac, who cares not at all what I do with women."

"I thought we weren't talking about us yet."

He pursed his lips, catching himself, but the mirth in his eyes did not dwindle. "Go on. Tell me more about your solution to Radha's problems."

Aviama took a deep breath. "It's only been three years since magic returned. Accidents are still going to happen. But in Jannemar, we've focused on education, training, and research. Incidents are already less frequent than they were, and they're continuing to trend downward since we've implemented some of these strategies. Perhaps you could reach out to my brother and sister-in-law, and they could help develop similar programs in Radha."

"That…is a very interesting proposition." Shiva ran a hand through his hair. "Do you think they'd be open to it?"

"If Jannemar wasn't interested in partnering with Radha, I wouldn't be here."

It wasn't strictly true. Jannemar was primarily interested in keeping Radha from sweeping in by force, and was too broke after the war to insult the greatest naval force on this side of the world. But partnering could be mutually beneficial for both kingdoms. Maybe Aviama could secure a positive working relationship with the country and escape relatively unscathed.

Shiva reached a hand to her face, gently turning her toward him. "And what kind of partnership would you recommend?"

Adrenaline shot through her veins, a dangerous cocktail mixing with her somersaulting stomach. Aviama swallowed, searching his dark eyes in the starlight. Alarm tensed every muscle in her body. The queen's nightmare came alive inside this room in this moment, and the queen's man stood just outside.

Something told her to run, but as his hand slipped to the nape of her neck, and his gaze drifted to her lips, she leaned toward him. With Radha's military strength, Jannemar could recover from the war without fear of invasion. What if an alliance with Shiva—not just some agreement to be easily broken, but a blood union—what if this was exactly what she'd come for? What if it was better than espionage, and she could change Radha from the inside out? Change Shiva, showing him more about melders until he was safe enough to reveal her own powers?

"Princess Aviama." Prince Shiva shifted closer on the bench until their thighs touched from hip to knee. "I would love nothing more than to choose you. To take your hand in mine and work together for a new world. A stronger Radha. To put an end to the disasters of The Return."

Aviama's chest tightened. Her breath quickened. She searched his face. His palm warmed the back of her neck, his satin embroidered tunic fitted to showcase his strong chest and arms. Shiva leaned in just a hair, and her lips parted before she could think.

He held himself there, his nose brushing hers. Hesitating. A current ran across her skin, the kind that wanted to pool in her palms and fingertips and escape in a wind. She squashed it down, hardly breathing.

"Only one thing gives me pause to this agreement." Shiva pulled back, and Aviama swallowed. "You know our country's history with magic. It's what's made us so cautious. It's taught us to fear any magic at all, but especially..." Shiva's voice trailed off, and he shook his head. "I would never partner with unclean magic, Aviama. I wouldn't train it; I wouldn't use it; I wouldn't encourage it."

Aviama nodded. Of course, that was the only reasonable position to take. Her older sister had embroiled herself in using housing artifacts to manufacture sifal magic, and paid the price—she still suffered the poisoning effects of its use.

Shiva took a breath and continued. "Your sister-in-law. Semra. I heard she was sick, in the final battle just after The Return. That even the dragons were sick, and one of them never recovered. I don't mean to accuse, but I would be remiss not to ask. Are we sure they are not sifal, that it's truly natural tabeun magic at play? Perhaps she was sick from the use of dark magic. You were there. What else could it be?"

Rumor. In the lack of any real information, the world went wild with it, theories becoming more believable than truth. Anything was better than a question left unanswered. Perhaps Shiva was right to protect appearances. Perhaps even so was his mother, on occasion.

Is this what people thought of Jannemar? The kingdom with the young, orphaned king and his dragonlord queen, steeped in sifal magic, chasing power for the sake of power— one dragon exchanged for another. Was it of any consequence whether the dragon at Shamaran Castle was blue or black, if the rulers on the thrones were after the same thing?

But they weren't the same. And Aviama's own older sister, Avaya, had been so kind as to provide a clear contrast. Aviama clenched her jaw. It was all wrong. And if the smallest dose of truth might divert the Tanashai family from destruction and invasion to partnership...well, what choice did she have?

Aviama steeled herself and lifted her chin to look Shiva full in the face.

"You say Radha has had a sordid past with magic. Well, we have more recent history. Not six hundred years ago, but three. Three years." Aviama winced. It was too short a time. "My sister wanted power. She had her reasons—I suppose everybody does—but nothing would sate her thirst for the vision in her mind. She resorted to siphoning magic from housing artifacts, as I'm sure you've heard about from your own history. Avaya has improved, but they say she will never fully recover from siphon poisoning."

She paused. Shiva's face was unreadable, but he seemed hardly to breathe lest he miss a word she spoke. She continued. "Semra, on the other hand, is in excellent health. She doesn't need a siphon. Her magic is natural, somehow coming from the bond she shares with the dragon. The mark of the dragon's kiss, they call it. It is tabeun."

"No. No, I don't understand." Shiva shook his head and ran a hand through his hair. "Word is that Her Majesty the queen was incredibly sick. So were the dragons, and your sister. But no one else. How could it be tabeun?"

"*Konnolan.* It's a substance that targets magical essence, but is inert on non-magical entities. Like magna, but instead of deadening the power in an isolated way from the person, the whole person or creature is impacted. It's severe, but acute. Both she and the dragon are completely fine." Aviama gave an encouraging smile. "See? Tabeun. Safe. She would never have allowed magic back into the world if it were only going to poison everyone."

Shiva smiled back, his tense shoulders dropping in relief. "Yes. That is precisely what I needed to know."

His arm slipped around the small of her back, and as he drew her toward him, that satisfied smile took on a sly quality. Pain squeezed her throat tight as disbelief and shock washed over her. The twinkle in his eye tonight was born not of joy or even mischief, but of conquest.

Aviama had been working under the assumption that there were three Shivas—the romantic one, the diplomatic one, and the threatening, dangerous one. But no. A tree had many branches, but they served the same trunk, were fed by the same nutrients, and grew in the service of one driving seed.

The three Shivas were not different Shivas at all, but branches serving a core that was stronger and more dangerous than any she'd identified before. She'd come for information, but in the end, it was Aviama who had given up her nation's secrets. In one fell swoop, with misplaced trust and a single sentence, she'd handed Crown Prince Shiva of Radha the keys to destroying Jannemar's greatest defenses.

Konnolan.

30

―――――――

Aviama stiffened just as Shiva's mouth crashed into hers. Bile rose up to choke her, and she pushed against him—but his arm tightened around her waist and his hand at the nape of her neck forced her to him. His lips moved against hers, all signs of tenderness replaced with a jubilant victory.

He was the lion, she the mouse. A hunter with his prey. And he liked the feeling. He was hungry for more, gloating her destruction as her breathing came frenzied and her hands batted uselessly at his iron chest.

Shiva tangled his hand in her hair and pulled her head back. "Is this not what you wanted?"

Aviama gasped for air, terror paralyzing every muscle. The wind begged to come to her aid, but if she used it against him now, she would be dead by morning.

And she'd just told him how to incapacitate melders.

Shiva's grip loosened in her hair, but she dared not move. He brushed his lips to hers, murmuring against them in the quiet dark of the room under the stars. "We can find Darsh.

We can find them all. Why wait for melderbloods to announce themselves when we can test their lies?"

"Shiva." The word came out as a croak. She was shaking. "Shiva, that's not what I meant."

"No, see, but it's what you *should* have meant." The corner of his mouth tipped up, and he twined a lock of her golden hair through his fingers. "You and I are a great team. You have information and experience I need. And I have both vision and money, in spades."

A tear slipped down her cheek. Shiva examined it, then wiped it away with his thumb. "No need to fear. I see no reason to over-involve women in politics. You won't be over-burdened. Wives should be like housing artifacts. Beautiful, useful, strategic, and an excellent bargaining chip."

Aviama ripped free of him and launched to her feet, nostrils flared, hands clenching to fists. "That's not a marriage. And I would never marry you."

Shiva clucked his tongue and shook his head, as though she were nothing but a disobedient schoolchild. "Now, now. Let's not be rash." He stood before her and raised his hand toward her face. Aviama swung at him to bat his hand away, but he snatched her wrist in a firm grip, and his expression instantly turned to stone. "I would not do such things if I were you."

The threat fell like a blanket, looming over Aviama like a storm cloud, a rolling thunder bringing lightning ever nearer. Her skin was white where he'd grabbed her, and he lifted her wrist in between them, arching an eyebrow to emphasize his point.

"This must never happen again. And *never* out there. We are to be married, you know. We are the picture of bliss, and your family must believe it."

Aviama's heart stopped. Every vein turned to ice, every

drop of blood fleeing her face. "Marry Marija. She's more than willing."

Shiva released her wrist and wagged a finger. "What Marija wants to give me I can find on any streetcorner. What *you* have, darling, is special. Jannemar has opened the door to magic, and it seems *you* hold the keys to safely controlling it. Who dares cross Radha on the open sea? Only ancient magic limits us there, but with the proper knowledge, all of the Aeia Sea will be ours. Keket will bow, and the Iolani will pave our way. Dragons will herald our coming to the south, and our neighbors will trip over themselves to bring us tribute. Ah, yes, with magic—who dares cross Radha at all?"

Nausea rocked her, and she wavered. Aviama threw a hand out to steady herself on the wall, and Shiva caught her. "Shhh, shh. It's okay. You are about to become part of the greatest empire in the world. We don't need to be at odds. I meant it when I said we were a good team. Accept me."

"Is that a proposal?" Aviama choked out.

Shiva shrugged. "Sure. It's why you're here, isn't it?"

"I thought you were reasonable before."

"No, you didn't. You thought I was debased, but still I caught you stealing glances." Shiva caught a stray hair and tucked it behind her ear, his touch lingering along the healing gash on her temple. "Perhaps, as your sketch might suggest, I was not the only one with a fire kindled."

Aviama's cheeks burned, and her stomach dropped. "I thought you might come to understand. I thought perhaps we could come to a place where we could work together."

Shiva took her hand and kissed it, giving her a sweeping bow. "And so we shall."

Aviama lifted her chin. Ire ate at her from the inside out, a fury only tempered by the fear of what she'd done. She should have let Darsh kill him in the pit.

"Dearest lilac." Shiva looked her up and down, drinking her in as though she were an exhibit on display. A cocky smile twisted at his mouth, sending a stabbing pain to her gut. He winked. "I do love you in purple."

A shiver of dread rippled down her spine as he opened the door and vanished without another word. Aviama squeezed her eyes shut against the rolling wave threatening to pull her under. She pressed a hand against her chest, trying to feel the beat of her own stampeding heart, to remember that she stood in a room in a palace, in a point in time, but all she knew were visions filing into her consciousness one after the other.

King Dahnuk, gripping the collar of the servant from the seats at the pit. *He's a melderblood.* The king again, after her rescue from the collapsed tunnel, with a simple plan to solve Radha's melderblood problem: *We kill them all.*

Shiva's threatening voice when they'd argued on the terrace, and the inescapable force of his hands as he'd kissed her just now. The victory on his face when she'd betrayed her family and homeland, when he knew he had what he needed to destroy them.

Running. Shouting. A deep *boom,* and her father King Turian's body lying on the ground of the courtyard. Her mother, Queen Sharsi, in a pool of blood in the Great Hall. Semra, fighting in the woods to save Aviama's life as they fled the castle. Snatches of memories past.

Air. She needed air. *Can't breathe. Can't breathe. Can't...*

Aviama fumbled for her rings and tried to spin them, but hardly even noticed them on her fingers. The room spun, with stars above and stars in the mirror at her feet, a swirl of white and black. Polar opposites that should never fit together.

Her chest heaved, but her lungs burned. It wasn't enough. *Air.*

She was going to die here, without a pursuer in sight. How

Queen Satya would rejoice! Would her family ever know what really happened to her? What would happen to Murin? Would Shiva feel guilty at all?

"Your Highness!"

The sweet familiar voice cut through the air, muffled but earnest. Aviama opened her eyes. Murin stood inside the room, door shut behind her, pushing against a swirl of wind flowing like a whirlpool around Aviama standing at its center.

Aviama gasped and dropped the currents. Murin ran forward and gripped her shoulders. "Your Highness!"

But only one thought prevailed over the others. "Did Ishaan see?"

Did he see that I'm a melderblood?

Murin shook her head. "No, I don't think so. And I closed the door."

The door handle turned, and the women rotated toward it as Ishaan swung the door open and set himself in the doorway. He scanned the two of them standing together, then folded his arms. "I think you've had just about enough of your evening stroll, don't you?"

Aviama grimaced. "Yes. Yes, I believe I have. Would you lead us back to my quarters?"

Ishaan's every muscle tensed, and his eyes narrowed. "It's against regulation. You walk first. I'll tell you where to go."

Biscuits. Not ideal. Aviama nodded. "Of course."

Ishaan stood to one side, and Aviama brushed past him out of the dark room of stars and back into the hall. Murin followed, closer than protocol, and leaned in toward her as Ishaan fell into step at the appropriate distance behind them.

"Your Highness, you look as though you've seen a ghost. What happened?"

Aviama clenched her jaw and blinked back tears. She took

a steadying breath and pulled herself up straight just before they hit the main palace halls.

"I think I just received my death sentence."

The reality of her situation settled over her with the weight of a dozen chains pulling at her every step. Shiva planned to marry her, to usurp her knowledge of magic and connection with Jannemar to serve his grand vision of ultimate control in the region.

As horrific as a sham marriage with Shiva might be, she'd never make it to the altar. Queen Satya would have her killed long before any wedding could take place. Satya still believed Aviama was melderblood, and she'd made it clear the Tanashai royal line would be so polluted only over the queen's dead body.

Unfortunately, Aviama lacked the connections and resources to make that happen.

The queen's control also kept her isolated. Without any chance for mail or messengers of any sort in or out, Aviama was trapped, and Jannemar would be none the wiser. They wouldn't know of the threat, or of Radha's plans to use konnolan against Semra, the dragon, and their growing force of melder warriors in training, until it was too late.

Mere months from now, Aviama could be the only remaining living member of her family—and be married to the man responsible for their deaths.

She needed help, and fast. After the events of this evening, chances of escaping her room again were slim, and even now each step carried her closer to that prison. And with Murin so close to Aviama, she was a target, too. After all, Enzo was already gone. How would the queen react when Shiva decided to make their engagement official? What would happen if she said no now? Shiva struck her as a man that would not take to such news well.

To what lengths would he go to protect his image? After tonight, she wasn't sure the limit existed. The hairs on the back of her neck stood on end, and she shuddered.

She'd told Semra she didn't want to be shut up in her room for any more disasters, the way she had been when the battle broke out in the throne room back home. An army of assassins had descended, two dragons duked it out on a carpet of broken glass across the marble floors, and her father, the king, had been seized and put in chains—all while the princesses paced their lavish rooms, locked into a dungeon of their own and left to twiddle their thumbs.

But tonight, in this moment, she was free. Free to do something bold. Something rash. Something dangerous. Even if it landed her right back in that blue and white cell upstairs.

She could not stand by and do nothing. She *would* not.

Aviama quickened her pace, turning down this hall or that at Ishaan's direction. She reached up to adjust her hair, and when her hand came back down, one of her earrings disappeared into her palm. The courtyard would be next, on the left. The last courtyard before the stairs back up to the residence hall.

Her last opportunity. Aviama veered right, waiting for Ishaan to correct her. Clueless women rarely did any meaningful scheming.

"Left, Highness. Across the courtyard."

Aviama lifted her chin and changed course, sweeping across the floor with an elegance she far from felt. Her pulse pounded in her ears. *Now or never.*

She tripped next to the pool, and the earring skittered across the floor and down into the pool. "No, no, no! That was my mother's!"

Murin rushed forward, and they both fell to their knees at the side of the pool, plunging their arms in up to the elbow.

Orange and blue fish scattered at their disturbance, and the cold of the water bit at Aviama's skin. Curated flowers of every color graced the sides of the pool, and empty benches waited under the fruit trees for morning.

As soon as Murin was close enough, Aviama dropped her voice low and let hurried words pour out like a flood.

"Shiva knows about konnolan. He wants to marry me and use me to get to Jannemar, and they'll probably hit the Horon Mines first, from the northeast side." Even with Shiva's strategy to marry her in play, King Dahnuk's approach hanging on his office wall was likely their first move. Aviama raked her hand through the water. Ishaan was running forward. "Find the guard with the scar on his hand. Tell him the shadow has looked on him with favor, and you can get him in with Darsh's men—but he has to get you both out of the palace first, unseen. Find Darsh. Tell him he was right about me, and I want to help. Darsh will come for me. Once you've done that, find a way home to Jannemar to tell my brother what's happened."

"Your Highness, please, what—"

"If you care for me at all, Murin, you'll do it."

Ishaan came to a stop three paces from Aviama and planted his feet a shoulder's width apart. "We should be going, Your Highness. If you've lost something, I'll send one of the servants to look tomorrow."

"No. You'll send for them now." A tear slipped down her cheek. Letting a tear free was easy. Holding back from breaking down and sobbing was the hard part. She turned to look at him. "I have so few comforts here. Would you really begrudge an orphan her last tie to her murdered mother?"

Ishaan pursed his lips. *Biscuits*, was that a sliver of humanity? If it was, she couldn't trust it to win out over his typical apathy. Better to appeal to his pride. Aviama let her shoulders fall forward, her hand still dragging in the water of the pool, her skirts a puddle on the floor.

She wiped the tear from her face with her free hand and tilted her head up at him. "Is it my impressive musculature that concerns you? Are you so slow that you could not catch me if I was stupid enough to run? Where would I go, exactly, in this ridiculous labyrinth of a palace?"

The queen's man sighed. "I'm not letting you out of my sight. I'm going to the edge of the hall there, and if you so much as flinch, I'll have your wrist shackled to mine."

Aviama resisted the urge to roll her eyes. "As happy a scenario as that would be for the both of us, you will find me here, waiting for my mother's heirloom."

Ishaan's jaw clenched, but he dipped his head in a curt nod. "Fine. Don't move."

Murin gripped her arm. Ishaan turned his back and strode for the end of the hall, looking back twice on his way. Aviama took Murin's hand from her arm, squeezed it, and let her go.

And took off at a sprint.

31

Aviama flew across the courtyard, feet slapping the marble floors, fistfuls of violet skirts in her hands. Ishaan let out a shout, and his heavy stomping run thudded down the length of the room behind her. She'd be lucky to make it around the corner.

Shooting pain ran up her shins, reminding her that running was not her strong suit, but she forced her legs to pump all the harder. Ishaan was close behind. He shouted again, and an answering shout signaled a second man joining the chase.

Her stomach dropped as she turned the corner and dove for the first door she found. Buckets of cleaning solution stood beside a rack of mops and brooms and what appeared to be a service hallway running the length of the courtyard and disappearing somewhere behind the residence halls. Aviama snatched a mop off the wall, slid the rod through the door handle, and hooked the looping yarns on the end on the wall.

The door burst in, catching on the makeshift barricade with only a small gap from the door to the doorframe, as her hand was still on the mop.

Ishaan glared at her through the narrow space. "You've got nowhere to go. I know the service halls better than you know your own room, and there are only two exits."

Aviama pursed her lips. "Yes, but weren't you getting bored of standing for hours in one place?"

The door rattled again, and the mop head shifted on the hook. Aviama fled down the hall. Did he mean two exits total, or two additional to the one she came through? If the latter, Ishaan would cover one, the other guard would cover the second, and no one would be at the door she came through— or, someone would cover the door she left behind and only one of the exits would be covered. How much of a stir would Ishaan create to apprehend her? How obvious should it be that she was not free within the palace?

She'd be caught. That much was inevitable. But following the passage to its end gave Murin her best chance of escape. Aviama was the prize horse, the expensive pawn up for auction in this twisted charade. Every eye was on her. If the horse broke loose, they'd send ropes and riders after it. But nobody would notice the stable hand slipping away.

The more time Aviama could consume their thoughts, the better. As long as she remained useful, she stayed in the auction. If she became dangerous, she'd be put down.

Run and be caught. Be defeated and brought under control. But never threaten the crown itself, or the game is up. Living dignitaries could gain information. Living prisoners could escape.

Dead bodies were only dead bodies. Not dignitaries, not princesses, not prisoners. She could tug on her rope, but only so far. The ultimate question: *was she worth the trouble?*

So far, to Shiva, she seemed to be. Maybe he could protect her from his mother. Maybe not. But how would he feel about her latest escapade?

Aviama threw herself forward, the clatter of her shoes an

echo down the service hallway. She kicked off her shoes and listened. No sound from behind, no sound from in front. She was the mouse, and Ishaan was the cat.

Her legs ached, her lungs burned, and her breath came in gasps. It wouldn't take long for Ishaan to gather help and cover all three exits to the service hall. No use wearing himself out when it was only a matter of time.

What if he'd lied? What if there were more exits, and he'd only wanted her to give up?

Once he caught her, would he drag her back to the queen this very night, or wait until her hyena was particularly hungry?

Her mouth went dry. Aviama groaned and started off again, gathering her long skirts in sweating fists. Cool tile met the soles of her feet as she fled, step by step, into the arms of her captors. The walls caved in around her, the dim light of the moon and stars completely shut out. If there were lanterns in the hall, they weren't lit. Aviama threw out a hand and ran it along the smooth walls as she passed, searching for a break in its surface.

And there it was—smooth, cold exchanged for rough wood raking across her skin. Aviama skidded to a stop several paces beyond it and padded softly back to the wood, exploring it with her fingers. The knob turned freely, but she held it closed. Her heart beat wildly, and her muscles begged for respite. She could afford none.

Aviama pushed the door open. A dark room spread before her, cast in eerie orange torchlight. Pillars ran the length of the room, and the windows on one wall revealed the double doors led outside. The hall to her right probably led back to the courtyard and stairs up to the residence halls in the direction she'd come. How much had the hall curved as she ran?

She knew she would be caught. She knew she'd done all of

this for Murin to get out. But in this moment, there was nothing she wouldn't do to save herself.

Aviama bit her lip and scanned the darkness. The torch on her left crackled, and she jumped. *Biscuits. Get it together.* No matter how many exits there really were to the service hall, she had no doubt Ishaan did indeed know every one of them. But the room was empty.

Slowly, slowly, she latched the door behind her. She took a deep breath. *You can do this.*

Aviama left the cheaper tile of the service hall behind and stole across cold marble on her bare feet. She'd hide behind a pillar, and double back once she knew no one had—

A tall figure whirled from around the pillar, looming over her. His hand snatched out to capture her wrist, a gold band glinting from around his arm in the dimness of the torches. Not a servant. Not a guard.

Shiva?

Hardly thinking, Aviama jerked her arm back and rotated her body to throw her weight as she twisted her wrist down through the break in his grip between his fingers and thumb. Sweat broke out on her brow, and she swung at him. The man caught her fist midair and looped his free arm around her waist, lifting her from her feet and swinging her against him behind the pillar.

Aviama's fingers found smooth glittering stones laid in a glittering collar on her captor's chest, and realization struck. She raised her gaze from his chest and shoulders up past a short dark beard to harsh eyes glaring down at her.

Her lips parted in surprise. "Chenzira."

His grip tightened, and she winced. Chenzira's jaw clenched. "What did you do?"

"I have information," she blurted. "But I'm no good to you

dead. Get me out, and I'll tell you everything you need to know."

She *did* have information. Nothing about Darsh or the extremists, but Chenzira didn't know that. If he could get her out of the palace, she'd take her chances with his wrath. Maybe he'd settle for Radha's plan against Jannemar, and Shiva's plan to marry her. Besides, Chenzira struck her as a standard sword-slashing type, and she'd rather die by sword than by hyena.

His stared at her for a moment, holding her there, then released her waist and dragged her out from behind the pillar just as three soldiers rounded the corner. Her heart dropped to her toes, and a chill ran down her spine.

Ishaan led the pair of soldiers, and Chenzira was dragging her toward them. "I caught her for you. Next time, don't lose your charge."

Ishaan bowed to the foreign prince, his beady eyes boring first into Chenzira, and then Aviama. "Believe me, she'll not leave my sight again. Thank you, Your Highness."

Something in Aviama's chest boiled, and her face flushed hot. Her fingers trembled. She swallowed and folded her hands. *You knew you'd be caught. You knew it, dummy. Cat and mouse.*

"It seems your guest is not comforted by your presence," Chenzira mused, looking her up and down. He turned to Ishaan. "I'm shocked. You have such a pleasant disposition."

Ishaan's lips flattened. "Thank you, Your Highness. We'll take her from here."

Chenzira handed her over to Ishaan, and the bitterness of his betrayal burned the edges of her mind. As Ishaan's fingers closed around her upper arm, a steely resolve hardened the knots in her stomach into stone. Her quaking ceased, and a haunting calm settled over her.

They could take her guard, cut her off from her family, threaten her, scare her, chase her—but if they thought they could *control* her, they were sadly mistaken. Murin would get free. She would find the guard with the crescent scar on his hand, find Darsh, and get word to Zephan and Semra. And Aviama would cause just enough trouble to keep Radha focused on her.

Preferably without being killed.

Aviama lifted her chin and drilled Ishaan with a cool glare. "Walking beside me is against regulation."

"Nonsense, Your Highness. Your safety is in jeopardy, and therefore we will take every precaution to deliver you to your new room without delay."

Her stomach wrenched. "New room?"

"Naturally, Your Highness. The old one did not seem to suit you. We want you to feel secure and well-guarded."

Of course. The balcony was a liability. "Your thoughtfulness knows no bounds."

One of the guards behind Ishaan stepped forward and dipped his head in a short bow, extending a hand with the purple earring she'd kicked into the courtyard pool. "Your Highness, your mother's heirloom has been recovered."

Aviama leaned forward to inspect the piece of jewelry, straightened, and shook her head. "You must be mistaken, sir. My mother hated amethysts." She pulled herself up tall, doing her best to ignore Chenzira's palpable presence. Aviama angled away from him as best she could as she turned to Ishaan.

She'd never seen him so openly fuming. He'd nearly cut off all blood supply in her arm. She cocked her head and offered a congenial smile. "I'm anxious to see my new room. You've kept these gentlemen from their posts long enough, don't you think?"

A blood vessel bobbed on Ishaan's temple, and his grip grew tighter still. He pursed his lips, spun toward Prince Chenzira, and gave a deep bow, tugging her down with him. "Prince Chenzira. Your assistance in keeping the princess safe is much appreciated. My apologies for keeping you. Good night."

Aviama stared hard at the floor. She could feel Chenzira's eyes on her, but couldn't hazard a guess what he was thinking. She only knew what she was thinking. *We had a deal.*

We had a deal, and I needed you, and you sealed my fate.

Chenzira had his own reasons for everything he did. He was not above blackmail, just as Shiva and Queen Satya were not above it, all of them using leverage to their own ends. Why would she think him any different than them?

Aviama swallowed hard against the lump forming in her throat, relieved when Ishaan finally pivoted and drew her along out of the room, down the hall, up the stairs, and down a new corridor leading away from the blue and white room. The two soldiers Ishaan brought with him followed wordlessly. Two doors down, Ishaan opened a door on the left, away from the courtyard and the luxurious guest rooms facing it.

He flung her inside.

The door swung shut, and the wind of its closing snuffed out a dying candle. Darkness closed in around her.

She was alone.

32

Night ensnared the room in blackness when Aviama woke. She had no memory of falling asleep. She remembered sinking to the floor and wrapping her arms around herself. She remembered crawling past a dusty wardrobe, jumping at its shadow before identifying it. And she remembered the emptiness in her midsection as her body racked with sobs on the cold floor under a window that refused to light the room.

The stars had forsaken their light, and the low rumble of thunder rolled across the heavens. An ache in her core overtook all her racing thoughts, and exhaustion set in. The last thing she remembered was the pitter-patter of rain just beginning to fall.

Something cold dripped down on her face and slipped down the nape of her neck. Aviama squeezed her eyes shut and shuddered. She reached a hand up to wipe another raindrop from her face, and opened one eye to squint up at the window set in the wall next to her.

Biscuits. The thing was open. So much for Radhan hospitality. Maybe the sheets were motheaten, too. Was there even a bed? Aviama hadn't remembered seeing one, but she hadn't exactly looked either. So far, her entire impression of the room was that it was cold, dark, and dusty.

Lightning split the sky, and a human silhouette stood out in the window against the flash. A thundercrack rocked the air, swallowing her scream as the man dropped from the second-floor window onto the floor of her new room. Aviama shrank back, and as the lightning vanished, so too did the man in her room.

Either the queen had sent someone to kill her, or Darsh had sent someone to kidnap her.

"If you could stop screaming at everything, that would be great."

The voice set her nerves on edge. Chenzira. Aviama untangled her legs and rose. *How long had she been sleeping? How long has the window been open?* Her dress was completely waterlogged, and she was soaked to the bone. She wrapped her arms tight around herself and jutted her chin out at him in the dark.

"You're the one who landed me here, so you can keep your mockery to yourself. Get out."

"Don't be bitter. I'd never have been able to get you out, not like that. You're lucky I was the one who got to you first. Now. You said you had information. I've come to collect."

A full body tremor rocked her head to toe, and she ran her hand up and down her arm to quell the goosebumps. "What did you find out about my guard? About Enzo?"

Chenzira stepped closer and dropped his voice into a low growl. "You first."

Aviama shook her head. "Not a chance. My leverage may be limited, but I do intend to use it."

He must realize she had little to lose. Besides, would he really spread a rumor of the two of them together if doing so put him on the chopping block beside her? Chenzira's value to her now was in trading information. His blackmail strategy was losing power.

A boom shattered the silence, and lightning lit the room in a flash. Chenzira stood closer than she expected, drenched to the skin in a tunic clinging to the lines of his upper body. The intensity of his glare might have intimidated her yesterday, but today she was too worn out to care.

The next moment plunged them back into darkness. Aviama clenched her teeth to keep them from chattering and took a breath. "If you're waiting for me to notice you're bigger and stronger than me, and capitulate, you should know that you are not the first person—or second, or third—to threaten me since my arrival."

Queen Satya held that honor first, followed by Ishaan, and most recently Prince Shiva himself.

A beat of silence followed, and Chenzira shifted in the dark. "I haven't had much time to look for your friend. I haven't got anything definitive."

Aviama crossed her arms. Not that he could see to appreciate it. "I've just been swimming in time, myself. Just twiddling my thumbs over here. That's why Shiva's decided to *marry* me, and I expected you were coming to kill me."

"He what? Wait, why would I kill you?"

"Not *you*, you." Aviama ran a hand over her face and wrung water out of her damp, matted tresses. "Just whatever strange man was dropping down through my left-open window in my new prison cell here. You don't know the half of my last few days here. You don't know what the queen—"

"The queen? What's she got to do with—"

Ugh. Too far. Stay on task. Aviama waved a hand and cut him off. "Never mind. Never mind all of it. Just tell me you found something."

"It's not conclusive. But he may be alive, yes. Rumor has it they came to kill your man, and he was gone. If you think the queen was involved, that may narrow my search. From the looks of it, your guy had help. Darsh's men, if I had to guess, or sympathizers. In any case, your man disappeared without a trace. I'll need more time to get you anything better than that."

Aviama blinked. She had to admit, she was impressed. It was far more than she could have expected with such little time. He must have set out to solve her mystery almost immediately after they struck a deal in the tunnel beneath the palace.

He was holding up his end of the bargain. Now it was her turn. It wasn't good news.

"Radha knows how to defeat our dragon in Jannemar and incapacitate all melders." She winced.

"What? How did—"

"Not important." It was actually likely extremely important, but the last thing Chenzira needed to know was that Aviama herself had ruined all melders and betrayed her own family and kingdom. Her chest tightened, and she cleared her throat. "Radha wants the Horon Mines from Jannemar. And he wants to use me and my knowledge to control magic. There's a substance he can use to identify melders. He'll be able to test anyone he wants."

Chenzira swore. "Konnolan."

Aviama winced at the word. She would hate it forevermore. How could she have been so stupid? How could she have trusted Shiva? A chill ran down her spine, and her chin quivered.

Suddenly, Chenzira's hand seized her arm in the night, and she gasped as he yanked her forward.

"Why is he so convinced you can help him control magic? What did you tell him?"

"I—"

"Does he know? Does he know about you?"

Bang.

Aviama jumped as the door to her cell of a room burst open and slammed against the wall. Ishaan filled the door-frame, the red-orange light of a swinging lantern casting an eerie pallor to his hateful features. His mouth twisted in a wicked sneer as he took in the sight of the two of them standing together, drenched in rain from the still-open window.

"I do hate to break up a lover's quarrel." Ishaan jerked his head to someone outside, and four soldiers filed into the darkness of her room. "Why don't we continue this conversation someplace more comfortable? I suggest the throne room of the king."

Aviama froze, and Chenzira dropped his hand from her shoulder. "It's not a lover's quarrel." But his words were no more than a mumble. After all, were conspiracy and treason really preferable to a forbidden tryst? The truth was even worse, and no other reasonable explanation offered itself.

Guards filed in and seized Aviama and Chenzira by the arms. Rain still leaked down the wall from the half-open window, and the chill air of night wafted in on a breeze just as lightning lit the sky once more. Satisfaction had never played so plainly in Ishaan's beady eyes as at that moment. Aviama pulled herself up tall as she passed him, a guard at each elbow hauling her over the threshold and back into the corridor.

Nothing but death could await them in the throne room. Breaking the conditions of the contest for Shiva's hand was an act of aggression, and the only way to prove she wasn't in love with Chenzira would be to admit she was a spy instead.

Brilliant.

But that wasn't even the end of her concerns. Chenzira's

final question rang over and over in her mind. *Does he know about you?*

Ishaan might not technically know, but he had to have his suspicions—suspicions the queen, Shiva, and Chenzira all seemed to share. What would they do when they found out she was a melder? Did they have konnolan already, or would they need to fetch some? Perhaps they would merely chop off her head and be done with it. As long as they didn't feed her to the queen's hyena...

She hoped Murin got out of the castle, but at this point, the best she could wish for was her lady-in-waiting letting her family know bits and pieces of what happened to her after she was dead. The journey from Jannemar to Radha had taken three months. And Murin had no connections, resources, or identification on the streets beyond the House of the Blessing Sun.

It was an ironic name. In Aviama's admittedly short-lived experience, the palace had brought only curses.

Ishaan marched his prize prisoners down the corridor and down the stairs, then through the palace back toward the butterfly pavilion, menagerie, and rooms of state. Chenzira strode with his guards after Ishaan as though it were his own idea that they move in this direction, and Aviama wished she could borrow his confidence. Did he have a bargaining chip she didn't know about, or was he just as likely to die tonight as she was?

Aviama stumbled on the slick marble, her wet feet tripping over sopping skirts and leaving a trail of excess water on the floor behind her. Her mouth went dry, and she fought against a wave of nausea in her gut and the lump in her throat. The next moment, against all reason, her stomach growled. She moved to clutch her stomach as though to silence it, but

Ishaan picked up the pace, and her feet briefly left the floor as the guards dragged her along to match his pace.

Double doors with gilded pakshi-head door handles shone in the light of torches along the wall as they approached the throne room. Two men stood sentry on either side, snapping to attention at the sight of them. The man on the right sidestepped in front of the door, blocking their progress, and scanned their group.

"What is the meaning of this?"

"We come for an audience together with His Majesty the king and Her Majesty the queen."

The sentry's eyes narrowed. "I'll not be responsible for disturbing the king at this hour. Wait until morning."

Ishaan arched an eyebrow as if meetings of this nature were commonplace in the middle of the night. "If the kingdom required your intelligence, Gaurik, you wouldn't be posted outside an empty room all night. Wake them up."

33

The sentry's upper lip twitched in the slightest hint of a snarl before he turned on his heel and disappeared inside the double doors of the throne room. Chenzira stood with his two guards on one side, Aviama and her two guards on the other, as the remaining sentry awkwardly supervised Ishaan and his charges in the hall.

Aviama shifted her weight and tried to remind herself to breathe, but adrenaline shot through her body like a powder keg ready to blow. She gritted her teeth to keep from trembling and steeled herself against the cool of the night as it wafted over her wet hair and clothes. Torchlight tossed flickering orange and yellow light across an entryway dressed in the colors of the sunrise, a gradient of ornate patterns burning brighter and brighter and culminating in the glinting gold of the double doors.

Chenzira passed her a sideways glance just as a shiver danced down her spine. His arm twitched, but he looked away and said nothing. Aviama swallowed and followed suit, her gaze landing on Ishaan's foreboding glare.

A metallic sound interrupted Ishaan's derision as the

double doors swung on their hinges and opened wide. Never would she have thought the herald of her death would bring her such relief. Aviama let out a breath and willingly fled his unflinching glower as the guards at her arms tugged her forward.

Did the man even blink? When had he last slept? Surely lack of sleep would do nothing to improve his murderous demeanor.

A thin skylight ran the length of the vaulted ceiling beyond the doors, red ornamental carpets spilling down its center to break up the pure white of the floors. Gold filigree climbed up the columns, archways, and ceilings of the entire space, and three thrones set with luxurious crimson cushioning commanded attention from a dais at the far end. Smaller cushioned chairs lined the sides of the aisle down from the dais, presumably for members of court. Uninformed, sleeping, lucky nobles.

A single, enormous chandelier hung from the ceiling, where the glass skylight would pour sunshine down on the pieces like prisms, scattering a thousand rainbows across the room. But now, all the elegance and glory of the room carried a solemn ghostly air as thunder cracked overhead and heavy rain pelted the ceiling high above. Lightning doused them in light and was gone, leaving them once again to the dimness of torches lining the aisle.

Aviama's throat constricted as she walked, her feet still bare from kicking her shoes off in the service hall earlier that night. She hardly dared guess what the rest of her looked like.

Two doors slammed at the far end of the room, and the king and queen strode into the room from opposite directions, meeting on the dais and taking their seats. The king's throne was taller, more deeply ornamented, and sported carved pakshi on the armrests. The queen occupied the throne to his left, and the throne to the right sat empty.

King Dahnuk surveyed the scene before him and ran a hand over his face. It wouldn't take a genius to deduct the nature of the night's impromptu meeting. Princess Aviama of Jannemar and Prince Chenzira of Keket had met together in secret. As if their coffins needed any additional nails, they were the only two figures assembled who were drenched in rain like drowned rats.

The king gestured at the prisoners and turned to Ishaan. "What is this?"

"Isn't it obvious?" Queen Satya perched on the edge of her throne, knuckles white as her nails dug into the gilded patterns. Embroidered yellow draped her small frame, but her face was left unpainted in the haste of her summoning. Satya bore the kind of beauty one could hardly look away from, but never wanted to quite look at directly—for fear she might smite a person down over a sneeze.

Her eyes blazed, and she jabbed an accusing finger at Aviama's chest. "I told you, didn't I, my love? I told you they were together. I told you they would turn on us."

Dahnuk frowned, then jerked his chin at Ishaan. "Well?"

Ishaan bowed low, almost comically so after the curt head nods and blatant disrespect Aviama had become accustomed to from him. "Your illustrious Majesty, Her Majesty is correct. After His Royal Highness Prince Shiva met with Princess Aviama tonight, Princess Aviama ran through the palace like a stray cat with its tail on fire. She ran from me, blockaded a door, and rendezvoused with Prince Chenzira unsupervised in the dead of night. We found her in his arms, Your Majesty."

Aviama was going to be sick. Who would spin a more favorable tale of the evening's events? They had more than they needed to kill Aviama and wage war on Jannemar as it was. Or, if not kill her, keep her alive long enough to taunt her brother and draw him out before launching their offensive.

The king tapped his fingers along the armrest of his throne. "So. This is why you awakened me from slumber and brought them here for judgment, without waiting until morning."

"Your Majesty, if they had been caught only once, I would have waited to confirm suspicions, searching out the matter completely. But I'm afraid there is more." Ishaan licked his lips. "Not only have they been seen together before tonight, but after the incident of this evening, we moved the princess to a more secure room to ensure her safety. Only a select few individuals knew about the change beforehand, Your Majesty. Mere hours later, they were together again, Prince Chenzira braving the storm and circumventing locked doors and guards to get to her."

A foreign prince, stealing into her bedchamber in the middle of the night. Through a second-story window, no less. Aviama wondered for the first time how he'd managed it.

But if a love affair set the nails in her coffin, espionage would blow it to smithereens. At what point should she confess to the lie to preserve the truth? Did it even matter anymore, if she was going to die anyway?

"The Jannemari princess has broken the contest agreement, and the Keket prince has betrayed our trust." Queen Satya shook her head, eyeing Aviama like a crow might watch a bread crumb. It was only a matter of time before the crumb was gobbled up. Satya laid a hand on her husband's arm. "They must both be dealt with according to our traditions. Treason, Your Majesty. The pit, for her. Something more private for him—we have a relationship with his father, after all."

Panic leaped from Aviama's stomach and wound up to her

throat to strangle her. A curl of wind snaked through her fingers, and she clenched her hands into fists to quell the power pooling in her palms. *Don't make it worse.* But could it *get* worse?

WHAM.

Aviama snapped her head toward the sound as Prince Shiva swept into the throne room with all the power and pomp of a beast who knew no predator. Those piercing umber eyes she'd once found enchanting now struck dread to her core. His gaze landed on her and lingered, soaking in the fear radiating off her in waves.

She fought the urge to bite her lip and looked away.

Be royal. Be arrogant like Avaya, regal like Mother, confident like Semra. Just—don't be you.

Aviama straightened and stared forward at a particular swirl on the foot of Dahnuk's throne. *If you die, you die a princess. Not a scolded dog.* She lifted her chin.

Shiva stormed up the dais. "Why was I not invited to a meeting regarding my fiancée?"

Aviama nearly choked at the word, and the king and queen's eyes bulged. Satya leaped to her feet. "Your *what*?!"

Dahnuk sighed. "Welcome, son. Your mother was just offering me execution suggestions."

"And none of you thought I should be privy to matters I am critically involved in?" Shiva bored his parents with a cold stare, as if he were the adult and they, misbehaving chil-dren. "Father, did you not tell me—*require* me, in fact—to sit beside you to hear and consult on all relevant matters of reign?"

"Relevant matters under your purview," the king corrected.

Shiva swept an arm in Aviama's direction. "She's my fiancée."

Dahnuk slammed a fist on the arm of his chair. "She's

nothing of the sort. Not without my signoff. Last I checked, King Dahnuk Tanashai, not Shiva, sat on the Blessed Throne."

The Radhan prince clasped his hands behind his back as though preparing to launch into a treatise on routine subjects of governance. "I have information to share, Father. And by the time I'm done, you will gratefully throw this woman into my arms and sing my praises."

Dahnuk pursed his lips, his eyes darkening as he glanced Aviama's way. "I doubt that very much."

Her mouth went dry. She swallowed, but said nothing. What was he doing?

Shiva jutted his chin at the guards at Aviama's sides. "Release my bride."

They hesitated, but the king rolled his eyes and waved them off. They let go of her and stepped back. Shiva descended the stairs of the dais and crossed the carpeted floor, leaving Chenzira in the hold of his guards and ignoring Ishaan entirely.

Aviama stiffened as he approached, the memory of the taste of his mouth and the unyielding manipulation of his strength churning bile in her stomach. Was it only earlier that evening she had found him with Marija, and he had chased her down to extract her kingdom's secrets? Was it only tonight that she herself had set the trap bringing him to her, and he'd caught her in her own web?

She could feel the heat of every eye on her, the king and queen from the dais, Ishaan from its foot, and Chenzira and the guards from mere paces away. Shiva flashed her a smile, wrapped an arm around her waist, and kissed her.

Every muscle shut down, and she barely breathed. Her feet were glued to the floor, her chest heaving with the exertion of doing nothing. Her mind begged escape. *This isn't real, he isn't here, this isn't real, this isn't real.*

But it was real. And his kiss was as dangerous as a knife to the throat. She dared not move. Not here.

Shiva pulled away, and she clenched her jaw. A tear slipped down her cheek, and he shielded her body from his parents to wipe it away with his thumb. Shiva leaned in, commanding her attention, and dropping his tone low for only her to hear. "You're weak. Jannemar is vulnerable. And konnolan can take out your dragon and all your melderbloods. You are defenseless." Shiva kissed her again. "So be good. Because only I can save you."

34

Numbness threatened to take over as Shiva turned back to the dais. Aviama blinked back tears and leaned into the embers of anger broiling in her belly. It might not be wise, but the whisper of rage sending fury through her blood was the only grounding reality that could hold her.

Terror would send her over the edge. Power would rip the room apart. But if she could control her anger, perhaps it could keep the sadness from sweeping her away. Perhaps it could give her strength, if only for this moment.

Shiva's silky voice began to spin, and Aviama nearly blanched at the sound of it.

"In your wisdom, my dear Mother and Father, you have selected four women to be the potential face of a new alliance with Radha. Each union option offers new strength to the kingdom, hope for the people in the uncertain era of The Return. Their crown prince will secure the stability of the Tanashai line through heirs to the throne, and our power and influence over our neighbors only grows."

Shiva paced to his right, paused for effect, and turned.

"Vanina is unique, interesting, and strong, but Batal is untrustworthy and too protected. Tensions continue to rise, and they cut underhanded deals. How are we to know this lifelong investment would pay off? That they wouldn't cut Vanina off and end all trade agreements at the first sign of struggle? She's uncouth and wild. I don't need a feral thing as a wife, much less one without significant reparations in the form of resources for Radha. And Radha must command respect. Vanina will not do that."

"Darra is a perfectly acceptable option. Our relationship with Curion will be strengthened, our access to—" Satya pressed her lips together and sat. She'd said more than she meant to, in the presence of her enemies. "Darra is the ideal choice. We've discussed this."

Shiva shook his head. "Everything we want from them we can get without a marriage."

The king leaned forward. "And Marija?"

"I don't want Marija." The Radhan prince folded his arms. "And she lacks the advantages Aviama can provide."

Advantages. Like Aviama's continued betrayal of her family, with a knife to her throat for information. Like the appearance of peace, for an easy approach to an unsuspecting victim as the hammer swung down to crush Jannemar, take its mines, and destroy its melders.

He'd thought it all through, like a man at an auction analyzing cattle. No action, no breath was breathed without an ulterior motive. Without serving his agenda. Without gaining him power. Aviama glared at him. He caught her eye and arched an eyebrow. *Only I can save you.*

She masked a grimace and smoothed her expression into what she hoped was a cool indifference.

His voice in the room of the stars replayed in her mind, the feel of his grip on her arms creeping up her skin like spiders. *I have both vision and money, in spades.*

Well, that was for certain. But she had a reservoir of her own. What did she have in spades but fear, anger, and a resolve to set to rights the threat she'd allowed on her people?

A shift burned in her chest then. Anger gave her the strength to keep fear from running away with her completely, but it was purpose that would drive her now. Purpose could keep her head on her shoulders.

She would not let Radha destroy Jannemar. She wouldn't let them kill Zephan, Semra, and the home she loved. She wouldn't let them wipe melders from the land of the living.

Aviama might be dead by morning. But she wasn't dead yet. And she'd spend her last moments scheming freedom for her family and her people.

King Dahnuk leaned back against the crimson cushion of his chair. "I really don't think this is the time to debate the matter."

"Really? I thought the timing appropriate." Shiva spread his hands. "Debating the point after you let Mother kill her hardly seems practical."

The king's eyes darkened, and Aviama's blood went cold. There was more in his statement than mere words let on. Was she now to be a pawn not only to steal her kingdom, but to manipulate Shiva's family dynamics?

Queen Satya turned from her son to look full in her husband's face. "My love, if we do not follow through on the rules of the contest, we shall be the laughingstock of our neighbors. We will lose all respect, all leverage. Darra is easy to control, she's beautiful, she's pure-blooded. Trade will flourish, and she is good for the family line."

Aviama grimaced. Ah, yes. The breeding mare would pop out the desired number of babies, hamstring her relatives through a union with a power-mongering kingdom, and buckle under the queen's blackmail. But most importantly, she wasn't melderblood.

Was it all the woman cared about?

That, and power. Perhaps, in the queen's mind, that's what melders threatened to take from her.

Dahnuk considered his wife for a long moment, then turned to Shiva. "Your so-called fiancée was caught in the arms of another man not once, but twice, only tonight, and you insist she will be a worthwhile investment?"

Shiva walked back across the carpet toward Aviama. He lifted her hand and glanced at his father as if raising a glass for a toast. *See? Look what I can do. Look what she* lets *me do.*

But there was no *let.* Not with his foot essentially on her neck. Aviama's jaw clenched, and briefly the metallic taste of copper distracted her. She must've bitten the inside of her lip hard enough to draw blood.

Shiva kissed her knuckles, and she looked away—her gaze landing directly on Chenzira, still held by two guards only several paces away. He looked a different man than the one she'd first seen glaring up at her from the courtyard as she stood on the balcony that first day. She'd seen him brooding, teasing, mocking, even threatening as he made his demands in the king's private office and its connected underground tunnel.

But whatever possessed him now was something else entirely. Chenzira jerked once in the arms of his captors, then stilled, his eyes wild.

Aviama's heart battered her chest. She dropped her gaze to the floor, then back up at Shiva, letting all the hate seething in her stomach funnel into him. Shiva winked, and her jaw dropped.

Dahnuk pinched his chin, observing the situation with interest. "What do you propose we do about the Keket boy?"

Shiva shrugged. "Kill him."

Chenzira broke free from his guards and swung. Aviama hardly registered what was happening before Chenzira's large fist crashed into Shiva's jaw, knocking him backward. Satya started screaming, and the king bellowed something as four guards fell on their crown prince's attacker and ripped him backward.

Shiva stumbled back several paces, collected himself, and straightened. He stared at Chenzira, then wiped blood off his chin and cocked his head. "Turns out you're as useless as your father."

The Keket prince smirked. "I don't care. I've wanted to do that for three years."

That was the Chenzira she recognized. Not that she even knew the man, really. But had he really been in Radha for three *years*? What had he been doing all that time? Whatever it was, it had only taken her being there a few days to dismantle it completely. Her gut wrenched.

King Dahnuk shook his head. His face reddened, and his lips drew taut. "I'm disappointed in you, Your Highness. I had hoped for a partnership. Alas, now no one will learn what happened to the lost prince of the island nation."

Queen Satya crossed her legs. "He needs to die for treason, for attempted murder, and for—for meddling. For—"

"Dearest, if meddling was a crime, you'd have been locked away decades ago." Dahnuk patted his queen's hand, and she snatched it away.

"—For daring to *tamper* with international matters of state and allegiances that could impact our relations with Keket and—"

"Yes, yes." Dahnuk waved her off. "He will die. Perhaps I'll even select a method of your choosing, if that would make you happy."

"It's not enough. This is not a joke. You swore *aggressive* action against any contestant who broke the rules! Against any contestant who entertained a lover!" Satya stabbed a long, slender finger in Aviama's direction again. "She must pay!"

Shiva leaped up the stairs of the dais. "That would undermine all that we—"

"Silence!" Dahnuk leveled his wife and his son with a withering glare. Satya opened her mouth, but he held up a hand, and she closed it again. Dahnuk turned to his prisoners and guards on the floor. "Pardon our friendly debate over your fates. Our family values passion above all else. Do excuse us."

35

Aviama blinked back at them as the king ushered his family off the dais and out of the throne room without another word, leaving Aviama and Chenzira with the guards, under Ishaan's watchful sneer and the flickering of the torches. The flurry of rushing footsteps ended as a door opened and closed, and the Tanashai family hid away to privately debate how to kill them.

Aviama shifted her weight, standing on one foot to scratch an itch on her ankle beneath her skirts with the other. She spun the rings on her fingers and bit her lip.

"Are they never going to ask us what happened?"

All the guards' heads swiveled toward her as one, and Chenzira snapped his head up in surprise. It was the first time Aviama had spoken since entering the throne room.

"What happened doesn't matter. All that matters is how paranoid they are, and what they *want* to have happened. Whichever narrative best serves their purposes now."

"Enough." Ishaan cut him a cold glare. "The next person to utter a single word in this room will spend the remainder of our time here with their face under my boot."

Chenzira's brows soared in mock concern, but he resigned himself to silence nonetheless. Aviama ran her hands up and down her arms to keep warm, and wrung out the edges of her damp hair onto the carpet.

Ishaan bored daggers into her skull for daring to drip water on the carpet. She nearly stuck her tongue out at him in response. But before she could decide on an acceptable alternative, the doors opened, and the king, queen, and crown prince of Radha returned to the dais and took their seats.

Shiva leaned on the arm of his throne, eyes hard, avoiding looking at his father. Queen Satya pursed her lips on the king's other side. *Some meeting,* Aviama thought.

King Dahnuk tented his fingers and peered down his sharp nose at her. "Princess Aviama. Did Prince Shiva ever ask you to marry him?"

Was he serious? Was the king still pretending anything about the arrangement was voluntary? Or did his son not tell him a single thing about his plans?

Aviama shot Shiva a look, which he ignored. She looked back at the king and cleared her throat. "*Ask* is not the word I would use, Your Majesty."

"What word would you use?"

"Ordered. Commanded. Coerced."

Queen Satya's body tensed, and she clenched her jaw. Aviama tried not to imagine her enormous hyena ripping her to shreds. If she could deal directly with the king, perhaps she could circumvent the queen.

Dahnuk's eyes narrowed. The resemblance between father and son, sitting stone-faced on thrones beside each other, was uncanny.

"And in light of such coercion, did you agree to marry him?"

Aviama hesitated. "No."

The queen drew in a sharp breath, and Shiva edged to the end of his seat.

But the king was inscrutable.

"What is your relationship with Prince Chenzira?"

Aviama's lips parted, but no sound came. Beside her, Chenzira stared straight ahead as if his very gaze might burn a hole in the throne room that he could crawl into and escape through. To her left, Ishaan's mouth twisted into a hideous pretentious smile.

It was sink or swim, but she was already sinking. Her mouth went dry.

And then out of nowhere, a crazy idea dropped into her brain. Aviama rolled her shoulders back and leveled her voice with more confidence than she felt. "He's a visiting dignitary I have met several times in passing."

Satya snorted. "Are you really going to tell me you aren't in love with him? After we've literally found you in his arms twice this very night?"

Chenzira shifted uncomfortably beside her. He could only assume she'd lost her mind.

Aviama spread her hands. "In the first incident, I was running from Ishaan. I'd grown tired of looking at his face after my only comfort and safety in a new place was taken from me, my personal guard replaced with *him*."

She jerked her chin in his direction, and his smirk soured. Aviama continued. "Ishaan was shouting for help in the dead of night—you know, the sort of screams one wants when maintaining a low profile and trying to preserve appearances at the palace."

The king frowned, and her stomach dropped. *Too far.*

Aviama hurried on. "It was my understanding that Chenzira heard said screams and came to assist in apprehending me. Which he did. And I can tell you with all sincerity that the interaction did nothing to spark loving feelings." This last bit she said with a pointed look in Chenzira's direction.

He rolled his eyes.

The king rapped his knuckles on the arm of his throne, deep in thought.

Aviama held her breath.

It was a good start. Only a little more, and her explanation would be complete. Maybe even a good one. A hopeful confidence wormed its way into her heart, a sprig exposed to its first rain.

Queen Satya's eyes sparked with triumph, that same victorious one she'd seen on Shiva when he learned about the konnolan. Satya cocked her head. "You say you do not know him, yet you call him by his first name."

The sprig wilted.

Chenzira's shoulders sagged just a hair. Apparently, she'd managed to kill any hope he'd had, too. She blurted the first thing that came to mind. "*Prince* doesn't quite seem to fit, does it? The man abandoned his kingdom. Prince of what, exactly? Do we know he's not been stripped of his title?"

Aviama tossed a haughty look in Chenzira's direction. She was putting on a show for the Radhans, but he looked like he'd been stabbed. Guilt gripped her, but when she realized she had to twist the blade, she thought she might drown in it.

The king laughed. "You seem to have seen his true colors sooner than we did."

Shiva's jaw clenched.

Chenzira's lip twitched into a shadow of a snarl.

The queen scowled. "And the second time you were caught together? The one that brings you before us bedraggled and ridiculous?"

"After being tossed like a sack of potatoes into what appeared to be a dark, rejected corner of the guest wing, a strange man dropping in through the window was the last thing I expected." That wasn't quite true, of course. She had in fact expected someone might come to murder her before the sun was up, but there was no use mentioning *that*.

Aviama folded her hands and twisted her rings. "But he seemed as shocked as I when he slipped through. I had fallen asleep, and the rain was coming through the window. It was already coming down hard when the cold of it woke me up, and I discovered the *prince* in my room."

She leaned forward as if telling the juiciest of secrets. "I believe he was indeed there for some romantic rendezvous. Just not with me. Has that room been used regularly for anything, or is it largely ignored?"

The royals on the dais exchanged glances. A glorious sensation burgeoned in her chest at her success. They hadn't thought of that.

Neither had she, until two minutes ago. And the longer she thought about it, the more brilliant her solution became. In one fell swoop, Aviama had saved Chenzira and herself, even making Ishaan look stupid as the cherry on top.

If Chenzira was sneaking around with some other woman, as many of the men of court presumably did, there was no harm done. Not to the Tanashais, anyway. And if Aviama had no romantic attachments, she was only guilty of refusing their crown prince.

And running from Ishaan.

Dahnuk's head swiveled to Chenzira. "Well?"

Chenzira swore under his breath, and if Aviama hadn't come up with the lie herself she would have believed his confirmation of it. "It is as she says. I've promised to protect the identity of the, er, lady in question. But it's no one of consequence."

"Convenient." The corners of the king's mouth tugged downward. "And your relationship with Princess Aviama?"

The man drew back as if the mere imagining of them together sent knives through his eyes. "An unfortunate reoccurrence as our paths cross, nothing more. With no offense meant to His Highness's tastes, of course."

Aviama's face flushed hot, and her ring snagged on her dress. She yanked it free and set her jaw. When she returned her gaze to the dais, Shiva's dark eyes glinted at her in the dim torchlight.

"Princess Aviama."

She flinched at the bite in the king's tone, but turned to face him.

"Will you marry Prince Shiva?"

Aviama's chest tightened, and her throat closed. The man himself never asked, so his father was asking for him? Asking whether she would bind herself to the destruction of her people, to a person who relied on threats, blackmail, and lies as the foundation for a lifelong sham of a marriage.

Asking whether she would throw her life away...

The faithless silk of his voice, the calculated guile of the game he'd played with her filed through her mind in snatch after snatch of memory. How could she have learned to despise someone so much in so short a time?

The iron of his grip on the terrace. *I will not be made a fool of.*

His nodding in agreement as his father set the plan for dealing with Darsh and his melders. *Kill them all.*

The stone of his eyes and the cage of his arms as he forced her toward him in the room under the stars. *Wives should be like housing artifacts. Beautiful, useful, strategic.*

His despicable kiss in this very room, when her body shut

down and abandoned her. *You're weak. Jannemar is vulnerable. You are defenseless. Only I can save you.*

Even his positioning at this instance, lounging on his throne as he analyzed her, a dark, bitter brooding clinging to him like moths to a flame.

Her skin crawled just thinking about spending a lifetime with those eyes.

The king leaned forward, and his voice pulled her back from her thoughts. "Your Highness?"

"I am not a housing artifact." A lump lodged in her throat. She raised her eyes to meet the king, pushing through the burning ache to say what she now felt compelled to say. She hadn't felt she could say something then, in the frozen terror of the dark room with Shiva.

But she would say something now. Aviama stepped forward. "I am not a bargaining chip. I know princesses often are exactly that and little else, but Jannemar does things differently. And as the birthplace of the magic Radha so desperately fears, you might consider taking notes. Jannemar is *not* defenseless. There is no single tool that could dismantle that great kingdom. Even if that tool, in your eyes, is me."

Queen Satya threw her hands up. "Your answer, girl!"

Whatever the consequences, whatever the cost, there had to be another way. She'd make things right. Somehow.

But not like this.

Aviama steeled herself and looked Satya dead in the face. "No."

The queen's face turned beet red, and Shiva jumped to his feet. Aviama flinched backward at his movement, but recovered as the king threw out a hand to stop him from whatever he'd intended.

Satya's voice ticked up to a shrill pitch. "If you do not

marry Shiva, we will kill Prince Chenzira. What do you say to that?"

Aviama pursed her lips. *I thought it was over your dead body that I would marry your son.* But the queen would never admit it. Not here.

Was her only tactic to threaten to kill people? Enzo, Aviama herself, and now Chenzira? Then again, death was probably a decent motivator for most.

Perhaps she was bluffing.

Aviama shook her head. "Only this, that it is imprudent to kill any royal without due cause. And you have none."

King Dahnuk regarded her with something between anger and interest. For a fleeting second, she thought maybe he would let her go, but the words he spoke next dashed all hope to pieces.

"Nevertheless, this is the choice before you. You will marry my son, and save the dignitary with whom you are on familiar enough terms for first names—or not, and he will die, and you also will die, in the manner we deem most fitting. If you choose to marry Prince Shiva, you will also agree to the responsibilities assigned to you in that role and swear on the graves of your parents to behave. If you reject us, the stench of konnolan will so fill your homeland that every melderblood chokes on it, and they will curse you as they die."

Dahnuk gave a signal, and the guards stepped forward and took hold of her once again.

"You have until morning."

36

The guards dragged them from the room and marched them down a familiar hall. Sentries opened the main doors to the menagerie, and Aviama realized she'd never actually entered it through those doors. She wasn't supposed to have ever been in there. Had Shiva told his parents about his little rebellion taking her there?

The tingling feeling of the magna suppressing her tabeun powers ran along her skin as she crossed the threshold. Two guards led the way with torches, bathing the floor before them in orange and yellow. Aviama caught glimpses of beady eyes and snatches of fur or feathers, twigs or hay as they passed. Monkeys screeched, and a zegrath gave a shrieking roar at their disturbance. The glorybird of paradise raised her head from underneath her wing and fluttered to the far side of her enclosure.

A cage had been cleared out on the left side, across from the mermaid. On one side, all four of the zegrath's ears swiveled toward them. Its hackles raised like a thousand spears, and a rumble emanated from a deep, muscled chest. Aviama looked away, but the sight on the other side sent a chill down her spine. Two ciraba monitors lay curled in the corner. Their monstrous talons reminded her of Semra's dragon Zezura. One of them opened slitted eyes to take her in, snapping its jaw at her with a hollow clap that sent her mind reeling in memories of the pit.

Darsh. Coarse sand. Teeth, scales, eyes. Aviama shuddered.

The guards threw Aviama and Chenzira into the empty cage between the zegrath and the cirabas and shut the door with a clang, then they receded back down the hall of the menagerie, and the double doors swung shut, taking the light of their torches with them. The scraping and shifting of beasts she could not see set her teeth on edge, and she shrank back against the stone wall. Aviama's bare feet touched something gooey, and she yelped. She shifted over a step and sank to the floor. Her stomach grumbled.

"Why the menagerie? Why not the dungeon?"

Chenzira ran his hands along the bars, tapping and shaking them one by one. She didn't bother guessing what he thought he'd find. "You're a melder."

"Stop saying that."

"You've never denied it."

"Why are you so sure I am?"

Chenzira laughed. A hollow, mirthless sound. "I'm not an idiot. And there's no way you got up over your balcony by yourself. You're not particularly strong, and you don't strike me as agile."

Aviama scowled. He was right on all counts, of course. But did he have to *say* it? She looked away.

You asked, dummy. Right. Biscuits. She folded her arms.

"They said we have until morning, but it's got to be almost sunrise by now. That's not very long."

Chenzira rattled another cell bar, and a thud told her he'd thrown his weight against it. "I'm sure Dahnuk feels no obligation to meet your expectations. He'll get us when he feels like it, and not a moment before."

The bite in his tone took her aback. Aviama's throat constricted, and the air grew stale around them. "You're mad at me."

"I'm not."

Aviama bit her lip and stared down at her fingers in the darkness. She plucked at her damp skirts.

"You are. And I think it's stupid. Because I haven't done anything to you. You're the one who shows up everywhere I go, mocking me, threatening me. All I did to you was save your rear end just now with a lie that makes sense. You're welcome, by the way."

Chenzira groaned. "Not everything in the world is about you. Maybe I'm mad that I'm in here at all."

Aviama ran a hand up and down her throat, but the pain there did not ease. She blinked back tears and set her head back against the wall. Was she as selfish as he thought she was? Maybe. Maybe years of being catered to as a princess had ruined her. *Or maybe you're mad at me.*

But why should she care? If he wanted to be unreasonable, he could be unreasonable by himself. After all, they'd probably both be dead soon anyway. Did she really want to spend her last moments squabbling with a stranger?

Chenzira struck the bars. She flinched, and a squawk and furious chittering rolled down the menagerie. A ripple of water mixed with the rattle of a cage door. Two minutes passed, and the animals resettled. Chenzira let out a huff.

"Maybe I'm mad because I've been in Radha for four years

now. *Four years.* I set up connections for myself, came up with a plan, and came to the palace three years ago as a royal prince on the run." He paused and sank down against the bars opposite her. "They gobbled up my story, and I was doing just fine before you came along. No one suspected me. But then *you* show up, and years of work spin out of control in the blink of an eye. So yes. Maybe I'm mad at you. Maybe I have a right to be. You've ruined everything."

Aviama pressed her lips together. Her stomach hardened, and she swallowed. "Maybe you got sloppy. No need to blame me for your problems. I didn't tell you to crawl through a second-story window."

The gray of early morning shifted down from behind dark clouds, lifting the menagerie from the deepest dark of night as soft rays flitted in through thin windows at the ceilings. Chenzira twisted away from her, hiding his face, and plucked at a piece of straw on the floor.

"If you didn't want to know, you shouldn't have asked. I didn't *have* any of these problems before you. I'll stop blaming you when you stop making my life miserable."

The timing was unfortunate, she had to admit. But how was she supposed to know he would be here in Radha? How was she supposed to know he would be snooping in the king's private office, or would catch her when she ran from Ishaan, or would break into her bedchamber? She'd never given his existence more than a passing thought before coming to Radha. How could she already be ruining his life?

A new thought crossed her mind, and she glanced up at him. "Is it because of what I said? In the throne room, I mean. I didn't mean it. I don't even know you. I only said the first thing that came to mind to get us out of there."

His fingers stilled on the straw he was dismantling. Then he ripped it to shreds and tossed it through the bars. "It doesn't matter. You were right." Chenzira took a breath, and she had to strain to hear his next words. "I did abandon them."

Aviama winced, and a pit formed in her stomach. Her fingers found the edges of the rings on her opposite hand, tracing the lines of the gemstones and their settings. Whatever he'd done, it couldn't have been as bad as betraying her family, home, and all melders by handing Shiva the key to destroying them all. She was the real villain. Her throat constricted, and she swallowed.

"Aren't you're supposed to be telling me to marry Shiva so you don't die?"

He turned from the bars to meet her gaze. "I won't be telling you to do anything."

"That's why they put us together. For you to convince me to do what they want."

Chenzira shrugged. "It's not my life."

Aviama cocked her head. "It *is* your life. Literally. Your life is at stake."

The man before her sighed and stretched out his legs. "They've threatened me with death, not a lifetime with a pig. It's not the same."

"I see," she said, though she didn't. "I suppose I should just let them kill you, then."

"Maybe you should."

Aviama stared at him, and he looked away. What was she supposed to do with that? Where was the fire she'd seen in him all this time? And most importantly, why wouldn't he *help* her think of a way through the mess they'd found themselves in?

The dim gray lifted around them under a dusty morning sun, light particles dancing in the rays falling from the windows along the ceiling. Animals shifted as they woke, pawing at each other, leaping up the sides of their cages, or crawling under a rock to pretend the morning had not come. Aviama wished she could do that. Her time was almost up.

Aviama shook her head. "I can't marry him. But I can't *not* marry him, either, can I?"

Chenzira ran a hand over his face. "You strike me as someone who causes trouble. People who cause trouble get killed. If it's not today, it'll be tomorrow."

Aviama glared at him. "This was precisely the ray of sunshine I've been hoping for. Thanks. You really gave me confidence in my decisions."

"Happy to help."

"I was being facetious."

"So was I."

Aviama groaned.

Chenzira rotated to face her and leaned back against the bars, examining her with genuine interest for the first time since they'd been deposited in the menagerie.

"How did you get into the king's office? It's been driving me crazy."

Aviama grinned. "I'm a melder. Obviously."

He laughed then, and the warmth of it made her glad she'd told him. Chenzira picked up a fresh piece of straw. "All that hedging just to tell me now? Is it because I looked all pathetic and sad?"

The corners of her mouth tipped up, and she shook her head. "It wasn't pathetic. And I just think we have more in common than I first realized. Not to mention sharing this lovely guest room." She gestured at the cage around them.

"I see." He fought a smile. "So how did you get in?"

"The window by the trolls doesn't have any bars. I unlocked the troll door through the window with my hand outside the menagerie and the reach of the magna, then fell through. I picked the lock at the door."

"Yes, I heard that part. You're terrible at it." Chenzira eyed her. "Windcaller?"

Aviama gave a short nod.

Chenzira slapped his knee. "I knew it! You used it in the pit, and got away with it because Darsh is a windcaller too. They thought it was him." He took her in for a long moment. "Maybe you're not a complete moron."

"Thanks ever so much." She tried to look offended, but couldn't help the smile that crept over her face.

"Why'd you run last night? Shiva demanded you marry him, and you just sprinted out of there? How did you think that would end?"

Aviama pursed her lips. "I won't tell all my secrets at once. I've told too many to the wrong people as it is."

Murin needed as big of a head start as possible. She wouldn't tell a soul until she was sure her lady-in-waiting had made it off the palace grounds.

Chenzira's lips parted. "The earring. The guard tried to give it back to you, and you didn't want it. You knew you'd get caught, and you ran anyway."

Aviama looked away. If Chenzira could read her so easily, Ishaan probably could too. Murin might already be dead.

Or maybe she'd had just enough time to slip out before they realized what had happened...

Aviama bit her lip, released it, and stared down at her lap. She turned the rings on her fingers. *Get home, Murin. Get home safe.*

She wiped a tear from her face and looked back up at Chenzira. "It's my fault they know about konnolan. It's my fault they're going to invade Jannemar. They've got far more resources than we have, and their navy is unmatched. I think I killed my family last night."

Chenzira gaped at her.

She clenched her jaw and swallowed hard against the lump lodging in her throat. *He hates me. He should. I deserve whatever's coming.*

The creak of metal hinges pulled her attention to the front of the room as the double doors to the menagerie opened.

The wait was over.

37

Half a dozen soldiers accompanied King Dahnuk, Queen Satya, and Prince Shiva into the menagerie.

Chenzira launched upright. He twisted back toward Aviama and kept his voice down. "Don't do anything stupid."

"That ship has sailed," she mumbled. He shot her a look, but she ignored it as she unfolded her legs and scrambled to her feet.

The king marched down the corridor, scattering a colorful school of fish in the aquarium across the aisle as he neared them. A flash of silver caught Aviama's eye, and the mermaid who had tried to choke her to death popped up with her elbows on the edge of her watery habitat to watch the show. Regrettably, she remained a safe distance away and held no seaweed. Such a shame she wouldn't use her skills for good.

Dahnuk came to a stop in front of Chenzira and Aviama's barred cell, set his feet a shoulder's width apart, and crossed his arms. "My son would like the chance to marry you. My wife would like the chance to kill you. Neither of them seems to care much about the truth of what happened last night. But I do."

Shiva folded one arm across his body and pinched his chin with the other, observing them as if estimating the value of a misbehaving stallion. He stood just behind his father's right elbow, maintaining his appropriate station by a hair. Queen Satya carried a gem-studded goblet, and swirled the liquid twice before taking a sip. As bored as she looked to be there, Aviama guessed she had demanded to be present.

Aviama took them in at a glance, and placed herself two paces down from Chenzira—not so close as to look like she required his comfort, but not so far to the edge that she aroused the interest of the ciraba.

"You came for a contest, and a contest you shall have." Dahnuk clasped his hands behind his back and paced the length of the short cage. "We shall treat our guests to an unprecedented display of the menagerie like none have seen before. We will not have just one remarkable beast facing off with a single criminal. Instead, we shall offer up a demonstration of skill and show off the creatures in my collection by having two contestants fight *through* various monsters to get to a final ring. You'll find the pit new and improved."

King Dahnuk paused, turned on his heel, and drilled Aviama with a cool glare. "Princess Aviama traveled for three months to accept our invitation to be considered as the crown prince's bride and to forge an allegiance between our kingdoms. Beyond all logic, when the moment came, she rejected my son's marriage proposal. Despite this, Prince Shiva insists her background in Jannemar has given her great knowledge of magic, and to that end, Princess Aviama will demonstrate her skill over magical creatures in the arena."

Shiva was expressionless. Queen Satya took a sip of whatever was in her goblet. Aviama's stomach dropped. She'd never survive in the pit alone. Even working with Chenzira, what were the odds she'd make it without exposing herself as a melder?

Dahnuk returned to his pacing.

"Prince Chenzira is guilty not only of trespassing in halls he is not permitted in, but of conspiracy, based on what we found in his room this morning. Prince Chenzira is an accomplished fighter, and his expertise with a battle-ax will put on quite the show."

Chenzira stiffened, and the taut muscles of his arms gave Aviama the feeling he was angry rather than ashamed. He hadn't had anything in his room to find.

But there was no arguing, and Dahnuk had already launched into the rest of his monologue. "If all this was not enough, Ishaan says your closeness is more than the story the two of you have fed us. I am inclined to believe him, which would lean us toward treason. Since we cannot know for sure, I'm leaving it up to fate.

"Whoever gets to the ring first will have his or her pick of weapons. You fight to the death. Win, and I will congratulate you with leniency. Lose, and your blood is on your own head."

Aviama's chest caved in. A suffocating weight bore down on her, and her head swam. She threw a hand out to stabilize herself against the bars. Chenzira was shouting. Shiva was shaking his head, his first expression of any kind since entering the menagerie. And the queen was sipping from her goblet, a twisted smile at her lips.

"Show me the evidence! Prove what I've done wrong! You have *nothing*. Nothing!" Chenzira slammed his fists against the bars, their rattling rousing a clattering and clanging throughout the menagerie as the animals spooked and reacted to the commotion.

But Aviama knew Radha thrived more off rumor than fact.

And the queen of rumor stood before them, laughing at their demise, cradling a goblet in long fingers.

They had more than they needed to indict them.

Because they needed nothing. They needed only to manufacture.

"Pair me with a warrior. Toss me in with the cirabas." Chenzira stepped back from the bars and swung a fist at Aviama's head, stopping centimeters from her temple. Aviama flinched, and Chenzira dropped his hand. "Don't insult me with a woman."

"Look how loverboy comes to her aid," Queen Satya cooed. "It's almost endearing, isn't it?"

"I don't have to be in love with the girl to tell you how idiotic this is." Chenzira swept his hand to gesture head to toe at Aviama's small frame. "She's *half* my weight, with *zero* of my skill! Is this what Radha calls sportsmanlike? Is this a show, or an execution?"

King Dahnuk pursed his lips. "If my son is right, you may be underestimating her."

Aviama shook her head. As pathetic as it felt to have Chenzira assess her uselessness in combat—and prove it with her flighty flinching—he was obviously in the right. Pitted against Chenzira, Aviama would die in seconds.

Or was that the point? To see if he would kill her, or spare her? But no decent man would slaughter defenseless prey. Did they simply mean to demoralize him? To send a message to other contestants or nobles? Why bother?

Aviama swallowed. "You won't need to finish renovations on the pit. I don't know how to fight. I'm slow. I'm uncoordinated. If you're wanting to punish me for running from Ishaan—"

But she never finished. Chenzira yanked her back from the bars, gripping her hard around the waist and snaking his arm around her throat, cinching it tight around her esophagus. Aviama couldn't help but appreciate the irony. The red ring around her neck, courtesy of the mermaid, had yet to full heal —and here she was again. Was the menagerie cursed to keep her close to death?

She could feel his jaw move against her hair as he taunted their captors. "Why go through the charade? I'll kill her now and be done with it."

Ice shot down her spine. So much for having things in common. Shiva stepped forward, and Chenzira hauled her backward, her feet barely brushing the ground as he dragged her further from the Tanashai family. Aviama's ribs ached where iron fingers dug in, and she pried helplessly at the elbow around her neck.

No. They were not the same.

The tingle of magna suppressing her magic ran like a current over her skin, but nothing happened. Shiva took another step forward, but his father put a hand out to stop him.

Aviama formed words she wanted to say, needed to say, in her mind. *I can't breathe. Chenzira, please.* All that came out was a choked croaking sound.

She reached up to feel for Chenzira's face, hoping to dig her nails in his eyes, but he only twisted his face away. She scratched somewhere on his neck instead. Black spots filled her vision, and a dizzy spell took her. Aviama started to sag against him. Almost reflexively, the hold around her throat eased.

Relief washed over her, and she shifted her weight to stand upright again. Nearly as good as gaining her first ragged breath of air in was the realization that Chenzira still didn't want to kill her. *But that doesn't mean he won't. He's testing options.*

"Don't be rash," Dahnuk warned.

"On the contrary, it's hard for a dying man to be too rash." Chenzira adjusted his grip on her waist, and Aviama lodged her fingers over the crook of his elbow, wedging them as best she could between the skin of his arm and her throat.

Shiva ripped the sword from one of the guards' sheaths and held it out toward the couple in the cage. "Put her down, or I skewer you where you stand."

Aviama sucked in a labored breath, and his hold tightened again. She dropped her weight, and Chenzira swore as he yanked her back up in front of him.

"Stop moving," he hissed. "You're my body shield and the only leverage we've got."

"Only leverage *you've* got," Aviama rasped. "I'm dead either way. Just trying to breathe as long as possible."

As far as the arena spectacle was concerned, she already knew her mantra—*dead if I do, dead if I don't.*

Apparently, Chenzira had the same idea. He raised his voice. "You kill me now, or a ciraba kills me later. What's the difference?"

Shiva whirled the sword in a low arc, and this time Dahnuk let him pace forward to face off with Chenzira. "Kill her now, and I kill you before she hits the floor. Play the game, and you have a shot at life."

The king snapped his fingers at the swordless guard next to Shiva. "Send for archers." The guard ran from the hall, and the king turned back to Chenzira. "Is this how the son of Samir Bomani dies? Wringing the neck of a princess like a goat, and falling dead on top of her corpse?"

Chenzira shrugged. "A public display seems even less desirable."

"Let him do it."

All eyes turned to the queen. She swirled the liquid in her goblet and drained it to the dregs. "He's bluffing."

Shiva's jaw clenched. "What if he isn't?"

Satya arched an eyebrow. "We'll all weep bitterly at her death, and then force the Keket boy into the ring anyway. But we'll reach out to his family first to let them know where he's been all this time. And perhaps with the Jannemar girl dead, we can take the Keket girl instead. She wasn't invited, but only on the esteemed Prince Chenzira's advisement."

The queen turned to Chenzira with a smirk, a light in her eyes at whatever expression Aviama couldn't see that painted his face. His fingers dug harder into Aviama's midsection, and she grimaced. Satya's smirk blossomed into a nauseating beaming smile. "Ah. See, something motivates him still."

Aviama stilled. Chenzira was a brother? Was he warm and loving with his sister, as Zephan was with Aviama? Protective and kind? Fun-loving? Of course, there was no reason he *shouldn't* be a brother. She'd known that—because he wasn't crown prince. He was the second-born. But older brother to a sister? She couldn't picture it.

King Dahnuk looked between his captive and his wife. He pursed his lips and gave a curt nod. "Unless you want to die right here on this floor, Prince Chenzira, and for us to invent creative horrors for your family to believe about what happened to you, you will participate in the game. This is not optional. There are more ways than one to rule the seas, Your Highness. If this contest does not go the way we intend, we will summon your sister. And she will come."

The double doors opened, and the swordless guard ran in leading four archers, bows drawn, with arrows on the string.

Chenzira dropped his voice at her ear, for her alone. "See how they stand? They don't mind shooting me, but they won't hit you. You're more valuable than I am." His breath tickled her neck, and she winced as his arm tightened around her once more. "Dahnuk wants you for the game, but Shiva is still set on marrying you. Remember that. You have leverage."

Chenzira released her, but his next words would haunt her waking hours. "Do everything you can to get out of this. You don't want to meet me in the arena."

38

You don't want to meet me in the arena.

No. No, she definitely didn't.

But after those words had left his mouth, the cage door had been opened, and Chenzira had been dragged from the cell. The Tanashai family and armed escort withdrew, and Aviama had been left behind in her own personal prison. Twiddling her thumbs. Spinning her rings. Dismantling bits of straw.

No genius escape options presented themselves, and the harder she tried to think of something, the dumber and more far-fetched her ideas got. It didn't take long for her thoughts to be disrupted by the banging of mallets and sawing of wood and whatever else the workmen used to repair the tunnel damage and upgrade the pit.

Across the aisle and down three enclosures, long snake-like bodies with barbed tails and wings fluttered up against the mesh of their confinement. They were relatively small, maybe half a meter. She'd rather face them than the monsters on either side of her. Bright purples, pinks, and greens flashed in the morning light as they danced about. They were odd, but beautiful. Maybe they were poisonous.

Next to the flying snakes, lemurs climbed up a structure in their cage, and beyond them, an enclosure filled with rocks, brush, leaves, dirt, and a small pond. Whatever lived there was hidden, and that mystery burned her up more than the knowledge of any of the rest.

Were these all the animals? Were there any beasts that didn't fit in the menagerie? Surely not all of them would be used. Would the king risk his entire collection?

The cirabas seemed plentiful enough. There were two in the cage next to her, and neither of them had the battle wounds from being attacked by Darsh or crushed by the tunnel. So the king must have had at least three to start with. The zegrath in the cage on the other side of her was alone, and the thing was truly massive—nearly the size of a horse. She knew from her reading that they were solitary beasts and might not play well with others of their kind, but zegraths came from mountain areas in the far west. Aviama seriously doubted that Dahnuk had got his hands on more than one.

Aviama's stomach growled. Someone came in with a cart of buckets and bins, tossing raw meat, grain, and whatever else the different creatures required through the bars. But they didn't look at her and left without a word. No gruel or grain for her, apparently.

An hour later, the double doors opened again, and Aviama craned her neck to see who it was. The repair work was still clanging obnoxiously loud, so it couldn't be ready for the contest. She wondered how much more work they had. Maybe the king had doubled or even tripled his workforce to get it done faster. He'd seemed eager to get to his precious death match.

But the two sets of footfalls that came toward her were

light and clipped along at a brisk pace. Aviama grimaced as her guest came into view. Queen Satya marched up to her cage and planted her hands on her hips.

For the first time, Aviama was grateful for the bars between them. She crossed to the back wall of her cage and took a seat on the dusty floor, leaning back against the wall with as unconcerned an air as possible.

The queen gestured at the cages up and down the menagerie. "What do you think of your competitors?"

Aviama pressed her lips together. No need to show weakness. If fear was Satya's currency, Aviama would pay no tribute. "I think they've been stolen from what could have been a good life, and that they'll be wasted in an arena."

"My hyena is quite the specimen. I had to leave him behind this morning, as he's quite aggressive and sees everything in here as prey. Do you think I should allow my husband to show him off in the competition?"

The hair on Aviama's neck stood on end, and she gulped as panic threatened to take hold. She tried to steady her breathing, but the queen's small smile told her she wasn't particularly successful. Of all the beasts in Radha, the queen's ruby hyena scared Aviama the most.

She took a breath and shrugged. "Your loss."

Satya laughed. "You actually think you're going to win?"

"No. But I think Chenzira will kill your hyena, and you'll never capture another one. I assume somebody got lucky and snatched it as a cub from its den? Did its mother come to save it? Could no one wrangle the adult hyena?"

The queen's cheeks flushed, and her mouth twitched. Aviama's breathing eased at the sight. Seeing Satya rattled—rattled by *her*—had a calming effect.

Satya adjusted a bulky gemstone necklace and peered

down at Aviama from beneath long lashes. "We found your girl. She's dead."

All the air fled her lungs like a slug to the gut. Aviama's hands shook, but she spun her rings and took three long breaths. No, she couldn't afford to believe it. If they'd caught Murin, wouldn't they have kept her alive to blackmail Aviama? If she were dead, wouldn't the queen have brought proof, to gloat? Radha might thrive on rumor, but Jannemar waited for the evidence.

Aviama lifted her chin and met her gaze with fire. "If you did as good a job killing her as you did killing Enzo, I can live with that. He sends his regards."

Queen Satya stiffened, and her lip curled. It was all the confirmation Aviama needed. Enzo was alive indeed.

Adrenaline ran through Aviama's blood. Let the queen believe that Enzo was not only alive, but in contact with his princess. Let her believe that her spiderweb of spies in the palace had failed her. She was not so powerful as she claimed.

The queen glided up to the bars, but Aviama refused to rise to greet her. A slap in the face for any royal. Satya's nostrils flared, and she crossed her arms.

"You've broken our arrangement."

"The one where you threatened to kill me like you killed Enzo, when you didn't kill him at all? Oh, what I would give to receive the same punishment, roaming free beyond the palace walls!"

Satya drummed the fingers of one hand against her arm. "You think I have no say in what happens to you now that you're in the menagerie. You think you only need to worry about the king. You're wrong."

Aviama arched an eyebrow. *Correct.*

"Who do you think arranged for your new room? Who influenced the king to have a competition in the first place?

Me. I may not sign decrees into law, but I influence the mind that does. And I have my own guards and servants answering to me and me alone."

She was reaching. Aviama could see that now. The queen did have *influence*, but the king was still the king. Otherwise, Aviama would have been executed in the throne room.

Still, perhaps if Aviama looked worried, looked controlled, she would learn something new.

Satya waved a hand. "No matter. I shall give you one more chance to escape the contest."

Aviama leaned forward, widening her eyes and parting her lips in rapt attention.

Satya's eyes lit up in response, and her slippery, silken confidence oozed back over her sour countenance. "My son is easily bored. He finds you *interesting*. Your task was to be boring and stupid and to lay low. An easy assignment. You wound up a top-notch imbecile, but you did it in a way that made you into a puzzle. And so, my Shiva's interest was piqued." Queen Satya folded her hands. "If he comes to you, I want you to assure him you'll never willingly marry him. Offend him, hurt him, whatever you need to do to repulse yourself to him. If you do this, and he gives up the chase, I will see that you survive the arena."

"And Chenzira?"

"Chenzira will die for his crimes. He was caught stealing information, and of course sidling up to you, against all propriety."

Aviama leaned back against the wall again. "If you're so influential, prove it. Stop the contest altogether."

Satya shook her head. "Too late for that. Think about what I said. I can save you."

Biscuits, everybody wanted to be the one with the power to save her. To dangle life over her head like a carrot. Aviama turned her head and stared out past the queen at nothing, as Satya backed away from the bars and floated back down the hall where she'd come. The double doors opened and closed, and she was alone again.

Time passed, and still, viable escape options eluded her. To her left, the zegrath crunched through the bone of whatever he'd been tossed for breakfast, and licked blood off the floor. To her right, one of the cirabas got too close to the other, and the larger one attacked it, pushing it back until satisfied that his position was secure. A soft ripple of water rolled across the surface of the aquarium, followed by three small jumping fish and a meter-long black one snatching them up in its jaws.

Aviama hadn't given much thought to what other dangerous creatures might live in the aquarium aside from the mermaid. She scanned the water, and found the mermaid an instant later—peering at her through the glass.

"Hey!" Aviama scrambled to her feet and ran to the edge of her cage, resting her arms on the horizontal bar running partway up. "You understand everything I'm saying, don't you? You're not just some mindless beast. You're not like the rest."

The mermaid's tail flashed a shimmering shower of pewter silver and white scales through the water in response, her perfectly white hair flowing out behind her. She sailed up through the water to crest the surface, and perched her elbows on the edge of the aquarium. Aviama had never seen anything so graceful in all her life. The mermaid flicked her tail, her gaze never leaving Aviama's face.

Aviama licked her lips. "You hate Radha. You hate Shiva. I don't know how you got here, but you're not like any other prize in the king's ridiculous zoo."

The mermaid didn't respond, but her lavender eyes remained fixed on Aviama. Another ripple of water coursed along the top of the water, and understanding hit her like a ton of bricks. She sucked in a breath.

"You warned me. When I broke into the king's study." The splash of water, the king's shout. "You warned me he was coming."

The creature watched her for another long moment. The silence stretching between them was palpable. Every ounce of Aviama's focus was trained on the mermaid's face. She cast a furtive look to either side of her aquarium and opened her mouth as if to speak.

A thrill ran through Aviama's body. *Yes! Talk to me...*

Just then, the double doors opened once more, and the mermaid flipped into the water and was gone. Aviama slammed her hand against the bars. *"No!"*

"My apologies, were you enjoying the quiet?"

Aviama jerked toward the voice. Shiva strode down the center of the menagerie, dressed in his typical embroidered finery and carrying a platter of meats, fruit, and bread. Bitterness roiled in her belly at the sight of him, but the platter gave her pause. She hesitated. Her mouth watered.

He saw her attention shift, and smiled. Shiva crouched on the other side of the bars and slid the platter through a slat against the floor. Aviama sank down, snatched the platter into her lap, and folded her legs underneath her. She was surprised the queen had been right about him coming.

Aviama popped a grape into her mouth and waved a hand at the menagerie around them. "This is what you think of me, isn't it?"

"Exotic, beautiful, and interesting?" Shiva winked, and Aviama's stomach soured.

"Flattery seems to be beyond us now, don't you think? The blatant threats, blackmail, and death glares really killed the romantic facade you had going."

Shiva shrugged. "Force of habit. And the romantic facade, as you call it, is far more pleasant than the threats. I much prefer it, and may dip into it now and again. To avoid those blatant threats you mentioned."

"How chivalrous." Aviama ripped a piece of bread off with her teeth and swallowed a bite so big it hurt on its way down her throat.

Shiva arched an eyebrow.

"You're acting like you haven't been fed in days. It's been a single morning."

Aviama shot him a venomous look. "False. I also didn't have dinner last night, thank you very much."

Shiva leaned his shoulder on the bars and tilted his head at her. "If you're offended by death glares, it's a good thing you don't have a mirror."

Aviama gritted her teeth and tossed another grape in her mouth.

"I'm allowed to give death glares. Death glares are all I have. There is no follow up, no execution. For you, the glare is just an appetizer."

At least glares were honest. His softness was a lie, to manipulate her for her secrets. To use her to invade Jannemar and kill her family. When he seemed least hateable, she needed most to be on her toes.

"Perhaps a romantic facade would be more enjoyable for you too."

"Shiva, I'm eating. Don't make me nauseous."

Shiva's hand shot through the bars and ripped the roll from her hands. "At the end of the day, Highness, a facade is just that. I do still require respect."

"What are you going to do, kill me?" She did her best to look unbothered, but she shifted to shield the rest of her meal with her body—and to cover up the quiver in her bones. "I'll be dead soon anyway."

"Maybe. Maybe not." Shiva reached into the sash at his waist and produced two throwing knives. He held them up. "I brought something for you."

Aviama swallowed a chunk of meat and stared at him. "You're giving me weapons?"

"Not for free. It's a trade."

Her eyes narrowed. "I'm not agreeing to marry you." And it had nothing to do with the queen's empty threats.

The corner of the prince's mouth twisted up into the kind of crooked smile that might make a lady swoon if she didn't know it was laced with poison. "I wouldn't dream of it."

Aviama gestured at the empty cage around her. "I haven't got anything."

Shiva leaned his head against the iron bars and leveled her with a piercing, unblinking stare. "I want you to kiss me."

Aviama choked on her own spit and swallowed. Bile rose in her throat, and she gaped at him. "Excuse me?"

"You're excused." He smiled. Politely. Like a politician.

Aviama furrowed her brow. The man made no sense. And she hated him. Because he was loathsome. It was wildly annoying when he tried to be normal, after everything that had happened.

When she didn't say anything, Shiva spun the knives in his fingers and continued. "I want you to give me a kiss on credit. I'll give you the knives now to up your chances of making it to the final ring to fight Chenzira. If you survive, you agree to give me one kiss."

She snorted. "Sure. If Chenzira and I face off to kill each other, and *I* win, I'll give you a kiss. At a later date. That is not now." Whatever landed those shiny blades in her hands.

Without them, she was a sitting duck. *With* them, she was probably *still* a sitting duck.

Shiva nodded. "Excellent." He grinned and passed her the knives.

Aviama eyed him for a moment, half-expecting him to jerk them out of reach again as she moved to take them. But he only patiently held them through the bars until she plucked them from his hands. Shiva went back into his sash and pulled out two long strips of cloth. "Here. To secure them to your forearms."

"Thanks. I think." She wanted to ask him why he was doing any of this, but she wasn't sure she wanted the answer. And she *did* want the knives. Aviama snatched the strips of cloth and scooted back from the bars.

"You're welcome."

It wasn't until he was gone that she realized he'd never answered her question.

39

The mermaid didn't surface again, and Aviama had no more visitors. Three days passed, a servant eventually bringing her meals. The banging of the workmen never stopped, day or night. On the first day, Aviama decided to try to talk to the zegrath and cirabas. Maybe if they got used to her voice, they would be less likely to kill her. She knew it was a fool's errand—the delusional hope of a woman under a death sentence. And the beasts never responded, except once when the larger ciraba charged the bars and snapped its jaws at her.

She bound the knives to her forearms, far enough up inside her sleeves to keep them hidden, and occasionally practiced with them in the air. Semra had been an excellent teacher, but Aviama was only moderately good as a student. Her melder power lessons with Frigibar had been more profitable, though they were useless inside the magna-lined menagerie.

On the fourth day, half a dozen guards trooped into the menagerie to extract her from her cell. Ishaan led them, and he bound her hands behind her back before escorting her through the halls of the palace. Clearly, a narrative had been spun. Princess Aviama of Jannemar, the criminal betraying Radha's trust by consorting with men.

Ishaan paraded her through the halls in her filthy, disheveled state, intentionally walking her through common areas stocked with people. Men shot her dark looks, and women whispered to one another behind their hands. Aviama's tangled tresses resembled the bird's nest it had been when she arrived, but with the added accessory of four days living next to animals without access to hygiene, after being drenched in rain and losing her shoes.

The queen would have her rumor. She would further besmirch the princess's fragile reputation in Radha and ensure the people would be against her. Originally, Aviama hadn't been sure the people could be more opposed to her than they were already. But the march through the palace proved her wrong.

They arrived at the dusty corner room in which she'd been deposited after running from Ishaan, and he opened the door wide. Three women servants stood beside a steaming bath, hands clasped before them, inclining their heads in minimal respect before the foreign captive princess. Tea and cakes adorned a side table, and fresh clothes were set out on the bed.

Aviama was surprised to recognize the woman in the middle. Sai, the servant she'd bumped into when she'd first arrived. The woman who'd come with the laundry cart, and somewhat unwittingly pushed Aviama out of her bedroom chamber.

Sai gestured to a divider standing to one side. "You can undress back there."

The guards untied her and closed the door, leaving her with the women. Aviama stepped gingerly behind the screen and glanced about the room. An empty desk, a stripped bed. No vases, no lanterns, no hiding places for anything. The place was as bare bones as a room could be.

Aviama cleared her throat. "I'd like to bathe alone."

The oldest of the servant women spoke up from the other side of the barrier. "I'm afraid that's not possible, Your Highness."

Great. Aviama unbound the knives from her forearms. They were a comfort while she had them, but they'd be confiscated before she even reached the arena. Aviama undressed, tucked the knives inside the folds of her ruined dress, and set the bundle on the floor.

Her pulse pounded in her ears as she crossed the floor naked and sank into the perfumed bathwater. The older woman and a young servant with a sharp nose came forward to rub her shoulders with oil and wash her hair, and as her sore muscles eased into the hot water, she had to admit there were worse ways to be caught smuggling weapons.

But as the older woman and the sharp-nosed girl took over responsibilities at the bath, Sai retrieved Aviama's old dress. Aviama kept a keen eye on her as she carried it over to the couch, slipped something free of the dress, and adjusted the clean outfit draped over the edge of the couch. When she was done, she dropped the old dress into a bucket that Aviama assumed meant the dress would be burned rather than washed.

So. Sai was loyal to Shiva, not the queen. And she knew to watch for the knives.

Aviama finished bathing and stepped out of the tub. Sharp Nose wrapped her in a towel, and Sai collected the new clothes and wordlessly handed them over. Aviama followed suit, taking them without a word and returning behind the screen to change.

She unfolded a gray pair of billowing pants that tied again at the ankle, and a top to match, with billowing sleeves that gathered again to tie at the wrist. The pants provided the answer to her unasked question—the competition was today.

And these may well be her burial clothes.

Aviama lifted the top for a better look, and the knives and strips of cloth Shiva had given her came tumbling out. She sucked in a breath and snatched at them as they fell, clutching uselessly at the air before finally stopping them centimeters from the floor.

"Your Highness? Is everything all right?"

"Yes, yes, just contemplating my upcoming death," Aviama snapped. "I'm allowed a few extra moments to dress for that, aren't I?"

The servants rewarded her with silence, and Aviama returned her focus to her task. The outfit was more functional than long skirts when one was expecting to be running for one's life, but she had to admit it was still feminine. Aside from the drab gray, it was almost attractive. And the sleeves would leave room for hidden knives. She'd have to leave them untied at the wrist to access them, but that would be no problem.

Aviama set down the top, wrapping the knives inside, and opened the pants to pull them on. When she did, a slip of parchment drifted to the floor. Honestly, was she expected to open each fold with such care? She picked up the crumpled parchment and unfolded it.

Lilac,
Magna is dissolved in the tea. Don't drink it.

She'd almost forgotten about the tea, but now that Shiva had said not to drink it, tea seemed like just the thing. No one else would have called her Lilac.

Aviama finished getting dressed, mulling over the note. Based on the queen's comments and Shiva's appearance at the menagerie, Chenzira was right. Shiva was very much invested in keeping her alive, if possible. And yet, he couldn't openly interfere with what his father had decreed. Just like the queen, or whoever else might be trying to slip chemicals in her tea, both played their games beneath the surface.

A pawn in an insane family game for power. An exhibit in a menagerie of foreign creatures. Aviama pursed her lips and secured the knives to her forearms, tying her sleeves at the wrist to cover them. When she looked in the mirror, they were indiscernible.

She stepped out from behind the screen and reached for the tea. Sharp Nose waited by the desk with a comb—there was no vanity—and the elder of the servant women busied herself with an array of face powders and paints. Sai.

No one seemed to notice her small action. But if Shiva had planted a servant in her room, so had his mother. And they would be watching. Aviama lifted the cup to her lips, mimicked taking a sip until she felt the heat of the tainted liquid inside.

Her mouth watered, but if there was any chance drinking it would take away her one true chance at protecting herself, she'd forego it. She set the teacup back on the saucer and reached for the cake. The note had said nothing about cake.

Of course, if she *did* reveal herself as a melder, all bets were off as to any of the shaky parameters the king might have made over the contest in the arena. If she won using melder powers, she'd probably still die. Unless she could do it surreptitiously enough to avoid suspicion.

It had worked with Darsh. Maybe it could work again. Although, Chenzira had caught on, and Darsh had been openly using his powers as a windcaller when she amplified his work with her own.

Aviama popped a piece of cake in her mouth and carried the rest with her to the chair waiting for her by the desk. The three servant women arranged her hair into complicated braids pulled back from her face and trailing down her back —a practical but elegant solution for a princess assigned to wrangle monsters.

Hair, makeup, and clothes complete, Sharp Nose went to the door and rapped three times. Ishaan opened it and looked her over, giving a curt nod after his assessment. "Ready?"

Aviama spread her hands. "Does it matter?"

Ishaan smirked. "Not a bit."

Her hands shook as she crossed the threshold of the dusty corner room. Half a dozen guards fell in around her and Ishaan as they left all semblance of normalcy behind and walked toward the pit.

No more bars. No more prison walls. This was it—the beginning of the end.

Would the king keep the competition private or make it a spectacle? Was he hoping for individual punishment or to send a message to anyone who dared defy him and disrespect his crown? Had the queen added her hyena to the circus, or had Aviama threatening its life with Chenzira's skill scared her off?

The Keket prince seemed gentlemanly enough. Maybe he'd be quick. Maybe she could even request the death she would prefer. Decapitation was fast, but she'd heard the eyes still saw and blinked and responded for some seconds afterward. Would she see her own body bleeding out before she died? She shivered. Creepy.

But it was preferrable to being run through and left to die slower. Also, if there was any water involved—as there would have to be if the mermaid was to participate in the showing of the king's collection—she did *not* want to be drowned. Aviama could think of few deaths as terrifying as drowning.

Maybe Chenzira had a better concept of what would be fastest and least painful. Maybe he'd just break her neck and be done with it.

Maybe one of the beasts would get her, and she'd never even reach Chenzira.

Nausea rocked her, and she swayed on her feet. Ishaan glanced at her, but did not slow their pace. Aviama had lived with the fear of her fate ever since the king declared his plans for the contest in the menagerie. The strength of it had ebbed and flowed over the past several days. But as they walked down the halls now, her face made up, her lips painted, her hair braided, knives hidden on her arms, true terror settled over her like a blanket of fog.

The halls had grown familiar over the short time she'd been in Radha. Aviama came to expect the greens, blues, and reds at each turn, the ornate patterning and delicate gold foil flashing in the light as the sun poured in through windows and open courtyards. The sound of her slight leather footwear was completely drowned out by the heavy boots of the men surrounding her. The guards' armor clinked as they walked in unison, an ominous drum beating out the quickly depleting time.

Aviama gasped as they turned the corner, passing the room next to the menagerie. The wall was much further in than she remembered, making the pit far larger than it used to be. How many people had he employed to throw up such significant changes so quickly? And how big was the arena now?

Ishaan escorted her past the opening, past the menagerie doors, and down a flight of stairs to a corridor so dark the guards lit torches to lead them. The hollow click of the guards' boots on marble exchanged for a swallowed thud against dirt. Several metal doors were set into the side, but they continued past them all. The tunnel looked to have been made long ago, except for new support beams partway down and fresh construction at the end.

A roar went up somewhere overhead. Thunderous clapping, calling, stomps, and whistles. Aviama's mouth went dry. She had the answer to one of her questions. King Dahnuk had chosen a spectacle.

Ishaan rapped on a metal door at the end of the passage, and a guard on the other side opened it. A ramp led steeply upward to ground level, and every step crushed Aviama's heart to dust within her chest. A muffled voice called out an announcement to the people, but as she approached a final door, she began to make out the words.

"...accused of trespassing, theft, and treason. Today, he demonstrates the skill of the island nation of Keket. May the sun shine, or hold its light."

Deafening whoops, hollers, and boos rocked the arena on the other side of the door. Aviama's stomach dropped. How quickly the favor of an audience could be bought and turned. Chenzira had been one of them for three years at the palace.

Though, he *had* been spying. They might not have manufactured the charge, but at least that accusation was accurate.

The announcer's booming voice carried through the arena again. "And Her Highness, Princess Aviama, charged with treason against Radha and for operating in bad faith, repaying the generosity of the crown prince with wickedness. May the sun shine, or hold its light."

The metal door rolled upward, and Ishaan shoved her through the opening into the bright light of day. No more secret messages, blackmail, or veiled threats. No more pretending, sneaking, or facades.

All that was left was to fight—and to die.

40

A small space greeted her, walled on all sides, and a guard by the door gestured her up a ladder to a platform. Aviama swallowed hard and climbed the rungs, emerging at the top to the same hollers and boos Chenzira had enjoyed moments before.

The arena had quadrupled in size since she'd last seen it—rectangular on one end, with what looked to be the original circular sand pit set on the far side, though she couldn't see down inside it. The platform on which she stood was only about a meter square, set before a mud pit that could only have been worsened by the recent rain. A mesh ceiling was erected six meters over it, sealing in a flurry of the vivid winged snakes Aviama had seen in the menagerie. The mesh ended at a short wall on the other side, dropped away to something she couldn't see, and ran up against a large, enclosed box that blocked her view of the remainder of the arena.

Beside her and twenty paces over, Chenzira stood on a second platform identical to hers. He wore gray pants in the

Radhan style, his bare chest and arms glistening in the sun. Somehow, he looked even stronger and more well-muscled than she remembered, seeing him in the courtyard from her balcony that first day. Her heart lurched to her throat, and any optimism she'd hidden in her belly utterly failed.

Chenzira looked at her, and she winced. Did he pity her? Was he sizing her up to kill?

The announcer's voice called Aviama's attention to the gallery. She shifted her weight under the gaze of the crowd, following along the fringes of jeering faces until she landed on the royal family's observation box. King Dahnuk stood under the shade of the box, his queen leering down at the arena from his left side. Prince Shiva was barely in his seat, leaning over the edge, his eyes trained on Aviama.

He didn't look victorious. His jaw clenched, and she couldn't tell whether he was angry at something between him and his parents, or anxious over the fate of his latest toy. Darra perched beside him, biting her lip until Aviama thought it might fall off. Vanina sat beside her, and Marija stewed on Vanina's far side—probably upset she'd been positioned so far from her target.

"Esteemed guests." Dahnuk spread his hands and smiled, and the crowd fell silent. "Ladies and gentlemen, we have set before you today a vast array of exotic delights. From diamond gliders, to cirabas, and the mighty zegrath—well, why spoil the fun? Let's leave some room for our contestants' imagination. We present to you a show of epic proportions, with demonstrations of skill mixed with beasts and creatures in action like you've never seen before."

Aviama had never seen the man so animated. He was a regular showman, gesturing and waving. She felt sick.

The king lifted his hand to quell the swell of applause.

"Our contestants have one objective: survive. The rules are simple. Each contestant must cross five obstacles to get to the other side of the arena, and may not interfere with one another until they reach the sand pit at the end. The first contestant to reach it gets first pick of the weapons on display." Dahnuk gestured at the archers stationed around the rim of the arena. "Any contestant that attempts to leave the arena will be shot. The contest ends when one contestant is dead. The winner will live."

Aviama grimaced. What did that mean, exactly? Exiled? Left to rot in a dungeon? She glanced at Chenzira, who'd sunken into a low stance as if ready to spring. His eyes were scanning the mud bog before them, already analyzing their first obstacle. Aviama dropped into a similar position and tried to do the same, but the king's voice pulled at her focus.

"Today we hand judgment over to the arena and let the sun shine on whom it will shine. Sit back, relax, and enjoy. And may truth reign." He paused, then waved his hand at a servant standing by a gong to one side. "Begin!"

The gong sounded, and Chenzira was off like a shot, ripping open the mesh door before him and diving headlong into the mud. Aviama hesitated. That was it? No countdown? They'd started?

The crowd roared, and Shiva frantically shooed at her from the box. His mother reached across the king to swat at him, and Aviama blocked them from her mind to lift the mesh door and jump down into the first obstacle. Brown sludge swallowed her legs nearly to the waist, locking in her knees. She moved in slow motion, every movement labored. The flying snakes—or diamond gliders, as she now knew to call them—descended en masse.

Aviama untied the loose sleeves at her wrist, letting them

flow free, but the gliders were upon her before she reached her blades. Flashes of gold, violet, and sapphire streaked across her vision. Wings beat the air about her ears, and she swung at them madly. On the other side of the bog, Chenzira pushed through to the other side, swatting at the gliders only when they got too close to his face.

Don't just stand there. Move.

With a grunt, Aviama obeyed the voice in her head and struck out for the other side amid the hissing cacophony assaulting her ears. One crimson glider dropped into a dive at her eyes, and she squealed before clocking it straight in the face. It dropped to the mud, and the others pulled back for a moment before batting themselves around her again.

But it was a win, and one she sorely needed. Mud oozed between her shoes and her feet. Not three steps in, and she'd lost the first shoe. Aviama raked her skinny ankles through the slime and slapped at a green glider that had gotten a bit too close. She could see why Chenzira didn't bother with them. They were annoying, but less aggressive than she'd anticipated. Maybe they were planning on working them in slowly.

Chenzira had almost made it across the bog. Aviama was barely a third of the way there. A sting surprised her from behind as fangs sank into the back of her arm. Pain shot up to her shoulder. She tried to shake it off, but it would not move. Aviama reached across her body and over her right arm to seize the snake's jaws with her left. *Just a little burst...*

Wind seeped from her palm and shot straight into the glider's open mouth. It released her with a hiss, and she whipped its body through the air to smack at the others. The gliders lifted, except for the one still firmly in her hand, and a thrill of victory ran through her chest.

A shout of dismay carried from the other side of the bog,

and Aviama snapped her gaze to Chenzira. He looked to be straining against something, but try as he might, every muscle taut, he did not budge.

A rumble moved through the crowd. Aviama plunged forward through the mud, angling toward him ever so slightly. She lifted her voice to call out to him over the crowd above them.

"What is it?"

He swore. "Snakes."

Aviama slung the green glider at a brave yellow one getting too close, and it abandoned course. "That's the whole point. The whole obstacle is full of glider snakes."

Chenzira jerked his hand above the mud and thrust it down again, running it this way and that. Searching. "Not gliders. *Snakes.*"

And then she saw it. A bubble in the surface of the mud. Aviama spun this way and that, but the rest of the entire bog was calm. Another bubble broke the smooth surface, followed by a rolling wave—like a fallen log pressed upward by some unknown force. Her stomach squirmed, and her throat constricted. Chenzira stumbled, and Aviama stepped on something slippery.

But it wasn't just slippery. It was a sliming, *moving* coil of pure muscle. Aviama snatched her leg up and off the thing as fast as she could, but a slithering mass ran itself over her other foot as she searched for traction against the bottom of the mud pit.

This was no glider. It could hardly be considered a snake, as her foot felt no end to the thing. She slogged at a funeral pace inside a trap with a serpentine monster.

Aviama threw herself toward the other side of the bog with a disappointing squelch, slowing her frenzied shove forward to a snail's speed. Her blood ran cold. *Squilch, squelch, squalll-*

llch. Her second shoe abandoned her in favor of the glopping grime.

A thick band the size of her thigh wormed its way around her waist. She cried out, beating in vain against the scaly hide. And then—*jerk*—she was plunged into darkness.

41

———

Cold enveloped her. Darkness blotted out the arena as every square inch of her submerged in thick mud. She'd never even got a glimpse of the python before it wrapped itself around her midsection and ripped her from her feet. But now, as it snaked around to eclipse her body in scaly coils, there could be no mistaking the monster's purpose.

Goosebumps fled along her skin as the blood in her body turned to ice. Aviama writhed in its grasp. The glider had slipped from her grasp in the attack, and now she flailed empty hands in every direction.

She tugged at the snake's body, but it only cinched tighter around her. She hadn't gotten a proper breath before being dragged under. Her lungs burned. Slowly, the snake pulled her along under the surface. Aviama pulled and pulled, but in vain. She tried sneaking her arm inside the coil to alleviate the pressure on her torso. The beast's hold was too tight.

Aviama's head ached, and dizziness hit her like a crate of bricks. Her racing thoughts slowed to a murky crawl, and her heart ticked loud in her ears. *Lub-dub, lubb-dubb, lubbb-dubbb.*

One thought crested the swirl in her mind: *knife.*

Aviama reached across her body and into her sleeve, but her fingers hardly had the energy to grip the handle. The snake jerked, and Aviama whipped through the mud—up into the air in a blast of sunlight, and down again into the dark. A single gasp in the light was all she needed. Aviama gripped the knife handle, ripped it free, and stabbed straight down into the body of the snake.

The python writhed, loosening only briefly before reclaiming its hold. Aviama ran her hand along the snake's lithe coils and stabbed repeatedly, hard, as hard as she could. The snake constricted around her. Pain screamed from her ribs at the pressure of it. In a final stroke, Aviama took hold of the knife with both hands and plunged it straight down toward herself into the belly of the beast.

Twisting, curling bands of snake loosened, and she thrashed into the bog, free at last. Aviama struck out with her feet and found the bottom of the pit, lurching upward and breaking the surface with a spray of mud that smelled of rot. Pure air rushed into her starved lungs, and a roar went up from the crowd.

Gliders hissed and flapped at the mesh ceiling, clearly uninterested in meeting the fate of their green friend. The presence of the python had terrified them almost as much as it had Aviama, and in that moment, there was little she would not have done to gain wings and join them up against the mesh.

Chenzira threw his arm into a pummeling downward blow against something in the mud, and spun to unlatch the gate to the next obstacle. Slick, slimy scales slid over Aviama's foot again, and she surged after the gate on her own side. She still had a third of the pit to cross.

A huge serpentine head dripping in oozing brown mud

rose from the bog next to Chenzira's gate. The beast weaved its head back and forth and lunged. Chenzira dove through the opening, a rasping roar emanating through the gate.

Only ten paces separated Aviama from freedom. The snake's head smashed into the latched gate half a second after Chenzira latched it behind him. The creature shook its head. Its long, forked tongue tasted the air. A coil of the snake's long body swept Aviama's leg, and she fell.

Every muscle in her body burned. Her ribs still ached from the python's grip, and her breath came with a wheeze. Aviama's shins were heavy as lead, pulling her down and slowing her progress. Her heart lurched to her throat as she fell into the mud again. The audience hollered and shouted, but she only half-registered the sound. She was more focused on the serpent's head, easily the size of her entire torso, whipping toward her from the other side of the bog.

Aviama wiped layers of mud from her face and slung it back into the pit. *Splat!* The beast hissed. She adjusted her grip on her knife.

The python darted forward with an open mouth. Aviama lifted her knife. The snake's fang met her slight steel with a clack that sent the blade flying. A collective gasp rose from the crowd as she dove to one side, snatching her second knife from her other forearm just as the python's fang grazed her shoulder.

Power pooled in her palms, but she braced herself against it. What would the archers do if she proved herself a melder, in the presence of the king?

The python reared back its head, and Aviama's heart sank. Without it, she had no chance. Unless...

The snake wrapped a coil around Aviama's body and lifted her out of the mud, tasting the air as it sized her up with slitted eyes. Her legs dangled, toes kicking little splashes in the surface of the bog. Her chest heaved and her throat constricted, but her blade remained fixed in her hand.

The python's mouth yawned wide to strike, and Aviama threw the knife. It only took a little spin of windcalling magic to propel it forward at twice its speed and angle the trajectory to correct her poor aim. The blade sank into the soft flesh at the back of the snake's throat.

Aviama dropped like a stone back into the brown ooze. Her first knife lay next to the gate on her side, only half-sunken in the edge of the mud. She pitched herself forward, snatched the handle, and stabbed downward just as the tail of the serpent extended toward her again.

Heavy mud clung to her as she hauled herself over the edge of the pit with a grunt, unlatching the gate and stumbling through it to the other side. The gate clicked shut, sealing the monster python behind her. But just as the gate shut the snake out, it shut Aviama *in*. The reality of the contest struck her then, like a slap in the face. She'd only just survived a single obstacle.

Low brush and small plants haphazardly littered a dirt floor, accented with several half-rotted logs. A single door marked freedom perhaps forty paces off in the center of the wall to what looked like a large box four meters high. Aviama groaned. No, not to freedom. To whatever next horror the Tanashai family had in store.

There was no sign of Chenzira. She could only assume he'd conquered every hideous beast and lay half-asleep on a pile of weapons in the pit, waiting for her to catch up so he could end her miserable life.

A hoarse hissing sound set Aviama's teeth on edge, then ended abruptly with a snap. She froze. One of the logs had moved. Now that she looked again, she saw that two of the five logs in the space were not logs at all, but cirabas. And both had their sights set on the slovenly mud-caked princess.

She knew she should move. It was only a matter of time before the cirabas attacked. But instead, she stood frozen, with her stomach in her toes and her heart in in her throat. The ciraba on the left eased up over one of the logs. The one on the right snapped its jaws and bobbed its head up and down.

Aviama hadn't a clue what that meant, but she didn't get the chance to think about it. An apple sailed through the air and landed on the log just in front of the ciraba. Aviama turned to see where it had come from. Marija twirled a pastry in long fingers, but that didn't mean she'd thrown it. From the box, Shiva drilled her with a stare and made a back-and-forth gesture with his hand. What was that supposed to mean?

The ciraba charged, one running into the other in its haste. Realization struck. Their awkward limbs and lumbering lizard bodies couldn't make tight turns. Shiva's hand motion suddenly made sense. *Don't run in a straight line.*

A dark flash in her peripheral vision snatched her attention back to the arena. It was too late. The ciraba was already upon her. Aviama swung her knife and jumped back, but the first ciraba smashed into her legs, and she buckled.

The dirt met her with a smack that reverberated through her bones. The ciraba opened its mouth wide, revealing long rows of dagger-sharp teeth, when the second ciraba latched onto it. So little of a threat was she, that they apparently prioritized taking each other out of the running. Aviama grabbed at a plant to pull herself out of the way of the beasts' battle, but the plant came up with her hand, roots and all.

The hurried construction of the pit hadn't leant itself to firmly rooted foliage. Aviama lurched to her feet and flew across the open space toward the door. A tug yanked her backward, and she fell—a tangle of cloth snagged among the teeth of one of the cirabas as it snatched at her pants.

Aviama threw the plant at the animal's face, sending a shock of air into its eyes. The ciraba recoiled, and Aviama gathered her feet. If she was strategic, maybe she could use her windcalling more than she'd thought. She lunged again for the door when the second ciraba slung itself over the dirt twice as fast as Aviama's legs could carry her.

The door was only three paces away. The mud on her feet did little for traction, and she slipped again on the dirt as she ran. At the last second, the ciraba launched itself over the last of the logs just as Aviama turned the handle. Aviama turned and thrust the knife down on the ciraba's head, throwing her whole weight into the blow.

It wasn't enough. The knife glanced off the creature's tough hide, and with a twist of its head, the ciraba knocked the blade free of her grasp. Her weight barely managed to redirect the ciraba's trajectory as it landed on her feet. The second ciraba crowded her at the door, and there was nothing left for her to do before they tore her apart.

Aviama wrenched free of the first beast, turned the handle of the door, and threw herself headlong into the mysterious abyss beyond. The cirabas pursued her, but out from under the supervision of the crowd, Aviama let the wind pool at her palms. The air answered her call, pressing back against the beasts—not enough to send them flying, but just hard enough to push them back from the door.

She strained against the door, throwing herself against it as she pushed the beasts out of the way. With a final shove, Aviama latched the door and sagged against it. Two obstacles down. Three to go.

A low rumble and a hollow creak echoed off the walls of the pitch-black box, then dropped away to a troubled silence.

Aviama bit her lip, then spit the grime she found there out of her mouth. A great rolling, pounding sound broke the stillness.

Aviama swallowed.

And then the ground shook.

oom.

CRACKKKK!

Something collided hard with the wall ten paces to Aviama's left, and a squeal escaped her lips before she could stop it. Aviama sprinted along the wall to put distance between her and the precise place where she'd announced her location, when another tremor rocked the ground beneath her feet and pitched her sideways.

Her fingers clawed the dirt.

Whump, whump, whump.

Footsteps. Huge, heavy, inhuman footsteps.

"Get up."

Aviama flinched away from the low growl in her ear. Her stomach dropped and her chest burned. How had he gotten so close? She hadn't the slightest inkling Chenzira was even in the box, much less a hair's breadth away.

She rolled to one side and sprang to her feet, feeling for the wall in the dark. The air was set with a stale chill, an odd contrast to the heat of the sun outside. Her pulse pounded in her ears, and a bead of sweat trickled down her brow and into her hair.

Whump, whump. CRASH.

This time, a bellowing cry accompanied the commotion, sounding somewhere between a shriek and a thunderclap. Trolls.

A hand clapped over her wrist and jerked her to one side, then shoved her in the opposite direction. Aviama careened through the air into the deep dark of the box, tripping over her feet as panic snaked its way up from her belly to her throat.

Chenzira's voice hissed at her again, this time from the other side. "They're stupid, but they're strong. Don't stop moving."

How did he do that? How fast was he moving? Aviama wiped her mud-caked palms on her mud-soaked pants, but it did little good. She ran forward, her eyes straining in the dark, but she couldn't make out anything.

Another crash, another roar. The ground shook again, this time so strongly she could have sworn the dirt itself tilted beneath her feet. Were the trolls big enough for all that?

Chenzira popped up beside her again, this time snatching her wrist and dragging her to the wall. She'd never been so comforted by rough wood at her fingertips.

"They've punched the door so badly it doesn't open."

Aviama gasped. "We're trapped in here?"

"I mean, so far, we are, yes. I was hoping you could help."

Why did his voice bring her so much relief? She nearly curled into his chest. Or would have, if she'd been able to locate it in the dark. Aviama steeled herself, angry at her own stupidity, and set her jaw.

"Shouldn't you be trying to kill me?"

"Not until the sand pit." He jerked her to one side, and the ground moved again. "Keep moving."

I would, if I knew where the walls were. Or the trolls. Or literally anything. Aviama pursed her lips and hovered behind her best guess for where Chenzira was standing. "I didn't think you were such a rule follower. Maybe it was the sneaking and spying that gave me that impression."

"Takes one to know one."

"I never denied it."

Chenzira found her wrist again and ran with her through the dark. Aviama's eyes were starting to adjust, and as they neared the exit door, she could just make out the shapes of the young trolls plunging after them. Ugly, contorted stone faces charged toward them. Chenzira let go of her to draw the big one away, darting in and out around him until the troll roared his rage.

The small one was still impressive, and faster than its companion, rolling into a ball to whirl its way over the hard-packed dirt. The troll popped up in front of her and swung for her head. She screamed and ducked, diving between the stony legs and rolling to her feet on the other side. A rocky fist slammed into the wall next to the door, leaving a splintering dent in the wall.

Chenzira appeared at her side again, but the larger troll snatched her by the ankle. A throaty chuckle mocked her as Aviama found herself hanging upside down, swinging back and forth as the blood rushed to her head. The troll stuck its tongue out at her and wound up its fist.

The smaller troll charged up, and the larger one turned toward it. Aviama winced as her head bonked the dirt floor, and gathered her strength to pull at the air around them. A sweeping motion caught her eye in the dim light to one side, and the ground trembled again.

The troll stumbled and dropped Aviama. The truth of what had just happened sank in the back of her mind even as she struggled to her feet and ran to the door.

Aviama threw her hands up toward the door, and Chenzira stepped into the space between her and the trolls. "Keep them busy."

"I've been in here twice as long as you," Chenzira grumbled. The trolls chased after him, and he danced in and out among them, breathing hard. "Just get the door open!"

Power pooled in her palms, waiting for her signal. She drew more and more air from under and around the door, joining the growing, swirling currents around her hands. "If I do this, the jig is up."

"If you don't, your secret dies with you. I'm getting tired. They don't get tired. All they've got to do is wait long enough, and we're toast."

"What about yours?" She didn't wait for an answer. She didn't expect one. Aviama swept her hands in an arc and let fly with a blast of air that tore the door from its damaged hinges.

The larger troll fled from the light as it poured in the doorway, but the smaller troll was caught in the path of the sun. It solidified mid-stride, Chenzira still half-wedged in the circle of its arms.

He clawed at the immovable arm around him and grunted as she glanced back at him. "A little help?"

Aviama couldn't help but grin at the warrior prince, dangling from a troll statue like a flopping fish out of water. She shook her head. "You're supposed to kill me today. I don't mind putting that off."

It wasn't like he was in any danger. As long as the door was letting in the sun, the troll couldn't move. And if the second troll came close enough to cause a problem, it would be solidified too. Chenzira would wiggle his way out eventually. In the meantime, Aviama would take any head start she could get.

He shouted at her as she strode from the dark box, and a twinge of guilt stirred in her gut. But the next obstacle might well kill her before he got the chance, and he'd be vindicated.

A murmur and shout rose from the onlookers as they caught sight of a contestant finally making it out of the hyland troll obstacle. Between the two contestants, they clearly weren't expecting Aviama to emerge first—if at all. Her knives were lost, and her bare feet padded over the dirt. Repeated tumbles on the ground had brushed off the bulk of the mud, but a stubborn remainder still formed a crinkly, half-dried second skin over patches of her chest, arms, and legs.

Aviama walked out into a modest space, maybe ten paces across, that butted up against a sparkling aquarium. She winced and rubbed her neck, memories of the seaweed rope infiltrating any hope the troll victory had won. A single, narrow ladder went up six meters high, overlooking the obstacle. Fish sparkled past her in every color of the rainbow.

They looked harmless enough. But they only set the stage alongside more sinister occupants. The mermaid was in play.

She was likely the main event of this obstacle, though Aviama wondered what other water menace might be hiding somewhere beneath the twist of rock and seaweed along the bottom. Aviama put her hand on the ladder. She glanced back through the open door to the trolls. Chenzira was slowly easing himself out of the statue's grasp. A head start wouldn't do her any good if she was too afraid to take it.

Aviama took a deep breath and climbed the ladder. Hand over hand, step by step, she rose eye-level with the observation box. Marija wiggled her fingers at Aviama in a bemused, patronizing wave that made Aviama wish she still had one of her knives. Vanina leaned forward, concern etched on her face. And Darra hid her face in Shiva's shoulder, but he couldn't have looked less interested in her if he'd tried.

A strange expression crossed his face. Was it possible that what she saw there was pride? What sense did that make? Her stomach twisted, and she grimaced. Her motive was survival, not proving her usefulness so the prince would win some twisted family wager.

But if the Tanashais had placed bets, the queen's nasty snarl indicated she might not be happy with how hers was panning out. Aviama could have told her not to worry. The sand pit at the end would solve all her ills.

Aviama turned away from the observation box to evaluate the obstacle before her. The aquarium was split into two sections, an upper portion where she was now, and a drop down to a smaller portion half its height. A ladder led out of the aquarium on the far end.

A dozen men stood on narrow platforms lining the sides of the aquarium. At first, Aviama thought it was to make sure she and Chenzira couldn't escape, but the edge of the arena was too far a jump to have to worry about that. And they were armed with harpoons.

Aviama scanned the water. Fish of all kinds swirled throughout, diving here and there into holes among the marine plants and large rocks along the bottom. A ray cut through the water in a graceful glide, its flying wings like silk rolling in a summer breeze. And the mermaid played with an oyster shell on the far side of the high portion, pretending not to notice Aviama's presence.

Nothing else of any substantial size inhabited the water at all. One of the guards shifted on the platform. Something white and fluffy caught her eye, stuffed in his ear. Aviama glanced down the line. Every single one of the dozen guards with harpoons on the edge of the pool had their ears stopped up.

A tingling shock shivered down her spine, and her lips parted. The silver-scaled creature in the pool was not just any mermaid. If it weren't for Dahnuk's desperate craving to show off, there would be no question whether to use her in a public event like this. No one would. She was by far the most dangerous of all the king's menagerie, and the guards were meant to safeguard against her song if she chose to go rogue and try to kill everyone.

Because if she did, she just might succeed.

The mermaid was a siren.

43

———

The Radhan guards remained stoic, for the most part, but as Aviama watched them, she caught their furtive glances and quick breathing as they stood stock still in their positions. Aviama shook her head. They were afraid of their watery charge. And they should be.

Not only could the mermaid understand everything Aviama had ever said to her, but she could talk. And sing. And it was probably the most hauntingly beautiful thing one could ever hope to hear before one's death. Legend had it that sailors went to sirens with a smile on their lips, only realizing their fate too late, as they were dragged into the depths and their screams were cut off by the sea.

Aviama swallowed. The mermaid tilted her head and bored into her with an icy stare, her perfect face a wavering illusion through the crystal water. That gaze was anything but friendly. Aviama's heart hammered in her chest. Visions of seaweed and silver scales and strangulation flooded her mind.

She wasn't ready. But she'd also never be any *more* ready, so it didn't make much difference.

Aviama dove into the pool.

The siren dropped the oyster, and the shell drifted away. The seal pelt covering around her chest and over one shoulder was accompanied this time by an accessory—a loop of braided seaweed slung across her torso. The mermaid reached back and snatched it over her head, and Aviama reeled backward in the water. When her hand reappeared, she sported the long wooden stick of what was most likely a stolen torch, with a seaweed-reinforced handle and a jagged, pointed shell fixed to the tip.

Aviama spun away from her, surging downward. She was already a siren. They didn't bother searching her for weapons? How much of an advantage did the mermaid need?

Her eyes burned in the salt water, but she couldn't afford to miss a shred of her surroundings. Aviama kicked hard, rotating away from the makeshift spear and straight into three rows of razor-sharp teeth zipping through the water straight for her. The long slender body of a menacing, meter-long fish had appeared out of nowhere, jaws open wide, four times as fast underwater as Aviama could ever hope to be.

Aviama punched it in the nose, and pain rocketed up her arm. But the fish only came again. A pins-and-needles feeling exploded into a ripping sensation along in her forearm, a pair of craggy teeth grating through her skin just as the siren's spear sank into its eyeball and shoved it backward. Blood spilled from her arm, staining the water with red.

Motion stirred the sand and rocks at the bottom of the aquarium, and a flurry of strange, ebony, stick-sized fish the width of her thumb shook free of their hiding places and rose through the water. Flat along the body, but with a bulbous head on the end, and nearly indetectable buried in sand. Blood lampreys.

Their hideous heads spun up toward the red mist, revealing circular jaws in a sucker-like ring stuffed with a hundred knife-like serrated nubs. Bubbles of precious air escaped her mouth with a short underwater scream. Wind-calling would do her no good in the water, but she was no match for a school of twenty lampreys.

The mermaid slung the long fish through the water on the end of her spear, streaking fresh blood in its wake, dragging it in front of Aviama in a barrier between them and the lampreys. Half the lampreys latched onto the fish, and the mermaid whirled the spear in a spinning, whirling arc, keeping the rest at bay. She lunged, pulling her lips back in a snarl and letting out a series of clicks and a shrill, piercing call that cut through the water like butter.

A chorus of little high-pitched shrieks answered, and the remaining lampreys fell back. The siren held her short spear out from her body and slung her muscled tail down on the fish, knocking it free of the tip so that it sunk to the bottom for the lampreys to feed. Two lampreys fell off as the mermaid's tail hit the fish, revealing two perfectly circular gashes where they'd been attached.

Aviama's eyes bulged, and her pulse hammered. Her lungs burned, and she left the staggering sight behind her. She needed air.

Aviama rose to the top of the water and broke the surface with a gasp. A raucous din flew up and around the arena of people, but her attention was snatched back to the pool as the mermaid crested the water with her. Lavender eyes peered at her from a single meter away, only just beyond her reach. Her skin glistened, almost glimmered, in the sun, as if the incandescent quality of her scales reached into her human half. The white of her hair lay tight to her head as she'd pulled herself out of the water and flowed out around her in a glorious wave the instant it met the surface.

Gratitude and wonder blossomed in Aviama's chest at the

mysterious creature before her. Lovely, terrifying, powerful—and somehow on her side. The siren had saved her twice now. Aviama wanted to thank her, to ask her why she did it, to—

The siren's gaze drifted over Aviama's shoulder, and her expression hardened. Aviama turned around in the water, and a cursory glance at the observation box told her all she needed to know. The king was shouting. Prince Shiva was toasting the siren with a piece of accursed geyser shrimp. And the queen was on her feet, glaring daggers at the mermaid and flicking scales off a strip of flayed fish skin.

Aviama's stomach dropped. The siren had been double-blackmailed. What leverage could one hold over a mermaid? Better food, or a larger aquarium? The chance to live outside the bounds of the magna? Or simply the tried-and-true threat of death?

A shadow flickered across the mermaid's face, and Aviama couldn't help but assume it was a shadow of indecision. Whose deal would she uphold? Shiva's, to leave Aviama alive to watch him invade Jannemar? Or the queen's, to strike her down?

Or had the king made his own deal? Perhaps to put up a fight and ensure a show for his guests. To challenge the contestants.

Perhaps the mermaid had saved Aviama because she had picked a side. But Aviama didn't even *have* a side to pick. She was reduced to a pawn yet again.

She wasn't sure what bewitched her to do it. But in that moment, staring into the agonized, mesmerizing face of the most magical musical prowess the world possessed, Aviama opened her mouth and sang.

It was almost a dare, she supposed. *Do it. Kill me, but let the Tanashais die with me. With us.*

And though her fear of drowning was greater than her fear

of dying by any other means, Aviama thought perhaps the chance to sing with a siren—however inferior her own contribution might be—would soften the dying blow. Nothing brought her solace like a song. Nothing touched her soul like harmony.

The melody had no words, no distractions, nothing but the lilting roll of a long note rising and falling at her whim. The onlookers had yet to hear her, still screaming their shock and displeasure, but the siren snapped her sharp eyes back to Aviama's face. Aviama let the note build, a low plea picking, weaving its way through the air.

Don't pick a side.

The note dropped lower still, then jumped and swelled, Aviama's eyes locked on the mermaid, and the mermaid locked on Aviama. *Don't look at them. Look at me.*

Sing with me.

A thrill ran through her body as the siren opened her mouth and a celestial sound poured out. Captivating, otherworldly composition blended with hers, a sound pure as refined gold, anticipating the movement of Aviama's song and winding around her own notes in transcendent harmony. Aviama couldn't help but smile through the notes as they climbed and twisted about one another, dancing close, then far away, in creative chords that felt like they'd been dropped from the heavens.

The guards on the platform stiffened, and Aviama's eye flitted to the man on the end. His fingers twitched on his harpoon. A clawing stir in her belly threatened to turn her inside out. Aviama glanced around them at the edges of the arena. All sound seemed to drop away before their song. Not a soul moved, or hardly even breathed, as the princess and the siren harmonized from their position in the aquarium. Every eye stared in rapt attention, stupefied, hanging on each haunting note.

The guard adjusted his grip on the harpoon. His ears were stopped up. All he saw was a siren, *singing,* and everyone around them spellbound. Aviama felt no desperate pull to the depths, no magical compulsion to act beyond her own will. But the guard couldn't hear. How would he know the difference between an innocent song, and the siren's lullaby of death? Perhaps he expected any moment for his king, his queen, and the entire watching court to fling themselves from their seats into the aquarium and follow the song to their demise.

Aviama's throat constricted, and the note faltered. A twitch here, a shift there—tension fell thick on the guards of the pool. Her gaze swept to the other side, and with a start, she noticed a new observer to the spectacle. Chenzira stood at the top of the ladder, his gaze transfixed on her face.

Aviama stared at him, each of them frozen as if by enchantment. The mermaid's tail flicked into her tired legs as she treaded water, pulling her focus, and Aviama spun away from Chenzira and back to the mermaid. The mermaid's face was taut, even as her song floated up to impossible notes. She was on edge, glancing around at her captors, and scared—just like Aviama.

In a swift motion, the guard on the end raised his harpoon. Without thinking, Aviama reached out and grabbed the siren's hand like she would an old friend, jerking her toward the center of the pool and away from the wall. The mermaid recoiled at her touch, but then twisted to see the guard just as he released his harpoon.

Aviama threw up one hand, a burst of air flying from her palm and knocking the harpoon just off course as its tip hit the water and the siren seized her by the wrist. Cool water rolled over her as the mermaid yanked her beneath the surface and dragged her down to the bottom of the aquarium along a glass panel separating the high and low portions of pool, scattering a school of blue and yellow fish.

Spshhh. Spshhhhh. One, two, three harpoons plunged after them as the mermaid's powerful tail propelled them through the water and into a narrow tunnel leading from one pool to the other.

Splooosh. Correction. Four harpoons. Aviama jerked free of the siren's grasp to catch the shaft of one of the harpoons, then kicked to re-enter the tunnel at the base of the pool, but her lungs were already burning. Time was running out. And eight harpoons were still in play.

The water caved in around her, washing the mud from her skin but failing to shake the sense of doom hovering over her. The queen wanted control, and she'd gotten it. She'd said she was at the heart of what really went on in the palace, and she'd been right.

Queen Satya had declared that Aviama would die. And so, her wish was granted.

Aviama's heartbeat pounded in her ears, a drum breaking up the rushing of the water swirling about her. Her knuckles were white on the harpoon, and her chest hitched with a desperate, vain plea for air. She squeezed her eyes shut.

Maybe if she swam to the surface, promised to play along, she could save her skin. Maybe by giving up her freedom, she could assuage the queen's anger...

But she knew the answer. Aviama could no longer escape the fate of the menagerie than she could make the water dry. Even if she could, she didn't deserve it. She'd earned her death fair and square.

Aviama had forsaken her country, her family, her home. She'd handed over the keys to victory over Jannemar. If Aviama's family wouldn't survive the Tanashais' greed, why should she?

An image of Satya flicking scales of the flayed fish skin floated to the forefront of her mind. That's how the queen treated everyone around her. Blackmail. Fear. Subterfuge. Perhaps even the king was a victim of his wife's schemes, though he might not realize it.

Family by family would fall at her hand. Aviama thought of her parents and the great love they had shared. It had been generations since the king and queen at Shamaran Castle had shared the same room at night, most unions resulting in absorbing themselves with their duties and distractions in their own quarters. But Turian and Sharsi had shared a love for the ages, and Turian had passed down that ability, that model, to his son. Zephan and Semra now ruled in their stead, honoring them beautifully. Their parents would have been proud.

Love deserved to be protected. Life. Freedom. Radha would undo all of Jannemar's progress. All because Aviama had been naive and stupid, and trusted Prince Shiva when she should have been shrewd.

With no one to oppose her, Queen Satya would rule in the background, in the shadows, turning the kingdom this way or that way to fit her vision like a rider steering a horse. And her vision? To blot out melderbloods from the world. To grow Radha's power, and *her* power, by climbing the fallen corpses of her adversaries.

Unrivaled power, by conquest and death.

And she would kick it all off with Aviama's death.

A lump rose in her throat, a ridiculous, unwelcome lump. She didn't deserve even this moment of self-pity.

Dizziness swept over her, and her grasp on the harpoon loosened as her body began to give up the fight. Cold sank into her bones, and her lips parted, as if to welcome in the air of salvation.

Burning, burning, burning.

The scream of her lungs enveloped her mind, and it was all she could do not to pull in a drag of water. Only seconds from now, she'd be forced to try it, as the pressure of the water and the cry of her lungs took over.

Aviama snapped her eyes open, welcoming the sting of the salt. No, she didn't deserve to live. But if she was going to die today, it wouldn't be by drowning. She'd spend the rest of her miserable life fighting to displace the queen from her position of power. To prove her wrong. To upend her plans.

Whatever it took, the queen must not win today. The king could win. Even Shiva could win. But the *queen* must not.

The time had come for Aviama's final recompense. And she would chase it, at any cost.

44

A current of energy ran over Aviama's hands, prickling her palms and tingling her skin. She could almost feel the air pressing up against the surface of the water above, worrying its way against the rippling waves as the guards waited her out on the platform. An idea struck her in the gut like lightning, and she abandoned the harpoon to lift empty palms toward the surface of the pool.

Why hadn't she thought of it before? Had any windcaller ever even tried it? She'd heard of crestbreakers capturing air and bringing it down into the water, but never a windcaller pushing air down into it. Aviama wasn't sure why. Theoretically, it should work.

Aviama pulled the air toward her, but the surface of the water resisted, bowing before the water and dancing outward in little choppy waves. She tried again, more forceful this time, and a small bubble appeared just under the surface. Her mouth opened again, chest hitching in retching-motions.

AIR.

In a final desperate attempt, Aviama raised her hands further and slung them down into the tunnel, summoning a whirling plunge of air spinning down through the water in a meter-long, meter-high bubble. The bubble surged to the base of the aquarium and into the tunnel with not a moment to spare, Aviama's lungs sucking life back into her body like a sponge.

Coughs racked her shoulders, and she collapsed against the bottom of the tunnel. The bubble around them wavered, and Aviama threw a hand back up to maintain the position of the air around her to breathe. The siren gaped at her. It was the first time Aviama had seen shock register on the mermaid's flawless face.

Aviama took long gulps of air and steadied herself, repositioning her body as her legs still drifted in the water beyond the bubble. A splash behind them made them both jump, and they twisted backward toward the sound. Chenzira had left the ladder, and swam toward them with strong, expert strokes.

She almost groaned. Of *course* he was a good swimmer.

Her throat constricted as panic and relief fought for prominence. Would he help her, like he had with the trolls? Or had he kept her alive just long enough to open the door, and would turn on her now to secure his own life?

Aviama twisted to the siren, her voice rushing out in a rasp. "You're scared. I know you are." She cleared her throat and licked her lips, willing the shrill terror in her voice to melt into something with a calming effect. Aviama still needed the siren's help. "Chenzira doesn't want to hurt you. I don't think he *wants* to hurt anyone. We're all pawns in the queen's game. But you struck a deal with Shiva, too, right?"

The siren swallowed and nodded. The mermaid probably hadn't realized Aviama noticed the look she'd given the queen and the prince at the surface, much less guessed at its meaning. But Shiva loved making coerced "deals." A wave of nausea ran through her at the thought. Even with Aviama behind bars in the menagerie, he'd struck a deal to give her the knives. A kiss on credit...

Aviama shook off the thought with a shiver and dipped her head. "Good. I want to ruin the queen's day. I hate Shiva. I hate his manipulative, two-faced...face." She grimaced at the weird word choice, but the corner of the mermaid's mouth twitched. Aviama stared out through the glass of the tunnel, up through the distorted view of the aquarium to the observation box where the royal family and the other poor idiot princess pawns sat on the edge of their seats.

"Let's lean into Shiva's deal, then, shall we? And I'll devote the rest of my life to destroying any ounce of power that woman holds over the palace—and the menagerie." Aviama lifted her chin. "They want a show. Let's give them a show."

The mermaid pulled her lips back into a hissing snarl toward the observation box, then melted into a mischievous smile playing across her lips. A thrill ran up Aviama's spine. She'd just recruited a mermaid as her ally.

Chenzira burst into the air bubble just as a fifth harpoon and a shout cut through the water of the aquarium behind him. He pushed into the small space, squishing Aviama tight between him and the mermaid. "Thanks for leaving me in the lurch with the trolls."

"You mean blowing the door off and saving you?"

He pursed his lips, but was fighting a smile. "Yes. That." He poked at the water outside the bubble, and waved his hand from dry air to water, and back again.

Aviama quirked an eyebrow. "And the air."

"That too. Nice trick." He eyed the mermaid warily, and she drilled him with a stony glare in return.

Aviama shifted uncomfortably between them, one arm

pressed up against Chenzira's side, the other brushing the mermaid. "We can't stay here forever."

"Excellent observation."

Aviama gave him a look, but Chenzira pretended not to notice as he scanned the platforms of the higher and lower pools. He gestured above them. "They've got seven harpoons, and the last guy was yelled at for losing his in pursuit of me. They were already terrified of *her*"—here, he jerked his chin at the mermaid—"and now that you've exposed yourself as a melder, and an impressive one at that, they don't know what to do."

The mermaid let out a sudden hiss, and Aviama nearly jumped out of her skin as a net descended behind the siren. On their other side, behind Chenzira, three guards were stripping off their boots on the platform in preparation for a dive.

Aviama's heart sank. "Looks like they *do* know what to do. Time to go."

The mermaid caught Aviama's wrist and pressed their hands palm to palm, staring intently at her in some meaning-laden symbolic moment she wished she could appreciate. The siren searched her face earnestly, then spoke the first words Aviama had ever heard her say.

"Tabeun sister."

Aviama gaped back at her, a twisted, gut-sick bittersweetness churning her insides. Here, at the brink of life and death, she'd made the most unlikely of friends. Aviama nodded. "Tabeun sister."

With that, the mermaid flicked her tail and was gone from the bubble.

"Wait! What's your name?"

But the mermaid didn't look back, diving out of the tunnel and out into the second, smaller pool where the net had now been stretched across the entire opening of the surface. Aviama reached for the harpoon, but Chenzira snatched it before she could.

"Not a chance. You've got the wind. And I've got a better arm."

She made a face, but took a deep breath and spun into the pool after the mermaid. He was right on both counts, after all. Never mind his own shenanigans with the trolls.

The mermaid's strong tail propelled her to the surface well ahead of Aviama. She seized the net with both hands and thrashed against it, tugging it under the surface. The guards strained against her efforts, planting their feet on the platform. One slipped but recovered just before toppling into the pool.

Aviama pushed the net back up to the top, the mermaid letting go as she realized the humans needed air. Aviama broke the surface, treading water under the net as the mermaid focused her efforts on the edges of the net instead, targeting a single guard at the end and reaching up to yank at the cords running up to his hands.

Chenzira thrust his harpoon through the break in the net, hitting the first guard in the leg. Aviama shoved her hands up above the water as best she could as the net pressed over her head, but only gathered a weak breeze around her fingers. Her head dipped below the surface again, and she let out a grunt. Aviama took a breath and swam to the far side of the tank to the ladder, clinging to it with both hands and pulling herself back up above the water.

"Chenzira! Get the net off me!"

He turned to see her predicament and retracted the harpoon, knocking his man off his feet as he did so. The guard tumbled off the platform to the angry roar of the crowd, and

Chenzira swam to her side. The three guards Aviama had seen at the upper pool moments ago were missing, and she scanned the water.

Aviama's stomach lurched as she caught sight of three dark forms from beneath. They were already through the tunnel, armed with harpoons. Aviama shouted at the mermaid, and she turned just as the first drew back his weapon.

The siren released the net and dove underwater. Aviama did not envy the guards in the aquarium. Without air, a strong fish tail, or the element of surprise, they had little chance of success.

Chenzira lifted the net just high enough over Aviama's head that she could come up and use her hands. Aviama drew a long pull of air around them like a lasso and launched it at the second guard. The man toppled off the platform into the water, ripping the net from the hands of the next guard as he landed on top of the net and pressed it down into the water.

Aviama slung another burst of air at the next guard, down the line until one by one they fell into the aquarium. Chenzira gripped one side of the net, and the mermaid swam up with the other end so that seven of the guards were caught up in it together. Aviama turned her hands up to the men in the net, a great wind pushing them to the side of the pool. She didn't want them getting out anytime soon, but they were only doing their jobs. She didn't want to kill them.

The three divers lay at the bottom of the first segment of the pool, one with a harpoon still sticking out of his chest. The siren apparently did not share Aviama's sentimentality—nor was she limited to her lullabies to kill.

Shouts rang out from the seats surrounding them, mingling with the din of splashing, screaming guards in the aquarium around Aviama. She glanced up. Twenty archers had arrows notched on the strings. The entire audience was on their feet, the queen screeching at the archers to let fly, and the king yelling to be heard above the racket of his guests and the supposed criminals in his arena.

Shiva was clutching the rail, leaning halfway out over the arena, and Aviama almost wished she could do to him what Darsh had done to her—to somehow rip him over the wall and down into the pit. But that would not serve her purpose. The archers weren't the only ones who didn't know what to do with the situation, and she did not intend to give them time to figure it out.

Aviama whirled for the ladder. A hand shot out from inside the net and seized her by the hair, and she squealed. Not the sound of an impressive warrior, or anyone of fighting repute.

Pain radiated across her scalp as her neck jerked backward toward the net. The siren burst upward into the man's arm from the water below, ripping his hold from her head. The mermaid gripped Aviama by the torso, propelled her to the ladder, and deposited her on its rungs.

Aviama pulled herself up over the wall and turned back toward her. She opened her mouth to thank the mermaid, but it was the mermaid who spoke first.

"My name is Makana."

In a flash of lavender eyes and silver scales, Makana disappeared into the water. Aviama leaped dripping wet from the aquarium into the final obstacle. It would take more than a few dead guards to defeat the queen's vision for her fate.

Her bare feet landed in peach-fuzz moss next to a leaning, poorly transferred tree that looked like it might fall over if she sneezed on it. Aviama tuned out the crowd and searched the space. Four trees, three boulders, patches of dirt and moss. One final obstacle before the pit.

I'm still in the game. Let the contestants play.

An unearthly screech split the air before melting into a long, hoarse roar. Aviama flinched, but she planted her feet and raised her hands.

Let's play.

45

The zegrath leaped up onto one of the boulders, and Aviama felt rather than heard the collective gasp of the onlookers. But they were none of her concern. Not now.

Chenzira dropped to the ground beside her, showering her with a fresh douse of cold aquarium water. He still wielded a harpoon. What would the king think of having his impressive menagerie reduced? Had he even considered it as an option that the animals might not all survive his sporting event?

The zegrath's four ears twitched, the front two trained on Aviama and Chenzira, the second pair swiveling to take in the surrounding noise. Talons like a dragon's claw adorned massive paws scratching against the rough planes of the rock, its deep chest taking in slow, measured breaths. Spines ran raised along the back of its neck and hackles. The beast dropped its weight, snapped its jaws, and launched itself off the rock.

Aviama summoned a whirl of wind, throwing the zegrath off its trajectory, but it wasn't enough to take the animal over the wall. Chenzira rushed forward, and this time Aviama caught the subtle hand motion he flashed as he ran in the light of day. The ground shook as the zegrath landed, knocking it off balance.

She ran after him, and he threw a hand out to sweep her behind him so that he stood between her and the zegrath. "I knew it," Aviama hissed, keeping her voice low. "You're a quakemaker. You did it to the trolls, and you did it just now."

A snarl ripped from the zegrath's teeth with a shower of spittle as it flipped over and gathered its feet. Chenzira glanced back at Aviama and jerked his chin at the far wall. A square opening was set in the wall a meter up from the ground. From the look of it, the space was too small for the broad-chested zegrath to fit through. Aviama nodded back. That was their exit.

Chenzira lifted his harpoon. "I used it when you were in the pit with Darsh, too."

Aviama blinked. Her lips parted. "You collapsed the tunnel."

The beast zeroed in on the Keket prince, and Chenzira dropped his center of gravity. The zegrath stalked two paces to one side, then flew at them, claws barely touching the ground in its long leaps. Aviama let out an unearthly screech and commanded the wind almost on reflex.

The wind hit the animal square in the chest just as Chenzira's harpoon drew blood from its neck. It tumbled backward and slammed into the boulder.

Chenzira swore. "Stop screaming! That was right in my ear!"

"Sorry."

"And no, I didn't collapse the tunnel. Not most of it." Chenzira hesitated. "The guard was almost on you, and Darsh is jumpy, like you, but holding a blade to your throat. You were seconds from death. I just rocked their footing a bit."

Aviama gaped at him, and her stomach flopped. "You...you saved me. Even back then."

Chenzira adjusted his grip on the harpoon, never bothering to look back at her. "Don't flatter yourself. You were a pitiful mess of mishaps. It was like saving a child."

She pursed her lips. He'd risked a lot to save her, and by then Prince Shiva and the royal guards were both working to get her free of Darsh's grasp. Then it hit her—the way he'd said Darsh's name just now, the familiarity. The way he knew Darsh was *jumpy.*

Chenzira knew him. The criminal leader of an extremist group of melders, wreaking havoc in Radha and bold enough to make direct attacks on the palace. Chenzira had been operating as a spy in the palace for three years. How long had the extremist group been active?

Was Chenzira part of the shadow network, the one the rogue guard had mentioned to Murin?

Why would the disappeared, second-born prince of a foreign nation be so interested in espionage for Radha? What if the rumors that he'd been cut off from his family were true, and he wasn't spying for his homeland, but for this shadow network, this radical group of melderbloods?

Aviama eyed him in a new light, the man blackmailing her in the king's office, the diplomat slinking up the ranks of trust in the Radhan court. How far would he go to ensure his mission succeeded? Could it succeed if he were not alive to carry it out? *Biscuits.*

"What are you going to do with me when we get through that window?" *After all this, are you going to decide to kill me?*

"I haven't thought that far."

Her mouth went dry. She swallowed. "Well, luckily, I have. Don't be stupid. And don't use any melder powers."

"Says the woman whose only hope of survival is killing me. I *will* protect myself."

An interesting phrasing. He didn't say he would kill her. Only that he would defend himself.

Aviama planted one hand on the ledge of the opening and hoisted herself up. The zegrath shook off the shock of hitting the boulder, roared, and charged. Its beady black eyes flashed, black fur and glossy spines shining in the sun. Aviama slipped as she tried to scramble through the exit, clutching with both hands at the stone to keep from falling.

Her hands were occupied when the zegrath attacked. The beast plummeted down on Chenzira. Guttural snarls tore through the air, human and zegrath locked in battle. Chenzira plunged the harpoon toward the animal's chest, but it twisted its head and snapped the shaft in two with powerful jaws. Razor-sharp talons raked across Chenzira's bare chest as he landed on his back with the zegrath drooling and snarling on top of him.

Aviama's heart twisted, and she ripped one hand free from underneath her, reaching toward him on instinct. A small voice whispered in the back of her mind. *Win the contest. Let him die. This is your salvation.*

But she knew she never could. Aviama dropped back to the ground, her hands free from the opening once more as she turned back to the beast and hurled a blast of air in its face. The zegrath snapped its head up, cruel, soulless eyes trained on her small frame. She'd need something stronger if she hoped to survive.

Aviama sidestepped away from Chenzira and called to the wind, every muscle straining at the effort, adrenaline coursing through her veins. *Come to me.*

The wind gathered on her palms, and her damp hair

whipped in its swirling power. The zegrath was enormous. She would need a lot of strength to bear its weight.

The monstrous creature abandoned its injured prey in favor of its latest insult—the rail-thin princess standing off to the side. Chenzira struggled to his knees with a groan. Aviama lifted her hands higher and screamed at him through the wind.

"Get to the pit!"

He wanted to resist. She knew he did. But a moment later, he was clambering through the opening in the wall. And the zegrath was launching at Aviama's throat.

Aviama aimed for its neck and released the wind on the zegrath. She'd hoped to snap its neck, but it toppled over mid-leap and fell to the ground with a resounding thud, still very much alive. That would have to do.

Aviama spun to the exit and threw herself through the opening, her hips landing on the stone ledge, her upper half starting to dangle down into the sand pit on the opposite side—but not far enough. Her feet kicked uselessly in the air on the zegrath side, and panic reached up through her gut to swallow her whole.

The zegrath pounded across the ground behind her, the rasp of its heavy breath coating every taut muscle in Aviama's body. Chenzira clasped her wrists and yanked her the rest of the way through the opening, stumbling backward as the two of them collapsed into the sand of the pit. The zegrath's snout and head plunged through the opening, but its body was caught at the shoulders.

It let out an infuriated yowl, and the keen look in its pitch-black eyes made Aviama sure that without being melders, the zegrath would have been the most imposing creature of the menagerie. Second only to the siren, perhaps, if she had been inclined to kill them.

Aviama rolled off Chenzira's chest, blood from three long, zegrath talon marks transferring from his body to her clothes as she did so. Her pulse pounded in her ears, and her breath came in short gasps, but there was no time to lose.

The weapons display on the far side of the pit held battle-axes, knives, swords, and three different maces. She couldn't allow Chenzira to reach it, and she couldn't let him reveal himself as a quakemaker. Not if her final plan had any shred of a chance at success.

She grimaced. It was a terrible plan. But it was also the only one she had.

Aviama ran to the weapons display and ripped a sword from its place. Chenzira lurched to his feet, clutching a dark bruise at his side. He wouldn't understand she didn't mean to kill him. How could he?

And if he thought she was going to kill him...

He would defend himself to the bitter end.

46

———

The sand beneath her feet shifted unnaturally in the subtlest of ways, and Aviama threw up her palm, knocking him flat on his back with a whoosh of wind. The sword felt awkward in the grip of her right hand, but the swirling air in her left gave her confidence. Aviama strode toward him, the wind pooling in her palm blowing her blonde hair back over her shoulders.

Chenzira raised his hand, but Aviama sent the wind to blast his wrists into the sand at his sides, invisible tendrils of rope bearing down on him. His eyes blazed into her, but she only shook her head. Her chest tightened to see him on the ground at her feet. Her throat ached around the lump that lodged there, and unshed tears gathered at her eyes.

Aviama dropped to one knee, leaned down for only Chenzira to hear, and searched his face. "If this works—if this works, and you get out—find Enzo and Murin, my lady-in-waiting. If she's still alive, Murin is with a defected guard with a moon-shaped scar on his hand. Make sure she gets free of Radha to take a message to Jannemar. Please."

Chenzira furrowed his brow, his face darkening as he tried

to understand what she was doing. A tear streaked down her cheek and down on his chest as she rose. Aviama raised the sword over her head, released the wind holding Chenzira's wrists, and drove the sword down into the sand a handsbreadth from his face.

Aviama spun to the crowd gaping at them from the arena seats overhead and spread her hands. Her hands shook, and she only hoped she was far enough away that no one in the stands could see it. Red-faced screams and fist-pounding thuds rocked the arena. Whooping hollers competed with passionate boos, and looks of disgust mixed with impressed fascination painted a spectrum of reactions on the spectators' faces.

She clenched her jaw, took a deep breath, and dropped into a deep curtsy toward the observation box. Prince Shiva arched an eyebrow. Queen Satya looked down her nose at Aviama, swirling a goblet and pretending not to appear desperately interested. And King Dahnuk leaned forward on the edge of his seat, the lines of his brow deepening with every second.

"Truly, Your Majesty, your genius knows no bounds!" The archers lining the arena swung their weapons in her direction. The king's eyes narrowed. She gulped. "I know you are a just and fair king, a land where the Blessing Sun shines its light all the more brightly for your presence in it."

Queen Satya moved to speak in her husband's ear, but the king held up a hand, his gaze fixed on Aviama. Aviama glanced between them and hurried on before he could change his mind.

"You wanted to test my mettle. You wanted to see if I deserved to marry Prince Shiva. And why wouldn't you? Prince Shiva is the kind of man any girl would fall over themselves to marry."

Shiva cocked his head, his umber gaze asking the question she herself had been pondering. Chenzira rose to his feet behind her and growled the same thought out loud. "What are you doing?"

But Aviama ignored him. "The truth is, you thought I refused to marry him. Your Majesty, nothing could be further from the truth."

A murmur rolled through the crowd.

The queen sipped from her goblet and raised her voice. "You lie! You came to us in bad faith!"

Aviama's stomach twisted. She shook her head. "Prince Shiva is an innovator, like his father. His firm hand and strategic wisdom are second to none. Jannemar would be honored to link itself to such a man. But I would not be linked to Radha as a bargaining chip, as a weakling desperate for aid. We, too, have something to offer. And I thought it best to participate in the contest to prove it."

Dahnuk drew a hand through his beard and crossed his arms. "Explain."

"My land is the birthplace of magic. I have much to teach, much to share. Jannemar desires a true partnership."

Shiva's mouth twisted into a nauseating smile. *Appearances, appearances.* She'd offered the king a way to preserve their lives while saving face—and she'd slathered Shiva's name in butter like a perfect golden bread roll. No matter how much Aviama hated herself for spewing such filth, flattery was a powerful tool.

Chenzira took three steps toward her, shaking his head. Aviama held up a warning hand. *Please.*

He searched her face. The muscles of his arms flexed as he clenched his hands into fists. *Don't be stupid.*

But could he have come up with a better solution? No. Or

he would have done it. And this way, they might both live out the day.

Aviama turned back to the Tanashais. "I propose a new deal. But there is one contingency. Let Prince Chenzira go."

Dahnuk laughed. "He is a criminal!"

"You are in love with him!" Satya spat, but her husband silenced her with a glare. Such a public outburst was unacceptable.

"I am not." Aviama took a step forward. "I am not, and I never was. Just as Prince Chenzira has not stolen from the honorable Tanashai family. The evidence is contaminated, Your Majesty. He is not deserving of death. I only hope to avoid unnecessary killing—messy killing that may upend the stability in the region."

Stability that Radha was more than happy to destroy. But the people didn't know that.

King Dahnuk pursed his lips. "You hold your own life in your hands. You could have won the contest and secured your own life. What motivates such charity?"

Aviama bit her lip, then spun the rings on her fingers. Visions of Azi, her murderous dragonlord uncle, and her parents' dead bodies filed through her mind. She lifted her chin. "I've seen men kill recklessly. Wastefully. I'll gladly be struck down before I play a part in that."

The weight of that silence was palpable. Not a soul dared to move. Aviama shifted on her feet. Chenzira crossed his arms in her peripheral vision, but she refused to look him in the eye.

The king jutted his chin at Chenzira. "What makes you judge over him?"

Aviama curtsied again. "You yourself handed over our judgment to fate in the menagerie, Your Majesty. The menagerie has decided. And I am ready to make you an offer. Or, more accurately, to make your son an offer."

King Dahnuk arched his eyebrows. He glanced at his son and gestured at Aviama. "Make your offer."

Aviama pivoted to face Shiva. Her breath came fast, her thoughts spinning in a whirlwind too disorganized to catch. Sweat beaded on her brow as she met his unflinching gaze. She couldn't do it. She couldn't bind herself to a controlling maniac, a manipulative monster.

But she had let the monster free. And if she didn't find a way to warn Jannemar, if Murin couldn't make it out of the city, if no one stopped the queen—everyone she loved would die.

So Aviama lifted a trembling voice to the man who'd made her a traitor. "A life for a life. I saved you in this pit once. Let Prince Chenzira go, that I might live with a clear conscience. Do this, and I will marry you."

Chenzira seized her wrist, and she twisted toward him with a blast of air to the chest. She'd made the move on instinct, but guilt still tore through her gut as he stumbled backward.

Dahnuk's face reddened, but Shiva's eyes lit with the spark of conquest. The king opened his mouth to object, but Prince Shiva shoved to his feet with that slimy, twisted smile Aviama used to enjoy. "I accept."

Relief and dread overwhelmed her at once. Above her, Darra reeled backward in the seat beside Shiva, and Marija's face contorted in revulsion with an audible gasp. Against all reason, Vanina laughed, perhaps merely enjoying Marija's displeasure.

Aviama weaved on her feet, and Chenzira caught her elbow. "You idiot. What did you do?"

"How else..." Aviama's mumbling voice trailed off, and she

winced as the dizzy spell slowly washed over her. "How else could we both survive the arena? I can't fight them all."

The crown prince signaled the guards surrounding the observation level. They glanced at the king, but he gave a reticent wave of acknowledgment, and they let down rope ladders from the top of the arena. It would hurt the king's image, and show of unity, to oppose his son's enthusiastic acceptance of her offer now.

A dozen soldiers dropped down into the pit, and moments later Prince Shiva himself landed in the sand. Aviama swallowed. This was her choice. The right one. The only one. She was going to be sick.

Aviama's only consolation as her fate was sealed was in the sight of Queen Satya, her goblet falling from rigid fingers. The queen looked on as her son, the future king, crossed the sand and spread his hands to greet his betrothed—a *melderblood*.

"My champion!"

Prince Shiva snapped his fingers, and two guards stepped forward, taking hold of Chenzira by the arms and pulling him away from her. Every one of Aviama's muscles went rigid as Shiva looked down on her. Her chest squeezed tight, and her breath came in panicked snatches.

Shiva slipped an arm around the small of her back, pulling her toward him, and caressed the side of her face with the other. A chill ran down her spine, and he smiled. "I'll have that kiss now."

She tilted her face up to meet him, but in that moment the reality of what she'd done settled over her like storm clouds. And it was already starting to rain.

The queen had lost the battle at the arena, but with Aviama trapped indefinitely within her reach in the House of the Blessing Sun, every ounce of her energy would be devoted to regaining control.

If Aviama was right about Chenzira's connection with Darsh, she'd just freed him to continue working to destroy the Tanashai family—and placed herself squarely in his crosshairs by tying herself to Shiva.

Weddings took time to plan. Aviama would play the game just like she'd played the arena. *Her* way. And when the time was right, she'd have everything she needed to repay Radha for their treachery.

Shiva's voice clung to her memory even as his lips pressed into hers. *What Marija wants to give me I can find on any street-corner. What you have, darling, is special. Jannemar has opened the door to magic, and it seems you hold the keys...*

Aviama pulled back from their kiss, searching his eyes in as romantic a look as she could muster—an act for the crowd. "You only want me for your menagerie."

"Nonsense. I'm not my father." Shiva leaned in to kiss her cheek and hovered at her ear. "I don't hide my collections for special occasions. I wear them. And I will wear you on my arm."

The secret was out. Aviama Shamaran, princess of Jannemar, was melderblood.

Continue the adventure with the second book in the series,
Shadow Caste...

The queen wants her dead. The prince wants to usurp her magic. And her only hope lies in a violent shadow society that would rather kill her than help her.

Scan the QR code to start reading.

THANK YOU FOR READING!

Thank you so much for reading *Melderblood,* book 1 of *The Melderblood Chronicles*! I hope you enjoyed reading it as much as I enjoyed writing it.

If you did, would you be willing to leave a review? Reviews help enable authors to continue doing what they do, and help other readers to find books best suited to them.

If you'd like to leave a review on Amazon, scan the QR code.

THE BLOOD & FLAME SAGA

This explosive new dragons and assassins series is about to become your new addiction.

Are you ready to ride dragons and unravel the mysteries of a land steeped in magic and betrayal?

Scan the QR code to start reading.

Magical bargains, high-stakes heists, and lovers who could
kill each other just by falling in love...

Read on for a fast-paced romantic fantasy full of curses,
cons, and a love that could kill.

If he loves her, she'll die. If she loves him, he'll die. But only by
working together can they stop a vengeful mage from rising
again—and lift the curses that bind them both.

Scan the QR code to start reading.

ABOUT THE AUTHOR

Author of *The Forgotten Stone* and *The Blood and Flame Saga*, E.A. Winters loves pouring a hot chai tea latte and delving into creating epic fantasy worlds for you to enjoy.

Erin lives in Virginia with her husband and two boys. When she's not writing, she sees clients as a Licensed Professional Counselor, and spends time with her family. She loves playing board games and reading, whenever the elusive "free time" opportunity arises.

- Website and newsletter: eawinters.com
- Facebook: facebook.com/eawintersnovels
- TikTok: @eawinters
- Instagram: @e.a.winters

Also by E.A. Winters

Blood & Flame Saga

Raised by a dragonlord to kill without question, one girl discovers the truth —and risks everything to bring down the man that made her into a weapon.

Book 1: Dragon's Kiss

Book 2: Broken Bonds

Book 3: Noble Claims

Book 4: Crimson Queen

The Melderblood Chronicles

In a palace of gowns, secrets, and betrayal, one princess walks the tightrope between duty and death... while magic simmers beneath her skin.

Book 1: Melderblood

Book 2: Shadow Caste

Book 3: Wraithweaver

Book 4: Reaverbane

Heist of Hearts

If he loves her, she'll die. If she loves him, he'll die. But only by working together can they stop a vengeful mage from rising again—and lift the curses that bind them both.

Book 1: Heist of Hearts

Book 2: Oath of Odds

Stand Alones

The Forgotten Stone

When a tavern girl angers the realm's fiercest warrior, she flees straight into a legendary quest—and discovers that destiny doesn't wait for the qualified.

Browse All Titles by E.A. Winters by Scanning the QR Code Below